PRAISE FOR

Under the Rose

"Deep within the Rose & Grave secret society at Eli University, the secrets even members aren't privy to make Peterfreund's second novel impossible to put down.... Peterfreund offers an intimate view of the modus operandi of a college society.... Readers will be absorbed by the juicy romance plots."—*Publishers Weekly*

"Diana Peterfreund has performed a minor miracle; she has created a sequel that works. The entire cast is back from *Secret Society Girl*, and boy, are they hiding some secrets.... Ms. Peterfreund has also managed to weave a very credible, complicated mystery into the plot, with more twists and turns than you would believe. *Under the Rose* is definitely worthy reading for this summer."—*Romance Reviews Today*

"Cross Dink Stover with Nancy Drew and Bridget Jones and you get Amy Haskel, the sarcastic senior at transparently disguised 'Eli University' who briskly narrates this winning mystery."—*Yale Alumni Magazine*

"Peterfreund pairs romance and suspense in a picaresque university setting with a few surprises thrown in for good measure. Readers who picked up the series debut will be excited to continue the adventures of Amy and her cohorts. The author doesn't spend too much time rehashing the first book, but new readers will get swept up in the sexy story in no time."—*Booklist*

"*Under the Rose* is every bit as involving and hard-to-put-down as its predecessor—perhaps even more so.... If college life is a kegger, Peterfreund's series is a cocktail in a sugar-rimmed martini glass, sophisticated and easily gulped but delivering a satisfying kick."—*Winston-Salem Journal*

PRAISE FOR

Secret Society Girl

"The action is undeniably juicy—from steamy make-out sessions with campus hotties to cloak-and-dagger initiations."—*Washington Post*

"[A] tell-all book about secret societies at Ivy League schools . . . Think *The Da Vinci Code* meets *Bridget Jones*."
—*Toledo Blade*

"*Secret Society Girl* succeeds. . . . Ms. Peterfreund's descriptions of the ambitious Amy Haskel's collegial life are both vivid and amusing."—*New York Observer*

"Cheerful, sensible, with just enough insider's scoop to appeal to the conspiracy theorist in everyone . . . Readers will cheer on the not-so-underdog as she faces male alumni and finds that membership does indeed have privileges."
—*Tampa Tribune*

"Thanks to a quirky, likable protagonist you'll be rooting for long after you've turned the last page and a provocative blurring of fact and fiction, *Secret Society Girl* provides the perfect excuse to set aside your required reading this summer and bask in a few hours of collegiate nostalgia."
—BookReporter.com

"Fun to read—full of quirky characters and situations."
—*Booklist*

"A frothy summer read for anyone interested in the collegiate antics of the secret rulers of the world."
—*Bloomberg News*

"The plot is a winner."—*Kirkus Reviews*

Rites

of

Spring

(Break)

AN IVY LEAGUE NOVEL

Diana Peterfreund

DELTA TRADE PAPERBACKS

RITES OF SPRING (BREAK)
A Delta Trade Paperback / July 2008

Published by Bantam Dell
A Division of Random House, Inc.
New York, New York

Book design by Carol Malcolm Russo

Delta is a registered trademark of Random House, Inc., and the
colophon is a trademark of Random House, Inc.

Library of Congress Cataloging in Publication Data
Peterfreund, Diana.
Rites of spring (break) : an Ivy League novel / Diana Peterfreund.
p. cm.
ISBN 978-0-385-34193-6 (trade pbk.)
1. Women college students—Fiction. 2. Greek letter societies—
Fiction. 3. Spring break—Fiction. 4. College stories. 5. Chick lit.
I. Title.
PS3616.E835R57 2008
813'.6—dc22
2008006628

Printed in the United States of America
Published simultaneously in Canada
www.bantamdell.com

BVG 10 9 8 7 6 5 4 3 2 1

For Mom and Dad, who made me a Florida girl

I hereby confess:
Even the secretive
and the powerful need vacations.

Not all tropical islands keep their treasures buried, but for those that do, no map will help. Take, for example, a tiny strip of land off the coast of Florida. It has long been understood by those who care to keep track of such things that this glorified sandbar, this unassuming key, heavily wooded and lacking more than a single decent beach, is actually a lush and luxurious retreat for the members of one of the most notorious secret societies in the world.

Yet Cavador Key is not listed on any map, whether those commissioned by the state, or the penciled sketches of shallows by a dock-bound old salt. The locals won't speak of it in voices raised above a whisper. No charter company will take you thither, and when emissaries from the island come to the mainland to pick up supplies, they are silent as the grave about their employers and those employers' mysterious pursuits.

What happens on Cavador Key? Rumors abound, but few have seen the rituals up close. Anyone boating near the island is given stern warnings to stay away, and if un-heeded, these warnings turn into threats. Several rooftops peek out from the ground cover, and grainy photos reveal evidence of people scurrying from building to building, wrapped in dark, hooded cloaks in spite of the warm Florida weather. Recently, access to satellite photos re-vealed still more: a helicopter pad, the remnants of an airstrip, and crisscrossed pathways surrounding a somber, windowless structure. Those who have made it close enough report strange sounds, and stranger lights. Those who have made it closer still are never heard from again.

So next time you're out on your boat, a little sunstruck and with way too many piña coladas on your tab, don't make a decision you'll regret. Cloak-and-dagger govern-ment cabals, clandestine midnight rituals, and inexplicable disappearances aren't on your Spring Break itinerary. You don't want the kind of trouble an unplanned excursion like this can bring you.

But hey, is there an offshore island paradise that *doesn't* hold a secret?

Trust me on this one. Some of us know the truth about Cavador Key. But we're few in number, and we keep our secrets close, just like we were taught by the Order of Rose & Grave.

———

Don't believe me *yet*? Do you think, perhaps, that I'm just spouting the party line? Or maybe you suspect that even a dedicated Digger like me doesn't know everything about the organization to which I've pledged my all, and even less about the property we call our most sacred retreat.

Interesting theory. Shall we put it to the test?

The Rose & Grave Club of D177

1) Clarissa Cuthbert: *(Angel):* Cavador Key
2) Gregory Dorian *(Bond):* Yaddo Writer's Conference
3) Odile Dumas *(Little Demon):* ~~Cavador Key~~ Filming Motion Picture
4) Benjamin Edwards: *(Big Demon):* Cavador Key
5) Amy Haskel *(Bugaboo):* Cavador Key
6) Nikolos Dmitri Kandes IV *(Graverobber):* Beachside Mixologist externship
7) Kevin Lee *(Frodo):* Cavador Key
8) Omar Mathabane *(Kismet):* Chairman of the International Prospective Students Week
9) George Harrison Prescott *(Puck):* Cavador Key
10) Demetria Robinson *(Thorndike):* Cavador Key
11) Jennifer Santos *(Lucky):* Cavador Key
12) Harun Sarmast *(Tristram Shandy):* Cavador Key
13) Joshua Silver *(Keyser Soze):* Art Tour through Spain with barbarian lover
14) Mara Taserati *(Juno):* Research Assistant for Groundbreaking Volume on Domestic Policy tentatively titled *Why All Liberals Should Be Set Upon by Wild Dogs*

I hereby confess:
I'm not cut out
for a life of crime.

1.
Crooking

Some people pledge to lose weight for their New Year's resolution. Others quit smoking, or promise to do their homework before Sunday night, or swear that they'll never again, no matter how many pomegranate martinis they've imbibed, give in to temptation and drunk-dial their ex-boyfriends, ex-lovers, or ex-friends-with-benefits and invite them over for a nightcap.

Instead of resolving any of the above (and that last one sounded pretty good), I promised to commit a felony.

On December 31st, as the clock struck twelve, I held aloft a glass of champagne and solemnly swore that I'd join my secret society brothers in their quest to steal back one of our treasured relics from a rival society. At the time, I thought it would be a relatively straightforward operation. Sneak into the Dragon's Head headquarters, snatch back the knee-high stone statue of Orpheus, and hightail it back to Rose & Grave's High Street tomb, booty in tow.

Wrong.

Dragon's Head had grown suspicious over Winter

Break, indulging their more paranoid sides. I knew from intimate association with my fellow knights that no one in our crew could have tipped them off on purpose, but perhaps we weren't as discreet as we should have been during one of our many reconnaissance missions to their York Street abode. Perhaps they had as many hidden cameras trained on our tomb as we had on theirs. Whatever the cause, intel showed, clear as infrared, the Dragon's Head members removing the purloined Orpheus statue from their courtyard late the previous night. If they were worthy of their admission to Eli, they would have hidden it out of reach in their house's safe, a move that would make things tricky—but not impossible—for us thieves.

Wait a second. Reconnaissance? Infrared? *Intel?* What's going on here? I was a Literature major, for crying out loud, not a CIA recruit. And yet, in the nine months since I'd been tapped into Rose & Grave, my inner spygirl had gestated and emerged as a black-clad, code-speaking, secret-handshake-knowing, card-carrying acolyte of the New World Order.

Or at least, the wannabe New World Order. Despite all the 007 talk, this mission of ours cut a little closer to fraternity prank than military coup. But whatever the flavor of the operation, the practicalities were the same: I was spending my first night back on campus lying in the slush in an alleyway behind the Dragon's Head tomb, waiting for orders, while my black ski mask painfully crushed my ponytail holder against my scalp.

However, that wasn't what was causing my headache.

"I say we go now," said the society brother lying in the slush to my left.

"Bond directed us to wait for his signal," said the one on my right.

From the left: "Listen, old-timer, maybe in your day, you sat around waiting for someone to hand you an engraved invitation, but that's why we're running the show now. Your ways are out-of-date. Don't you agree, Bugaboo?"

I shifted in the slush. Time was, I would have made precisely that statement, and had. But last semester I'd been involved in espionage activities with the guy on my right, and he'd proven quite handy in a pinch.

Whereas the guy on my left was mostly all hands and pinches.

"Listen, *Junior*," hissed the party on the right from behind his ski mask, "I concur that we don't see eye-to-eye. About anything. But if you move now, you're going to throw off the whole group. Wait for the signal."

The guy on my left rolled his copper-colored eyes and sat up. "I'm no one's junior," he threw over his shoulder. "Dad's middle name isn't 'Harrison.'" He sprang into a crouch.

Poe leapt across me to grab Puck before he could give our position away, but it was too late. Puck had already jumped to the top of the wall that separated the Dragon's Head property from the alleyway.

"Middle name should have been *Asshole*," Poe grumbled.

In place of a response, I coughed, politely, and he seemed to notice that he was still lying on top of me, his hands resting in places that weren't exactly public access.

"Oops." He stood, and brushed snow off of his pants. "Here's an idea for next year's taps, Bugaboo," he said, and pulled me to my feet, making as if to brush snow off me before I gave him a warning swat, "only tap the ones who are interested in keeping your secret operations *secret*."

I laid a finger against my ski mask–covered mouth. I

was to blame for many things involving George Harrison Prescott, but not this. "Remind me who it was that tapped our dear Puck?"

"I liked it better when you were playing mute."

"You always have," I replied, as the alarm went off.

Alarms in most buildings on campus might bring a few offhand observers, perhaps some threatening glares from light sleepers or heavy studiers, and campus security. Alarms at a secret society bring *reporters*. And since the offices of the *Eli Daily News* were right next door, I'd say, Winter Break or not, we had approximately eight seconds before our masked countenances turned downright conspicuous.

"Jump!"

"Right. New signal." Poe jumped. I followed, missed the ledge, and proceeded to scrape elbows and knees on the stone as I slid down the wall.

Poe's face shot over the ledge, silhouetted against the purply-orange sky, a signature of overcast New Haven nights. "Can't take you anywhere, can I?" He reached down and gave me a hand.

I looked over the wall at the virgin snow on the ground inside. *Crap*. Could we make the leap all the way over to the cleared walkway in the center of the yard? Did it even matter anymore if the Dragon's Head knights knew where we came from, now that the alarm was blaring loud enough to be heard up Science Hill?

Poe jumped down from the ledge and landed in the snow, and I saw black-clad figures doing the same all around the yard. Guess not.

We convened at the kitchen entrance near the back. "What brain donor was responsible for moving in early?" asked Thorndike, a.k.a. Demetria Robinson. She was rocking her set of broken-in breaking-and-entering duds and picking the lock on the Dragon's Head back door.

Poe and I pointed at Puck, who gave us the finger.

Angel arrived. The New York socialite most called Clarissa Cuthbert was almost unrecognizable with her fall of blond hair tucked under her ski mask. "That was...unexpected. Lucky almost had the alarm system disabled. Bond's furious. They'll be along in a minute." She stared at our motley crew. "Where are the others?"

"Forced to abort." Lil' Demon, known to her legions of fans as bad-girl starlet Odile Dumas, leaned against a wall and attempted to catch her breath. "I tried to wave down Tristram and Frodo, but they were totally zoned out." She squinted at Poe. "Who brought him?"

I shrugged. "He brought himself, as usual."

"I don't blame the boys for getting distracted," said Angel. "We've been waiting for half an hour. I almost forgot what we were doing myself."

"I think the term is 'woolgathering,'" said Poe.

"Yeah, if you're my grandmother," said Thorndike, and the door popped open.

"Wait," I said. "Wasn't your grandma a Black Panther?"

"Okay, so not *mine*, exactly. She skipped the tatting lessons in favor of showing me how to crack safes. Let's go."

We slid inside the building, taking up positions in the main hall according to our pre-arranged plan—a plan that now seemed to contain several obvious and glaring holes. Lil' Demon, in possession of the two-way radio, directed us to keep our headlamps off for the time being and peeked through a scratch in one of the blacked-out windows to assess the damage.

Dragon's Head, unlike most of the dedicated society buildings on campus, is a retrofitted frat house. Instead of the windowless, mausoleum-like tomb we members of

Rose & Grave enjoy, their building is more of a Tudor mansion. Back before all the frats were kicked off campus and the society had taken over the property, you could be a member of the fraternity that called this place home and, in your senior year, of Rose & Grave as well.

To wit: We know every crevice of this house. Because past generations of Rose & Grave ceded their loyalty to us Diggers, we know the location of every secret room, every back stair...every emergency exit. And we'd probably need each one if we still wanted to pull this caper off.

"Crowd's forming," whispered Lil' Demon. "Bond says the rest of the crew was forced to give up or be recognized. He's trying to mingle and keep giving us updates."

"Perfect," I said. "So we're down to what, Ocean's Six?"

The alarm died.

"Ocean's Seven," said Lil' Demon with a laugh. "Lucky came through after all."

"Either way," said Poe, "we're not going to have time to get Orpheus and get out. I bet they've got security on the way. I know their caretaker will have been roused, and any members already on campus."

"So you think we should abort?" I asked.

"I think it might already be too late to make a clean get-away."

"Spoilsport." I almost stuck my tongue out at him, then remembered the mask.

"I think that title belongs to your friend." He gestured to Puck, who'd taken up residence on one of the leather wingback chairs and looked relaxed enough to pour himself a drink. "He's the one who got us into this mess."

True. Okay, time for some decisions. I addressed the group. "Here's my thought: The same crowd that's keeping us from getting out might be helpful in preventing the members from getting in. Too many witnesses. I say we're made whether they catch us inside or outside. So let's keep to the plan. All in favor?"

There was a chorus of "Aye"s in the darkness. Poe crossed his arms, but his expression was unreadable beneath his mask.

Puck clapped and rubbed his hands together. "I love it. Let's go get arrested."

Lil' Demon looked around. "Where's Thorndike?"

"Already working," came a voice over Lil' Demon's two-way. "And I've got good news and bad news."

"Lay it on me," Lil' Demon said.

Thorndike's voice crackled through the radio: "The bad news is, I'm not going to be able to open the safe. The good news is, I found something even better."

———

"Impossible," said Poe, shaking his head, so the beam of his headlamp swerved like a lighthouse ray.

"I'm with him," said Puck. "Weird as that sounds."

Angel peeked into the hallway and down the stairs. "There's no way we're moving it without a dolly and about seven burly men."

Lil' Demon stood speechless in front of it. "What . . . what is it?"

To hazard a guess, I'd say the Maltese Dragon. The statue before me was about six feet tall, plated with gold leaf, and encrusted all over with semi-precious jewels. Lapis eyes flickered in the glow of the LED headgear a few of us wore, and ivory fangs jutted out from carnelian jaws. Jade scales mixed in with the gold. It was, without a doubt, the most precious thing in the society's possession. (It was also way nicer than the tiny marble statue we'd come here to reclaim.)

I'd been through most of their house by now (I can't

call this windowed Tudor a "tomb") and, nice as it may be, their headquarters held none of the grandeur of the Diggers' own home base. Their meeting room was cozy and well appointed, but enjoyed neither walls covered with expensive antique oil paintings nor a painted dome ceiling, like ours. Of course, I'd memorized their floor plan, but seeing the rooms in person gave a different impression completely. The whole building had a far less grandiose air than the only other tomb I knew.

It only stood to reason. Dragon's Head was almost a half century younger than Rose & Grave, and though generally well respected (hey, anything we deign to consider a "rival" is okay by us), it boasted fewer alumni gifts, a smaller trust, and, perhaps as a consequence of both, a lesser cachet in the campus pecking order.

Or at least, it had until this year. The scandals that had rocked Rose & Grave during the last two semesters had tarnished our reputation somewhat. I'm sure the Dragon's Head's (or Book & Key's, or Serpent's) sales pitch to potential taps this spring would sound something like, "Rose & Grave is going to pot. Look at how many times they've been in the tabloids this year. You sure you want to hitch your wagon to that falling star?" Which made tonight's expedition all the more important. Pull off a good crook, and we'd prove our mettle once again.

Unfortunately, our chances of departing without a police escort, never mind scoring any booty, looked slimmer than the cut of Angel's jeans.

"Bet it's heavy," said Thorndike, leaning a bit on the beast's long, lithe body. The pedestal base barely jiggled. "But what a coup, huh?"

"Really puts the 'grand' in grand larceny." I shook my head. "There's no way we can take this with us. Are you sure you can't open the safe?" I directed the beam of my headlamp toward the enormous safe set into a recess in the far wall.

"Nope," said Thorndike. "I've never even seen a lock like that before. Sorry to let you all down." Apparently, our safecracker hadn't spent as much time studying with her grandmother as she had preparing for her SATs. Couldn't blame her, to tell the truth.

"Great," said Puck. "All this trouble for nothing."

"At least you can afford a good lawyer when we get caught," I said. "I doubt these charges will look good on my graduate school applications."

"Don't worry about it," Angel scoffed. "New Haven cops never take these pranks too seriously."

Poe, as usual, was standing somewhat away from the rest of the group, studying the peeling wallpaper in the bluish ray from his headlamp. Suddenly, he stiffened. "Someone's inside. Quick, we've got to hide!"

We all froze, straining in an attempt to hear whatever clue Poe had that we weren't the building's only occupants. I looked around. Where would we hide? This room was cluttered with various knickknacks and furniture, but nothing that would conceal six college kids (no matter how petite certain starlets were).

But Poe was straining to lift the upright piano in the corner by the safe as quietly as possible. "Someone help him," I whispered, though I really had no idea what he was trying to do.

So I asked him. "Um, if we're trying to steal something heavy, I think it's best we go with the dragon."

In response, he grabbed my arm and shoved me behind the piano. "Get in."

There was a thigh-high hole in the wall, and from the

cobweb-covered opening came a distinctive draft. Great. Spiders and cold air and blackness. I reeled back against him, standing up. "No way!"

"Now," he hissed, pushing me back down.

"Crawl space" is a generous term for the damp, grimy cavity my companions and I presently found ourselves crowded into. Poe squished himself inside and began tugging the piano back into place. "It won't budge," he said, a note of real fear entering his voice at last.

Angel, who was closest, began pulling on it with him, and as the back of the upright snapped against the wall, the two of them tumbled across the unfinished floorboards and hit the wall opposite with a crack.

We all stopped breathing. Could whoever was downstairs hear that?

"The lights!" Thorndike's warning came on a breath, and around me, LED headlamps extinguished one by one. And then, from a distance, we heard a rhythmic pounding. Footsteps on the stairs. We lay completely still, heedless of our awkward positions and the way we were all jumbled together in a heap.

"Did they get anything? Search all the rooms."

A chorus of voices began to ring out from all around us. "All clear here." "Nothing here." "I don't think they even made it up here." And then, one voice, louder and clearer than all the others. "I'm in the treasure room. They took the cover off the dragon." A sliver of light sliced into our hole from the crack between the piano and the wall. In its blaze, I saw Poe's eyes, wide and almost silvery inside the eyeholes of his mask. They met mine and we simply stared at each other for several long moments, not blinking, willing in unison for the light to vanish before it gave away our location.

More voices joined the first. "Did they open the safe?"

I heard the rapid-fire clicks of the lock spinning. "They didn't get it," a voice said, and someone sighed loudly with relief.

Inside the wall, we were still a long way from that point. I glanced away from Poe, and then, after a decent interval, looked back. He was still staring at me.

"I think they set off the alarm and ran," said one at last. "They didn't have the chance to steal anything."

"We'll get them back, though," another cut in, his voice low and threatening. "We can't let this kind of affront stand without a counterattack."

Puck jerked in place, and several pairs of arms clamped down on him before he could rally to the Diggers' defense.

"Yes," said the third voice. "But how? We can't get into their Inner Temple. We've tried."

They had? That was news. I could feel, in the infinitesimal shifts of my companions, how they were taking this information, and predicted a sudden increase in our tomb's security. If we had any say in the matter, they'd continue to fail at breaching our sacred spaces.

Another voice joined in. "They aren't here. We've checked all the rooms."

"Even the back stairs?" said the scary voice. "You know they know where all of our secret places are. Damn frat boys."

Poe's eyes glinted slightly, and I fought to keep from giggling.

It seemed like hours later that the Dragon's Head members finally left the room in darkness, and hours more before any of us felt comfortable enough to move. I spent the time trying not to think about spiderwebs or rats' nests or how many creepy crawlies were sharing this space with me. I think Thorndike fell asleep. Puck did something that made Angel knee him in the balls. Lil' Demon almost had a heart attack when her two-way radio beeped on, but she shut if off before anyone could transmit.

Finally, Poe broke the silence. "We should make a break for it . . . soon."

"How did you know about this place?" I whispered back.

He shrugged, a move I could feel in the close quarters. "Didn't. But the safe was in a recess. Stood to reason there'd be a space, and I thought I could feel a draft from behind the piano. My main worry was that they knew it was here, too."

Thorndike roused herself from slumber. "You're the go-to guy when it comes to secret rooms on campus, man."

Poe fell silent, and I didn't blame him. When last he'd commandeered a secret room, it had almost torn our society apart at the seams. Of course, Poe was only one of the men who'd been involved in the society-within-a-society of Elysion last semester, and, as a group, we'd risen up and nipped the experiment in the bud well before Winter Break. Still, I swallowed the impulse to respond on his behalf. If Thorndike was still pissed off, she wasn't alone, and she was well within her rights.

Also, I wanted to defend Poe like I wanted to make this hole my new summer home.

Slowly, we pushed the piano away from the wall and squeezed out, stretching our cramped limbs and breathing deeply at last. After our long confinement, even the dim glow filtering in around the edges of the window seemed enough to define every detail of the room. We'd spread out, relieved to finally be able to have some space to ourselves. Lil' Demon was doing lunges, Thorndike had gone back to examining the dragon, and Poe leaned against the wall, his hands pillowed behind his head. Angel once again checked the status of the hallway. "I think they're still here," she whispered. "I can hear a television on down-stairs."

Crap. So we were still stuck, and still without a prize for all our trouble. I stared back at the hole behind the piano, and suddenly got a great idea. "Let's steal the dragon."

"What?" said Puck. "No. Trying to go forward anyway is what got us into this mess."

"No, you jumping before the signal is what got us into this mess," Poe offered from against the wall.

"Forget it, Bugaboo," said Thorndike. "There's no way we can get it out of here."

"So we don't get it *out*," I replied, feeling a grin tugging at the corners of my mask. "Hidden is as good as gone for our purposes. We pull a *Thomas Crown Affair*."

"The original or the remake?" asked Lil' Demon.

I furrowed my brow. "There's an original?"

Poe chuckled softly. *"Children."*

Hollywood history aside, my plan was quickly ratified and, with no little difficulty and a good deal more noise than we hoped, we got the giant golden dragon hidden inside the crawl space we'd so recently vacated.

"Doesn't have the same sense of victory as if we actually *took* the item we're supposedly stealing," Angel whispered, when at last we had the piano pushed back in place and the entire area dusted to ensure that our tampering wouldn't be detected.

"It works, though," said Thorndike. "When they notice it's missing, they'll know it was us. We can still bargain with them to get our little statue back."

"Don't celebrate yet," said Lil' Demon. "We still need to escape, or did anyone fancy spending the rest of the semester in the Dragon's Head tomb?"

In the ensuing silence, we all tried not to look at the one patriarch in the room. Poe was, after all, the go-to guy when it came to finding secret passages. We stood in silence for a full ten seconds before his sigh floated over from the position he'd returned to, holding up the wall.

"Okay. I'll help you guys out, just this once."

———

"Did he have to be so holier-than-thou about it?" Angel asked me five minutes later, as we sneaked down the back stairs into the kitchen. "Every time I start to think he might be okay, he turns around and acts like a complete jerk."

And every time I decided he was a complete jerk, he turned around and did something decent. Poe kept his sheet pretty well balanced.

We broke out into the yard and sprinted quickly for the nearest wall. This time, I made my leap on the first try, but it took three attempts for Poe to reach the ledge. We hauled him over the top and into the safety of the alleyway beyond.

Thorndike pumped her fist in the air. "Success!"

We hurried back to the street, and Lil' Demon pulled out her walkie-talkie. "I'll see if they're still waiting up for us. This calls for pizza and beers, I think."

"I think they're paying," Puck said. He whipped off his ski mask and let out a primal shout to the sky. His hair was plastered to his face and wet with sweat. "Man, what a rush!"

I pulled off my own mask and fluffed my hair. I'm sure I looked just as gross, but I felt just as exhilarated. I wanted to dance, to run, to scream. Angel and Thorndike were tangoing in the snow, and Lil' Demon laughed and snapped pictures with her cell phone to send to the knights who'd missed out on the adventure. I turned to Poe, grinning. He'd removed his own mask, and ran his fingers through his wet, dark hair, then lifted them into the light. I saw a flash of red before he caught me staring and whipped his hand behind his back.

Euphoria leaching into the air, I rushed over. "You're hurt. What happened?" I reached for his head and he wrenched it away. "When you cracked your head against the wall in the crawl space..."

"Presence of real genius, Bug'boo."

I shook my head. He'd been hurt all that time, and hadn't said anything. "If you're still bleeding...My God, Poe. Let's call Lucky and get her to give us a ride to the hospital."

He moved another few steps back. "'m fine. Go get your...pizza." He waved vaguely at the retreating group.

"You're not fine," I argued. He was slurring his words. He'd been leaning against the wall while we'd been in the treasure room. He hadn't been able to jump over the ledge. "You're still bleeding. You could have a concussion. *Probably* have one."

"Yo, guys!" Puck called. "Let's get a move on! There's a pitcher of beer at Sicily's with my name on it."

I looked at the others, then turned back to Poe, holding out my hand. "Come on. Stop being so difficult."

"Right, 'cause the perfect ending to me tagging along, *again*, is ruining your vict'ry cel'bration with a trip to the ER."

I laughed in disbelief, hoping it would set him at ease. "Please. You're talking crazy. We only made it out tonight because of you."

He wadded up his ski mask and held it against his head, then turned south, which was not, thankfully, in the direction of his apartment, but rather of Eli–New Haven Hospital. Still, it was a half hour walk, a hike I had no intention of letting him take alone. Or at all.

"Poe, wait up already!" I hurried after him.

"Where are you guys going?" I heard Angel call.

"Check out Bugaboo, hooking up with the freaks," Puck said. But I barely noticed. In the golden glow of the sodium lights, I could now see that the back of Poe's black sweater was soaked with a dark liquid I doubted was sweat.

I skidded to a stop on the icy walk before him. "Stop. Now. You're in no condition to walk."

He looked at me with unfocused eyes. "Christ, Amy, you're such a bossy bitch."

And then he collapsed.

I hereby confess:
I didn't realize
how much I'd missed him.

2.
Mistakes

THINGS THAT HAPPENED
IMMEDIATELY AFTER

1) Clarissa screamed.
2) Odile rushed to the nearest blue emergency phone and called campus security, the irony of which was not completely lost on us.
3) Poe woke up as we packed snow and ski masks against his head wound, and mumbled incoherently about "Discretion" and how I couldn't fine him for using my real name, since, officially, our society mission was over. (Or, for the purists, *Jamie* woke up . . .)
4) Demetria concocted some cock-and-bull story for the paramedics about how Poe slipped on the ice.

5) I got blood all over my favorite pair of Converse sneakers.

6) George hit on the ambulance driver.

Poe flatly refused to let any of us accompany him to the hospital (though I think George would have loved to log some time with the cute paramedic) and the ambulance left us standing in the snow, kicking slush over the circle of fresh blood on the walk beneath the street lamp.

"Do you think he'll be okay?" I asked.

"More to the point," said Clarissa, "do you think, in his state of mind, he'll give us up?"

Demetria put her hand on my shoulder. "Head wounds bleed a lot, but I bet he'll be fine. My biggest concern is that there aren't any pieces of wood embedded in his skull—"

"Gross," said Odile.

"—which will show the doctors we were lying about how it happened."

"Screw the doctors. We'd better hope Dragon's Head's forensic capabilities aren't top-notch," I added in self-recrimination. "I bet Poe bled all over the house." How could I have been so dense? I'd been so intent on getting that statue hidden, I hadn't even noticed he was bleeding out where he stood.

I called the hospital the next day, and they told me that Mr. James Orcutt had checked out. I left him a voice mail, but he never called back. And he didn't show up at the Rose & Grave tomb as usual in time for our first society dinner of the semester, leaving me to wonder if he'd

a) finally gotten a life outside of Rose & Grave

b) realized that no one in my club wanted him around

c) was lying unconscious and concussed, alone, in his
shabby apartment.

Unfortunately, something else did show up at the tomb
that night, and it shot to hell all my fantasies of a happy-
go-lucky last semester at Eli. We'd spent most of the
evening congratulating ourselves on a raid well done and
regaling one another with stories of our Winter Break adventures. Toward the end of the evening, there was a soft
knock at the door of the Inner Temple. Soze stepped outside to speak to Hale, the tomb's cook and caretaker, then
returned, a somber expression on his face, and held up a
large manila envelope. "We have a problem."

Immediately, the chatter and backslapping stopped.

"The following was delivered to Hale by the caretaker
of Dragon's Head." He slipped two sheets of paper out of
the envelope and laid them on the conference table. One
was a grainy, shadowed photo of black-clad figures in ski
masks climbing the wall around the Dragon's Head tomb.
The other was a page from our class's Freshman Facebook.
My photo was circled in red.

My heart sank into my sneakers and I pressed closer,
trying to get a better look. "How did they know?" I whispered. Very few barbarians were aware of my involvement
with Rose & Grave. There was Brandon Weare, my ex-
boyfriend, but he'd have no cause to share the information
with anyone. Lydia, my roommate, but she'd never do that
to me—or to my fellow knight Soze, who'd been her boyfriend since the start of the school year. And finally, there
was Genevieve Grady, the old *Eli Daily News* editor, whose
place in Rose & Grave I'd inadvertently swiped last year.
Could she have let it slip?

Soze pointed again to the photo, and I noticed a faint
red pen circle around one of the figures' footwear.

"How many seniors have yellow Chuck Taylors, Bugaboo?"

Oh, crap.

Everyone now leaned in to look.

"You gotta be kidding me," said Puck. "How can they even tell the color in the dark?"

Angel put her hands on her hips and faced me. "We were *supposed* to wear all black!"

"Well, some of us don't have your shoe collection," I snapped. "I can't exactly climb walls in sequined black pumps or knee-high black stiletto boots."

"No, but I'd pay to see you try," drawled Graverobber.

"Me, too," said Puck. He winked at me. "Knee-high stiletto boots? You were so holding out on me."

Lucky snapped her fingers in his face. "Focus." She turned to Soze. "What do you think they mean by this?"

Soze sighed. "It's a threat. They're saying they know which society is responsible for the raid, and, more to the point, they know the identity of at least one of the knights involved."

"So?" asked Thorndike with a shrug. "We want to negotiate with them anyway. Our statue for, uh, the location of theirs."

"But that was before they could pick Bugaboo out of a lineup," said Bond. "Now they could force us to return the dragon without giving up our statue in return."

Man, and here I thought we'd make it through the end of the school year sans any more barbarian scandals. "How?"

"I don't know," said Bond. "But whatever it is, they'll do it to you."

———

The missive from Dragon's Head dampened the mood of the evening, and no one felt much like hanging out once the meeting dismissed. After taking a rain check on a planned game of Kaboodle Ball (despite protests from George) the members of the club headed our separate ways. Josh accompanied me back to Prescott College, on a pretense of seeing his girlfriend and my roommate.

"Feeling okay?" he asked.

I shrugged inside my winter coat. Once again, I'd shown how very appropriate my society name was. I'd screwed up the raid for everyone. Poe had cracked his head open for nothing. "Do you think Greg was right, that they'll come after me unless we give them what they want?"

"Probably," Josh said in a hushed tone, as we passed the Dragon's Head tomb.

"I hate the idea of capitulation." I kicked the snow, caught sight of my sneakers, and grimaced.

"Really? Wait, you wouldn't be Amy Haskel, by any chance, would you?" He grinned. "I'm inclined to say it's up to you what we do. I don't want to give in either, but then again, I'm not the one with the target on my back."

"But what could they actually do to me?" I asked, swiping my proximity card at the Prescott College gate. "What would we do, if the situation were reversed?"

"The usual: murder, mayhem, total annihilation of our victim and anyone she's ever loved."

"That's it? Piece of cake."

We walked up the steps to the suite I shared with Lydia. Josh paused at the door. "Seriously, though, they'll probably start by publicizing your Digger status."

I twirled my finger in the air. "Whoop-de-doo. Worse things could happen. Heck, it might even help me get into grad school."

"Or . . ." He hesitated at the door. "They might press charges against you for breaking and entering."

That one stopped me in my tracks.

"And the related theft," Josh added. "They have a picture with identifying features, you probably left fingerprints somewhere in the building, and I don't want to know how valuable that dragon is."

"That probably *wouldn't* help with my grad school apps." I could feel a headache coming on. "But wouldn't they have to let the police into their tomb, let all sort of stuff become public?"

Josh sighed. "I really don't know how the rules work at Dragon's Head. I know the policy of the Diggers is to keep as many of our activities below the radar as possible—not to involve the barbarian world in whatever happens on the inside of our organization. We wouldn't risk opening the tomb up to scrutiny to get a statue back. We'd find another way to deal with it. But Dragon's Head? Who knows?"

"Okay, okay," I said, grasping at straws. Orange jumpsuits weren't really my thing. "But I thought the cops tended to look the other way when it came to society pranks."

"Yes. *Tend.*"

"Josh, I must say, you aren't exactly the embodiment of comfort at this moment."

The door flew open and Lydia stood on the other side. "I beg to differ," she said. "He's my favorite bodily comfort. Now, exactly how long have you guys been standing here, hatching secret plots?"

Josh kissed her on the forehead. "The real question is how long you've been standing here listening to us hatch our secret plots."

"Not long enough, unfortunately." She pulled his head down for a real kiss.

I trailed the sickeningly sweet couple into the wood-paneled common room, dropped my coat on the couch, and followed after it. Josh took the recliner on the other side of the coffee table, and Lydia perched on its arm, resting her hand on the back so as to be in easy finger-twirling distance of her boyfriend's hair.

Do I sound bitter? I don't mean to. But here are the things you need to know about Lydia:

1) She's been my best friend and roommate for years, and we've seen each other through everything—I mean *everything*—from highly inappropriate relationships with T.A.s (not mine!) to regrettable anonymous one-night stands (guilty as charged).
2) Up until this past fall, her love life was every bit as disastrous and strewn with little pieces of ventricle and aorta as mine. Then she met Josh, a man whose own romantic history left much to be desired, and they both fell hard.
3) Ever since, she's been engaging in the type of coupley behavior we used to scoff at: hair-twirling, lap-sitting, "honey-bunny-ing," and other nonsense.
4) Once, during exam period in December, I even caught her laundering his boxer shorts.

I love the girl, but she needs to remember that this is New Haven, not Stepford. As they cuddled, I put my feet up on the coffee table and toed off my sneakers. Josh cast them a pointed glance.

"Perhaps a change of footwear for the time being?" he said. "No point making it worse."

I sighed and looked at Lydia with imploring eyes. "Josh says I can't wear my sneakers."

Lydia traced her fingertip around his ear. "Since when do you get fashion advice from Josh?"

"Since now. Can I borrow your fabulous brown boots?"

"No, because they *are* fabulous and I want them to stay that way at least until Easter. The slush outside will ruin the finish in a day and a half." She looked from me to Josh and back again. "Is this one of your new rules? No metal, no sulfur, and now...no sneakers?"

"Could tell you, but then I'd have to kill you," Josh replied with a smug smile.

This was par for the course in our suite since the big reveal in November. Lydia teased Josh and me mercilessly because she knew we were in Rose & Grave, and we, for her amusement, played the parts of obnoxious, secretive society types. At times, Josh even affected an accent he said was James Spader–esque but I insisted was a lot closer to adenoidal.

On the whole, however, I considered myself pretty lucky that Lydia had picked Josh as my roommate-in-law. I had friends whose inter-suite romantic trauma had been so intense, they'd actually made their bunkmate choose: either the suite, or the significant other.

"Speaking of Easter," Lydia said, tiring of the game a little early tonight. "We need to finalize those plane flights before the prices go through the roof."

"Flights?" I asked.

Lydia looked a little guilty. "Yeah. Josh and I are going to Barcelona for Spring Break."

Some might be surprised to learn that the look of betrayal on my face was not directed at my roommate and best friend, with whom I had spent my last three Spring Breaks. I'd told her back in the fall semester that I'd be occupied.

But *Josh* was supposed to be occupied right along with me.

"But..." I began, then broke off. What could I say? *Oh, Lydia, don't be silly. Of course Josh isn't going with you, his loving girlfriend, on a romantic getaway to Europe to consume gazpacho and rioja and dance to guitars on streets covered in bougainvillea and orange blossoms. He's got to go hang out in an undisclosed and possibly underground location with the Diggers, none of whom is giving him sex or rioja, and discuss those secret world domination plots of ours. Sounds fun, huh?*

"Wow," I said at last. "How exciting."

Apparently, Lydia wasn't entirely convinced by my ecstatic tone. "Well, you said you couldn't—"

Yeah, but I didn't realize how much the idea of my best friend jaunting off to Spain with her *lovah* was going to hurt. All of a sudden, I felt very hot inside my turtleneck sweater. I wanted bougainvillea and orange blossoms. I wanted rioja and gazpacho. I wanted to know why the hell Josh was ditching the Diggers. Wasn't he supposed to place us above all others?

"What, I'm not enough for you, Lydia?" Josh cut in before I could grill him. "I thought this was supposed to be a *romantic* getaway you were dragging me on."

"With all the museum trips you have planned?" Lydia rolled her eyes. "Guernico is not romantic."

"It's *Guernica*, and that's in Madrid, so don't worry about it." Josh pulled her onto his lap. "You're thinking of Gaudi, whose art we will be seeing a lot of, and whom you shall learn to love, my sweet. *La Sagrada Familia. Colegio Teresiano. Palau Güell...*" He began to nuzzle her neck.

Hint taken. Plus, if possible, I was even less interested than Lydia in a lecture about Spanish art, so I chose that moment to adjourn to my room. No sooner had the door shut behind me than I heard Lydia hiss in a whisper to Josh, "Don't do that in front of Amy."

"Why not?"

"Because..." She hesitated. "I feel bad. She hasn't had a boyfriend in a while..."

Oh, no. I sank into my desk chair. They weren't going to be one of those couples who liked to gossip about a single friend's lack of love life behind her back, were they? Of course, Josh knew exactly how long it had been since I had a date—he'd even warned me against my short-lived affair with George last semester. But still, it rankled. Especially if they were going to talk behind my back *within earshot*.

"She's got bad luck with men," Lydia continued.

"I beg to differ," said Josh. True. A lot of women I knew would think I'd been very lucky indeed to snag George, even for a little while. I rolled closer to the door to listen in.

"Don't you know any nice guys for her?" Lydia was asking. "We could double date."

"Look," Josh said, a note of annoyance creeping into his voice, "it's not my responsibility to play Cupid for my—er—girlfriend's roommate."

"She's not *just* your girlfriend's roommate, though, is she?" Lydia cajoled.

"This conversation is officially over."

Hey! No! It was just getting good! Why didn't Josh want to set me up with anyone? Didn't he think I was cute enough for any of his friends? Or did he have another problem with me? Was it my, um, *experience* with George? I was ready to burst back out and ask him what he meant, when Lydia spoke again.

"No need to get bent out of shape. I can understand your concern. She does have a tendency to self-sabotage all of her relationships. Like last year, she was seeing this great guy—"

"Brandon."

"Right, of course you know."

And he had made several vows to the effect that he wasn't supposed to let anyone *know* that he knew! Josh! Man, I had him so bad. The fines I'd level on him at the next meeting—he'd better hope flights to Barcelona weren't pricey!

"Anyway, you should have seen them together. They were so perfect. But of course she botched it up," Lydia added. "Oh, that reminds me." She shouted, "Amy!"

I waited a few seconds before opening the door, so they wouldn't realize I had been right behind it. "Yes?"

"Brandon called."

I blinked. I hadn't known what Lydia wanted with me, but a phone message from my ex-boyfriend and ex-friend-with-benefits (if not ex-friend, full stop) was not at all what I'd expected. Brandon never called. In fact, the last time I'd spoken to him at any length, he had said the ball was in my court as far as future contact went.

It was a ball I'd dropped, as Brandon's Amy-free life seemed to make him perfectly happy, and Brandon's very non-Amy girlfriend was beautiful, accomplished, crazy about him, and singularly unimpressed with me.

"What did he want?" I asked, or rather, croaked. My mouth had gone inexplicably dry in the last two seconds.

"Um . . . to talk to you?" She pointed at the phone. "You still have his number, right?"

Yes, I still had his number. And I still had a lot of baggage to lug around regarding our broken relationship. After sleeping together for several months last spring, Brandon had finally talked me into becoming his girlfriend for real, only to discover that I was no more committed to him than I'd been when I hadn't called him my boyfriend, and he broke it off.

I'd been more hurt by the loss of his companionship than by anything else. He'd mostly kept his distance ever since, but every time we did see each other, the air was charged with unfinished business.

My hand hovered indecisively over the phone, as if each of my fingers had taken a vote, decided that calling Brandon would be a poor plan, and mutinied. "It's probably too late."

"It's barely eleven," Lydia replied. "Early evening in college time."

I willed my fingers to retrieve the phone then beat a hasty retreat into my bedroom.

"See what I mean?" I heard Lydia say as I shut the door.

I'd show her. I dialed his cell phone from memory, and Brandon picked up on the first ring.

"Hi, Amy."

I was so unprepared, I couldn't think of a response. "You rang?" Ugh. Well, that was rude of me. Not even a *Hi, Brandon, how was your Winter Break?* No wonder his girlfriend thinks I'm a bitch.

"Yes, I did, though I should have known you wouldn't be home. It's Sunday, after all." He chuckled. Everyone on campus knew that Sunday nights were secret society meeting nights.

Time to get back on subject. "So, what's up?" I kept my tone light. "Have a good break?" There. I could be polite.

"Wonderful. Felicity and I went to Tahoe."

"Oh," I said, and dropped onto my bed. "Nice."

"Her family has a house out there. I was worried that I'd embarrass myself on the slopes, since she's been skiing since birth, but...you'd never believe it. Did you know

I'm a naturally talented skier?" I could hear the smile in his voice.

"I had no idea." But it didn't surprise me. Brandon was a natural at whatever he put his mind to. It was one of the things that made him so attractive. That and his complete lack of pretense. He was brilliant, but didn't brag, popular, but not cliquish, comfortable in his skin, and utterly forthright about his needs and desires.

I know what you're thinking: *You idiot, Amy.* It's okay. I think that often enough myself.

"What were you up to?" he asked.

"The usual: family, carols, tree, stockings, too much fruitcake."

"Any fruitcake is too much."

"Agreed...I went to a party with some friends in Manhattan for New Year's."

"Nice. Anyone I know?"

"Maybe," I said coyly. It was indeed possible he knew some of the Diggers in a barbarian capacity, but I wasn't about to name names.

All in all, I was starting to feel okay about the conversation. Maybe we could move beyond our shared past and be friends, the way we used to be before we'd made the mistake of sleeping with each other. Once upon a time, he'd been among my closest college chums. But that was before Rose & Grave. Now I wasn't sure anyone could take the place of my society brothers in my heart.

"So..." He hesitated. "I was wondering if you wanted to have lunch sometime soon. We have a lot to talk about."

"We do."

He was silent for a moment. "I mean, I heard through the grapevine you're going out for some fellowships this semester. I am, too. I thought maybe we could help each other with our applications."

Oh. "That would be great," I choked out. But it would also be an exercise in humility. Last time Brandon and I had been in competition for something (the editorship of the *Eli Literary Magazine*), he'd almost beat me out *while* finishing a huge project for his Applied Math major. Seriously, the guy had brains in his toe joints. "You think you want to keep studying literature?"

"No, these are math fellowships. I just thought—"

"Yes. Sounds great," I said, before he could change his mind. Whatever it took. The opportunity to hang out with Brandon was not easy to come by these days.

But why did he want to work with me instead of with Felicity?

"Good." He sighed into the phone, as if he'd been holding his breath. "How about lunch tomorrow? I'm free at noon. Want to meet at Calvin College?"

His college's dining hall. Interesting choice. There was a decided connotation associated with the location and timing of a dining hall date, and modern Eli students recognized the distinctions as easily as their forebears once understood the difference between events that called for them to dress in morning coats, dinner jackets, or white tie:

DINING HALL DATE RULES

	Mutually Neutral Dining Hall	One Party's "Home" Dining Hall
Dinner	Closest thing to a real date, except cheaper for everyone involved. Possibility of seeing/sitting with an acquaintance: negligible.	Almost as bad as brunch in a Home Dining Hall (see below). Possibility of playing off as "just friends," if necessary: high. Possibility of sitting with a group of Home Party's friends: very high.
Brunch	Either a business meeting or the aftermath of a one-night stand. You don't want anyone to see you.	Official announcement of coupledom to the Home Party's entire acquaintance. (This goes double if either Party has wet hair.)
Lunch	What the asker angles for if he or she can't get the other Party to agree to a real date, or even a Dining Hall Dinner.	So aboveboard, it's sickening. Might as well have a sign saying, "Nothing to see here, just grabbing a bite before our next class." Possibility of sitting with friends: medium.

"Sounds good," I said. "Remember to bring your apps."

After we'd said our good-byes, I unearthed my applications from my pile of start-of-term paperwork and attempted to make it look as if I'd been doing serious work on them for the last few weeks. I made little headway, however, as my brain's computing power was focused on Josh and Lydia and what they'd been saying about me. Naturally, it's far worse to hear unpleasant things about yourself from people you know love you, because they aren't saying it to be mean, nor are they prejudiced against your shimmering personality. No, your friends are telling the truth that you know deep down anyway—and my friends were saying I sucked at romance. To the point that they wouldn't even try to set me up on a date. Wouldn't risk subjecting their other friends to the horror that is me.

Cheer up, Amy. It's not like this is anything new. I am well aware of my limitations when it comes to forming healthy relationships with the opposite sex. It's why I'd tried to keep Brandon at arm's length to start with. I knew getting involved with him would wreck our friendship, and it had. Last year at this time, he'd been buying me dinners at Thai restaurants. This year, I was braving my way through a cafeteria lunch where he had home-court advantage.

And I wouldn't even have the comfort of my favorite pair of sneakers.

Later, when I headed to the bathroom to brush my teeth, I noticed that Lydia and Josh were nowhere to be seen, and later still when I tucked myself into my narrow, extra-long single dorm bed, I heard them whispering softly through our shared wall.

Had things gone differently, would it be Brandon and me whispering late into the night? Would we still be together if I hadn't accepted the tap from Rose & Grave? Would I be planning a career in publishing instead of looking at graduate fellowships? Would we be booking flights to Barcelona for an extended double date with Lydia and Josh?

Stupid to play *what if* games! I loved being a Digger. I loved my brothers, and the tomb, and the activities. I loved our tricks, and our raids, and our silly society games. I loved everything I'd learned about myself as a result of joining Rose & Grave.

But right then, one room away, there were people *in* love, and I'd never felt so alone in my life.

I hereby confess:
It only takes two.

3.
Conspiracy

Since my morning lecture in the English department building ended at eleven-thirty, I had the dubious pleasure of cooling my heels in the Rose & Grave tomb for half an hour before I was due to meet Brandon around the corner at Calvin College. I spent the time whipping myself into a frenzy of nerves and second-guessing my choice of outfit—which, Josh would be pleased to know, did not include my yellow sneakers. I fully admit that I'd dressed with more care than usual this morning, and even blow-dried my hair to give it extra body and shine.

After all, when one hangs out with one's ex, it's important to look as stunning as possible.

I wonder if boys even notice the machinations we go through on their behalf? Are they aware of the subtle but significant difference between your everyday jeans and your very best pair, the fact that this particular color scarf makes your eyes look green, or the light layer of mascara designed to enhance the entire ocular region? Back when Brandon and I were an item, he'd been known to tackle me on occasions where I was wearing sweatpants and fluffy socks, so my guess is that he doesn't care at all.

Bummer.

I repeatedly checked my watch, the face of the grandfather clock in the Grand Library, and the digital readout on the room's single computer screen, until they all agreed that it was time for me to head out. Exiting the Diggers' tomb mid-day is a somewhat delicate operation, but in my tenure as a member, I'd figured out the trick of it, and managed to escape the property undetected by any of the barbarian students milling around the Art History building.

Brandon was waiting for me in the Calvin College common room. I pasted an awkward smile on my face in preparation for the inevitable awkward hug.

But when it came, it wasn't awkward in the least. Brandon enfolded me in his arms and dropped his chin onto my shoulder and I almost gasped from the sudden, overwhelming sensation of *fitting*. With it came the memories: how Brandon wasn't all that much taller than me and I hadn't had to tilt my head up to kiss him; how every curve of his body seemed to fit perfectly against mine. I stiffened, steeling myself against the impulse to press against him, and pulled away. "Lunch?"

We engaged in idle chitchat all the way through the cafeteria line and the salad bar, and then Brandon directed me to an out-of-the-way table with only two chairs. Well, that answered my first question. We wouldn't be sitting with his buddies.

As soon as we got settled, Brandon launched into a description of the various programs he planned on applying to and I responded in kind, all the while wondering how he expected me to know anything about what universities were looking for in a candidate for their Applied Math programs. I hadn't taken a math class since high school. I'd earned all my Group Four—Eli-speak for science and math—credits in the natural sciences. What use would I be to him reviewing his applications? What was I even doing here?

"...though I really like the work they're doing at the Courant Institute," he was saying.

I shook my head. "I'm sorry, Courant is where, now?"

"NYU, Amy."

"Right. Well, the one where you go to study in Antarctica sounded—"

Whoosh! A deluge of icy liquid spilled over me, soaking my hair, my clothes, everything! I jumped, but not quickly enough to dodge the shower of soda, pink lemonade, water, and juice.

"Oops," said a smug voice behind me as I yelped. Antarctica, indeed. I whirled around, to see an unfamiliar kid standing above me, holding a tray covered in about ten tipped-over, extra-large dining hall glasses and the remains of their liquid contents.

The dining hall went silent as everyone directed their attention to our table. So much for flying under the radar.

Brandon had yanked a wad of napkins from the dispenser and was trying to mitigate the worst of the mess. "Say you're sorry, jerk, and give us a hand."

The guy shrugged. "You probably shouldn't have left your bag in the aisle."

I held my sticky, frigid shirt away from my chest and tried to mop up the puddle in my lap. "My bag?" I looked down and discovered that the damage to my person was nothing compared to what had happened to all my newly bought books and school supplies. "Oh my God," I wailed, reaching for the sopping straps. Everything was ruined. I touched one sodden, pulpy pile. "This textbook was eighty bucks!"

"You disparage my aim?" the guy drawled.

"You're saying it's *my* fault you tried to turn me into a human soda machine?" I snapped.

"What the hell were you doing with all those drinks anyway?" Brandon demanded, using up the last of our table's supply of napkins and starting anew with those swiped from the table next to us. Some nearby diners had pitched in to help stem the flood, and I felt carbonated beverage seeping into my underwear.

"I get dehydrated," said the guy. He craned his neck over my shoulder to look into my bag. "Look on the bright side: Your computer wasn't in there. I'd say you got off lucky, Amy Haskel. This time, at least."

My mouth dropped open and my eyes shot to the collar of my assailant's jacket, where a tiny, gold reptilian face leered. He turned and walked off before I could push away the hands that were wringing out my scarf and go running after him. *Dragon's Head!* It was starting already?

I rose and tried to follow him, but the move dislodged several wayward ice cubes that immediately found their way into my crotch. I attempted a subtle jiggle (unsuccessful, I might add), and stopped walking, for fear the ice would shift left and press against spots even more sensitive than my inner thigh.

"What an asshole," Brandon said. "Look, let's go. Our lunches are drenched, and you need some dry clothes."

I nodded, poured the excess liquid from my bag into a nearby cup, and let Brandon bus our trays of ruined food while I prayed for the ice to melt as quickly as possible.

Of course, ice in my pants was the least of my problems. Even my gorgeous new camel coat—a Christmas present from my grandmother—was stained with star-bursts of orange soda and...was that fruit punch? *Great. Just great.* I gingerly tried to slip my arms into the sleeves for the trip outside, but Brandon stopped me.

"It's too cold for you to go out all wet. Come on, we'll get to my suite through the basement."

I followed him down into the tunnels that twisted below each residential college. This was where they kept all the goodies reserved only for their residents—everything from laundry rooms and student-run burger joints called "butteries" to bowling alleys and squash courts. We wound through the narrow, dimly lit hallways and I began to shiver.

Wait until the other Diggers heard about this! And where was I supposed to find the funds to replace the sticky mess Dragon's Head had made out of my course materials? I wondered if Rose & Grave had any kind of emergency scholarships for knights who were victims of another society's taste for vengeance, since I couldn't picture explaining to my parents what I'd done with this semester's book money. And let's not start on my coat.

Ahead of me, Brandon stopped and turned. "Amy, you okay?"

"Aside from the obvious?" I wrapped my arms tighter around my torso.

I felt his fingers on my chin, and he tilted my face up to his. "Your teeth are chattering."

They were. I clenched my jaw. "I'm fine. Just cold."

He said nothing, just stared at me.

Um, hello, cold? Maybe we should keep going until we get out of these tunnels? But I didn't say that, because under his gaze, I didn't feel chilly at all anymore. Nope. Downright warm.

"Amy—" he whispered.

I stepped back, and the—feeling, the moment, whatever it was—fell away. I hugged myself even harder, trying to quell the need to get close. "I could, um, really use some dry clothes right about now."

"Of course. Come on." He put his hand on my shoulder to guide me up the stairs to his entryway. I could feel humid, sticky heat burning through the material of my sweater and deep into the flesh of my arm.

The first time Brandon and I slept together had been Valentine's Day, almost a year ago. There'd been none of that weird, first-time-with-a-new-girl fumbling on his part. Like I said: The guy was a natural. Such a natural, in fact, that I'd put up little resistance when he'd repeated the persuasion act several times over the next few months. But he'd wanted a real relationship, and I'd resisted. Logical as the Applied Math major was, he had a mental block regarding my deplorable girlfriend potential, probably because we got along so well as friends. And yet I had no problem with the sex; bed was the one place where all the Brandon/Amy equations balanced perfectly.

He showed me into his unfamiliar suite and made a beeline for what I assumed was his bedroom. "I think I've got some spare sweats it wouldn't embarrass you too much to wear," he called back.

"I appreciate you doing this for me." I stood in the center of the room, recalling the odd bit of furniture and some of his posters from before. Though tempted, I tried not to touch anything. My fingertips were sticking together. My hair was plastered to the back of my neck. My soft, makes-my-eyes-green cashmere scarf was hopelessly destroyed. I also tried not to think about Brandon's bedroom. Instead, I started making a list of what I'd do to Dragon's Head. They wanted a war, they'd get one.

As Poe was fond of saying, I had a way of making trouble for people.

Brandon popped his head out of his room. "Do you want to hop in the shower first and wash some of the stickiness off?"

I hesitated. "Maybe I should just run home..."

"Don't be silly. You're still shivering. You're not hiking all the way back to Prescott like that. It's not a big deal."

"Getting in your shower isn't a big deal?" And *all the way back*? It was a block and a half.

"Well, it's not like I'll be there." He checked his smile. "Is this too weird for you?"

"No." It wasn't weird *enough*. I put my bag down and held out my hands. "Fine. Toss me some towels."

But I did little more than rinse. Brandon's shampoo and soap smelled too familiar to risk; I remembered too many other showers, too many other afternoons spent smelling like him. I dried off and headed back to the suite, praying his suitemates wouldn't see me in towels.

The common room was empty, even of Brandon, but I saw that he'd cleaned out my bag and hung it to dry over the radiator. A pile of used paper towels sat next to a neat stack of my ruined textbooks. Beyond, his bedroom door was open, but I couldn't see anyone inside. Perhaps he'd gone to a bathroom on another floor to wash his hands.

I closed the door behind me and sat on his bed. I knew this comforter well. He'd laid out a worn Eli T-shirt and a pair of drawstring sweatpants for me to wear. I picked up the shirt and held the softness against my skin. Forgoing the soap had been a useless effort. His clothes smelled like him, too.

And I'd have to wash them before I returned them, even though I'd only be wearing them for the trip back to my place. Not to get too blunt about it, but my underwear was in the same condition as the rest of my clothing: covered in soda. I had no choice but to go commando.

I dressed, then stuffed my sticky outfit into an empty shopping bag. Shouldn't he be back by now? As if on cue, there was a knock at the door. Brandon was always so polite.

"Come in," I called.

Of course, it wasn't Brandon. Felicity stopped dead on the threshold and gaped at me. In her boyfriend's clothes. On her boyfriend's bed. With my hair leaving wet rivulets all over her boyfriend's shirt.

This isn't what it looks like is so cliché, but it's the only phrase that popped into my head at the moment. Luckily, I was spared speaking it aloud, as Felicity regained her composure and asked, in a surprisingly reasonable voice, "Why, hello, Amy. Brandon around?"

I rose. "I think he must be using a downstairs bathroom. I'm sure he'll be right back."

And then, because the room didn't seem large enough for both of us, I squeezed out into the common room. Felicity stood by the door, watching as I assessed the damage to my schoolbooks. "What happened?"

"Some guy spilled a bunch of drinks on me at lunch."

"A *bunch* of drinks?" She raised her eyebrow. "How... odd."

Chick had no idea.

Brandon returned to rescue me. "Lis," he said, his eyes wide.

Lis? What kind of nickname was that? Better than "Fell," I suppose. And man, that was a guilty tone he was using. Curious. Brandon wasn't the type to expect anyone else to see impropriety where he saw none.

"Hi, sweetie." Felicity crossed the room, placed her hands on his chest, and kissed him like she hadn't seen him in months. "Amy was just telling me what happened to her. It's so awful. Do you know who it was?"

Brandon shook his head. "He's not in Calvin. Amy, did you know him?"

"No," I said. But I knew where he could be found on Thursday and Sunday nights.

"Sucks," Felicity went on, moving closer to me. "You should try to track him down if you can. He should be forced to pay you for those books." She toed at one of my stickier texts. "They're unusable."

Thanks for the tip, bitch. Never would have figured that out myself.

She straightened. "It was good to see you again, Amy. I just have a short break before my next class. I was hoping to duck in here and take a nap." She smiled at Brandon. "Maybe you could join me."

Brandon restrained his male hormones long enough to look momentarily taken aback by her audacity.

I swallowed. "I have to get out of here anyway."

Felicity smiled, sweetly. "Of course." *Of course, because I'm the girlfriend here. Of course, because I've made the fact that you're not welcome abundantly clear. You may have the sweatpants, but not their owner. Scat.*

I grabbed my still-damp bag and shoved my books inside. "Thanks for the clothes, Brandon. I'll get them back to you ASAP."

"Amy, we haven't even talked about these applications."

Or eaten lunch. "Rain check," I insisted, and ran.

I'm sure I hadn't reached the ground floor before she had him in her clutches.

———

I reported the soda dump to some Digger friends over pizza that night and basked in their appropriately appalled response. They vowed revenge, promised to protect me, and started up a pool to replace my books. We talked about letting Dragon's Head know the location of their missing statue, lest this incident was only the opening volley in a full-scale war on *me*. I liked having it as an option, but if anything, their little game made me even more determined to stand my ground and protect Rose & Grave—with my body, my textbooks, and my new camel coat.

Besides, there, in the bosom of my brothers, the whole affair seemed like a singular event, an isolated incident that would be immediately snuffed out now that the full weight of the society was bent on avenging the wrongs perpetrated against one of their own. Except, they couldn't keep their eyes on me at all times, and it seemed as if whenever the Diggers weren't watching, the Dragon's Head members were. And thus, over the course of the next few weeks, we had as many failures as successes.

The Eli Library suddenly reported that I owed fines in the thousands on library books whose due dates went back to my middle school days. Jenny Santos, computer whiz that she was, managed to fix the "problem," but lo, when the hold on my lending privileges was lifted, I discovered that all of the volumes I'd reserved had mysteriously gone missing in the stacks. So much for my research paper.

Two days later, I turned my back for five seconds in the dining hall and someone covered my salad with a spray of habanero pepper. A day after that, I was following my usual route home from class and passed underneath the Hartford College arch. When I emerged on the other side, I was met with another icy shower. (Luckily, I'd taken to keeping my valuables inside Ziploc bags inside my satchel.) By the time I looked up, I saw little more than two hooded figures disappearing back into their window, dragging a large empty tub behind them. Dragon's Head sure liked their liquids.

Greg Dorian said he admired the ingenuity of their multilateral attacks. (I thwapped him with the Kaboodle Ball in response.) Josh wondered if we should be keeping tabs on my transcripts, to avert any bizarre clerical errors, a possibility that kept me up all night. Jenny was constantly monitoring my computer, and reported three different attempts to send me a virus through bogus announcement e-mails from the Prescott College master's office. I only hoped she was good enough to catch them all.

And then came the superglue incident. And the Great Cricket Invasion of January 2008 (Lydia still won't sit on our couch). What was next, locusts to eat all my homework? I began to wonder if Rose & Grave pride was worth ruining my last semester at Eli. Nothing against taking one for the team, but it's not as if I could explain to my thesis advisor, the dean of the Lit department, or any potential graduate schools that the reason my work took a sudden nosedive was because I was fending off a secret society hell-bent on using me as a scapegoat for all the crimes the Diggers had committed over the past centuries. And even if I did manage to make this point without forswearing my own society's vows of silence, I doubt the faculty would believe me, or even care.

I was beginning to think our rivals didn't even need the dragon statue as an excuse. They wanted revenge on Rose & Grave, and since they couldn't get into the tomb, one innocent knight walking the streets of New Haven made a darn convenient target. Spring Break was still a month off, and this winter looked like it would never end.

So, in the grand tradition of stalker victims everywhere, I began to act like the hunted prey I was. I varied my schedule, turned down social engagements, took alternate and unfriendly routes around campus, and found excuses to stay home from class in the relative safety of my room. (I insisted Lydia double check all the locks every time she stepped out, and since there were still several dozen chirping insects hiding somewhere in the suite, she agreed.)

One afternoon, Prescott College held a snowball fight in the courtyard, but there was no way I'd brave the melee under the present circumstances. Who knew how many Dragon's Head members lay in wait, disguised as innocent Prescotteers, eager to pummel me into the slush? Instead I sat at the window, watching the festivities from afar, warm and dry and bored to the beyond. *There goes my last college snowball fight.*

I also missed my friend Carol's senior thesis play, and all the cajoling in the world on the part of Lydia and my other friends, barbarian or otherwise, failed to induce me to go to the Seniors' Valentine's Day Ball. Of course, as soon as I was left alone in the suite, it occurred to me that I'd maneuvered myself into another classic stalker-victim position—the isolated target. The only place I felt safe was in the Rose & Grave tomb's Inner Temple, because—you'll remember—Dragon's Head still didn't know how to breach our security. I packed my study materials into my bag (still mildly sticky, despite several washings) and furtively raced for the tomb, hoping my heavy winter clothing would disguise my identity from any Dragon's Headers who'd also stayed home from the dance.

I made it safely into the sanctuary and shed my coat in the front hall. Success. Relieved to be free of the constant pressure and vigilance, I practically skipped up the stairs to the Inner Temple. I even did a little pirouette on the landing.

And then I heard the clapping. Not a full-out round of applause, just a slow, sardonic smack. I froze, and slowly turned around. So, they couldn't make it into the Inner Temple. Didn't mean they didn't have access to other parts of the tomb.

"Nice, Bugaboo." Poe stood at the base of the stairs, unsmiling (as usual). "Planning an audition?"

I sank back on my heels, relieved to see him for perhaps the first time ever. "Just reveling in my freedom."

"From what?"

"Tyranny and terrorism."

"I assume you aren't talking in general terms," he said. "Otherwise I'd have to engage you in a political lesson."

"Dragon's Head." I clopped back down the stairs.

"Ah." He nodded. "I heard." I reached him and he leaned on the banister. "For what it's worth, I don't think you're to blame."

"Why not?" I was truly surprised. Poe *always* thought I was to blame. It was the foundation upon which our relationship was built.

"*I* didn't notice those sneakers."

I laughed. Right. And if Poe, the über-Digger, didn't notice it, then it was just a fluke they were identified at all. "I appreciate the support, but right now, it doesn't make a difference. I'm still wearing a bull's-eye on my back." I shrugged. "I can't even go to the V-Day Ball tonight."

"Here I thought it was because you were too much of a loser to get a date."

"That, too," I mumbled. I looked up at him. "What brings you here tonight? You've been MIA since—" since his recent brush with concussion "—all semester."

"Miss me?" he snarked.

"Hardly," I snarked back. "And you didn't answer my question."

He flashed a ghost of a smile. "Because it's none of your business."

"My tomb, my society, my"—I pointed at the black book he held in the crook of his arm—"archives."

"As well as mine. And trust me, this is nothing that concerns you."

"Why?"

"Because it concerns *me*."

Or maybe because I'd screwed up the last caper. "Right. The Bugaboo."

He rolled his eyes. "Okay. What's your opinion on current domestic policy?"

"Huh?"

"Exactly." He said nothing for a moment, just stood there, observing me in the unnerving way he had. "If this Dragon's Head thing is really bothering you, then give in," he said. "Tell those losers where we hid their precious hunk of metal."

I blinked in astonishment. *Poe* was telling me to put my needs above the Diggers'? Perhaps he'd hit his head harder than we thought. "Excuse me?"

"I'm serious. You don't have much time left. Don't waste your last few months on a battle that's not going to be worth it in the long run. If you're miserable, let it go and just . . . enjoy being a senior. Rose & Grave will survive a little more humiliation this year."

Oh, I got it now. "You don't think I can take it."

"No, I'm saying you shouldn't have to. It's misplaced pride."

"I can't believe you of all people would say that to me." I put my hands on my hips. "What happened to all that bull you spout about our oaths coming before anything?"

"I almost can't believe it myself." He shrugged. "But I've been there, remember? I have huge regrets about the things I didn't do when I was an undergrad. This is it, Bugaboo. This is your last chance. You don't have any more semesters, any more 'wait and sees.' Don't let it slip by while you ride this out. Trust me on this. It's not worth thinking about."

Now he sounded like Brandon, whose similar advice had tipped me toward joining Rose & Grave in the first place. Funny, I couldn't name two people less alike. Brandon was warm, where Poe was cold; Brandon friendly and open, where Poe was distant and unforgiving. Brandon had loved me, whereas the most I'd ever expected from Poe was a reluctant truce. Brandon was honest and forthright where Poe was—okay, he was honest, too, but he tended to say things I didn't want to hear. And he never spoke like this. Kind counsel wasn't Poe's usual style. I didn't know how to respond.

"Anyway," he said at last, "I should probably head home." He made for the door, then paused for a moment. "Of course," he said, "if you do roll over, don't expect me to let you live it down."

"Of course." *That* was the Poe I knew.

I spent the next few hours studying and musing over Poe's words. And in the end, I understood it wasn't snowball fights or even Winter Balls that I was missing, and that it wasn't Dragon's Head that was keeping me from it, either. I'd been afraid my junior year when I'd told Brandon that I didn't want anything more than a friendship-with-benefits. I'd been afraid last semester when I'd had my no-strings-attached fling with George Harrison Prescott. I was wallowing in fear every time I made fun of Josh and Lydia, or beat myself up over what Felicity had been able to create with Brandon. I'd been afraid of it for years, and I was about to graduate from college, still terrified of the idea of being in love.

Pathetic, huh? They teach us a lot here at Eli, but evidently not much about human nature. We're all so awash in our own ambition that we can't spare any attention for the ambitions of another. We can't afford to invest in relationships that will likely crash and burn. And we really can't allow ourselves to get distracted by the everyday drama of romance. There were too many other things to do.

But what about now? Arguably, I'd had a stellar college career. I'd run a publication, taken full course loads, drafted theses, joined a secret society, and taken on powerful conspiracies bent on my destruction—and no, that last one isn't necessarily in the Eli brochure for prospective students, but I did it anyway, and I kicked ass. I didn't regret one minute I'd devoted to these things.

I did regret screwing up with Brandon. I regretted that we were no longer close. If there was one thing I wanted back, in the twilight of my college career, it was him.

———

But I didn't expect it so soon. Because when I finally packed up my books around three and headed back to the suite, I found Brandon waiting for me on my common room couch—locks be damned.

It was as if I'd fallen through a time warp. This could have been last year, when Brandon was a regular fixture on this couch, waiting for me to come back from wherever I was. Loyal, devoted, like a puppy. Except now he wasn't puppy-like in the least. No, the energy he radiated was that of angry stray. Tonight, he was dressed in a rumpled suit, his tie undone, his dress shirt unbuttoned over a white tee, his dark, longish hair ruffled far past the point of respectability.

"Brandon?" I blinked. "What are you doing here?"

He looked at his hands. "I honestly don't know." He sighed, and stood. "This was a mistake. I'm sorry, Amy."

Now that he faced me, I could see that wrinkled clothes were the least of his problems. His usually warm, golden skin looked wan, his deep brown eyes were rimmed in red.

"No, it's fine. It's just...a little late for a social call."

He nodded absently. "Yeah, it is. I was beginning to think you'd be...out. For the night."

Like, with a guy. I could fill in that subtext all right. "And I figured that you'd be at the Ball...with your girl-friend."

He let that one hang in the air for a while. "Why didn't you call me...ever? After the coffee shop last fall? After lunch last month?"

So much for chitchat. "I don't know," I said with the type of honesty that can only come of being taken by surprise. "What would be the point?"

"The point would be *you* calling *me*." His voice was raw, like I'd never heard it before, not even when he'd broken up with me.

My eyes flashed to the door behind him. Could Lydia and Josh hear this?

He caught the direction of my gaze and waved dismissively. "They aren't here. They let me in and left. It's just us."

You mean just me, on trial. "What I'm saying is, what would be the point, with the way things are between us now?"

He took a few steps closer. "How is that, Amy? How are things between us?"

I watched him approach with trepidation. I heard the way he said my name with even more. No one ever said my name like Brandon did.

"They're...awkward. You have your girlfriend, and she doesn't like me very much."

"No, she certainly doesn't. Especially not tonight."

Tonight? But before I could say it out loud, I remembered. Valentine's Day. Our anniversary.

He looked down for a moment, took a deep breath. This wasn't like him. Brandon never hesitated to say anything. "The thing is, Amy, I'm really happy."

"I'm glad." Pure reflex. I was so lost here.

"I mean, really happy. This is my senior year, I'm acing all my classes, my badminton team has been kicking ass, I think that Calvin College might actually be in the running for the Tibbs Cup, and I have this gorgeous, amazing girlfriend who is very much in love with me."

Wow, when he put it like that, the best thing for me to do would be go jump off of something tall. "I'm ... glad," I choked out.

"So then, what's wrong with me?"

Nothing. Nothing was wrong with Brandon. He was perfect and happy. He had to be. I'd driven him away so he *could* be, in a way that wasn't possible with me. "What do you mean?"

He looked up. "Why am I always thinking about you?"

I hereby confess:
I blame the weather.

4.

Sin and Cosin

Late that night, it started to snow again. The flakes floated against the windowpane, flashing blue when they caught the reflection of the emergency call box outside the entryway. We'd turned off all the lights in the suite, since there are things you can't say if you're not in the dark.

Snow is a different substance at 3 A.M. It accumulated on the ground, glowing in the moonlight, coating the campus with an unearthly, radioactive radiance. Part of me wanted to go out and roll around in it, see if I could shimmer as much as the crystalline trees and the icy ground and the frosted, wrought-iron banisters. The other part never wanted to leave the room. In the post-snowfall silence, it was easy to believe that the night would never end, and I'd never have to deal with the consequences that waited beyond this moment, beyond that door.

The room was still dark when I opened my eyes the next morning. It might have been the sound of the wind that woke me. New Haven was in for a rotten day, to judge by the wet, angry howling on the other side of the glass. So much better just to snuggle back under the covers, which I did.

And jostled the body lying next to me.

"Hi," he said, and put his hand on my T-shirt-covered shoulder. "You're awake."

"How long have you been?" I whispered.

He shrugged, his arms brushing my torso beneath the covers. "A while."

"Doin' what?"

"Watchin' you."

I felt heat in my cheeks, and wondered if there was enough light for him to see me blush. The silence that followed his announcement was one in which, under normal circumstances, the girl would kiss the boy who'd wanted to watch her sleep, but these weren't normal circumstances, and even though the rules were only a few hours old, I understood them.

1) Look, but don't touch.
2) Talk, but don't taste.
3) Sleep together, as long as you aren't *sleeping together*.

Brandon wore the sweatpants and T-shirt I never had gotten around to returning to him. He shouldn't have stayed, and we both knew it. But our conversation had gone on so late, ending just as the weather had been at its worst, that the very idea of sending him out in it had seemed unconscionable. Why the perfectly serviceable couch in the common room hadn't been a viable option was a bit harder to explain away.

You know, if we planned to explain it to anyone. And I didn't know if we did. It hadn't once occurred to either of us to say *What are we doing?* or *What does this mean?*

And I didn't want to be the one to break that spell. Not

on this dreadful, bleak morning, cocooned inside my comforter, lost in the dreamtime of February. I didn't want to know the answer to those questions. Didn't even want to think the word *Felicity*, in case it was enough to crack this moment like thin ice.

But as I looked into Brandon's eyes, I ran out of synonyms for happiness.

"You aren't hungry, are you?" he asked me.

I rolled my eyes. Being hungry would mean getting up and going into public. And I never wanted to do that again. I wondered, idly, how long we could live on the Tic Tacs in my purse.

"Do you want to sleep more?"

I shook my head against the pillow, still not willing to speak. And now he was smiling. What a great smile he has. How in the world had I survived the last eight months without seeing it?

"Neither do I." And then he snuggled back under the covers as well. His hand slipped from my shoulder down my arm and past my wrist, and he laced his fingers with mine.

I shifted my face up again and met his eyes. We stared at each other as his thumb softly traced that sensitive bit of skin at the base of my thumb and forefinger. It was another moment where normal circumstances would prompt us to kiss, and again, we didn't. We didn't kiss, because that would cheapen the whole experience, turn it into some kind of rebound fling. It would be wrong.

And what we were doing felt so right.

————

The story came together courtesy of my various friends, each of which had their own version—not to mention their own take on the matter.

Of course, I'd heard Brandon's first, that night:

"I didn't even realize I'd been doing it until she started pointing it out after that day when you were in my room. But the more she kept bringing it up, the more she kept talking about you, the harder it was to overlook. And it doesn't make sense that..."

I didn't need him to finish the sentence. It didn't make sense that he'd be dating Felicity and thinking about me.

"The dance was the last straw...for both of us. She wouldn't stop talking about you. It wasn't even me, I swear. And when she started *screaming* at me..."

Poor Brandon. He looked so lost. No one could blame me for being a shoulder for him to cry on.

Lydia, of course, had her own perspective. As soon as Brandon left the next morning, she pounced:

"Amy, don't you think it's a *little* odd that after having a huge screaming match with his *current* girlfriend, in front of the *entire* senior class, about how he wasn't over his *ex-*girlfriend, the first thing he did was go to said ex-girl-friend's room?"

I also thought it was a little odd to be spoken to like I was a six-year-old.

"To be fair," Josh said without looking up from his *Wall Street Journal*, "it wasn't the first thing. We saw them fight at the dance, and judging from the state of his coat, he'd been walking around outside for at least an hour."

"Thank you, *CSI*." Lydia rolled her eyes. "The point is, I practically bruised my jaw on the floor when I saw him standing outside. I wouldn't even have let him in if it hadn't been for Josh making me."

"Making you?" I looked from one half of the couple to the other.

"He looked cold," said my fellow knight, with a shrug.

"But," Lydia pronounced, like a judge, "in the light of day, it doesn't look good."

"It looks like Felicity had a point," Josh said from behind his newspaper.

Yeah, she won the fight, but lost the boy. Some victory.

Lydia snarled at her boyfriend. "Someone's going to get hurt. It's too soon for . . . whatever they're doing."

"We're not doing anything!" I insisted.

Lydia rolled her eyes. "Well, that's good. Did he officially break up with her?"

I hesitated. We hadn't actually discussed that. Just as we hadn't discussed what *we* were doing. Everything else, sure. But not that. How had we spent so many hours together without it coming up?

Lydia knew me well enough to read my expression. "Just as I thought."

Josh looked up now. "Say what you will, Lydia. I think it's over. No man should have to put up with that kind of public humiliation. That girl is a harpy."

————

The harpy's childhood friend Clarissa had a decidedly different take on the matter. She breezed into the tomb at dinner that night, filled with stories about the recent scandal:

"So then, just as they are dancing to the new Bublé—"

"Oh, I love that song," said Lil' Demon.

"He makes some comment about Valentine's Days of yore—" at which, she flicks a hand in my direction. "I mean, can you believe it? Most romantic moment ever, and he's *still* talking about his ex. What do you expect a girl to do in a situation like that?"

Even I couldn't come up with a good response.

"So they broke up on the dance floor?" Lil' Demon asked. "Harsh!"

"Oh, no," Angel said. "They didn't break up. I mean, they may, but..."

But what? I bit my lip from bursting out—*But he spent last night with me!*—though I knew Angel would be obligated to keep my secrets, considering her oath. Soze glanced at me.

"No," Angel said. "In fact, I think they're supposed to meet for coffee later."

Damn these Sunday society meetings! If it weren't for Rose & Grave, I'd be able to stop him from keeping that coffee date. Unless he was using it to stage their official breakup. Yeah, that was it.

Juno groaned in frustration. "If we're all done talking about our love lives, can we get onto more serious topics?"

"What could possibly be more serious?" Angel asked.

Juno grabbed her bag and pulled out her laptop, opening the screen to reveal a news ticker. "World stage, people. Political upheavals. Empires collapsing. Citizens dying..."

Thorndike read the headline. " 'UPSET IN WHITE HOUSE STAFF ROCKS CAPITOL HILL.' "

The politically minded Diggers surrounded the laptop and started reading, but I couldn't muster up the interest. There was a new political scandal every day. I'd catch tomorrow's. Right now, I just wanted to figure out my love life.

"Look alive, Bugaboo, do you know who this is about?" Soze waved a hand in front of my face. I glanced down, halfheartedly, at the article on the screen.

Kurt Gehry.

What?

All thoughts of Brandon fled, and the entire tomb was in an uproar for the next few hours. Our planned program went right out the window as we researched, discussed, and debated the various details of the case. Seems that the White House Chief of Staff had quietly resigned last week, without a formal announcement to the press, without any fanfare at all. No one knew the reason. Nobody on the President's staff was talking about it, and Kurt Gehry himself was "unavailable for interview."

I almost felt sorry for Gehry, who was known to the Diggers at large as "Barebones." (His name in my club was mud, though, since he'd not once, but twice attempted to sabotage the entire class of knights in an attempt to reform the society in the image he found most suitable—one with no women in it.)

Speculation both in the capital and in the tomb on High Street ran rampant, and with it came an abandonment of any other topic. The job and thesis talk, which had made up the bulk of tomb discussions since consultancy and banking interviews had commenced in January, gave way to endless back-and-forths about why Gehry had really left his job and whether or not the President would tell Rose & Grave (if not the country) what was really going on.

One theory, popular among a certain breed of paranoid conspiracy theorists (but hey, they've been right before), promoted the idea that Gehry and the President had quarreled over Gehry's intervention in society matters last semester. In response to his attempts to undermine the society by siphoning off funds from the Trust to create a secret, males-only inner circle known as Elysion, my fellow knights and I had disavowed him as our patriarch, retroactively kicking him out of Rose & Grave for our year and any we tapped afterward.

According to the conspiracy theorists, the President of the United States, good Knight of Persephone that he was, could not bear to have on his staff anyone who was running afoul of Rose & Grave. Who knew a bunch of college kids had that much clout?

No one in my club, that was for sure.

"This is ridiculous," Josh said during a study session the following afternoon. He was showing a marvelous amount of aggravation for a man who'd just been accepted to Stanford Law School. (Lydia, also, had received a thumbs-up from our cousins on the Pacific, and I was positive she'd indulged in a couple of fantasies about the two of them becoming a power couple every bit as pedigreed as they were passionate.)

As for my couple status, it remained, much like my future, undecided. After the meeting last night, I'd waited up for Brandon, but he hadn't called. Who knew how long his conversation had gone on with Felicity? Maybe he hadn't felt up to seeing me directly after breaking up with her. His latest e-mail to me hadn't even mentioned the coffee date with Felicity that Clarissa had reported. He'd just asked if he could meet me in my suite after his afternoon lab. Of course I agreed.

"It's flatly impossible that no one knows anything," Josh went on. "I've shaken down every patriarch I can, and they are either stupid or playing so."

"I'd guess the latter, considering they're Eli alums," Demetria said. She and Jenny had spent the evening finalizing plans for the second half of Spring Break. Though we wouldn't all be visiting Cavador Key, the knights who were going to the island would be spending a week there, then renting a van, driving up the coast, and spending a week volunteering with Habitat for Humanity.*

---

* And people think secret societies are evil.

"I'd guess the former," said George, turning a page in his textbook, "considering most of them are inbred legacies with more money than sense." He looked up, an innocent expression pinned in place. "Wait. I meant, other than me, of course."

I rolled my eyes and went back to my work. Brandon got out of lab in forty-five minutes, and I wanted to make sure I had all my homework done well in advance. So far, I had three fellowship applications in, and four more in the works. I'd submitted one of my best term papers to two scholarly publications and a couple of conference listings besides, though I knew it would be a long shot. Still, anything would help beef up my grad school applications. So far the rolling admissions hadn't trundled in my direction, and I was hoping some last-minute additions to the package would help grease the skids.

The GREs had been a joke (ninety-eight percentile without even taking Kaplan) but I hadn't exactly distinguished myself in front of my professors the way I'd hoped. After all, it had always been my intent to go out into the workforce instead of staying in the Ivory Tower, and recommendations from crusty Russian Lit professors didn't carry much weight at Condé Nast. I hoped to get a few responses before Spring Break, but it was beginning to look unlikely. Landing a fellowship would vastly increase my chances of getting into the program of my choice. I still hadn't decided what the option was if I failed to receive admission at any of the A-list programs. Did I want to go to grad school enough to go just anywhere?

George dropped his book next to me on the table. "Stressed about the future?"

"Not really." I turned a page and typed another line into my file.

"You know, it occurs to me that we're the only two people in the club who don't have our futures planned out like a military invasion."

"Oh?" I said, looking up.

"Look." He began pointing. "Kevin's going to work for CAA, Clarissa's starting at McKinsey in the fall, Demetria got into Berkeley, Omar's headed to the Kennedy School, Jenny's starting that company of hers, Josh to Stanford Law, Odile to her next film, Ben to PwC, Mara to Wharton for her MBA…"

I wondered how long it had taken him to memorize that list for recitation. And to think that, last year, I chose him over Brandon. "We haven't heard from Greg yet."

"You think there's a chance he's not going to get that Fulbright? I'm just saying we're a dying breed." He tapped his fingers on the table. "And that I'm sick of it being all political scandals, applications, and interviews around here. Don't you think it was better when our weekly conversations were a tad more colorful?"

"No. I'd rather this than sit through another eight hours of your C.B."

Oops. That was a mistake. He leaned in. "Could have been longer." He'd spared me that humiliation at least. Sitting there while George kissed and told, and kissed and told, and kissed and told ad infinitum was a lesson in agony. The Connubial Bliss reports were a right of passage for every knight in Rose & Grave, but I had dreaded hearing George recount every sexual encounter he'd ever had for two reasons: First, I would learn exactly where I fell on his lengthy list. Second, so would everyone else. I had spent a week preparing to hear him report the gory details of our affair to our entire club. But he hadn't even touched upon it—for reasons that were still beyond my comprehension.

"I could always present a coda," he said. "If you think it's necessary."

"Is that a threat of some sort?" I asked.

"A threat?" He pressed his hand to his chest. "You wound me, Amy." He also hadn't called me "Boo" since I'd broken it off in November. It had been Amy outside the tomb and Bugaboo inside. He stared at me through his copper-rimmed glasses. His eyes, gorgeous as always, were steady and unblinking. "I wasn't even the one to bring it up. You're the one who has sex on the brain. Feeling frustrated? You can tell me."

I abandoned the table then and there. Maybe I was frustrated, but I also had a date that could, hypothetically, fix all that.

When Brandon arrived at my room, his face was practically glowing. "I got in!"

"To what?" I said.

"NYU. Math!" He grabbed me and spun me around. "I just had to tell you first."

I beamed. *Eat your heart out, George.* Knowing that Brandon wanted me to be the first to know his news was so much better than sex. "Oh, Brandon, that's amazing! I'm so happy for you!" I enclosed him in a hug. "I'm applying for some stuff in New York, too. We could be together there next year. Wouldn't that be wild?"

And he hugged me again, which was not really an answer, but never let it be said that Amy Maureen Haskel doesn't do denial with the best of them. I didn't even have the heart to ask him about his breakup conversation with Felicity after that. He was in such a great mood. Why spoil it with sad remembrances?

Brandon and I spent the rest of the evening in my room, talking about everything in the world but what was going on with him and Felicity, and doing everything in the world except the kind of activity that might lead to something I'd have to relate in a Connubial Bliss report. The rules, apparently, still applied.

Curious.

The pattern repeated for several days in a row. He'd come over, ostensibly there to help me out with my applications, but not a moment's work would get done. "This is boring," he'd say. "Let's put on a DVD. We deserve it." Which was all well and good, except I didn't deserve it yet. I still hadn't gotten into grad school.

Sometimes it felt like senior year in high school all over again. Once you got into college, nothing seemed very important. You'd skip classes, blow off homework, party on weeknights. Now, with most of my friends' futures secure, I was witness to much of the same behavior all around. Not that I indulged too much. After all, the shenanigans from Dragon's Head were getting more outlandish every day (I'd taken to keeping my shower supplies out of the bathroom, as the other day I'd found my conditioner bottle filled with blue dye, my soap covered in drain hair, and all the safeties removed from my razor blades), and I was a bit nervous about what they'd try on me if I ventured out and about.

My fellow knights were at a loss as to revenge schemes. Attacking one society member for the crimes of all of them was taboo in our little culture, and we were pretty sure Dragon's Head was keeping a close eye on their tomb after our most recent raid. Their attacks on me were reminiscent of the kind of pranks we pulled on barbarians, not other society knights. Our rivalries were held to a different standard of honor entirely. Dragon's Head was breaking the code by treating me like a barbarian. I admit I was beginning to pity—or at least empathize with—poor Micah Price, the last barbarian victim of Rose & Grave. The guy had been a first-class jerk, and had caused a huge amount of pain to both my fellow knight Jenny and the society as a whole. But, on the other hand, we'd filled his apartment with rats. Way worse than crickets.

I felt so left out that on Wednesday, when Brandon asked if I wanted to skip my Geology lecture in favor of taking a short afternoon nap with him, I acquiesced to his demands. After all, maybe this time we'd finally cross the line we'd set back on Valentine's Day.

We didn't. And we didn't again on Thursday after my society meeting, nor on Friday when neither of us were skipping any classes at all.

Meanwhile, every kiss we didn't share made the next one that much harder to resist. I was lying there beside him during these indulgent—yet platonic—afternoon naps, knowing that it would take little more than a swivel of my hips to bring our bodies into alignment, to cross that invisible and all-important line between right and wrong. So I dared not move, because I was terrified of what his response would be. I knew, somehow, that if anyone was to cross the line, it had to be Brandon, just like it had to be Brandon who came over that night, had to be Brandon to be the first to admit that he missed me, to say that he still wanted me, regardless of our past.

On Saturday, Lydia waylaid me outside my bedroom door.

"I'm worried about you."

Because I'd turned into a hermit? "I know I haven't exactly been a social butterfly lately—"

"No, Amy. *Brandon.*" She sat down. "When he came over the night of the Valentine's Day Ball, I was so excited. Everyone had seen his girlfriend storm out of the dance. I thought they were through, or as good as through."

"So?"

"So Clarissa apparently told Josh that they're not." She gauged my reaction, and I fought to keep it under control. "Josh thinks you don't care. But I said that couldn't be so."

Why did I feel a sudden stab of guilt for disappointing her? "Thanks for discussing me behind my back." Again.

"You're welcome. Isn't it nice to have friends who care? Now tell me what's going on. Are they broken up? And if not, why not?"

What was going on was that Lydia had gone and gotten herself a perfect boyfriend and had suddenly forgotten how complicated the battle of the sexes could be. "I don't know," I said honestly. Maybe they weren't broken up. Maybe they were, and he was just practicing some sort of . . . mourning period before becoming involved with someone else. Did I really want to know that answer? "It's complicated."

"Bullshit," Lydia pronounced. "It's easy. He wants you, or he wants her. They aren't married. They don't have shared property or children. They're *dating*. Sure, there are going to be hurt feelings, but that doesn't make it complicated. Awkward and potentially hurtful, but not complicated. 'Hi, Felicity, you've been grand and we've had a really good time together, but I don't think it's fair to keep dating you, since I realized I still have feelings for my ex— as you know—and she wants me back—as you may not know. I'm sorry; I'm a shithead, but you're fabulous and beautiful and I'm sure there's a line of amazing guys waiting for the day you're single.' See? Easy."

Felicity was indeed fabulous and beautiful. I didn't need Lydia or her imaginary suitors-in-the-wings to remind me of that.

"So I can't see why he's spending so much time hiding out in your bedroom and *still* dating her." Lydia shrugged.

"Why doesn't he make a choice? If it makes sense to you, please explain."

"It's just that…" *Okay, choose my words carefully here.* "We've had such a rocky past. We don't even know if what is going on between us now *is* a sexual, romantic kind of thing."

Lydia blinked. "It's not sexual?"

I ducked my head. "Well, no. It's, uh—"

"Don't tell me. *Complicated.*"

"Yes. For now."

"He's not being fair to either of you. But especially not to Felicity."

"So now you're the patron saint of girlfriends?" I said. Figures. Get a real relationship going and all of a sudden you have no sympathy for those of us on the outside. Wonder what the T.A.'s girlfriend would have said back when it was Lydia infringing upon *her* turf.

"Someone here has to be. Don't get me wrong: If you *did* want to steal some guy from his girlfriend, and I liked the guy and not the girl, I'd say go for it, as a friend. Ends and means and all's fair in love and war and a thousand other aphorisms." She shrugged. "But that's not what we're dealing with here. You're not, apparently, trying for him, and he's not, apparently, letting go of her. If you're in a relationship, you have to be in it. If you're unsure, then you have to be fair and end it. *Really* end it, Amy, not play two people off each other. Brandon, of all people, should know this behavior is unacceptable." And she fixed me with a look that was impossible to mistake:

Because it hurt him so much when you did it.

"It's not like what happened with us, Lyds."

"You're right. It's worse. Because Brandon and Felicity had a real relationship that you're messing with. Amy, you're *the other woman.* Things never end well for the other woman."

"I'm not! I told you, we're not doing anything." Not really.

Lydia was just shaking her head at me, disbelief rolling off of her in waves. "Right. All those hours in there, bedroom door closed, lights off, no sounds. Bet you're studying, huh? Bet whatever it is you're doing, you'd do it in front of your mother, in front of his girlfriend, in front of anyone who cared to watch, and you wouldn't think twice about it, it's so aboveboard."

I swallowed. How had this turned from *I'm worried about you* to an indictment of my behavior? "There are a lot of things I wouldn't do in front of my mother that are perfectly aboveboard."

But Lydia was on a roll. "Come on, Miss Digger. You of all people should know that the things you do in secret are private for a reason."

That was it. I stood, turned, and marched toward my bedroom.

Lydia called after me. "Amy, come back!"

I turned around on the threshold. "Please, Lydia. *You* of all people, with your well-researched secret society factoids, should know what happens when you drop the D-bomb in front of me." Lydia knew everything about societies, enough to have convinced me all last semester that she was in one. And when you used the name of a society in front of a member, they had to leave the room.

"Only when you feel like obeying that rule," she replied. "You usually just thumb your nose at all of them."

Oh, now we were getting down to it. Not only was she appalled by my current romance, but she was also going to get all bitter about the way I chose to handle my society membership. Couldn't I do anything right in Lydia's eyes?

Was I not so perfect as her darling Josh? He may have buffed up his relationship outlook for her benefit, but he wasn't a better Digger than I was, yellow sneakers aside.

"I really think that you should pick one thing at a time to be mad at me about."

"I'm not mad," she practically shouted. "I'm *concerned*."

"You're butting in is what you are," I practically shouted back. How dare she say such awful things about Brandon? Of course he was going to break up with Felicity! She clearly didn't know him at all.

"Weren't you storming out of the room in your little society huff?" my best friend said with a sneer. "Or should I help you along? Rose—"

"You've made your point."

"Don't think that this conversation is over. I'm not the only one who's concerned about what's been going on here."

"I really wish your boyfriend would stay out of my love life."

"Funny. I bet Felicity wishes *her* boyfriend would stay out of it, too."

I slammed the door between us.

I hereby confess:
There are some negotiations
for which no amount of
preparation is enough.

5.
Parley

The next morning, there was an e-mail from Lydia in my in-box. (You know you and your roommate are in a fight when you get e-mails from the other side of the suite.)

From: Lydia.Travinecek@eli.edu
To: Amy.Haskel@eli.edu
Subject: Last night

Honey, I don't know how everything deteriorated last night. I certainly wasn't looking to pick a fight with you. I'm sorry if you took my attempts to be a good friend the wrong way, because that's all I ever want to be for you. I love you and will always stand by you, even if I don't agree with your choices and no matter what kind of petty squabbles we have.

Love,
Lydia :)

Hmph. If she wants to be taken seriously in politics, she might consider nixing the smiley faces. And so like her to try to get the last word in, too!

Though, true to form, the more I began to ruminate on Lydia's words, the more I started to question the status quo with Brandon. I figured I was only being fair by not asking for clarification. After all, last year, when we'd actually been sleeping together, I'd kept Brandon on the hook for several *months*. What was a week, by comparison?

Still, I couldn't help running my mouth at our next get-together. Brandon was standing behind me, supposedly checking the essay I was editing but concentrating more on the neck massage I'd asked for. I'd even planted two spelling errors in the first paragraph, but he hadn't noticed.

"How's Felicity?" I asked, apropos of nothing and in the most innocent tone I could muster.

His hands stilled on my nape. Rule broken. "Fine."

"Are you still dating her?" The words fell like bombs, shattering our arrangement to bits.

He sat back on the bed. "I thought I wasn't . . . that first night. You have to know that."

"And since then? How can you *think* you're not?" I asked. "Aren't you smart enough to determine something like that beyond a reasonable doubt?"

"It's not that simple, and you know it."

Hadn't I just made this argument to Lydia? So then, why did it suddenly feel so hollow?

"The day after . . ." He gestured to the bed. "She came and apologized. She loves me, Amy. She loves me. And I . . . care about her, too. So she made me promise. That I'd . . . think about it."

"Think about not breaking up with her?" I asked. "Or think about getting back together with her?" There was a subtle but important difference.

He looked away.

I joined him on the bed, sitting as close to him as our unspoken rules allowed. His hand rested on his thigh, and I covered it with my own, splaying my fingers so that their tips spilled over onto his jeans. "I'm sorry," I said, softly, *sweetly*. "I shouldn't have brought it up."

But I wasn't sorry. My fingers moved in a subtle caress of his leg, and I watched him carefully to see how he'd respond. His back stiffened, his gaze flew to my hand. It had been a mistake, I realized, not to press the issue. A mistake that Brandon himself had made with me last year when I'd been the one unsure of where I wanted our relationship to go. I'd learned something from his failure: Don't take amorphous for an answer.

"More than anything, I don't want to put you in a tough position," I went on, and slipped my arms around him. I dropped my head to his shoulder and snuggled into one of our new, almost-over-the-line hugs. I ran my hands up and down his back, wondering what he would do if I slipped them beneath the hem of his sweater to touch his bare skin.

No, I didn't want to make his choice difficult at all. I wanted it to be so easy to pick me. And now I realized that if I wanted to, I could force a decision right here. I held him tighter. "This is *so* nice."

I felt his breath against my hair, and his lips brushed my temple. "Amy..."

Am I evil? No. So he had a girlfriend, marginally. Temporarily. So what? I don't know her. She's not a friend of mine. I don't owe her anything. I was with Brandon first, had known him far longer. And the way he says my name... no one says it like that. He could never say *her* name like that.

I felt him put his arms around me, felt his fingertips

trailing along the waistband of my jeans, into the gap between the top of my pants and the bottom of my sweater. I felt his hands at the base of my spine, covering the Rose & Grave tattoo I'd put there the weekend he'd broken up with me. As far as I knew, he'd never seen it.

I wasn't the same girl Brandon had known last spring. Now he was dealing with an Amy Haskel who ran with the big boys. I'd been around the block with George Harrison Prescott. I'd learned a thing or two about seduction.

Wouldn't he be surprised? I lifted my face, brought it close to his. I'd come so far, he could be the one to make that last step, to break the rules we'd never made explicit, but had followed nonetheless. "Brandon." The word was a breath.

"Amy, we should stop." But he wasn't meeting my eyes. He was looking at my mouth. His fingers tripped along my spine, beneath my shirt.

"I missed you so much." Another whisper, another murmur.

"This is wrong." Instead of pressing his lips to mine, he leaned in farther, rested his face against my jawline. Spoke the words into my cheek, into my neck. I could feel his mouth there, moving. But he was still only speaking. Not kissing. "We shouldn't . . ."

Hell yeah, we should. And we should have done it already. Man, if I were George, I'd already have my partner's clothes off.

If I were George . . .

Inwardly, I reeled. Outwardly, I somehow managed to keep from shoving Brandon across the room in an effort to put distance between us. But I did draw away, and as I did, I saw twin expressions of disappointment and relief on Brandon's face. What was I thinking? What had I turned into?

"I should go," Brandon said. "I have to—"

"Don't," I said. "I'm sorry."

"I have to think," he finished. "Please let me think about this?"

I shrugged, my eyes downcast. "Sure."

He cupped my face in his hands. "Amy, don't be upset. God, you're so amazing. I just have to think about how I'm going to . . . handle things. I want to be fair to her. She's been so good to me."

"Of course." Of course Brandon would think like that. He's such a nice person. And look what I'd just tried to do to him. He didn't need seduction and manipulation. He needed patience and understanding and to handle things in his own, gentlemanly way. I could give him that. "I'm sorry," I said again. "I don't know what came over me. I've just been so stressed recently."

"Applications?" he asked, sounding back on firmer footing.

"And other stuff." I laid my head on his shoulder. "I know we don't talk about it, and that's fine. I can't even get into it now. You'll just think it's silly."

"What?"

I laughed in self-recrimination. "It's just . . . society nonsense." *I'm being targeted by Dragon's Head as payback for the latest round of a fifty-year-old feud* sounded way too silly to speak aloud.

At the door, we held each other for a long time, breathing as one, doing everything that a kissing couple would do that didn't actually involve mouths. It was hotter than a lot of the sex I'd had. Then he left, and I floated back to my desk, relieved that we'd finally worked things out between us.

And then I didn't hear from him for days.

———

After the first day, I sent Brandon an e-mail, and then another two days later. In between, I left two messages on his answering machine. No response. There was no way the ball could be construed as being in my court.

When it came, his volley took an interesting form. On Wednesday, as I was working, a tiny IM window popped up on my screen.

B_Weared: Tell me about the "society nonsense."
AmyHaskel: Hey! Where have u been?
B_Weared: What's been happening to u?

Way to answer a question with another question. And happening *to* me? What was that about? He had no way of knowing I was being stalked.

AmyHaskel: Can't really talk about it, of course.
B_Weared: Does it have to do with the time in the dining hall? That guy who spilled the drinks on u?
AmyHaskel: Yes.

After that, he typed nothing for a good long while. And then:

B_Weared: I gotta go.

I typed a response, but it was too late, and bold red lettering told me Brandon had signed off. How odd was that? Three days of nothing and then random questions about my society feud? I skipped dinner, waiting by the computer for him to sign back on, but he didn't. Nor did he call, e-mail, or drop by my suite.

The following day, I went to class like a good little

student. I did all my homework by myself, worked on my last few applications—and did a load of laundry, to boot. February was ending, and I could no longer afford to pretend this semester was going to last forever. When the sun set, I bundled up, as interested in protecting myself from the weather as I was in disguising myself from any roving Dragon's Head members, and plunged into the night.

Hale met me at the door of the tomb, before I could meet the other knights in the Firefly Room for dinner. "Miss," he said. "A note arrived for you this afternoon."

"Just for me?"

"From the caretaker of Dragon's Head." He must have noticed my quizzical look, for he went on. "I suspect it is an offer of parley."

"But why to me? Why not to the whole club?" And why would they want to strike a deal? They were totally getting the better of me and they couldn't need some crummy statue they'd been keeping in their storage room that badly.

"Couldn't say, miss. But I suggest you let the Secretary know about it."

I tore into the letter, which had been sealed with a dollop of golden wax pressed with a reptilian face.

To the Thief Amy Haskel, so-called Knight of Persephone:

We issue an Offer of Parley. Meet with our Representative, alone, at Midnight in the Center Courtyard of the Library, and there endeavor to come to an Agreement over our Differences. In keeping with the long-standing Association between our Societies, no Harm shall come to you there.

If you do not come, it will not end.

If you bring a Companion, our Offer becomes Void and they shall share your Fate.

I shot a glance at the entrance to the Firefly Room, where I could just glimpse the other knights poring over the latest scandal sheets for news of Gehry. But who could care about one disgraced politico with all the drama going on in my life? I had a boy who couldn't seem to get back to me and a society that was dying to get back *at* me. Kurt Gehry was the least of my problems.

"Bugaboo!" Thorndike exclaimed, spotting me through the doorway. "Check this out!"

I shook my head. "No, check this out." I waved the letter at her, but she'd already refocused her attention on the computer screen. From across the room, all I could hear was snippets of the newscast that had my fellow knights so enthralled.

"For the past four years... Could be considered the new 'Nannygate'... Always a proponent of tough immigration laws... Though a federal crime... Claims the employees were hired through an agency that handled all financial transactions and paperwork..."

I drew closer and saw a montage of images of Kurt Gehry and the President walking across the White House lawn, a shot of a suburban home, its yard covered in news trucks and federal agents, the latter of which led two women and a man down the path. The footage gave way to a live shot of Gehry, in a coat and carrying a briefcase, pointedly ignoring the cameras and microphones being shoved in his face.

"Well, I guess we know why he resigned," Soze said. "You can't be a federal employee and break federal immigration laws."

Juno shook her head, and her curls bounced on her shoulders. "Let's not get out the tar and feathers just yet. Could be, the employment agency's to blame."

Bond cast her a skeptical look. "Easy enough to

determine that, don't you think? Ring up the employment agency. 'Hello, agency, can you provide the correct documentation for your staff? Thanks ever so.' No. If the agency is still an issue, it's because the Gehry camp is spinning it that way."

"Soze—" I started, but then was promptly shushed as Gehry turned to answer a reporter.

"My wife and children are currently visiting family abroad," he said, then spun on his heel and strode rather quickly inside the nearest building.

"Poor kids," Lucky said. "I don't feel bad for him, but those children..."

"Hey, Soze..." I tried again, but he was glued to the monitor as the talking heads started doing their thing.

"This is really big news, guys," Thorndike went on. "Gehry could end up in jail."

"Josh!" I cried. He turned to me at last.

"Two dollars, Bugaboo," Angel said.

"I need to talk to you. Now."

Soze followed me into the library, and I was pleased to see that Angel and Lucky could manage to tear themselves away from the news for five minutes as well. I showed them all the note.

"Well, this is good news," Angel said.

Lucky snorted. "You can't actually be considering this. After everything they've done to you, you want to go over there alone?"

"Well, that's what I was wondering," I said. "Does it have to be, like, *alone* alone? I mean, couldn't you guys just come and lurk in the shadows or something?"

"It's the shadow-lurkers I'm worried about," Lucky said. "I'm sure Dragon's Head has this place scoped out. How naïve do you really want to be about this? Considering everything they've done already?"

Angel studied the letter. "I don't know. There is a degree of honor between societies. If they say they want to parley, maybe they mean it."

"But why with Bugaboo alone?" Soze said. "Why don't they want to parley with all of us?" He glanced back into the Firefly Room. "Is there any way we can talk about this later?"

"Later!" I cried. "There's a 24-hour news cycle covering Gehry. I promise you, you're not going to miss a thing. The *parley* is happening now."

"But the Gehry situation is *unfolding* tonight," he said. Almost whined it, in fact.

Hale cleared his throat. "Should I serve dinner now? We're running late."

I appealed to the small contingent of knights. "Should I go? Should someone come with me?"

"I vote yes to the former and no to the latter," Angel said. "There *is* a code. Just because they haven't been following it so far . . ."

"Doesn't mean they'll start following it now," Lucky pointed out. "Stay far away."

We looked at Soze, who was clearly straining to hear the newscast from the next room.

"Well?" I asked.

"Go," he said in a distracted tone. "I'm sure it will be fine."

All three of us glared at him in frustration, and when he noticed our expressions, he threw up his hands. "Fine! I don't care, okay? These stupid pranks . . . they don't matter. There is serious stuff happening in the world and I'm sorry if I can't get all worked up over every little drama this society goes through. Sheesh!"

"Fine!" Lucky exclaimed. "Let her go, and if she winds up dead, it will be on your head."

"They aren't going to kill her," Angel said. "They have expulsion to think of, too, you know."

Some comfort. Over dinner, we discussed the parley offer with the rest of the club, and it was agreed upon (rather quickly, in my opinion, so conversation could turn back to Gehry's political and legal troubles) that Angel was right. I should follow the instructions on the note, despite the risk.

"Think of it this way," Angel argued, "if they wanted to 'get' you, they've been doing a bang-up job of it without arranging it with you in advance. If they're bothering to send a letter saying they want to parley, maybe they really mean it."

"Or maybe that's what they want you to think," Thorndike pointed out.

Finally, we decided I'd go, with a small contingent of Diggers waiting for me outside the library, and my finger poised over the *Send* button on Jenny's Push-to-Talk cell in case things got hairy.

At fifteen minutes to midnight, I left the tomb and began walking to the library. It was raining, the type of wintry, New Haven downpour that seems to come at you from all sides, thwapping at you with clammy bursts of wind and making every step away from shelter seem like a futile, if not downright insane, gesture. But I soldiered on and eventually made it across the campus to the steps of the library. The timing of this part of the journey was very important, since the library closed at midnight and they stopped letting patrons enter at quarter-till.

I made my way through the front door and into the splendid, Gothic-cathedral entrance hall. With the security guard and the research-desk employees looking on, I tried to casually gravitate toward the West Reading Room, which had, among its many desks, wingback chairs, and private nooks, a fire entrance to the central courtyard that was often propped open when the building's ancient heating system threatened to turn the Stacks into a sauna.

Tonight I was lucky. I sat and waited, wondering in turn how many of the library's remaining visitors were Dragon's Head spies and if a security guard would be along presently to kick me out.

At 11:58, I stepped outside into the cold rain, which felt that much worse after the dry heat of the Reading Room. As the golden light faded into blue-gray darkness, I strained my eyes to determine if there were any people waiting in the courtyard, but the only things I could see were stone carvings of grimacing gargoyles, winter-dead trees, and piles of grayish ice. I kept my gloved hand in my coat pocket, ready to press the button on the phone.

And I waited. And waited. It seemed much longer than 120 seconds before I heard the distant chimes from the clock tower. Midnight.

On my left, I saw a shadow move. It drew closer to me, but all I could make out was a vaguely human shape. Still ten yards away, the figure stopped and sat on one of the stone benches. It raised a hand and beckoned to me. I stepped forward, and as I did, the figure's features came into focus.

Felicity.

I hereby confess:
I'm the dumbest person
at Eli.

6.
Sweet Defeat

"Oh, come closer," Felicity said, as I struggled to breathe. "It doesn't count unless we talk."

"What…are…" *Get ahold of yourself, Amy.* "What are you doing here?"

"I'm here to parley, of course." Her tone was perfectly calm, perfectly kind. Perfectly perfect. I knew this unflappable socialite charm, had seen it at work in Clarissa—had hated it in Clarissa, long before I ever grew to hate it in Brandon's girlfriend. "As I assume you are."

"I'm here to parley with Dragon's Head," I replied.

She smiled and flashed me her pin. "Well, I'm in Dragon's Head, but I'm here to parley with *you,* Amy Haskel."

My name on her lips was a curse, the opposite of everything Brandon made it sound like. I swallowed my disbelief. "This never had anything to do with that raid."

"Of course it did," she said. She patted the seat beside her. "Come sit next to me. We're protected from the rain by the eaves."

"I'll stand, thanks," I said, though my teeth were starting to chatter as the water seeped under my collar.

"Suit yourself." She took a deep breath. "Here's the deal, and don't think it was an easy one for me to concoct. The members of my society will henceforth cease and desist from their personal campaign against you. And in return..." she paused. "...you will never see my boyfriend again."

"I'll *what*?" I cried. "You've got to be kidding me. I don't agree to that!"

Felicity's beautiful brow furrowed. "I'm sorry, perhaps my letter was a tad unclear. *You* don't have to agree to anything. I made this deal with Brandon."

I stood there, dumbstruck, wishing I had a bench to fall onto.

"You see, Amy, my boyfriend, for reasons passing understanding, took umbrage at the fact that we were, shall we say, persuading you to return our property." She paused. "You wouldn't be interested in doing that now, would you?"

"Over my dead body," I hissed.

She sighed. "At any rate, my boyfriend had this crazy theory that I, as the director of our little campaign of persuasion, had some sort of personal stake in the matter, above and beyond the usual society feud. Barbarians and their strange ideas! Of course, you and I know that's silly."

I personally didn't know anything of the sort. "Your *campaign*, as you call it, was a bit out of the mainstream."

"As is *everything* about your club," Felicity replied. "My boyfriend was under the impression that I had used his inexplicable lingering fascination with you to discover your schedule, habits, and even brand of shampoo."

"Which you did."

"Don't you find it odd that anyone would remember

someone's favorite brand of cheap, drugstore shampoo?" Felicity's smile remained sanguine, and my hands fisted inside the pockets of my coat. "And I don't even know my own roommate's class schedules."

"Brandon must really care about me," I shot back.

Here, her smile grew wide. "My boyfriend is a kind person." She kept saying that phrase, *my boyfriend*. She must have known how much it needled me. "And I really care about him. I love him. I love him ever so much more than I love some silly feud between two college clubs. I care about him so much more than I care about some silly college secret society." She paused. "I don't know if anyone else could say that."

The little bitch. Brandon had apparently told her everything about our breakup last year. She'd never needed the shoes to identify me. She'd always known I was in Rose & Grave. And she also knew I'd chosen it over Brandon.

"And it was surprisingly easy to convince my boyfriend of that fact. For him to give you up, I just had to promise that I would as well. Which I have."

"Your society won't accept that!" I said.

"Oh, we aren't letting go of the feud, or of our statue. The Diggers are going down, mark my words. We just won't be after you—specifically—anymore."

Frustration and rage bubbled inside me, cutting off rational thought, any argument. "I don't understand! If this was a decision made between you and Brandon, why this whole parley charade? Why drag me out here in the rain?" I mean, aside from the obvious pleasure of watching me look like a drowned rat.

"How else would you know?" she asked simply. "How else would you know that I won, and how I won, and how, now that I've chosen him over my society, Brandon loves me even more than he did before?" She rose. "Have a good night, Amy. I hope you get in safe from the storm." She brushed past me, and it took all my self-restraint not to pummel her into the mud. Girls like Felicity probably had years of kickboxing or Krav Maga training anyway. "Oh, and if I were you or any of the other Diggers, I'd be watching my back."

———

I stood there for way too long after Felicity left, not from any desire to savor the New Haven climate. I just didn't know what to do next.

Where do you go when everyone you know owes you a big fat *I told you so*? Where do you hide on a night so wretched that even Dickens wouldn't have chosen it to illustrate his character's desperation? Where do you run to the moment you realize that your SAT scores were a lie, your transcript obviously faked, your faculty recommendations the apparent result of a parental bribe, your acceptance letter from Eli University clearly some sort of cosmic joke, because there is no way that anyone in their right mind would mistake you for someone smart?

Someone with operational gray matter would never have let this happen to her. Someone with the intelligence of your average housefly would have put two and two together when Brandon had IM-ed her about "society nonsense." Someone who had spent a moment examining her history, her experiences, or even the rational order of the universe would have noted at least one of the following:

1) Mr. Let's-Define-Our-Relationship Weare had never professed any interest in discussing what we were really doing in our stolen afternoons.
2) The fact that after he told me he was going to make a decision, he never called again. Hello, clue phone.

3) Or how about the simple truth that when someone has the choice of the beautiful, polished, rich girl who has never broken his heart—the girl who would forgive his transgressions, would sacrifice her position in her society to make him happy—or the girl like me, it's a no-brainer. Whatever else I might be tempted to say about Brandon at this moment, I'd never insult his intelligence.

Where do you go when this is made obvious to you? Other than back to Ohio? Part of me wondered if it was too late to book a flight. I wanted to be far, far from campus right now. I wanted to climb into my dad's lap and hug my mom and act like I was still a teenager, instead of an adult who should have *so* known better. I wanted to hide, to flee, to pretend that I'd never even heard of Connecticut, let alone chosen it as a setting for such a humiliation. *How could he love her more?*

One thing was certain, I could not go back to my fellow knights yet. They were waiting for me just outside the library, but there was no way I could face anyone in my current state. There would be plenty of time to explain Dragon's Head's new strategy—after I dealt with my own state of mind. I pulled my coat's hood low over my face and rushed back inside the Reading Room. Out in the main hall, I turned right, toward the back, rather than toward the front entrance. There was a back way out, near the law school.

A security guard stopped me. "Library's closed, miss," but as soon as he saw my face, his expression softened.

"I just want..." I gasped. "The back door."

"Closed after midnight."

"I just want to leave. I don't have anything to check out...just..."

The guard relented and I rushed by him, practically sprinting on my way out the back. I shoved hard on the door and burst through into the cold alleyway beyond. I plopped against the nearest wall, heedless of the rain as it mixed with tears on my face. Great wracking sobs seemed to echo around the empty street, bouncing off stone walls and cobblestones. Yeah, there was no way I'd do this in front of the other knights. I imagined the patriarchs that had come before me weeping dignified tears over a lost comrade in war, or the death of a brother or a spouse. I couldn't see them acting so stupid. No, this kind of behavior would be reserved for the Bugaboo of the group.

"Why?" I said to the buildings around me.

How could I question his choice? Maybe it was best. For if I did love him, if I really did, wouldn't I have fought for him long before this? Wouldn't I have fought for him when we tried dating last spring, or when I saw him again this fall, or even the first time he told me he still cared about me? Wouldn't I have told him to stay with me that night, to really be with me, to tell Felicity right away that they were through for good?

If I'd really loved him, then I would have done what Felicity had. I would have picked him over Rose & Grave, I'd have put him first last spring, have shared my troubles with him rather than with the society brothers I'd only just met. I'd have called him back this fall instead of getting caught up in yet another society drama. I'd have run to him from the first moments of Dragon's Head's "little campaign of persuasion." Wouldn't I?

Eventually the tears dried, but I spent several long minutes just standing there, slumped, catching my breath, adjusting to this new reality, the one where I'd again added to my seemingly endless list of romantic mistakes. *Chalk another one up, Amy. Not only are you crap at having a boyfriend, crap at having a one-night stand, and crap at having a no-strings-attached fling, you're also crap at being the other woman. Pack it up, go home, commit to celibacy. You're one hundred percent, unequivocally awful at being with a man.*

I took a deep breath. *There. Fine. Now you know.* I looked up.

And saw Poe standing in the doorway across the street. I could make out little more than a glint of his gray eyes, the line of his jaw, his sharp cheekbones in his thin face, but still, I recognized him. His defiant stance, arms crossed over the chest of his worn wool jacket. I knew that pose. It was like the first time we'd met, when he'd interrogated me. Only worse, because here I was, as raw as hamburger, ready to crumble. My eyes began to burn, but whether it was a fresh batch of tears or suppressed rage, I couldn't tell.

Why was he here? Why was he always, always, always around? Didn't he have a life? Didn't he have anything better to do?

"I take it the parley went poorly?" he asked, coming toward me.

"What are you doing here!" I snapped.

He rolled his eyes. "Amy, there are two exits to the library. I guessed—and rightly so—that your club would forget that, and I wanted to make sure there was no funny business on this side."

"How did you even know this was going on?" I resisted the urge to run a hand across my no-doubt snotty nose.

"I have friends in the tomb." Of course. He and Hale had always been buddy-buddy. He held out a small white square. A handkerchief. When I took it, he added, "I thought I'd only get involved if they tried something."

"Otherwise you'd just sit here and spy?" I swiped at my

face with the handkerchief. Of all the people to catch me at my most vulnerable, why the hell did it have to be Poe?

"I was afraid to interrupt you by moving. Seemed the lesser of two evils." He stood there for a moment, hands in pockets.

"The greater being?"

"Leaving you here alone."

"Well, you can go now," I said, then realized how ungrateful that sounded. Even if he'd been sneaking around.

"That's the thing. I can't." Hands still in pockets, eyes still downcast. "Malcolm would probably kill me if I didn't, um, see to his little sib in her time of need."

"Then don't tell him." Malcolm was in Alaska and hadn't written me in a month. So much for big-sib solicitation.

"And then there's that whole pesky oath of constancy I took. I'm supposed to stand by you."

"You *would* think of that."

He looked up, met my eyes with his serious, gray stare. "So would you, Amy."

What a time to remind me. I hated my society oaths in this moment. I felt fresh tears and made use of the handkerchief again. I sensed his hand on my shoulder, and suddenly we were crossing the street to the alcove at the law school, and sitting on a sheltered bench, and he was . . . *patting me*, or something, landing awkward little strokes along my upper arm that were no doubt meant to be comforting.

"Calm down," Poe said. "The parley was supposed to make things better. What did they say?"

"That it's over," I sniffed.

"In exchange for what?"

I shook my head in misery. "Nothing."

"That's not true." He peered at me through the shadows. "What did you have to give them?"

"Nothing!" I repeated. "They got what they wanted without my help."

"They found the statue?"

"No. It had nothing to do with the statue." I hung my head. "You'll be happy to know that I've been acting like the brain donor you always say I am."

"I don't think you're stupid," he said. "A troublemaker, yes, but that's different." He let his arm drop to his side.

Well, I'd been causing trouble for Brandon and Felicity, that was for sure.

Poe cleared his throat. "Am I better off not knowing?"

Everyone in the world was. It was too humiliating. "Yes."

"Those attacks were . . . personal."

"Yes."

"I thought as much. It's not the usual society feud M.O. Was it an academic or romantic rival?"

Right. Because it was always school or love for an Eli student. Were our troubles as simple as that? I took a deep breath. "I thought I was heading toward something important with this guy, and I was wrong, and Dragon's Head used it to get to me. That's all." It was enough.

"George?" The word exploded out of his mouth.

"Does *everyone* know about that?" Guess it was silly of George to think that leaving it out of the C.B. would accomplish anything.

"We didn't become Diggers due to a lack of perception, Amy."

"Well, you aren't experts, either. That's been over for months." And while it had been going on, I knew exactly what I'd been doing. My heart stayed clear of entanglements with Eli's most notorious playboy. No, when I decided to get my heart broken, I took the road less traveled.

"Oh," Poe said. "Forgive me if I've failed to keep up with the latest in your love life."

"No one asked you to," I snapped, then instantly regretted it. He'd been attempting a wee bit of civility, which was pretty much a miracle when it came to Poe. I shouldn't wreck it. "Sorry," I said. "I'm a little sensitive at the moment."

"At the moment?"

I bit my tongue. "It's just been demonstrated to me, yet again, that I'm doomed when it comes to romance. I've got to prepare for a life alone."

Poe took a deep breath. "Listen, I have severe doubts that this is any of my business, but in the interest of fulfilling my duty, can I give you some advice?"

Advice from Poe. Romantic advice...*from Poe*. Okay. If nothing else, it would be entertaining. I nodded.

"I don't think that the way college dating works has any bearing on the real world. If you don't have a good experience for these four years, it doesn't mean you should start fitting yourself for a habit and enter a convent. I didn't have a girlfriend in college, and I turned out okay." He paused. "Okay, *you* don't think I turned out okay..."

I laughed in spite of myself. "I think you turned out fine," I said, mostly because etiquette demanded a denial. Mostly. Because really, who was the one in real trouble here? The guy who seemed comfortable with his desire to hang out alone, in the dark, in secret, or the girl standing in the rain, sobbing?

He shrugged. "Thank you for saying so, at least."

He looked down at my hands, which were currently twisting the life out of his handkerchief. I didn't know anyone our age who used handkerchiefs. And, oddly enough, rather than seeming like another example of his weirdness, it suddenly felt to me like something grand, old-fashioned, a little refined. As that thought occurred to me, I stopped wringing it, lest it tear in my fists. I held it up.

"Uh, keep it," he said.

"That's nice of you," I said.

"Not really," he said. "It's covered with your snot."

Did I say refined? I meant rude. *Rude.*

And that thought must have shown in my posture, because he backtracked. "That's not what I meant."

"Though it's true."

"Yes." He looked at me. "You get offended by some things that blow my mind, and then, sometimes, when I'm *trying* to offend you, you don't even notice."

"I notice. You can tell, because I bite back."

"Note to self," he said. "Pre-emptively, I'm not trying to offend you right now. If I do, it's accidental."

"So 'Brace yourself'?" I translated.

"I was just wondering, how much of this—" he gestured to the handkerchief and my tear-streaked face, "—is a result of losing this... guy, and how much of it is just losing?"

"What!" I hadn't braced for *that*.

Poe, being in for the penny, decided to go for the pound. "Maybe your heart is really broken. That's possible. Or maybe it's February, and you haven't seen the sun in weeks, and it's cold and icy every day, and you are trying to write a thesis and look your future in the face, all while hiding from a bunch of assholes who are turning this campus into a war zone for you. And now they've won."

The lump in my throat got so huge I could barely breathe. I definitely couldn't speak, couldn't respond to Poe's outlandish... accusation. How could he be saying that my feelings weren't my feelings? How could he be saying that Brandon and I... that it wasn't...

"I just find it surprising that you are in the midst of a huge romantic crisis but, as far as I can tell, it came out of nowhere."

"Out of nowhere!" I shouted past the lump. "What do you know about it?"

"Nothing." His voice was perfectly calm.

"Exactly," I agreed, then ran out of things to argue. "You have no idea what I'm dealing with."

"You're right." The pause that followed his words seemed full of unspoken thoughts, but I wasn't sure I wanted to hear any more of this patriarch's advice.

Slowly, it dawned on me that I was sitting in the dark, with Poe, discussing my love life. How weird would it look if another Digger were suddenly to walk by here, looking for me, and discover this little tête-à-tête?

"I should go," I said.

"Do you want me to walk you back to Prescott?" He obviously didn't disagree with me. Guess "sharing time" was over.

"It's out of your way," I said. Poe lived off-campus in the opposite direction.

"It's not a problem."

"It's pouring rain. You don't even need to be out here."

"I vastly prefer a society plot to hanging out in my dump of an apartment."

One word remained unspoken—"alone." I blinked at him. I don't think I'd ever heard him speak like that before. The standard Poe qualities of bitterness and sarcasm were there, but this was casual and matter-of-fact. It's like he had nothing to hide, as if he'd figured: I'd seen his apartment (maybe I was the only one who had), I knew what it looked like, so why bother putting up a front? Or maybe he was hoping I'd disagree with him, defend the "dump"? Or maybe he decided that letting me glimpse his feelings was only fair payback for my big revelation of the evening. Who knew? But he did have my sympathies. How many nights had I been glad that I had Lydia waiting for me, fun and funny and not at all like Poe's pet snake?

"Do you . . . want to grab a slice of pizza or something?" I blurted out.

He hesitated. "You want to be seen in public with . . ." a microsecond pause, ". . . your face looking like that?"

I cocked my head to the side. "The real question is, do you want to be seen in public with a face like this?"

"I'd consider it." He stood, his expression still wary.

I pasted on a weak smile. "Are you sure they don't do deliveries to the law library?"

"Yes, but I think I have a bag of stale Doritos in my study carrel."

"Pass."

So I had pizza with Poe. (Er, Jamie. But really, I have a hard time reminding myself of that.) And we didn't talk much at all. Just ate. It's surprising how ravenous heartbreak makes you. Also surprising is how long I'd been at Eli without discovering some of the truly bizarre items on the menu at one of our most classic restaurants. White clam pizza. Who knew? Total revelation.

When he dropped me off in front of Prescott College, he said. "Are you going to Cavador?"

"Yeah," I swiped my card at the gate. "There are nine from my club going. You?"

He nodded. "Cheapest vacation ever. And some of my club will be there, too. It'll be nice to see them again." He took another deep breath. "Amy, I know you don't want to hear this right now, but I think that when you come back from Spring Break, everything will be different."

"So I just need to make it through another few days and all my troubles will be over?" Yeah, right. Cavador Key was a retreat, not a miracle cure.

"It's possible."

Oh, Poe. If only he knew how impossible it would be.

I hereby confess:
Best to bear the ills you have
than fly to others
you know not of.

7.
Escape

Two days later (two days!), Brandon finally grew the *cojones* to e-mail me.

From: Brandon.Weare@eli.edu
To: Amy.Haskel@eli.edu
Subject: Things

Dear Amy,

Even after deciding that it had to be via e-mail, I still went through a dozen drafts of this letter. I apologize in advance for anything I fail to say, but I eventually realized that it was a far worse sin to not contact you than it would be to send you an imperfect version.

I can't imagine what you think of me right now, or what you have been imagining this past week. I am so sorry for the silence, and for everything I'm about to say.

We can't see each other anymore. (But you already knew that, didn't you?) I allowed myself to go to a bad place this month—why, I can't say—and I dragged you into it. I don't know what is to blame: the horrific winter weather? The nostalgia prompted by our imminent graduation? The fact that our "anniversary" (if you can call it that) was passing? I don't know. But I know that it's my fault. You and I have been over for a long time. I understand that now. And I do want to thank you for being there for me these past few weeks and for humoring me while I worked out my issues.

I wish you the best of luck with your applications. I know you'll do great.

Your friend,
Brandon

"He's so full of shit" was Lydia's pronouncement upon viewing.

"Agreed," Jenny said, digging into the family-sized pack of gumdrops on the bed. "Now explain again how the Gumdrop Drops work?" Lydia came over with a shot glass and perched near my pillow to show the Diggers' newest twenty-one-year-old our suite's signature drinking game.

Demetria, stomach squashing my corduroy husband, slammed back her third shot of vodka and rolled her eyes. (She'd decided to forgo the candy chasers.) "This is five classes of rhetoric and as many ounces of Absolut speaking, but that is one fine piece of work there. The way he seems to take all the blame upon himself while simultaneously practically calling you a slut? And 'your friend.' Unbelievable! Pièce de résistance, girl. Be glad you didn't fuck him this time around."

Jenny jabbed her in the ribs. "You're not helping."

"Are we even sure he wrote it himself?" Odile asked,

swooping in. The tips of her red hair brushed the keyboard as she bent over the computer screen and scrutinized the letter. "Maybe that bitch did it."

"She's not a bitch," Clarissa said from her position on the windowsill. Everyone else shot her eye-daggers and she put up her hands. "Hey! I said I was Team Haskel here, but that doesn't mean I'm going to commit character assassination. I can put Amy above all others without demonizing my barb—other friends."

Lydia rolled her eyes, handed Jenny a shot, and took off for points common room. "Gotta pack," she called back by means of an excuse. Rose & Grave was once again the elephant that lived, unremarked-upon, in our suite.

"I think Brandon wrote this himself," I said. "Let's not go all *Sense and Sensibility* here."

"Especially given that the names are all backward," Clarissa agreed.

I glanced at the e-mail again, my finger hovering over the *Delete* button. No, Brandon had written it, and I'd bet a fellowship spot little Miss Dragon's Head didn't even know about it. There was no reason to make him write me after her declaration of victory last night.

"Good riddance, I say." Odile poured herself another drink. "Shake him off, pack up your bikini, and blow this joint for a while."

My bikini was packed, but it was purely decorative. I'm no swimmer.

"She's right," Jenny said. "If it helps, focus on all the good we're going to do building the house with Habitat."

"I only wish I could go with you," Odile went on, "but I can't pass up this role." The starlet had, just last night, canceled her plans to go to Cavador Key. But since the movie she was supposedly shooting didn't seem to have a title, we all suspected she either had a hot new fling or a

VIP pass to some glamorous club opening. "One Spring Break à la Dumas, and you wouldn't even remember this prick's name."

"He's not a prick," I said stoutly.

"Amy," Jenny said, shaking her head knowingly. "He didn't pick you. That's total p-you-know-what territory." She paused. "At least for the moment."

"What's that supposed to mean?" Clarissa turned to Jenny. "Don't tell me you've started having tender feelings for Micah again." Micah Price had convinced Jenny to expose our society for the coven of devil worshippers he believed it was. When she refused to keep passing on secrets to a paranoid conspiracy theorist website, because, well, we *weren't* worshipping the devil, the jerk had broken her heart.*

The younger girl's eyes widened. "No. That's over. But until you forgive, how can you move on?" Forgiveness was a top priority for Saint Jenny.

"Move on?" Clarissa pounced. "So there's someone else? Has a rebound man stolen our little hacker's heart?"

Jenny blushed and tipped her head forward, though her stylish new pixie cut (complete with Eli-blue streaks through her black hair) did little to hide her expression.

"You can't keep secrets from us, you know," Demetria warned.

Jenny cast a knowing glance after Lydia, out in the common room. "I'm under no obligation." And considering that her C.B. had been back in December, we might never know. Jenny, as I'd learned last semester, had more secrets than any society.

"Just a little hint, then?" Clarissa was well into wheedling mode. "A student? A senior? What college?"

---

* But that's a whole other story, and the confessor knows you can read it elsewhere.

"Just tell me he's a barbarian," said Demetria. "We've had plenty enough society incest in this club."

I clicked back to my e-mail, hoping no one could see my face. George and I had done our best to keep our interludes a secret, but I guess we hadn't been as successful at fooling the other knights as we'd thought. Still, Demetria might have been talking about her own short-lived (and still only alleged) indiscretion with Odile, though both of them acted like it had never even happened. I wish George and I were so laissez-faire.

Jenny said nothing. Not even a flat denial.

Interesting.

Clarissa, clearly glad to be off the subject of Felicity, drew back the curtain and peered at the gray drizzle beyond. "Get me to Florida. Stat. When does our flight leave tomorrow?"

"Not soon enough," said Jenny.

"Speak for yourself," Demetria said. "I'm not sure I feel like intruding on the Gehry family's leisure time."

Four faces turned to her, mouths agape. "The what?"

"Gehry family," Demetria said with a shrug. "Didn't you hear? Our man Kurt left town last night to join his family 'abroad,' only he can't actually leave the country while he's under investigation. I don't think the wife and kids are in Europe at all. I think they're in Florida. And I'm not the only one." She rolled off the pillow, and commandeered my keyboard. A few clicks later, we were looking at an old photograph of my patriarch nemesis, standing with his wife and two children in front of a podium.

ATLANTA, Georgia (CNN)—Embattled ex–White House Chief of Staff Kurt Gehry has left the capital in the wake of his resignation and ongoing investigation into the possibility that he employed several illegal immigrants in his Potomac residence.

There is much speculation as to the current whereabouts of the President's most influential advisor, including an exclusive resort in the Florida Keys reserved for members of Rose & Grave, a two-century-old secret society on the campus of Gehry's alma mater, Eli University. The Chief of Staff has never confirmed his membership in the organization.

Gehry's absence during the investigation has dismayed his supporters in Congress, as well as those within the GOP. A representative for Governor Jacob Cabot said, "This resignation and the White House's reaction was handled in a secretive and unfortunate manner that gives the wrong impression to the people of the country. I hope we will all soon receive the answers we deserve from our nation's leaders." Cabot recently dropped out of the presidential race, citing family obligations.

White House spokesman Bob Gibson responded to the statement from the Cabot camp with a thorough defense of the Chief of Staff. "Kurt Gehry's wife and children have been unreasonably scrutinized in the last few weeks by the inside-the-Beltway media machine. As far as I know, they are currently enjoying a short family vacation."

Administrators at the National Cathedral School for Girls and St. Albans have confirmed that neither Darren nor Isabelle Gehry is an enrolled student for the spring quarter.

Was I really going to be spending my Spring Break with Kurt "Grade A-Asshole" Gehry? And his spawn? After our last dramatic run-in, when my entire club disavowed him as a patriarch, I figured any future meetings would be awkward at best.

"Great," Odile said with a huff. "Way to start a vacation. Maybe I'm glad to be skipping out."

"Forewarned is forearmed," Demetria replied.

"I'm not sure I understand," Jenny said. "How can the family be on Cavador Key? The wife and the kids aren't Diggers." I was relieved that she'd asked it, since I was usually the knight with the most questions about the way the society worked.

"No," said Clarissa. "You can take your family there if you want. They can't go to any meetings or ceremonies, and obviously they aren't supposed to know what the place is—though everyone does—but they can be there."

"Did you ever go with your dad?" I asked.

She rolled her eyes. "Why? We've got a great house in the Hamptons."

———

Twenty-four hours later, I wondered if the Hamptons might have been a better idea. I stood on the pier, duffle bag in hand, and goggled.

"You've got to be kidding me," I said, backing up a few steps. "There is no way I'm getting on that."

"How did you think we were going to get to Cavador, Amy?" George asked, swinging his suitcase out of the airport limo's trunk. "It's not like there's enough traffic to warrant building a bridge."

"And it's not exactly on the ferry route," Jenny added.

I backed up a few more steps, watching my fellow knights strip off their winter coats and don sunglasses, caps, and even (in the case of fair Clarissa) sunscreen. No one else seemed concerned that our transport to the island looked like little more than a toy boat.

A captain and a teenaged boy emerged from the pygmy cabin on the deck and smiled at the new arrivals. "Ready to get going?" the man asked.

Everyone else grabbed their luggage and hopped aboard. I watched as the tiny craft pitched and bobbed under the onslaught of all that extra weight. Waves splashed up and down the side of the craft, and some water even spilled on the dock.

"What's the holdup, young lady?" the man said.

"I was wondering," I said, "what's the weight limit on that thing?"

He threw back his head and laughed. "Plenty enough for you and your bag. Now hop on. We've got a schedule to keep."

I hesitated, then handed my bag over to the man. But I couldn't bring myself to climb aboard. "Is there a lifeboat or something?" I asked.

"A lifeboat?" George said from the deck. He laughed. "What do you think this is, Amy? The *Titanic*?"

It had better not be. I must have looked even more scandalized, because the captain snorted and shook his head at me.

"Will you feel better if I fix you up with a life jacket? I think I have one or two on board." He lifted his head. "Kid!" he cried, and the teenager looked up from where he was fiddling with some ropes on the deck. "Get Miss—" He looked at me. "What's your name, girl?"

"Amy Haskel."

"Get Miss Amy Haskel a life vest."

The kid shot me a quick, incredulous look and ducked into the cabin. Great. Now I was an object of mockery to an adolescent.

Even knowing that I was about to be stuffed into some neon nylon-and-polyurethane fashion disaster/safety device, I didn't want to get on board. Everyone was starting to make impatient noises. I looked up at them, standing above me on the raised deck of the boat, superior and smug because they had no problem with the bobbing and the splashing and the unfathomable depths of the ocean. I peered over the edge of the dock and caught a glimpse of seabed about four feet below the surface. Okay, well, maybe not unfathomable, but *still*.

The teenager emerged again and tossed me a cornea-searing orange vest held together with bright yellow straps. "That do?" he asked.

I slipped it over my head. The vest was made of two squares of foam sewn together at the shoulders, with a hole for my head. The straps went beneath my arms and attached in front with a big plastic buckle. I snapped myself in, feeling stupider by the second. And then I steeled my nerves and climbed aboard.

Okay, this wasn't so bad. Nice, even, what with the gentle rock and sway. I stood for a moment in the middle of the deck, hands splayed for balance. The spring sunlight flickered out from behind a cloud and spilled onto the skin of my arms.

Warmth. Why is it that sunlight warms so much more thoroughly than radiators? It was the first time in months that I'd felt that sensation, and I lifted my face to the sky, soaking it in.

There was a rumbling beneath my flip-flops as the boat's engine turned over. The deck pitched and I dropped into an alarmed crouch.

Clarissa laughed. "Midwesterners." She beckoned to me. "Come here. I'll keep an eye on you."

I rose and cast a quick look around. Most of the others

were enjoying the sun and the view and hadn't noticed my humiliating moment.

But at least one person hadn't missed it. Poe shook his head at me, one brow raised above the rim of his sunglasses, and turned away.

Whatever. I wouldn't let him see me sweat. Poe was the only one on the boat who really knew how much this experience freaked me out, and I intended to keep it that way. I took a deep breath and edged toward the railing near the—prow? front?—to join Clarissa and George.

Up here, the rise and fall of the deck was even more pronounced, and I gripped the rails securely. Just to the side, the railing gapped at the "entrance."* Only a thin chain dangled between the two bits of rail. I suppressed a shudder and huddled closer to Clarissa.

"...sailing," I heard George say.

"Right, tomorrow," Clarissa said. "I can't wait."

I could. I hadn't yet figured out what I'd be doing on the island all day while my brothers went swimming or jet-skiing or who knows what else. Hopefully, the sunbathing-and-catching-up-on-reading contingent would be just as popular.

Clarissa held her arms out over the abyss. "I mean, look at how pale I've gotten. I need a tan like no one's business."

As George and Clarissa compared skin tones, I tried my best to relax. I attempted to roll the tension out of my shoulders and neck, but the life jacket limited my mobility quite a bit. Not that I had any intention of taking it off until I was back on dry land. Safety first, and all that.

However, I had to admit that once you got into the rhythm of the boat—the way it smacked hard against

* The confessor is most frustrated by her lack of boating jargon.

the waves, then rose and swooped into the dips between the swells—it was almost fun. Like a little roller coaster. I could understand why folks of Clarissa's stock actually enjoyed this kind of activity.

And then I remembered that Brandon and Felicity had gone on a yacht tour of Fiji. Another example of why she worked so much better for him than I would have: boating trips. I would never suggest such a thing to him. I didn't even know he liked boats. (Just airplanes—and paper ones, at that.)

I loosened my white-knuckled grip on the rail a bit. Maybe if I'd been more adventurous, he would have . . .

No. Stop it. I'd promised myself that I wouldn't do this anymore, that I wouldn't spend any more time thinking about what I was lacking. I'd made mistakes with Brandon, but it didn't make me a bad person. Just a different person. A person who wasn't right for him.

Still . . . I moved my hands a few inches from the rail. It didn't hurt to try.

The boat pitched again and I tightened my grip. Maybe I should wait to try until we were closer to the dock?

The boy who'd given me the life jacket joined us by the rail, and George and Clarissa scooted over to give him room. I did not scoot. Someone else could stand by that chain-enclosed gap.

"Hi," George said, sticking out his hand. "I'm George. You the skipper here?"

The kid shrugged. "Today. Gets me off the island."

He'd been on the island for a while? Maybe . . . hiding out from the media? I looked at him more closely, trying to recall the photo I'd seen online. "Are you Darren?" I asked.

"And you're Amy," he stated, smiling.

"How did you know that?" Clarissa asked.

"The captain said it." He flicked a chip of paint off the railing and over the side. "So, are all you guys Diggers?"

"I don't think we're supposed to tell you that," Clarissa said.

Darren shrugged again. "It's pretty obvious with everyone else. You're either a Digger, or the girlfriend or wife or kid of one. But not anymore."

"What makes you say that?" I asked.

"Because they've got girls now. So you guys could all be Diggers."

"I'm just the boyfriend of one," George volunteered. As if he was ever the boyfriend of anyone.

"No," said Darren. "*You're* a Prescott. You I know."

Clarissa laughed. "Your reputation has preceded you even here, George."

I squinted through the sunlight at Darren Gehry, trying to find in him some resemblance to his father, but noticed none. Where Kurt was beefy, red-faced, and scowling, Darren was skinny, freckled, and had an easy, open (if vaguely smug) smile.

"How do you know Rose & Grave has girls?" I asked him.

"There's nothing better to do here than read up on you guys."

Funny, to talk to some of my fellow knights, there was nothing better to do than read up on his family back at Eli. I could see now why the Gehrys had spirited their children off to Cavador. There was no need to subject the kids to that sort of media frenzy, especially after they just lost their nanny!

"There's a lot of old records and stuff lying around." He peeled another strip of paint off the railing.

I feigned innocence. " 'We guys'?" I said. "I'm not one of them."

He chuckled.

"Still, you seem to know a lot about Rose & Grave for someone who isn't a member," Clarissa added.

"Are you saying you are one?" he replied.

She leaned in. "What do you think?"

The deck tilted as the captain started cutting to the side, and we all jostled against one another. I bit back a scream, since no one else seemed to be fazed by the movement.

Come on, Amy. Pull yourself together. I could do this. It was just a boat ride. I'd been on boats before.

Well, no. I'd been on a log flume once, where the water was about three inches deep. And I'd ridden the Pirates of the Caribbean at Disney World. And It's a Small World, too, come to think of it. But other than that, I'd led a pretty boat-free existence. How had I made it to twenty-two with so little experience? And here I'd thought myself so worldly.

The captain started calling for Darren, and he excused himself.

"Not a bad kid," said Clarissa. "Shame about the father."

"Is Daren really stuck down here, alone with his family?" George said. "That can't be fun. And what are they doing about his school?"

I nodded, not sure I could trust my voice as the boat began zipping across someone else's wake with several jarring slaps. Could that possibly be good for the hull? If I felt this kind of bumping in a car, I'd freak out, but apparently no one minded that every second it felt like we were about to break open and spill our contents right into the depths. I felt my stomach drop into my toes, then rise in my throat.

Great. Now I was seasick.

A few moments later, Darren rejoined the party.

"So," George said, "how much farther to Cavador?"

Darren pointed vaguely off into the distance, and the boat pitched again. He covered his mouth with one hand and gripped the railing with the other.

"You feeling okay, man?" George asked. Darren shook his head miserably. From my position on the other side of Clarissa, I sympathized. I wasn't feeling so hot myself. Maybe the captain should take it easy on us.

Suddenly, Darren reared up and spewed something white and chunky all over Clarissa. She screamed and flung herself backward, out of the splash zone, knocking into me. I lost my grip on the railing and catapulted backward. I made one grab, then another, reeling back, trying to find my balance on the ever-tilting deck. My hands closed over metal, and I heard a crunch.

The chain. The gap.

And then the world turned upside down.

I hereby confess:
I thought I was
going to die.

8.
Waves

It took forever for the splash.

In case you're wondering, water is not soft. The sea smacked me in the head as I landed. My breath whooshed out of me and I gasped, instantly swallowing a lungful or two of water.

I tried to move my hands, but they were tangled in something, and the pressure of the water made them feel heavy. Clumsy. There was something very loud nearby. The propeller? I kicked and felt my shoes fly off. When I tried to open my eyes, they burned and blurred.

I saw blue, then the shiny white boat, bathed in sunlight. Tiny colors clustered at the prow. Then blue again, as another wave hit.

I heard a scream. Not mine, of course. To scream, you must be able to breathe.

Thank God for the life jacket, I remember thinking. Right before I noticed I was no longer wearing one.

And then I did feel a scream rising in my throat. I kicked and kicked, and once again, the blue gave way to sunlight and boat. The same colors clustered on the deck, only now there were more of them, and they were pointing at me, and then I saw something black fly out. And then everything went blue once more.

Why couldn't I move my hands? Where were my shoes?

In the next second, there was something squeezing my chest, dragging me backward. I stiffened and then breathed air. Or something approximating air. My hair hung in my face like a wet blanket, wrapped tight around my neck. I choked and coughed, trying to get my arms free.

"Hold still, Amy," said a voice at my back. "The straps."

And then the water got a lot less heavy and I clawed at my face, scratching my skin with my nails as I scraped my hair out of the way. Yes! Air—cold, salty, but air nonetheless. I gulped it into my burning lungs, and started coughing again, jostling against whatever constrained my torso.

"Amy." The voice was as calm as before. "Stop struggling."

I went limp, and found that I wasn't sinking. Someone was holding me above the water. I turned my face toward the voice.

"Ah," Poe said. "She does know how to listen." There was a smear of watery red beneath his nose. Was he bleeding?

Something smacked against the water. A Styrofoam circle. Poe grabbed for it with his free hand and shoved it toward me. "Hold on to this." I reached for the lifesaver with shaking hands, and as soon as I took hold of it, he flipped the tube over my head and pushed me through. "Got it?" he asked, breathing heavily. I nodded, and another coughing fit overtook me.

Poe began pushing me and my Styrofoam tube toward the boat, asking me questions the whole time.

"Can you breathe?"

I nodded.

"Anything broken?"

I shook my head.

"Anything hurt?"

Another shake. Though that wasn't true. My head was pounding, my lungs burned, my throat felt raw.

"Can you *speak*?"

"What happened to your face?" I croaked.

"You kicked it."

"Sorry."

We'd reached the boat by then, and Poe pulled me beneath a fiberglass ladder built into the side of the hull. Hands were already reaching out over the edge, but I couldn't tell who they belonged to. Somehow, I pulled myself up onto the rungs. Somehow, I got over the side and onto the deck, trailing water, coughing and spluttering the whole time. Clarissa wrapped me in a towel. I could see vomit drying on the front of her shirt.

"Amy, I'm so sorry," she said. "I didn't realize you were standing so close to me. I feel awful—"

"It's not your fault," George said, placing a hand on her shoulder. "It was an accident."

"Where's Darren?" I asked. "Is he all right?"

"Fine. Seasick." Clarissa pulled her shirt away from her chest. "I'm going to go change."

Jenny took her place at my side. "You caught your life vest on that chain and it ripped right off," she reported. "I've never seen anything like it."

Harun stood above us. "When you went down again, we figured you'd hit your head or something. You just... sank."

Yeah, dude. That happens when one doesn't swim. But I didn't say that. I just hugged the towel more tightly around myself and prayed that this boat ride would be over soon. But how was I supposed to get off the island once I was on it? Another boat? Was there any chance I could be airlifted off?

My Capri pants and T-shirt stuck to my body, my hair hung on my face in clammy tangles. The right side of my head throbbed where it had smacked against the water, and I could feel bruises forming on my right shoulder and the top of my foot where (I suppose) I'd hit it against Poe's face.

Poe. Where had he gone? I looked around the deck for him, but he hadn't joined the others in seeing I was okay.

"When will we get to the island?" I rasped.

"Soon, Amy," Jenny said. She leaned in and dropped her voice to a whisper. "You don't swim, do you?"

I put my head down on my knees.

I heard her voice overhead. "Come on, guys, let's give her some space."

That's the last thing I noticed until the boat engines ground to a halt.

———

"We're here." Demetria's voice was gentler than I'd ever heard it. She touched my shoulder. "Wake up, Amy."

My clothes had dried somewhat, but were still damp and clingy in the back, under my arms, and, of course, near my crotch. Lovely. I pushed my tangled hair out of my face. "Thank God. Dry land."

"Well, come on, Kevin Costner, and enjoy it."

I looked up. Ugh. This was a mistake. I needed to get off the island, go someplace where there was no water for miles. I wondered if there were any interesting Spring Break trips through Death Valley.

"There's supposed to be some sort of tour for the neo-phytes," Clarissa said, crouching down to join us. I'd been huddling on a bench near the control panel, too afraid to go into the cabin but not wanting to get anywhere near the edge of the deck. Demetria and Jenny also stooped over me.

"So we're neophytes again?" Demetria asked.

"Well, it is our first time here." Clarissa looked at me. "But I bet we can take you straight to your room instead. I'm sure the last thing you want to do is spend time walking around, until you've gotten a chance to—"

"Change," Demetria cut in.

"Rest, I was going to say."

Hide out would probably be better.

Jenny appeared at the door. "Seems this is going to be more complicated than we thought."

"What do you mean?" Clarissa asked.

"There's some sort of issue with the sleeping arrange-ments."

"What?" Demetria said. "What issue?"

"Well, the island caretaker is what some would term a tad old-school. He says that he won't put us girls in the same building as the other knights. We have to sleep else-where."

"What?" Clarissa asked.

At this, I seriously considered staying on the boat.

Demetria frowned. "Are you sure it's Victorian sensi-bilities? Maybe there's something else going on here."

"What?" Clarissa asked. "Are you taking up the mantle of Amy's conspiracy theories?"

"Well, she's hardly in any shape to do so!" Demetria replied. She turned to Jenny. "Go back and tell this guy that Eli dorms went co-ed ages ago. We have gender-free bathrooms and everything."

"You do it," Jenny said. "Or am I the only one expected to get treated like a second-class citizen around here?"

"If the shoe fits," Demetria muttered. She'd never really forgiven Jenny for the whole website fiasco last semester.

"Guys," I said through my sore throat, "what's the problem here? Where exactly do they propose to put us?"

"Just another cabin. But it's kind of on the far side of the island. A bit out of the way."

"So what?" Clarissa said. "It's not like the island is that big to start with."

"It's the principle of the thing," Demetria said. "Why do we have to be the ones to go away? Put the boys there if he insists on separating us."

"And where's the principle of that thing?" Clarissa replied. Demetria appeared to concede the point.

"Also," Jenny said, "it doesn't have its own bathroom. We'd have to hike back to use the shower house near the kitchens."

"What?" I asked, while Clarissa shrugged and Demetria's expression grew mildly less combative. "What do you mean, no bathrooms? What kind of luxury resort is this?"

All three of them blinked at me. "What do you mean?" Clarissa asked. "It's our own *private island*. How much more luxurious can it get?"

And that was Miss Park Avenue talking. I instantly felt foolish.

"Yeah," Jenny said. "No other club on campus has an island to call their own."

What could I say to that? That I'd been expecting a fair approximation of the Ritz, on top of my own private island? I sank even farther into the bench cushions. Spring Break Score: so far, so crappy.

"Poor Amy," Clarissa said, sitting by my side and putting a hand on my shoulder. "Don't worry. If I'd been through what you had today, I'd be looking for some creature comforts as well. It's okay. As soon as this tour is over, we'll get you all settled in."

"I'll skip the tour," Jenny offered, crouching on my other side. "I'll find my way around later. Like Clarissa said, it's not like Cavador Key is that big to start with. Besides," she added. "I owe you one." True. I'd stood by Jenny during her nervous breakdown last semester.

"What about George?" Clarissa asked. "He's been here before. He can take her to her cabin."

"I'm sure the last thing Amy wants is to have George tuck her into bed," Demetria said.

"Maybe the last thing *you* would want," Clarissa said under her breath, but I heard it nonetheless.

Before I had a chance to react, I heard someone clear his throat, and then Poe was standing there, still sopping. His black hair was swept back from his face, except for a few lone strands that hung over his forehead like slash marks and left trails of water sliding over his cheekbones.

Had no one given him a towel?

"I came to see if you were all right," he said, as if the others weren't standing between us.

"She's fine, just shaken," Jenny said, her voice cold.

I opened my mouth to thank him for saving my life, but once again, my sore throat refused to perform.

"I'm taking Darren to his cabin," Poe continued before I had a chance to choke out my gratitude. "And I'll help get you to yours if you want. Let *our brothers*"—his eyes flickered momentarily in Jenny's direction—"go on the introductory tour."

"What about you?" Demetria asked.

"I've been here before. Patriarch, remember?"

Demetria's expression said it all. *Tough to remember when you're always hanging around.*

"Besides, I could use a change of clothes, too." He pointed to his sorry attire.

It was amazing how quickly their attitude to Poe warmed once it became clear that he was offering to take responsibility for me. And how could I blame them? There was Spring Breaking to get on with. They hadn't signed up to babysit a half-drowned brother who currently looked like a fully drowned rat. Within moments, the Diggirls had vamoosed, leaving me alone with Poe on the deck. I stood up at last.

"I just wanted to say—"

"That yours?" Poe interrupted, pointing to my yellow duffle. (It was the only one left on the deck.)

I nodded, noting as I did that Poe's only luggage seemed to be the knapsack slung across his back. Well, he never had been much for fashion. Still, I remained concerned about what would happen with the clothes in that bag, as the T-shirt he wore was still so wet that it molded to his chest and shoulders. I looked away.

"You have another pair of shoes?" he said, taking in my bare feet. "The paths are all made of crushed shell. They'll tear you up."

I knelt and dug in the duffle until I found a pair of ballet flats. So much for showing off my pedicure.

Poe had my bag on his shoulder before I even stood up. We met Darren on the dock, where he was leaning against a pylon, head in hands.

"Feeling any better?" I asked him.

He nodded slightly, but didn't look up. I wondered briefly if I should tell him that I didn't blame him for my fall, but I clammed up once I caught Poe's expression and the almost imperceptible shake of his head.

Of course. Poe would know. The last thing this teenager wanted from me was anything that carried a whiff of *pity*. He was already feeling guilty enough. I remembered the night Poe had ended up in the hospital after our crook. Nice to see he hadn't matured much beyond his teens.

But neither was I capable of rolling out one of those guys'-guy faux-threatening comments in my current mental state. I couldn't just laugh it off in any manner that would seem convincing. I think that ability was bundled with the Y chromosome.

And here we were always arguing for equality of the sexes.

So it was in silence that our little party trailed up the path and past the tour, where a man I supposed was Cavador's caretaker was busy enlightening a knot of my brothers as to the geologic history of the island.

Maybe I was glad to skip this tour after all. My Spring Break–enthusiast Diggirls looked bored to death. As we passed, a few of my fellow knights twiddled their fingers in my direction, and George gave me a thumbs-up and raised his eyebrows. I smiled weakly in return and he looked relieved.

I'd give Cavador Key this: It may not be a luxury resort, but it sure was beautiful. The spring sunlight filtered through the leaves of shrub pines and palm trees, and the gray-white path snaked through thick palmetto ground cover toward a cluster of buildings. To my right, I saw a mangrove stand hugging the shoreline, and there were red and pink hibiscus flowers as big as my head on bushes all along the path.

We stopped by a low house hugging the path a little away from the main cluster of buildings. "Better stay here," Poe whispered to me.

Must be the Gehrys' house. He and Darren headed up the walk, but I don't think the teen was interested in having the incident repeated to his parents, since he disappeared into the dark interior and shut the door in Poe's face. Poe stood there for a moment, clearly torn between knocking or letting the whole issue slide. Personally, I'd vote the latter. I didn't know if I wanted to know how Kurt Gehry would react to the news that Darren had almost killed me, accident or no.

He might be pleased.

After a moment, Poe returned to me. This of course is when I should have thanked him for saving my life. But for once, I, never at a loss for words, couldn't think of anything to say that would get the job done. Eloquence deserted me. Even fluency seemed to be taking a coffee break. So instead I decided to have another coughing fit.

Poe paused on the path a few steps ahead of me and waited for me to finish.

The island was bigger than Clarissa and the others had led me to believe. At least, it seemed to take forever for us to get to the girls' cabin. We trudged along in awkward silence, victim and savior, until finally we broke out of the scrub into a small clearing, and there it was, highly rundown, with dingy screens, a peeling green paint job, a sagging front porch, and a bright orange aluminum roof. I'd given up expecting luxury, and now merely hoped that the cabin would stand up to a rainstorm. (Doubtful.)

"There should be towels and sheets and stuff all set up for you," Poe said, breaking the silence like a spell.

"Thank you," I choked out. No. Not right. It sounded like I was thanking him for telling me about the linens. I reached out my arm. "No, really, P—Jamie. Thank you. How can I thank you? I could have died."

He just looked at me, and then hefted the bag in his

arms. "You're welcome. Do you want me to take the bag in?"

"No," I said. "I didn't even want you to carry it this far. I could have found this place by myself."

"It's not a problem. Like I said, I need to change, too. So, the bag?"

"I'm fine." I held out my hands. "Please."

He handed me my luggage, and once again I faltered. Saying thank you wasn't enough, even if I said it three times. Even if I said it three hundred. How could I let him carry my freaking bag after he'd saved my life? It was too stupid for words.

So it came out again. *"I could have died."*

"I know." He was quiet for a second. "That's what happens when you don't know how to swim." He quirked his head in the direction of the cabin. "Go lie down for a while. Dinner's not for hours."

I made it up the path, my face burning with shame. *Yep, way to thank the guy, Amy. And you're supposed to be a writer.*

But it wasn't as if Poe had helped any. I mean, what kind of guy starts lecturing you about your swimming skills when you're in the midst of confessing how you'd practically faced mortality that afternoon? Not the time, man, not the time.

The interior of the cabin was warm, and dust motes floated freely in the sunlight that sneaked through the slats and the screened-in windows. Three bunk beds were pushed against the wall, each equipped with fresh sheets, pillows, and sets of towels. There was also a lone dresser next to a sink. No closet. Lovely.

I dropped my stuff on one of the bottom bunks, then dug around in my bag until I found my pajamas and a fresh pair of underwear. I peeled off my still damp clothing, and set about seeing if the sink had hot water, hoping to save myself a trek to the shower house. Negative. I weighed the trouble of hiking back down the path against the hassle of a tepid sponge bath, and decided on the latter.

The towels were pretty scratchy and thin, but big, more like bath sheets. Beach towels, I realized. For people who go to the beach, who actually like the water. I wrapped my body in one towel, and my hair in another. Maybe I'd go sit on the porch until I felt warm again. I looked out the window.

And that's when I saw him.

Poe was standing on the border of the clearing, acting most peculiarly. He took a few steps toward the cabin, then paused, shook his head, and marched back out. He repeated the move a few times before stomping off for good.

I stood at the window, confused as hell. Why in the world ... and then it hit me, way, way harder than the water had when I'd fallen off the boat.

Poe liked me.

I hereby confess:
I had no idea how
to handle it.

9.
Expectations

My mind was still buzzing when the other girls arrived at the cabin.

"I owe you an apology," Clarissa said, struggling to heave her Louis Vuitton over the threshold. "You were right. This place is a dump."

I didn't even have the presence of mind to look smug. "How was the tour?" I managed.

"Snoozeville," Jenny said. "And did you know they don't have Internet access here? How do they survive?"

"On the upside," Demetria said, "I now know more about Caribbean air currents than I ever thought possible."

"No Internet access?" I said. "But haven't Mrs. Gehry and the kids been here for a while? That must suck for Darren."

"Yeah, he must be so behind on his MySpace updates." Clarissa rolled her eyes. "Perhaps he can entertain himself figuring out a way to get his spew off my shirt."

"How are you?" Jenny asked me. "I feel so bad that we dumped you on that jerk."

I shrugged, mind still whirring. Pour some rum into my skull and we could all have daiquiris at this rate. *Poe liked me?*

Clarissa was unpacking her second suitcase. "Don't worry about Amy. She's actually been known to seek out James's company from time to time, isn't that right?"

"I remember," Jenny said.

"It's Jamie." I clamped my mouth shut. Where did that come from?

"What?"

"His name. It's, um, Jamie." *And how long had he had a crush on me?*

"Oh." Clarissa turned back to brushing the wrinkles out of a silk sundress. "Whatever."

And how come I'd never noticed it before?

"Tell me how it happened," Jenny said.

I was curious about that myself. Poe hated me. He thought I was everything wrong with Rose & Grave. At least, that's what he'd said back in November. But, since then, well, I thought we'd graduated to mutual...respect and neutrality?

"Yo, earth to Amy." Jenny waved her fingers in my face. "The accident? How did it happen?"

Oh.

"I wasn't standing by the deck," Jenny went on. "Weren't you wearing a life jacket?"

"It ripped right off," Clarissa said. "It's my fault. Amy, I'm so sorry." She looked at Jenny. "I bumped into her and she lost her balance and fell right through the chain gate. And her jacket tore off. It must have gotten caught on something."

Jenny shook her head. "That doesn't make any sense. Those things are supposed to be all tough and made of rip-stop nylon and stuff."

Demetria cut in. "Well, Jamie brought the straps on deck with him. They were completely frayed through. I'm surprised they didn't fall off when you tried to buckle them. If you wanted to sue, you'd have a pretty good case on your hands. Talk about safety violations—life jackets that fall apart as soon as you hit the water?"

"Who would she sue?" Clarissa asked. "The Diggers? She *is* a Digger."

"And if she had died?" Jenny added. "Her parents aren't in Rose & Grave. They could sue."

I shivered. I didn't want to talk about dying anymore. "No one is suing. I just don't want to get on a boat again unless it's the one leaving this island."

"But what are you going to do?" Clarissa asked as Jenny returned to her unpacking. "Not go snorkeling with us tomorrow?"

"Blondie," Demetria cut in as Jenny started unwinding a long length of cable, "did you not notice the part where she almost drowned today? Cut the girl some slack."

I chose not to contribute to this conversation and watched as Jenny knelt on the floor and resumed unpacking. First she took out a laptop and a long stretch of Ethernet cable. So far, so normal. Then she took out a large silver bowl, a mess of aluminum foil, and a pair of wire cutters, and I started getting confused.

"What the hell are you doing?" Demetria asked. Her luggage, like Poe's, consisted of a battered rucksack. Of course, Jenny's suitcase seemed to hold more electronic equipment than actual clothing, so it seemed to be a trend.

"I'm getting us Internet access," Jenny replied, coiling one end of the cable around her cell phone. She lined the bowl with foil and placed the cord-wrapped phone inside. "Jerry-rigged satellite dish," she said, and plugged the other end of the cord into her laptop. "Now, let's see if we can't pick up any signals."

"Well, while you pirate wireless, I'm going to take a shower." Clarissa turned to me. "Amy? Any plans to wash your hair before the introductory dinner?"

I touched my salt-encrusted tresses. Okay, good point. I hadn't realized how gross seawater made your hair. But I wasn't sure I wanted to go to dinner, either. "Um . . ."

"Go take a shower, Amy," Demetria said, waving me off. "I don't necessarily think you need to get back on a boat, but you can't spend your Spring Break hiding in this dump, either. There's no water at dinner other than the kind they put in glasses."

Yes, but thanks to Dragon's Head, I knew exactly how unpleasant those glasses could get.

"Besides," Clarissa added, "you can't miss seeing how far the mighty Kurt Gehry has fallen. Aren't you looking forward to getting all smug in the buffet line?"

Would it be mean to admit I was?

"Here we go," Jenny announced. "It's weak, but it works. Anyone want to check their e-mail?"

———

Eventually the other girls impressed upon me the need to shower and make myself presentable for dinner. While we got ready, they filled me in on the least boring parts of the tour, as well as the loose itinerary for the week. (Unfortunately, it sounded like a lot of snorkeling.)

"And the rules," Jenny said. "Don't forget those." She handed me a crumpled sheaf of papers.

"Right." Demetria rolled her eyes. "*Comandante* Saltzman runs a pretty tight ship on Cavador."

"What a sweet job, though," Clarissa said. "I want to be

an island caretaker when I grow up." We lapsed into silence as we tried to imagine Clarissa playing servant to anyone.

RULES OF CAVADOR KEY

1) Barbarian names ONLY outside of the tomb or other official ceremonies. Remember, we're not all Diggers here.

2) Though most of the visiting barbarian family members are aware of this island's true purpose, there's no reason to go blabbing about it at random. Your oaths still hold.

3) Try to limit showers to ten minutes or less, no more than once a day. We are dealing with severe water shortages.

4) The generators will be shut off every night at precisely 10 P.M. Each room is equipped with candles and flashlights if you wish to stay up later than that. (Tomb excepted.)

5) Special dietary requests will be submitted, in writing, at least three days prior to your visit.

6) The only barbarians allowed on this island are the wives and biological children of active knights and/or patriarchs.

7) No, there is no pool. The ocean is a few feet away. Deal with it.

This went on in the same vein for several pages. At the bottom of the last sheet, there was a handwritten addition:

* No co-educational sleeping arrangements will be provided without proof of matrimony.

"I think we've found our new slogan," Demetria said.

The main compound of Cavador Key was composed of four buildings. One was the cabin the other knights were using, near the shower house. Then there was a larger building in a Key West style, with big windows, a sloping roof, and a wraparound porch. This, Demetria informed me, housed the kitchens, dining room, billiard and rec room, and "library." Upstairs, the main hall had a few small apartments for married Diggers and families, though Clarissa explained that they were all currently occupied, which was why we girls had been relegated to the distant cabin. There was also a small, windowless, stucco structure that served as the island's "tomb," and looked too hot to even think of entering ("Looks like a strip club," Jenny said). Finally, there was the little cypress-wood house where the caretaker lived. None of the buildings was particularly beautiful or grand, but each appeared well built and maintained. I wonder how much it cost the Tobias Trust each year to keep this island. Little wonder it was used for far more than a Spring Break hangout by the current club. That could hardly justify the cost. I gathered that patriarchs could drop in for some rest and relaxation anytime they chose.

What I didn't expect was to see my favorite of them all waiting for us on the front porch of the main building.

"Amy!" Malcolm cried, sliding off the steps and coming to meet me, arms outstretched. "I heard you took a dip on the way over."

I hugged my big sib hard. "What are you doing here!" He hadn't dropped any hints at all over e-mail. But maybe keeping this secret was why his communication had dropped off.

"Surprise!" He ruffled my hair. "Had about enough

as I could stand of Alaskan winters. And I'd thought Connecticut was bad." The recent Eli grad had been spending a gap year on a fishing crew before starting business school.

"I still can't believe you're here, though," I said.

"What, thought I'd prefer to take my vacation with my parents?"

I looked down. Malcolm was currently estranged from his father, an ultra-conservative state governor who didn't take kindly to the news that his only son preferred the company of men. "Still getting the silent treatment?"

"I figure they'll relent when they reach the age where I'll sock 'em away in a nursing home if they don't."

"Good idea."

"So tell me about your trip over here." I couldn't blame Malcolm for changing the subject. "What happened?"

"You must have already heard a dozen different versions."

"Yeah, but I want the one out of your mouth."

What, didn't he trust his buddy Poe's interpretation? Speaking of, where was Poe?

The other girls had wandered into the rec room to join the rest of the island's inhabitants. I caught sight of a television, a bunch of board games, a pool table, and a dart set, but nothing really held my interest until I saw the lone figure on a chair in the corner, in a dark shirt and a pair of khaki shorts, reading. Poe. I stopped short.

"Do you know how to play backgammon?" Malcolm asked, still headed into the rec room. "I think I've got time to teach you before din—" He noticed I hadn't followed him. "Amy?"

"Actually, can I talk to you for a minute?" I beckoned him back outside.

He furrowed his brow. "Sure. What's up?"

But I didn't say anything more until we were a safe distance from the crowd, seated on a picnic table bench on the far side of the porch. "I have a question for you, but it's kind of . . . um, personal."

"Yes, I'm gay."

"You really are a fan of saying that, aren't you?"

"Once you start, you just can't stop."

"Seriously, though, you can't laugh at me," I said.

He smiled. "I make no promises."

"Okay, fine. You can't make fun of me, then. And if I'm totally off base, you have to forget I ever said anything, and never tell anyone this conversation happened."

"I swear on Persephone. Now you've got me really intrigued." Malcolm leaned forward, his hands on the bench between us, his expression one of amused anticipation.

I took a deep breath. "Does P—Jamie . . . like me?"

Malcolm blinked. This was clearly not the kind of dirt he'd been expecting.

"I mean, *like me* like me," I clarified quickly.

"What are you, twelve?" he asked, incredulous.

"You aren't supposed to make fun of me!" I scolded.

"You never said you were going to act like a teeny-bopper. That's a special circumstance. Any judge would agree."

"Fine." I started to rise. "Like I said, forget I asked."

"Wait, Amy. Sit down," he said with a sigh. Malcolm was leaning his fists against the wood, staring down at his knuckles.

I sat. "What?"

He didn't look up. "This is all just between us, right?"

"Yeah."

"I wouldn't say he likes you."

"Oh." Oh. Of course not. How stupid of me. How ridiculous, really—

"He's pretty much in love with you."

"What?" I whispered.

"Amy, don't..." Malcolm's face had gone red. "He'd kill me if he knew I just told you that."

I jumped up. "Why didn't you tell me *before*?"

"Because you hate him, remember?" Malcolm grabbed my arm and pulled me back on to the bench, dropping his voice to a low growl. "Remember how you hate him? Remember how I had to send you about twelve thousand e-mails last semester before you agreed to even *talk* to him?"

"I don't...hate him," I stammered.

"Since when?"

Since last semester, actually, when I'd finally talked to him, but that was hardly the point. "I don't understand. How can he—" No way was I using the L-word. "—feel that way about me? We had a very strong mutual dislike, remember?"

"Yes," Malcolm said snidely. "I remember. I heard it nonstop from both of you."

"So what makes you think..."

"We're brothers; we don't do secrets. And something about the *manner* in which he conducted his nonstop complaining about you," Malcolm said, "tipped me off." Now my big sib leaned back on the bench. "You aren't the only one here who acts like a twelve-year-old when you've got a crush on someone."

"I don't have a crush on him."

"I know." Malcolm leaned forward. "And that's why this conversation has to end now. Amy, please please please don't let him know about this. Don't let him know you know. You may not like him very much, but he's a good friend of mine, and if you lord it over him, I may have to find a new little sib."

"I won't," I promised. "But you have it all wrong. We actually get on really well now."

"You're only saying that because he saved your life this afternoon."

"No! Well, maybe a little bit. But that's not all. We talk. We hang out." We *had* gone out for pizza that time.

"That's not what I hear," Malcolm said.

"Then you aren't hearing the whole story. Ask anyone in my club. They even—" *They even make fun of me for spending so much time with Poe.* But how could I say that to his good friend? And what had Poe been telling him?

And why did I care?

"I don't think I'm going around to the knights and canvassing for opinions about your relationship, but thanks," Malcolm said. "Just do me a favor and forget we had this talk, okay? Jamie's had a tough year where Rose & Grave is concerned. I don't think he needs any more humiliation."

"I wouldn't do anything, Malcolm. What do you take me for?"

"A knight of Rose & Grave. We're ruthless to our enemies."

But Poe wasn't my enemy. He was…God, I don't know what. This was all very disconcerting.

One thing was certain, I would not be able to talk to him until I figured it out. With any luck, we'd be sitting very far away from each other at dinner. My desire to give him a proper thank you was far outweighed by my need to get a handle on this revelation.

We moved inside. I listened with half an ear as Malcolm taught me the finer points of backgammon, and then I proceeded to really suck at the game, since I spent half my time thinking about the situation and the other half wondering if Poe was looking at us. On the upside, it got my mind off the whole almost-drowning thing.

So while Malcolm was bearing off pips or something, I was remembering Brandon. And not the way you think.

When had I figured out Brandon liked me? Or had I ever *not* known it? After all, our relationship had been fraught with flirtation since we first met. Such was not the case with Poe. In fact, I don't think he ever flirted with me. At least, not flirting as I understood the definition. Insults, threats, arguments: sure. If that was his way of trying to spark my interest...

But from what Malcolm had said, I doubted he was trying. And who knew what Malcolm had meant by "in love" anyway? We're talking about guys here. He was probably just attracted to me, and as unhappy about that prospect as I would be if I found myself attracted to him.

Speaking of...

But no. I wasn't going to look over there. What if he caught me sneaking a peek? He'd know for sure that I knew.

Still, I didn't need to look. A few very specific memories came unbidden to my mind. Poe, pulling his shirt off back in his horrendous apartment last fall. Poe, laying that asshole Micah Price flat with one punch. Poe, staring at me in the sliver of light as we lay together in the crawl space at the Dragon's Head tomb.

"Amy." Malcolm was waving his hand in front of my face. I rolled and moved a piece, blindly.

"You can't do that."

"Right, because...it's not an open point?" I said, hopeful.

"No, because it's my piece."

Crap. I stared at the board and made a different move. Malcolm sighed, shook his head, and sent me to the bar.

I needed a real bar. Were we getting cocktails before dinner? I swallowed, but my throat remained dry. Okay, so I wasn't *repulsed* by Poe. He was a young man, had all his limbs, no major deformities, and . . .

Oh, Jesus, Amy, who are you kidding? He's perfectly attractive. Not in league with George Prescott, of course, but then, who was? It was just tough to tell sometimes, what with that permanent scowl, and his ratty clothes, and his misanthropy . . .

Why was I even thinking about this? It shouldn't matter to me if a guy liked me, unless I was into him. Look at Brandon. I'd gotten involved with him because he liked me, and it all ended in tears. Never again.

I'd never been so relieved to head for dinner as I was that night, and I took great pains to fill my table with knights from my club so there would be no danger of sitting near the focus of all my recent thoughts.

The crusty caretaker made some sort of welcome speech (which I listened to as carefully as I had Malcolm's backgammon instructions) and then we poured the wine. Thank heaven. I filled my glass.

"Here's to an awesome Spring Break!" my brother Kevin said, raising his glass. "May it make up for all the Spring Breaks I've spent singing big band standards for Rotary Clubs from here to Kalamazoo."

"Here, here," said Clarissa. "And where is Kalamazoo?"

"Michigan." Kevin shuddered. "The Midwest."

"Hey!" I said, coming out of my haze enough to defend the flyovers.

"May this week be filled with new opportunities and experiences," said Harun, clinking his soda against the one belonging to Jenny, who sat beside him.

"May we all survive being unplugged," she added begrudgingly.

"May I not be sober again until classes restart," George said, already refilling.

"Agreed," Demetria said. "And may Ben finally agree to take me on in tennis."

"You got it, Billie Jean," Ben said. "Prepare to be annihilated."

"Billie Jean won, moron."

"Oh."

Clarissa raised an eyebrow in my direction. "And may we all convince Amy to get back up on that horse. Or boat, as the case may be."

I almost spat my wine at her. "Hell no. I'm heading up the landside sunbathing team."

"Awww, come on, Amy," George said. "Don't be a loser. What are you going to do back here on the island by yourself all day?"

"Vacation?" I replied coldly. "Eat junk food, catch up on my reading, just chill?"

"Leave her alone," Jenny said, and I took the opportunity to excuse myself and head for the salad bar.

But George, as I well knew, was not one to be sidetracked. He caught up with me between the croutons and the chickpeas. "I need to talk to you," he said softly, loading up on romaine.

"So talk." Did anyone really like canned beet slices?

"Are you angry at me?"

"No."

"Are you sure? Because you've been acting like a bitch."

"*Now* I'm angry at you." I stabbed the tongs into the cucumbers much more violently than they deserved. "Me not wanting to get on a boat again has nothing to do with us."

"I mean in general. Can't you let bygones be bygones?"

"Not when you're holding it over me. Last time we

spoke, you as good as threatened to tell everyone in the club about our little...thing."

A young patriarch's wife was picking through the tomato wedges on the other side of the sneeze guard. I smiled at her, but she only had eyes for George's megawatt grin.

"Hi there," he said, and as she moved on to the dressings, he turned his attention back to me. "Come on, Amy. I was *joking*. Besides, you already know why I left it off the C.B."

"Enlighten me." I rolled my eyes. "Wait. Don't tell me: I was *special*."

"No, because everyone knows. It's not a story."

"Everyone knows you slept with half the girls in our class, too. You told *those* stories."

"So the only other option is that I'm trying to blackmail you?"

I'd reached the end of the salad bar. There was no way to continue this conversation without moving on to the dessert table, which brought with it the base instinct to smack George in the face with a cream pie. Tempting.

"What exactly is it that you fantasize I'd be blackmailing you to do, Amy?"

I wasn't about to dignify that with an answer, so I just picked up my plate and left. Barely two steps toward my table, I froze. Malcolm and Poe had drawn up chairs and were squeezing into a heated argument about the current Democratic National Platform.

Oh, well. At least it wasn't snorkeling. But between trying to keep up with the debate from folks who were way more politically savvy than I (Malcolm's background gave him an unfair advantage, I think), and avoiding eye contact with Poe, I had a tough time following everything.

Eventually, I gave up and resorted to familiarizing myself with the china pattern.

Some Spring Break. First, I'd almost drowned, now I was in the middle of a big steaming pile of *awkward* with approximately one-fourth of my companions. What else could possibly go wrong?

"Do you think the Gehrys will come to dinner?" Kevin asked.

"I doubt it," Clarissa said. "He'd have to show his face in front of us, and he's in as much disgrace with this club as he is with the rest of the country. I was surprised the Gehrys even let their son on the boat today, considering the risk."

"What risk?" Jenny asked.

"Of one of us telling him exactly why they're hiding out here," Clarissa said, casting a quick glance in Demetria's direction.

"You don't think he knows?" Kevin asked.

"I doubt it," Clarissa said. "At least, I didn't get that impression this afternoon. And I heard the wife and kids left town before the whole immigration thing blew up. If your kid's nanny was about to be deported in a huge public blowup, don't you think you'd want to shield your child from all that?"

"If so, then it's really shocking that Kurt Gehry would leave his son alone with your club," Poe said. I didn't dare look up. "Everyone knows how much D177 hates him. Why would he risk giving you that kind of ammo?"

Demetria didn't miss a beat. "Why would it be *our* club in particular?"

"Only your club disavowed him," Malcolm argued. "He's still our patriarch, and thus, we're still obligated to keep his secrets."

"Come on, Malcolm," I said, trusting myself enough to speak to my big sib, if not his friend. "Don't tell me you like Kurt Gehry."

"Who cares whether or not he likes that slimeball?" Demetria asked. "It's not a society secret if it's being looped on CNN."

Malcolm only laughed and leaned back in his seat. "If it's a secret from someone in particular, though, I'd say we have an obligation to a fellow knight."

I noted the way his hand rested on the back of Poe's chair. Was that a hint? Like I said, Malcolm was very well politicized. He knew how to make comments without making them.

And Demetria was no fool, either, though she misunderstood the message completely. Recalibrating her missiles, she turned to Poe. "Well, *brother*? Gehry screwed you over, too. Broke his oaths to you. Can you think of any reason to keep his secrets for him?"

Poe acknowledged her question with the ghost of a smile, but returned to his rice pilaf and said nothing.

"Well," Jenny said. "There's the obvious: It might hurt the kids. That's one bit of advice that even the barbarians here would follow. You don't say nasty stuff about a kid's dad in front of the kid. Come on, Demetria. You didn't go up to Darren this afternoon and say, 'Hey, too bad about that nanny of yours, huh?' "

"True," Poe said.

But Demetria wasn't finished with him. "Okay, fine. No one here is into humiliating a child. But forgive me if I want to know exactly what's going on in that family, and how they're all dealing with the fallout." She aimed her fork at Poe. "And I think you know more about it than you're saying."

"Forget it, Dee," George said. "Poe would never go against the party line. He really likes having secrets. It's the only way he can get anyone to pay attention to him."

You could sense the shock around the table. It wasn't like George to be so cruel.

But Poe took it in stride, meeting George's gaze with a look that said, *Do you really want to take me on?* I had no doubt that Poe could out-insult anyone. Especially someone with so little practice as George. "Exactly. I'm always looking for attention. So flashy. Man, I'm obvious." He looked at George for one second more, then returned to his food.

"Do you think they're going to fix the boat railing before tomorrow's snorkeling trip?" Clarissa asked, whipping out her best charm-school voice.

"We're not going on that boat," Ben answered, obviously more than happy to follow Clarissa's lead. "One of the patriarchs brought a yacht to the island, and he's lending it out."

"Cool!" Clarissa said. She turned to me. "You have to come now. It's not even the same boat."

I didn't care if it was the *QE2*. I wasn't setting foot on a boat deck until it was time to leave, and that only by necessity. "Sorry," I replied.

The conversation turned to other topics, and soon after, Poe finished his food and carried his dinner plate to the counter near the kitchen. I expected him to return to the table, maybe grab a cup of coffee, but he left the dining room.

And in that instant, my decision was made. I stood so quickly I almost knocked my chair over.

"Whoa, Amy," Malcolm said, catching my chair by the armrest and righting it. "What are you doing?"

"I have to..." I trailed off. *No, Malcolm. Don't look at me like that.* He made a grab for my arm, but I shook him off and headed after Poe.

He was out of the building and halfway across the path to his cabin by the time I reached the porch. In the fading evening light, everything had turned violet. The crushed shells beneath our feet, the grass, his shirt, his hair, the hands he was jamming into his shorts pockets.

"P—Jamie," I said in a voice that wasn't quite normal volume but fell way short of a shout.

He turned. "You're going to slip up one of these days."

"Well, I'll expect you to keep track." I jogged to meet him on the path.

"What do you want?" He cocked his head. "To *thank* me again?"

Give it a rest, Poe. "Whence the hostility?"

He said nothing, but he didn't need to. It had been our default setting for so long that whenever we broke through and actually communicated, it was as if by accident.

Time for a change. "I was actually wondering if you were planning to go on that snorkeling trip tomorrow."

"Why?"

"Because I'm not. Obviously." *Deep breath, Amy.* "And I thought maybe if you were staying behind, we could hang out. You and me."

He didn't react, so I kept going.

"I have no idea what to do around here. I missed the tour. But you've been here before, so I'm sure you have some ideas."

"It's not that big of an island." He pointed. "House, games, library, beach. Those are your choices."

Ouch. Time to retreat. "Okay, well..."

"Eleven o'clock?"

What? "Okay."

He nodded. "Meet me here. I'll have something for us to do. Wear walking shoes."

"Okay," I said again.

He started to turn away, then stopped, smiled a little, ducked his head, and reached into his back pocket. "Amy, here." He tossed me a small package. "Just in case."

I looked down at my hand.

Life Savers.

I hereby confess:
Even in Florida,
they know who we are.

10.
Left Behind

The rest of the evening was spent in the game room, where the main topic of conversation was my near-drowning and Poe's rescue. Clarissa and George even performed a two-person reenactment with the help of the edge of the billiard table and a few too many glasses of wine. The patriarchs present were utterly enthralled.

I sat to the side, adding commentary and applause where necessary, but mostly keeping my hand wrapped around that package of mints.

How cheesy was that? I mean, Life Savers? What a dork.

But I still held them. So what did that make me?

I crashed early, picked my way back through the woods to the girls' cabin, and slept like the dead* for the rest of the night. Later, Clarissa told me that the others had arrived back around four in the morning, drunk (except for

---

* Not surprising, given the confessor's busy day, near-death experience, and boy-related stress. And she thought fellowship applications were tough!

Jenny, who had stuck to soda) and singing some Diggers tune from the Roaring Twenties (including Jenny, who'd honed her pipes through years of choir practice). But it would have taken a whole corps of moonshiners to rouse me from my slumber.

Unfortunately, my early-to-bed behavior meant I was up at the crack of dawn.

Mindful of my unconscious bunkmates, I dressed in the dim light filtering through the window screens and slipped out into the morning. A thin layer of mist lay over the island, blanketing the path with dew and muffling the sound of the waves on the shore.

Because the morning was a tad on the chilly side, I wore a lightweight hoodie over my shorts and tank top combo. As Poe had instructed, I'd chosen sneakers rather than ballet flats—my only other option since my flip-flops had found their way to Davy Jones's footlocker.

Poe. Was I really going to spend the day with him? And was it like...a date?

Well, if it was, it was my fault. I'd asked him out last night. Well, asked him to *hang* out, anyway.

Ugh. What was I thinking? I didn't ask guys out. I'd never done so. Call me old-fashioned. And if I was going to start, Poe wouldn't be my choice.

But the facts were incontrovertible. I'd asked Poe to be with me today. Poe. Not Clarissa, not Malcolm, not Jenny, who owed me sitting out a snorkeling session or two, and not George, who may or may not be interested in kissing and making up. Poe. Jamie. Whatever. *Him.*

Why? Maybe I'd been suffering the aftereffect of some near-death brain chemical? Perhaps it had impaired my decision-making skills. Or maybe it was even worse than that. Maybe I'd been all giddy and power-drunk off that little tidbit Malcolm had given me about Poe. It wouldn't be the first time I'd played fast and loose with someone's feelings.*

Without realizing it, I'd broken into a jog, disturbing slumbering seabirds as I pounded through the underbrush in an attempt to escape this unfortunate line of thought. No! I hadn't made a plan with Poe because Malcolm told me he liked me. It was because I'd wanted to talk to him ever since he saved my life.

Right, Amy. Because gratitude is a much better motivation.

I ran faster, but pretty soon I was going to run out of land. My chest grew tight, and I regretted not having made it to the gym as much as I should have since December.

When I reached the docks, I slowed and rested, looking out over the mist-shrouded water. There was an easy solution to this. Cancel.

But that one didn't appeal to me at all. I remembered our impromptu pizza party, long before I'd known he liked me, long before either of us had gone overboard. I'd had fun that night. Maybe we'd have fun today. It didn't have to be a date. He was a patriarch, I was a knight. That was plenty of reason right there that it wouldn't be a date. I had firsthand knowledge of how bad society incest could get and I was never going there again.

Even if we weren't talking about Poe.

Malcolm didn't seem to think there was any real potential, either. He'd said as much last night. There was too much water under the bridge between Poe and me. Maybe he had some sort of bizarre crush on me, and maybe I thought he was attractive on the few occasions that he wasn't actively scowling, but neither of those things is groundwork for a relationship.

---

* The confessor might consider working a little harder on that whole goal of forgetting Brandon.

Thus decided, I headed back toward the main compound. Thin sunlight had started seeping through the overcast sky, leading me to suspect that it would all burn off later in the morning. Good. I hadn't come to Florida only to get more gray weather.

I took stock of the buildings. The boys' cabin was dark, as I'd expected, as were the caretaker's cottage and the upper floors of the main building. I heard someone banging pots and pans around in the kitchen, probably getting ready for breakfast. The tomb, of course, was still and silent. I wondered if the Cavador Key version retained any of the grandeur of the New Haven original. Nothing to do at the moment but find out.

Unlike our tomb's giant double doors with the copper book-shaped handles, this tomb's more modest entrance reflected the Spanish style of the architecture. It was an arched doorway, with a door of simple painted aluminum, whose only embellishment was the painted ironwork grate in front, patterned in a mix of swirls, flowers, and little hexagons. The latch featured an analog keypad.

I stared at the numbers. Could it be that simple? I tapped out *3 1 2*.

Nothing. This was probably information they gave out on the tour. Bummer. Oh well, I guess I'd have to come back later, after I'd been enlightened.

"Young lady!" A hand clamped down on my elbow. "What are you doing?"

I whirled around—was whirled around, to be more precise. The caretaker was glaring down at me, a vicious-looking machete in his spare hand.

"Let go!" I cried, wrenching free from his grip and backing up, right into the wrought-iron grate. Great, the Diggers employed sword-wielding maniacs. I was going to die, and my parents thought I was in South Beach.

"What are you doing?" he asked again, and I noticed in retrospect that he hadn't actually *raised* said machete. Up close, Saltzman didn't strike me as the despot the other Diggirls had painted him to be after yesterday's tour. He seemed to be well into his seventies—though it was difficult to tell how much was age and how much was weathering—with the sort of burgundy leather skin that was a result of several decades spent in the sun. His nose was a mass of bumps and scar tissue that spoke to more than one surgery for basal cell carcinoma, and each eyebrow sported enough white hair for four. His eyes were blue, his manner cautious and crotchety, but not altogether unlikeable.

I straightened, remembering that this guy worked for *me*. "I'm looking at the tomb," I said, in a voice as haughty as I could muster, given the circumstances. "Be so good as to give me the pass code?"

He switched hands with knife and gave me his right. I rolled my eyes and provided him with the proper society handshake. Then, for good measure, I lifted the edge of my shirt so he could see the pin stuck through my belt loop. "D177, Saltzman."

"So I see." He seemed to relax. "I apologize, miss. It's just instinct. I'm not used to seeing females around here who aren't wives or daughters. And the tomb is off-limits to *them*."

"Well, times are changing."

"Don't go getting defensive with me, missy. I have no problem with the new policy. Makes things a bit complicated around here, but it's just one of those things. I'm sure we'll all adjust just fine." He gestured with the machete as he spoke, which spooked me more than a little. "You're the one who missed the tour, huh?"

"Yes. Amy Haskel. I had an . . . emergency."

"So I heard. Well, no time like the present. I like that you don't spend all day in bed like some of them."

I didn't know exactly how to respond to that.

He reached past me for the gate. "It's 3122, see? The second tomb."

How creative. I followed him inside, and watched as he lit a few sconces on the wall. The yellow glow flickered over the walls and he turned to me. "What do you think?"

As I've said before, I'm no actress. Even if the Eli drama department weren't one of the best in the country, I'd hardly be commandeering roles that weren't of the "Girl on Left" or "Apple Tree" variety in campus productions. But I plastered a look of wonder on my face and went, "Wow."

The Cavador Key tomb was decidedly not wow-worthy. There was a simple table in the center, sporting a scratched surface despite the layers of finish meant to spiff it up, and the chairs surrounding it included a few hardwoods, a mildewed wicker rocker, and three folding chairs. There was some art on the walls, grimy with smoke, and the upholstery on the armchairs and couches around the perimeter was faded.

I reminded myself that however unimpressive this building was, it represented a second property belonging to my society. The whole island, the free food, the fact that we employed this man to take care of it all—all spoke of a more-than-ample income. So we used folding chairs instead of the fine carved teak I was used to in New Haven! So what? We used it, as Clarissa had pointed out, on our *own private island*. Dragon's Head couldn't hold a cricket to that.

I began to grow very nervous about my future earning potential. What could I do for a living that would provide the type of spare cash that Rose & Grave no doubt expected out of their patriarchs? Jenny was already a millionaire, Clarissa an heiress, Odile a movie star. What could I do to make myself half as worthwhile?

"You haven't even seen the best part," he said, tossing his machete casually to the table. (Well, that would explain the scratches.) He crossed the room to a large hutch on the opposite side and flung the doors wide. "Look at this!"

I'd blown my wad on the first "wow." But this was the one that actually deserved it.

"Those are swastikas," I said, my voice flat. I was shocked the china had survived Demetria taking a look at them.

"Word is, one of our boys swiped them right from Adolf's compound when they invaded Berlin."

I wasn't quite sure what to say. That we had Hitler's dishes sitting in a hutch seemed perverse to the extreme. "Why?" I finally managed.

"Why else?" Saltzman asked. "Because we beat him!"

Battle spoils. I nodded. I remembered Malcolm telling me about this one time. Still, I had no intention of ever eating off them. Gross.

The caretaker closed the hutch doors again, locking them with a tiny gold key. "Yep. There are lots of people who would do anything to see what we have hidden away here on Cavador Key. So you can see why I have to be so careful about who I let go sneaking around the place. I didn't know you were a knight this morning."

"Right." Was it a little stuffy in here?

"I'm dead serious. You've got to keep constant vigilance around here. I catch trespassers all the time. I've made a proposal to the board about a couple of guard dogs."

I pictured packs of pit bulls roaming the beach, with the machete-wielding Saltzman close behind. "That would be..."

"Especially recently." He nodded. "What with all the troubles our poor Barebones has been going through."

Barebones. Kurt Gehry.

"Too many people saw the family arriving at the airport down here, and it's well known in town what we are. Ever since they got here we've been fending off boats loaded with photojournalists. There were even a couple of news helicopters."

"Really?" Demetria had clearly been barking up the wrong tree last night. She should have been nicer to the caretaker. He seemed more than ready to talk about the Gehrys' presence on the island.

"Vultures. Parasites." He picked up the machete again, hefted it in his hands. "I'm sure our man's got an excellent reason for his sabbatical."

Our man. I began to wonder what Saltzman's deal was. Not even Hale was this devoted an employee of the Trust. The caretaker of the New Haven tomb regularly called us on our bullshit. If we were too loud, or left a mess in the kitchen, or dared to skimp on coaster usage in the library, we were sure to get an earful in the next memo sent to our private Phimalarlico e-mail accounts.

"Have you been getting it bad up at the school?" he asked me.

I furrowed my brow. "What do you mean?"

"You know. For jumping to his defense and all. You're the newspaper girl, right? Any backlash in the letters column?"

Um . . . "Backlash?"

"For your articles."

Oh. My theoretical articles defending him. Of course. Well, this one didn't require a lie. "I actually worked on the literary journal. We . . . stay out of politics, for the most part."

"Oh." He frowned. "Literary journal? That's a new one for us, isn't it?"

He had no idea.

"You might think about doing something, though. I'm sure the *Eli Daily* would take a guest editorial."

"I'm sure," I agreed, turning toward the door. Get me out of here. "I'm going to go check out the library. Thanks so much for showing me the tomb, sir."

"Anytime, young lady," he waved at me with his knife. "I'm going to get back to trimming those weeds."

I guess that was indeed the proper purpose of a machete. Oddly enough, it was the least sketchy thing about the man. At the door, we went our separate ways, and I walked a little more quickly than necessary up to the main house, hoping that someone else had woken early.

Turns out, someone had. I entered the rec room and found Darren Gehry idly racking up the balls at the billiard table.

"Hey," I said, stopping short just inside the room.

"Hey," he replied.

"How you doing?"

He shrugged. "You okay?"

"Are you kidding?" I smiled. "I'm totally a celebrity. No one could stop talking about my little adventure yesterday."

"Oh." He looked down at the cue ball. "That's . . . cool."

I pointed at the table. "Want to play?"

"Do you think we'll be too loud?"

"Good point." I imagined the crack of the balls shattering the stillness of the Florida morning. "Darts, then?"

As Darren set up the board, I sifted around for topics of conversation that didn't start off "So, sucks about your dad, huh?"

"Didn't see you at dinner last night," I finally said.

"We eat as a family," he said. "We've got our own kitchen and all."

"Oh. Cool."

"Mom doesn't wake up till late, though, so I usually get breakfast down here when the kitchen is serving. It's much nicer. French toast and stuff." He flicked a dart at the board, and it landed in double twenty. I had a ringer on my hands. "They're supposed to do pancakes today."

"Ooh, pancakes. Sounds great." I watched him throw two more darts in quick succession, all closer to the center than I'd have predicted, then took my place at the line. My first throw went wide. "You're much better than me," I admitted.

"Nothing to do here," he said. "I practice a lot."

"What are you doing about school?" Oh, crap. I shouldn't let on that I knew he'd been taken out of his school back in D.C. My second dart bounced off the board and landed in the carpet. I suck.

He frowned. "I'm not really supposed to talk about personal stuff."

If I were his age, would my parents trust me with the kind of truth the Gehrys were facing? And regardless of the adults' wishes, would I have the right to know? "Sorry, I don't mean to—"

"Whatever. I'm homeschooled for now. But it's pretty much a joke. I'm not doing anything. It's not like we have a chemistry lab in the house. I do some math problems, read a couple of books."

"What are you reading?" My third shot hit the mark underneath the three. Woo-hoo!

He gestured to the shelves around us. "You're looking at it. Actually, I'm supposed to be picking something new right now."

So I was contributing to the delinquency of a minor.

Though I doubted this was the first time he'd played darts rather than reading. "Do you want any recommendations? I'm a Literature major, so I've pretty much read it all." I retrieved my darts and wrote down my pathetic score.

"Sure." Darren took his place at the line and I wandered over to the bookshelves. "Not now, though."

"Why?"

He gestured with the dart. "I wouldn't want to hit you."

Right. I backed away and watched Darren hit two more doubles and one in the outer ring of the bull's-eye. This was going to be a massacre.

"Are you going on the snorkeling trip today?" I asked him as he retrieved his darts and made marks on the scoreboard.

"There's a snorkeling trip?" he asked.

Well, that answered that. God, this kid had to be going stir-crazy. He wandered over to the bookshelves and I took it as a cue to delay my turn at the board, since if he was worried about hitting me, he had to be terrified, given my wild aim.

"So what do you suggest?"

Go with the obvious. *"Catcher in the Rye?"*

He snorted. "Everyone says that. I read it, like, three years ago."

Oh, a challenge. I smiled. "Did you like it?"

"It was okay. I'm reading Nietzsche right now."

Like good disaffected fourteen-year-old boys everywhere. "Which one?"

"Genealogy of Morals."

"How are you liking that?"

"Easier going than Kant."

I laughed, and, as he'd moved away from the board, risked making a toss with the dart. It landed right outside the outer bull's-eye ring.

"Good throw!" Darren said.

My next shot hit right above the "4" in fourteen. "I had a German Lit prof who said it was easier to learn German, *then* read Kant, than it was to read him in English."

"Well, I'm not going to learn German on this island."

Especially if he didn't make it into the tomb here. "I specialize in fiction anyway. I mostly only read philosophy for background material. My Aristotle is less morals and more poetics."

"I hate Aristotle. I find his tone to be remarkably jejune." He looked at me as if I was supposed to contradict him. To act shocked. Yeah, this was the kid of an Eli student. A Digger, too. I don't think I'd even seen that word since I took the SATs.

I threw my last shot (wide) and went to collect my darts. "Let's see, what should you read?" I wandered over to the shelves. Who stocked these things? The bulk of the titles were your usual paperback thrillers of the Clancy and Grisham variety. Stephen King. Heinlein. Krakauer. Beach reads for boys on vacation. No romance, but I didn't expect it, what with the usual demographics of the island's visitors. Farther along were a few hardcovers of the classics. *Tristram Shandy*, of course. I'd have to show it to Harun. A dusty copy of *Pilgrim's Progress*. Gag. *War and Peace*, my old nemesis. Several Dickenses, *Tom Jones*, *Robinson Crusoe* (natch!)—

I caught sight of a dart whizzing past from the corner of my eye. "Hey!" I cried, turning around.

He lifted his shoulders. "Oops. Sorry. I forgot."

I looked back at the board. He'd hit the bull's-eye. "Good shot." I held up a thick paperback. "What about *Catch-22*?

He looked down at the darts in his hand. "Do you think—?"

The door opened. "Amy!" Demetria called. "There you are." Half my club trooped in, looking famished and beachy. Everyone wore bathing suits and the appropriate cover-ups (except for Clarissa, whose itsy-bitsy pink bikini and white mesh cover-up were hardly G-rated), sunglasses, and hats, and smelled strongly of suntan lotion. Ben even had zinc smeared on his nose.

I suddenly felt way overdressed in my shorts, sports bra, tank top, and sneakers.

"Clarissa figured you were hiding so we wouldn't force you on the boat," Jenny said. "Do you know when break-fast is?"

Darren checked his watch. "About fifteen minutes." He walked over to me and looked at the book in my hands. "I read Heller last year. Try again."

This was trickier than I'd thought. Darts forgotten, we traveled down the length of Cavador Key's collection, which I noticed was pretty much devoid of women writers (with the exception of Ayn Rand, who was present in an al-most unhealthy abundance). No Austen, no Alcott, no Ahrendt. And that was just the As. No Brontë, no Behn. Somebody needed to shake up these shelves. Mary Shelley was there, thank goodness, along with a slim volume of Emily Dickinson. But all in all, a pathetic turnout for fe-malekind.

Figured.

Darren vetoed *Animal Farm* and *1984* ("I mean, it obvi-ously *didn't* happen, right? So what's the point?"), looked skeptical about Kafka (and who could blame him?), made a face at Flaubert ("So, she's a madam? Like a hooker?"), and seemed only moderately intrigued by *Crime and Punishment* (which I thought, but didn't say, was too old for him).

"You'll love it in about five years," I said, placing Dostoyevsky back on the shelf. Nearby was a volume of the complete works of Edgar Allan Poe, which only made me think of the one Digger who hadn't yet come by for breakfast.

It's fine, Amy. It's not a date.

"Okay, last suggestion, and then I'm out." I pulled down a hefty volume. *"The Count of Monte Cristo."*

"What's it about?"

Had he not seen any of the movies? "It's about a guy who is betrayed by his friends and winds up in this island prison for ages, until he escapes, finds a buried treasure, and gets revenge on everyone."

"Hmmm..."

"Lots of swordfights. Swordfights and opium and lesbians."

"I'm in."

"Good lad." I handed him the book and patted him on the shoulder. Yep, the old lesbian ace in the hole. Better than Nietzsche for the teenaged boy. Demetria would *not* approve.

Soon after, breakfast was served, but still Poe failed to appear. I tried to concentrate on my pancakes, which should have been easy, given how delicious they were, but my eyes kept sliding to the door of the dining room, waiting for my date to arrive.

No. Not my date. My, uh, appointment. My eleven o'clock appointment.

Breakfast ended and the others started to gather their things together for the walk to the yacht.

"Are you sure, Amy?" Clarissa asked.

I patted my bag. "Absolutely." Where was Poe? "I have all kinds of reading to catch up on." I wasn't about to tell Clarissa I'd made a non-date with everyone's second-least-favorite patriarch on the island.

She peeked into the mesh sack. "Longinus? Hell no. If

you spend your Spring Break reading literary criticism, I'm going to have to kill you."

"If you make me get on that boat, you won't have to. I'll die of fright all by myself. Really, Clarissa. I'm much happier this way."

"Okay," she said warily. "But if I don't see a tan on you this afternoon, we're revisiting this topic."

"Absolutely."

Everyone filtered out the door, including Malcolm, who gave me little more than a friendly wave, and I settled into my rocker with my *On the Sublime* and wondered what the author would have thought of a Florida island in springtime. The earlier mist had completely burned away by this time, leaving nothing but warm, lemony sunshine, blue skies, soft, salt-scented breezes, and the sound of singing insects. All I needed was a hammock.

It was so peaceful that I'd almost forgotten I was in waiting mode by the time a shadow fell across the pages.

"Hey."

I looked up and there was Poe, in a dark bathing suit and a smoky blue T-shirt that made his eyes look almost silver. He wore a faded pair of running shoes and smelled of sunscreen.

"Are you ready?"

No way.

I hereby confess:
It was __so__ a date.

11.

Lessons

Like many young adults my age and occupation, I suffered from the occasional recurring nightmare of walking into class and finding the other students occupied with taking an exam that I had not only not studied for, but that I had no idea was even on the syllabus. Occasionally, it would be for a class I had no recollection of enrolling in. Such dreams always elicited a peculiar feeling of dread in the pit of my stomach, one quite distinct from the queasiness inspired by heights, deep water, scary movies, or bad eggs. There was dread, and then there was the specific dread of being unprepared.

I had that feeling now.

Poe, on the other hand, looked as if he'd spent the past week working up flash cards and doing timed practice tests with a study group.

I stood up, narrowly avoiding spilling Longinus onto the porch. *Do not say you were worried he was going to stand you up.* Being "stood up" sounds very date-like. Or not, as the case may be. But certainly not *not-date-like*. "I didn't see you at breakfast," I said, and hoped he'd get my point.

"Indeed. Did you like it?"

"Breakfast? Yeah. Why?"

And now he smiled, just a little.

"You made breakfast," I realized.

"Just the pancakes."

"Why?"

"I was feeling pretty guilty last year, about the free trip to Florida and all. So I kept offering to do things, as if I could balance the debt through some sort of bizarre work-study program. Salt wouldn't let me do yardwork, which you know is my specialty, but Cook let me in the kitchen at breakfast. Just breakfast, mind you, because she had some strange idea that I was a tad on the antisocial side and would hide out in the kitchen for as long as she'd let me."

"Imagine that."

"But since my pancake recipe was better than hers, she made me promise to give her a refresher when I came back." He shrugged. "No one knows that, by the way. Malcolm just thinks I skip breakfast."

"And if word got out, you know we'd all be roping you into tomb brunches."

"Not your club, no. I think they'd be afraid I'd slip strychnine in the batter." His tone was light as he said it, but I had to wonder, why would Poe keep his pancake recipe a secret, unless it was to quietly lord it over the others that the breakfast they'd so enjoyed was made by the guy they weren't altogether too fond of?

Still, that didn't explain why he'd keep it a secret from Malcolm, nor why he'd confess it to me. Maybe he really was embarrassed by his plebeian roots. Or maybe he was just kidding himself that his richer friend wasn't completely aware of what made Poe tick.

And yet, I still wasn't sure what kind of person he was. Wasn't that the reason I was doing this? To figure it out? The funny feeling in my stomach intensified.

"So," he said. "What are you up for this morning?"

"I was hoping you had a plan, seeing how well you know this place and all of its inhabitants."

"Oh, Cook doesn't live here. She only comes in for high-volume weeks."

"And no doubt Cook isn't her given name, either."

"No," he admitted. "It's Berta."

"I see why she goes by Cook."

Darren wandered out of the library onto the porch. "You're still here?" he asked. He held the copy of Dumas in his hands.

"Yeah. I'm skipping out on the snorkeling today," I said. Poe waved at him.

"Oh?" He looked hopeful.

"Jamie and I were going to..." Do what? I looked to Poe for help.

"I'm taking her over to the sanctuary," Poe said. "We'll catch you this afternoon, Darren." He started down the steps and I followed him.

Okay, so we were going to the sanctuary, whatever that was. We hiked down the path in silence for a few moments. As soon as we were out of earshot of the porch, Poe spoke again.

"Are you sorry?"

"For what?"

"Not inviting him to come along." He cast me a sidelong glance.

POSSIBLE ANSWERS

1) "Yes. He seems awfully lonely."
2) "No. Do we look like babysitters?"
3) "Nah, baby, three's a crowd."

Each was partially true. I placed a hand on my stomach, where the unease had evolved into butterflies. If anything, the fluttering scared me even more. Not having made a decision was one thing. Making it brought a whole new snarl of nerves.

"Do you think Mr. Gehry appreciates you befriending his son?" Poe asked, saving me an answer.

"I didn't really think about it," I admitted.

"I believe that." But it was said without rancor. "I bet he's thought about it."

"Darren?"

"His father."

"Well, that would explain a lot. Maybe if he'd spent less time thinking about a bunch of college students and more about the laws of the nation he worked for, he wouldn't be in so much trouble."

"That's probably very true," Poe said. "But do you believe he should think about it more than about the well-being of his family?" He met my eyes, and once again, I reflected on how hard it was to read this boy.

Was he talking about hiring illegal help at home or letting Darren talk to the likes of me? I shrugged and refocused on the path. "My opinions of Kurt Gehry don't have anything to do with how I treat his son."

"That's a nice illusion."

"What's that supposed to mean?"

"I mean that it's pretty tough to disassociate a person from what they stand for."

"Darren Gehry is a teenager. He doesn't stand for anything."

"I disagree."

"Yeah? What is he to you?"

"The guy who almost got you killed yesterday."

I stopped short, but Poe kept going, and I practically had to run to catch up to him.

"Poe."

"Two dollars." And he kept walking.

"Jamie."

"You still owe."

"You don't blame Darren, do you? It was an accident."

He slowed down but kept his face turned toward the ground. "People are still responsible for accidents. Someone is always at fault."

"Yes, but I'm not angry at him, so why are you?"

"I'm not."

"You just said that you can't disassociate him from the fact that he made me fall off the boat yesterday, which, I might add, is just as much Clarissa's fault." If she hadn't been so squeamish . . .

"That doesn't make me angry at them." And with that curious statement, we reached the end of the path. Beyond us was only woods. "Watch out for snakes."

Snakes? Some sanctuary. I started picking my way in after him. "So who are you angry at?"

"If you keep talking, you won't see anything." He put a finger to his lips. "Just look."

So I looked. By this time, the sun had done its duty, bathing the island in warmth and bright light. The patches of sky I could see between the treetops were a deep, opaque blue. Presently, the trees thinned and we broke out onto a narrow, unkempt beach, marred with bleached driftwood and piles of dried seaweed.

"What are we looking for?" I whispered.

He pointed, and out of the trees shot a flash of brown and white. I watched it soar over the water, circle around a bit, then drop like a stone into the waves. A minute later, it rose, clutching something floppy in long, hooked claws.

"Watch where it goes."

The nest was pretty easy to spot, as it was perched at the top of one of the tallest pines in the stand, dripping with needles like a beard in need of a trim. The bird circled the tree, letting out a long shriek, then landed. Its back and wings were dark brown, its underside pure white, and even from the ground, I could see its enormous golden eyes and the sharp curve of its large talons. It looked around, as if aware that it had observers, then occupied itself with the fish.

"Not an eagle," I said. I knew next to nothing about raptor species.

"An osprey. It's breeding season. I was hoping the nests would still be here."

"It's really beautiful," I said. Bird sanctuary. Of course. A moment later, the osprey's mate joined him at the nest. I listened hard for the sound of cheeping, but if there were any babies in the nest, the wind carried their voices away.

We sat in the sand and watched the birds in silence for a while longer, and then Poe said, "So that's the last thing there is to do on the island. You can swim, hang out in the rec room, or see the birds."

"That seems like plenty to me."

"Come on, Amy, don't kid yourself. You'll go as stir-crazy as Darren in a matter of days."

"Then it's good I'm only staying a week." I watched the osprey make another trip to the water, looping in wide circles for a long time before diving again. Imagine being as comfortable both in the air and in the water as this creature was.

Poe seemed to tire of antagonizing me. "Did you talk to Salt yet?"

"He's pretty interesting . . . gung ho."

"That's a kind way to put it." He stretched his legs out in front of him. "Couple years ago he wanted to chop down the trees, chase off the ospreys."

"Why?" I asked, stricken.

"Nesting pairs like this are quite the draw to bird-watchers. The last thing he wants is trespassers on Cavador Key."

"So he mentioned."

"Funny thing is, the folks who'd come for the ospreys couldn't care less about the society. They really, truly just want to watch the birds. Wouldn't even get near the compound. One group sent all kind of letters to the Trust promising as much. Said they'd stay right here on this beach."

"What happened?"

"TTA let them on. Three weeks later, a conspiracy-theorist group showed up, dressed as the bird-watchers, and broke into the main house."

"You're kidding!"

"Yeah, they stole some photo albums and some of our other stuff. Ever since then, Salt's been pretty militant about not letting anyone on the island, no matter what they said they were here for."

"What a shame."

"You want to see them?"

"The bird-watchers?"

"No, the conspiracy nuts." He stood, brushed sand from his shorts. "They're camped out on the next island

over. Always are around this time of year, since they know
Spring Break is high season. I bet there are even more of
the campers this year, watching for the Gehrys."

We picked our way across the beach until we reached a
small cluster of mangroves. Poe claimed you could see
them better from the far beach, at the tip of the island.

"Yeah, but won't they be able to see us?"

"Like I said, there isn't a whole lot to do around here.
One night, we'll amuse ourselves by playing dress-up and
giving them something to actually look at."

"How very John Fowles of us."

We moved inland around the mangroves and spilled
out onto another beach. This one was shaped like a large,
open crescent. On the far side of the lagoon, I saw a tiny
sandbar, and beyond that, the expanse of the sea, with a
view of another island in the distance.

"You can't really see," I said, shooting Poe an ac-
cusatory glance.

Poe was taking off his clothes!

"What are you doing?" I asked, as his T-shirt hit a rock.

"You have to get out to the sandbar to see. Take your
shoes off."

I shook my head violently. "What is this, an ambush?"

"Amy, it's not deep. You can wade." He pulled off his
sneakers, then his socks, laid them side by side on the rock.

How could I make this any clearer? "I don't like the water."

"And I don't like that you almost drowned yesterday.
Let's see what we can do about those things, shall we?"

"No thanks." I turned, fully prepared to storm back
into the woods, but he grabbed my arm.

"You wanted to know who I'm angry at?" he asked.
"I'm angry at you."

"What!" I whirled.

"It's unbearably stupid that you don't know how to swim. You have no excuse."

"I have a phobia."

"You're too smart to have phobias."

"You're too smart to think you can get away with telling me what to do!"

"No," he said. "I know that really well. You've made it perfectly clear since the moment we met. The most I can hope for is convincing you to listen to reason." He let go of my arm, appeared to wrestle with himself for a moment, then spoke. "I didn't mean to scare you so badly, Amy."

What?

He ran a hand through his hair, looked everywhere but at me. "That night, at the tomb. I didn't know how bad it would be."

At the initiation, when he stuck me in a coffin, flooded it with a Super Soaker and threatened to dump it in a pool. "That was ages ago."

"Didn't seem like it yesterday. You looked just the same. Terrified."

"A lot wetter."

"I'm sorry." He lifted his gaze to mine. "I'm really sorry, but I can't see you—you can't imagine how I felt on that boat. Like I'd made it worse for you." His eyes were filled with guilt, and all of a sudden I understood that it wasn't just me he was angry at. My going overboard was a reminder of how he'd hurt me last spring. "You want to thank me for jumping in after you yesterday? Do me a favor and take off your shoes."

Damn him. I took off my shoes. Poe was down to his bathing suit, but I hadn't worn mine. Not that it would matter if all I was doing was wading. My shorts were of the gym variety. I glared at him through the sunlight and reached up to tighten my ponytail. Thus girded for battle, I stood. "How deep is it?"

"Depends on the tide. Your clothes are going to get wet."

Well, I wasn't stripping down to my panties! I pulled my shirt off, hoping that the gray sports bra wouldn't turn translucent in water.

"Would you feel better holding my hand?"

"Over my dead body."

"Suit yourself." I watched him walk down into the water, all black hair and broad, winter-pale shoulders. He still wore the tiny sack-turned-backpack, suspended from those shoulders by two small straps. This was the worst date ever. I considered shouting that to him and taking off for the forest.

But instead, I followed him into the water. The sand shifted and squished below my feet, and the water was still plenty chilly. A few feet out, I was only up to my knees, but the ground fell away swiftly after that. "P—Jamie!" I called.

He waded back toward me. "I'm starting to think my name is Pajamie."

"Your name should be Pajerky. You said it wasn't deep."

"Pajerky?" He gave me a skeptical look. "That's Pa-thetic."

"We'll see how smug you are once I'm on dry land."

He took my hands in his wet ones, started walking backward. "Come on. I got you."

The water rose over my thighs and crept up the hem of my gym shorts. It slipped over my crotch and I rose onto my tippy-toes, but still, Poe drew me forward.

"Slower," I said.

"Slower is harder," he said.

"Do you say that to all the girls?"

He ignored that. "You feel the cold more."

"And again I ask..."

We were more than halfway to the sandbar by this time. The water lapped against my stomach, then my rib cage. I got another shock when it hit my elbows, and tightened my grip on Poe's hands, sliding my fingers up his forearms. Two steps later, it covered my breasts.

"This is deep enough," I said. "I can't go any farther."

"Okay," he said. "We'll rest here a minute." And true to his word, he stopped. I spent the time trying to slow my heartbeat. He watched me, his face calm and inscrutable. (This wasn't doing anything for my heartbeat.) Standing as we were, with Poe in deeper water, we were the same height. The tips of his shoulders peeked above the surface, giving him the appearance of a classical statue bust. Several times I almost said, *Take me back*. And several times I stopped.

"I'm ready." I said.

"Whatever you want." And he took another step backward.

I panicked. I couldn't touch! "Stop! Stop!" I cried, kicking with my feet. My hands slid back down to his fingertips as my toes searched for the sandy bottom.

"Amy, I've got you."

"Please!"

He sighed and guided me back into shallow water.

"See!" I seethed. "I can't do this. Do you think you're the only one who has tried? What's next? Showing me how to blow bubbles?" I folded my arms across my chest and turned toward land.

He bobbed close to me, his brow furrowed. "What if I carry you?"

"I don't want to."

"Are you going to spend the rest of your life like this?"

"If necessary."

"That's tragic." He swam a little circle around me.

I scowled. "Shall I tell you what's tragic about the way you live your life?"

"You don't have to." He rose before me, dripping water down his chest, and extended his arms. "I've already got a pretty good idea what you think. Please. Give me one more chance. I promise that I won't let anything happen to you. You're in charge."

He had no idea what he was asking. Neither did I, for that matter, but I put my hands in his anyway. This time he slid his hands up my arms until he held me just above my elbows.

"Put your arms out, like an airplane." And back we went, into the deep, Poe giving me instructions every five seconds:

"Don't think about where your feet are." Easier said than done.

"Breathe in. Your body is more buoyant than seawater. Can't you feel yourself floating?" Um...no?

"Flap, like a bird." More like a fish on a hook.

"Cup your hands."

"Keep breathing."

"Kick."

Enough! "Stop...telling me...what...to do!" I hissed. I reached my foot back down, felt nothing and freaked. "Ack, take me back!"

"Amy—"

I made one more desperate try for the ground with the tip of my toe, but it wasn't there. So I reached for the next best thing. Poe. I wrapped my arms around his neck, my legs around his waist, and held tight.

"Uh, hi," he said in my ear as I clung to him.

"Take me back!" I cried.

"Amy, you can touch here." I pulled away slightly and saw that it was true. The water only reached to Poe's chest. "You were swimming. That's why you didn't feel the ground." Beneath the water, his hands slid around and rested on my hips.

Maybe it was the adrenaline, but those butterflies were back. And I wasn't moving, wasn't letting go of him. But, considering the position of his arms, he didn't want me to.

"You did this on purpose," I said in an accusing tone.

"You're right," he said. "I arranged all of this so you'd jump on me. I'm diabolical."

"You're a Digger."

"As are you," he replied.

Yes, and therefore capable of being every bit as manipulative. Of stripping down and getting in the water and finding the perfect way of creating proximity, regardless of my fear, regardless of the water's depth. I thought about all the times I'd wanted to turn back, and didn't. *I'd* done this on purpose. It made no sense to have reached for him otherwise. It made no sense not to let go now.

I was in charge. I was fully rational. And I wasn't an idiot.

So I kissed him.

I hereby confess:
I may have seen it coming.

12.
On the Beach

This is what I remember about that moment:

1) Poe tasted like salt and suntan oil.
2) His hands stiffened on my hips. Not tighter, not looser, just...frozen.
3) The water made little squelching sounds as it flowed between our bodies.
4) It took a second or so for him to start kissing me back.
5) The kiss went on a lot longer than a second or so.

Poe finally pulled away and we blinked at each other in the sunlight. Quickly, I disentangled my legs from around his waist, but before I could let go of him completely, he'd covered my hands with his own. "Wait."

And then we were kissing again, only this time our bodies were pressed together, and I could feel the silky sensation of his wet bathing suit on my legs, could feel the skin of his stomach rubbing against mine, and I realized he had his hand splayed against my back, holding me tight as the water swirled around us, and when I came up for air I saw that we were floating, that Poe had taken the opportunity to push off from the sandy bottom into the deeper arc of the lagoon, and to take me with him.

And for once, I didn't freak out that I couldn't touch the bottom. He pulled through the water with one hand and both legs, and I must have been holding my breath or something because I was floating along with him, skimming between the surface of the water and the planes of his chest.

Finally, he straightened, and once again, my toes sank into wet sand. I dropped my hands to my sides. Poe was breathing hard, his chest rising and falling in the water, and I wasn't exactly calm myself. And since neither of us seemed to have any inclination to speak, I just walked up past him onto the sandbar.

The contrast between the coolness of the lagoon and the sun-warmed sand was extreme. I wrung droplets out of my hair and walked to the far end of the sandbar, looking out over the waves to the other island. As promised, I could see colorful tents clustered on the shore, the smoke from a cooking fire, the movement of tiny figures. Were they really conspiracy theorists? Were they watching me now? And if so, what did they think of the utterly pedestrian sight of a girl in a sports bra and gym shorts and a boy in a bathing suit kissing in the Florida surf? How could they spin that into their fevered fantasies of a New World Order?

And could they provide me with any interpretation I could use?

Poe joined me, still silent, then pulled off his backpack and dug around inside. He handed me a bottle of water, slightly warmed by the sun. The label had turned gummy in the sea, but I drank happily, washing away the flavor of salt. Funny how sweet plain water can be.

I passed the water back, swapping with Poe for a plastic baggie filled with grapes. I nibbled on the fruit, still tasting brine and a slight grittiness from the sand on my fingers. Poe sat down, and I joined him, side by side. Our hips touched, our arms brushed.

It no longer felt awkward not to speak. Rather, it seemed like a competition. The first person to say something would be responsible for putting it all into context.

I kept my mouth filled with grapes instead.

Poe lay back on the sand and I followed suit, only to discover he'd extended an arm for me to use as a pillow. I turned my face toward him and found he was looking at me, too. The chorus of *Oh-my-God-what-are-you-doing*s that had taken up the bulk of my consciousness for the last few minutes faded away. I wanted to kiss him again, so I did.

I don't know how long we lay like that, sharing grapes and kisses. Water evaporated from my skin in the sunlight, and heat seeped into my flesh, driving off the chill of winter and the trauma of February. Against the elemental forces of earth and sea and Poe, Eli was a chimera. Who cared about fellowship applications, about society feuds, about the Ivory Tower or the even more fantastical "real world" that awaited when it crumbled? The very idea of debating Book 3, Canto 2 of Spenser, or doing yet another problem set on the reactions that cause ozone layer depletion, or writing Eli's thirtieth paper on the role of Persephone in feminist literature seemed ludicrous. Pointless. The life of the mind held not the slightest fascination for me.

Poe's skin was warm and smooth, and all I could hear was the sound of the waves. I wasn't overthinking. For once, I wasn't thinking at all.

Spring *Break*. I get it now. Only took four years.

More time passed, and my brain started up again, but slowly, with none of the frenetic, stressful ferocity of its usual pace, just softly batting around bizarre contemplations and idle curiosities. One flitted to the surface.

"Can I ask you a question?"

Poe was running his hand up and down the length of my arm. At the sound of my voice, he stilled. "Okay?" he said warily.

"Why do we have Nazi china?"

He burst out laughing, and I was so relaxed, it took me a moment to realize why. He thought I was going to ask about *this*.

"I don't know," he said at last. "I find it really creepy myself. It's supposed to be some sort of war trophy from some old patriarch, but it's gross. Let's go smash it."

I looked at him, eyebrows raised, but he wasn't kidding. His eyes sparkled.

"Seriously. Turn the whole collection into dust. Or better yet, we'll sell it off to skinheads at high profit and donate it all to...the Anti-Defamation League or something."

"Salt would not be happy."

"We'll blame the conspiracy theorists." He grinned and cocked his head toward the other island.

I shook my head, incredulous. "What about tradition?"

"Screw tradition."

This was *the* Poe, right? "You've gone crazy."

He thought about that for a moment. "You're right. I have. You're contagious." He leaned over me and kissed me quick and it may have been the sun, but I think my entire body blushed. We'd wound up talking about *this* after all. But lying beneath Poe was another new sensation, and I devoted most of my attention to that for the next few minutes.

I don't know what tipped me off. Perhaps there was some material change to the sound of the waves against the shore, but I looked up and saw it a moment before he did.

The yacht was rounding the tip of the island! It was still pretty far from the sandbar, but if you squinted, you could make out the figures on deck, and as I watched in horror I saw a blond one in a bright pink bikini walk to the nearest rail and peer out over the water. She raised an arm and pointed at us. A moment later, a brown-haired man in a red bathing suit joined her. The sunlight hit them and bounced off the rim of his copper frames.

Crap!

I scrambled out from under my companion with the speed and agility of a fiddler crab and rolled to the side. My eyes still on the boat, I clutched my knees to my chest and willed them not to come any closer. They must have recognized us. Must have seen.

Without a word, Poe slung the bag back over his shoulders and waded into the lagoon.

"Hey!" I started to follow him. "Where are you going?"

He didn't dignify that with an answer. I splashed in behind him, all the way up to my waist. Clearly, he was setting a new pace.

"What, am I on my own now?" I asked.

Now he turned and his cold expression said it all. "Don't you want to be?"

I waded out farther, and he stopped. He didn't return, but he stopped, just a few feet out of reach. And as I floundered toward him, he moved back at the same rate.

"Poe, don't..." I said, dog-paddling.

"Two dollars. And I'm right here."

We made it halfway across the lagoon like that. It wasn't pleasant. I was breathing hard and I'm sure my terror showed on my face. Eventually, Poe took pity on me and pulled me the rest of the way to the shallows, but as soon as I'd found my footing, he took off again.

"Please stop," I begged him. And he did. His expression was cold, his eyes unreadable slate.

"What is this?" he asked, wading toward me, the water churning around his thighs. "Are you *grateful*?"

"Yes," I admitted, then added, "but I wanted to kiss you."

He shook his head and returned to the shore. I splashed up onto the beach after him, but it was as if the sun had gone behind a cloud. I copied him as he brushed sand off his feet then shoved them back into his sneakers. He skipped putting his T-shirt back on, but I covered up with my tank top and did what I could to squeeze the water out of my shorts and ponytail.

"That was a shit move," I said at last, not looking up.

"Yours? I agree."

"No, yours! You marooned me out there!"

He snorted. "No I didn't. I was right next to you the whole time. You *can* swim. And even if I weren't right there, you could have walked around." And he pointed at the left side of the crescent, where the sandbar was closest to the island. "It's about knee-deep the whole way."

I clenched my hands into fists. "We could have gone that way the whole time? I didn't have to swim?"

"Yep. I tricked you...into all of it." He shrugged, all smug, and I shivered, suddenly wishing I had on more than a damp tank top. The boat had sailed on, and now I knew I wasn't imagining things. The sun really had gone behind a cloud.

Poe stared into the forest for a bit. "Let's go back," he said.

"No."

"Just forget it, okay?"

"No!" I walked over and grabbed his hand, held tight when he tried to shake me off. "You didn't trick me. And I'm not *grateful*. And I'm sorry, but I didn't know what to do when I saw that boat. Did you?"

He hesitated. "No."

"So give me a break." But even as I said it, I knew that would be unlikely. Poe didn't give people breaks. He never had. Not even for himself. You were with him, or against him. Worthy of his notice, or beneath it.

So I wasn't surprised when he said, "Let's just go back."

And that was the end of the date. We walked back through the forest in heated silence, one fueled by friction and frustration as much as by our quick pace. There was no more talk of osprey nesting or destroying society heirlooms because we hated their origins. There was absolutely no discussion about what had transpired on the sandbar, though the taste of Poe lingered in my mouth and I knew that if I lifted my hands to my face, saltwater or no, I'd be able to smell him on my skin.

I left him at the entrance to the girls' cabin, and while I watched from inside, Poe strode off toward the boys' cabin, and didn't once look back.

Twenty minutes later, I'd washed off all traces of our interlude, and, dressed in my bikini and a fresh pair of shorts and top, I walked down to the docks to meet the boat.

Demetria was the first one off, and her face was like a

thunderhead. "Hey, Amy," she said, brushing past me. Jenny hopped down after her and shot her a concerned look.

"What's with her?" I asked. Had there been another boating mishap?

Jenny scowled and looked over her shoulder at the boat. "Long story. Back at the cabin."

My trepidation waned in light of whatever was bothering my fellow knight, and I'd almost forgotten it completely when Clarissa and George jumped down.

"You missed it all!" Clarissa said. "Some folks broke onto Cavador from the other island! I saw them on the beach. We're going to tell Salt." She clapped her hands. "You didn't see anyone, did you?"

I glanced beyond her to George, who remained uncharacteristically quiet, merely raising his eyebrows in my direction.

I swallowed. Exactly how good was his vision when he had those glasses on? Could he have recognized us? "No," I said, fighting to keep my voice light. "Hey, what's with Demetria?"

Clarissa lowered her voice and led me up the docks. "That patriarch's wife is a little whore, that's what."

"I don't know why she's letting it bother her," George added, bringing up the rear. "She's just a stupid barbarian. Dee says the word and we'll all go kick her ass."

"She won't do that," Clarissa replied. "She knows Kadie and Frank will leave and take the boat with them."

"Who gives a shit?" George said.

"I'm sorry, what's the problem here?" I asked.

"Racism," George said.

"Homophobia," Clarissa corrected.

"A little from column A, a little from column B," George guessed. "Bottom line is, Kadie wasn't exactly polite to Demetria."

"She freaked out when she discovered Dee had been using her snorkel."

Oh dear God. "That's ridiculous." What, did she think being a black lesbian was contagious?

"I think it's the last time we'll be using the yacht, that's for sure," Clarissa said. "What a bitch."

Back at the compound, someone had already notified Salt about the supposed "intruders" out on the crescent beach, and he was mobilizing for a full sweep of the island. I looked around, hoping to take my cue from Poe, but he was nowhere to be seen. George was looking at me with barely concealed interest, and when I raised my chin he just shrugged and smiled.

Ben came over to us. "I've volunteered to take the north part of the island. Want to come with me?"

"Nah," George said, obviously enormously amused. "I think I'll stay here, make sure the compound's safe. Whatever we saw, I don't think it's a big deal." He turned to me. "What do *you* think, Amy?"

"I'm not sure," I answered smoothly. "I wasn't there to see."

"Of course you weren't." He nodded.

"Well, I know what I saw," Clarissa claimed. "Two people walking right up the beach and into the forest. They're probably still here."

"I'd guess so," George said, and I resisted the urge to sock him. "From what *I* saw."

"Maybe you didn't see it right," I said to him. "Did you have your glasses on?"

"I've got 20/20," Clarissa said. "I saw it just fine."

"What the lady said." George's smile didn't get any less tempting with time. But now the temptation I felt was decidedly more violent than carnal.

"I'll come with you," Clarissa said to Ben, and I found it

expedient to join them lest I be left alone with George Harrison Prescott again.

To my surprise, the sweep turned up the remnants of a campfire (several days old, according to former Boy Scout Ben), six Budweiser cans, and a waterproof tape recorder that we promptly relieved of its cassette, though it hadn't seemed to record anything more than the sound of the waves.

"We've been bugged!" Clarissa exclaimed, vindicated.

I considered admitting that it had been Poe and me she'd seen out on the crescent beach, just to take her down a notch. In light of the evidence, however, I refrained.

The search party assigned to the aforementioned crescent reported traces of footprints but couldn't even ascertain the direction in which the parties had been moving and, naturally, they found no sign of the boat that the hypothetical trespassers had used to get onto the island. From this "evidence," everyone concluded that whoever they'd been, they'd left Cavador Key by now.

After that, we all had a late lunch, at which the majority of the conversation focused on our findings, and on how best to avoid Kadie Myer for the remainder of the trip. Luckily, she and her husband hadn't taken lunch in the main room, perhaps suspecting that she'd fallen out of favor with the knights. The entire meal was patriarch-free, as a matter of fact, and I was spared a run-in with Poe, as well as the no-doubt curious/accusatory presence of Malcolm.

I only hoped that wherever they were, they weren't together, and discussing me.

Apparently, the evening plans included a fully formal tomb meeting for all society members present, and there was much speculation among the knights about whether or not Gehry would show his face as the lunch morphed into a lazy afternoon. Clarissa took up a post on the sunny lawn beyond the porch and laid out with an impressive stack of gossip magazines. George and the other boys started a poker tournament, except for Harun, who was having an intense debate with Jenny in the corner. I came close enough to hear them only once, and the subject matter seemed to be theological enough to make me keep my distance from that point on. Demetria was on the porch steps, painting her toenails with rainbow colors. I thought it was some sort of statement, until I got closer and noticed the designs all featured smiling suns and flowers as well.

"You're pretty good," I observed.

Demetria wiggled her left foot. "Want me to do yours?"

"Little Rose & Grave symbols?" I suggested.

"Subtle, Amy. Real subtle."

I sat down and stuck out my foot. "Then you pick."

By now, George had been knocked out of the tournament*, and joined Clarissa on her towel, amusing himself with dramatic readings of the articles in her tabloids.

" '*It's been a nightmare for her. She's practically a prisoner in her own home!*' *claims a source close to the starlet.* '*He even tells her what she's allowed to eat!*' This is boring." George flipped through a few pages. "Are there any articles on Odile?"

"Try *Life & Style*." Clarissa tossed him another magazine. "According to them, she stole Lindsay Lohan's boyfriend."

"That's our girl."

Behind me, the porch door swung open, and Kadie stepped out. She glanced down at the steps, saw me sitting

---

* The confessor assumes that for a Prescott, it's all in or nothing.

with my foot in Demetria's lap, and let out the tiniest of sniffs.

Demetria's brush stilled on my nail. I looked up at Kadie. "Am I in your way?" I asked coldly.

"No," she said, but couldn't seem to make a wide enough arc around us. I watched her pick her way down the steps and onto the lawn. She looked back at us and rolled her eyes, but it was her mouth I saw moving.

Dykes . . .

And then she was splayed out on the lawn, spread-eagled and gasping for breath.

"Wow, are you all right?" George asked. He was closest, but didn't offer her a hand. "The path's a bit uneven here."

Clarissa buried her face in her magazine, but I saw her shoulders shaking. Had George tripped the barbarian?

Kadie rose and brushed away the crushed shells imbedded in her palms and shins.

"I'd be more careful around here if I were you," George added.

"Who do you think you are?" she sputtered.

George rested his chin on his hand and smiled sweetly at her. "Who do *you* think we are?"

Clarissa sat up and swept her hair over her shoulder so that the Rose & Grave tattoo on her shoulder blade was clearly visible.

The barbarian fell back a step or two, then cast a glance around the porch. Harun and Jenny were staring at her, and Kevin and Ben had put a hold on their hands. Outnumbered, she turned and stomped off.

"Bitch," Demetria mumbled, and returned to painting my toes.

Malcolm and Poe came up the path a few minutes later, and I found myself suddenly fascinated with Demetria's work.

"How's it going?" Malcolm asked, leaning against the nearest post.

"How would you suggest getting rid of a pesky barbarian?" George asked him, flipping another page.

"The usual. Sacrifice, altar, sacred knife, full moon. What do you think, Jamie?"

"Sounds good." I flinched at the sound of Poe's voice and Demetria tightened her grip on my ankle. "Who's the target?" Poe went on. I sneaked a look at him from the corner of my eye. His attention was on Clarissa, who was doing yoga. In a bikini. The tease.

"Frank Myer's wife," George said in a bored tone.

"Jeez, can I help?" Malcolm said. "I can't stand that bitch."

"Yeah, and she doesn't even know about you," I murmured under my breath.

"Not for long, kid," Malcolm said, and ruffled my hair. I looked up at him, and he gave me an easy smile. Maybe Poe hadn't said anything at all about our morning?

"Did you hear about our excitement?" Clarissa asked, from downward-facing dog. She swept into a sphinx pose. "Strangers broke onto the island this morning."

"Really?" Malcolm asked.

Demetria nodded and put the cap back on the nail polish bottle. "Yeah. Clarissa saw them from the boat."

There! There. The merest flicker in Poe's eyes. George looked up from his magazine, but he clearly couldn't read Poe as well as I could. I wondered what Malcolm saw on his friend's face. I forced myself to turn away from him, but every few seconds I couldn't help but glance up to see if he was looking in my direction. No, nope, and always negatory.

"What do you think they were doing?" my big sib asked.

"Who knows?" Demetria said. "They're gone now."

Ben joined us on the porch, poker forgotten. "We also found a tape recorder and the remains of a campfire. I think they've been here before."

Malcolm looked at Poe, who was drawing in the dirt with a stick. "What do you make of it?"

Poe shrugged, head down. "There's no fence around this island. I'm sure they can pretty much come and go as they please."

"Yeah," Jenny said. "But you know what these guys are like. They can be real creeps." She would know.

It may have been Poe and me on the beach this morning, but the tape recorder *must* belong to the people on the other island. I shivered. "I don't like the idea of people sneaking around here," I said. It reminded me too much of my recent experience with Dragon's Head. "You said stuff had already been stolen."

"What do you want me to do?" Poe asked, finally looking up. I felt myself shrinking under his steady gray gaze. "How do you propose we keep them out?"

"I don't know," I said.

"Well, neither do I." He went back to his stick.

"Whatever," George said. "I'm sure they're harmless."

"Okay," Demetria said, "you're done." She stood. "I'm going back to the cabin."

"Can I come, or will they mess up?" I wiggled my toes. New pedicure or not, I needed to extricate myself from Poe's presence.

Clarissa tossed me her flip-flops. "Here, borrow mine. You'll be fine."

Shod, I followed Demetria up the path. As we passed Poe, he shot me a brief, inscrutable look, and I hastened as much as one can while wearing wet paint and someone else's flip-flops on a sandy surface.

"I can't believe I let that bitch get to me," Demetria said as we walked back to the cabin. "Like I care what she says about me. And then George, of all people. Rescued by our great white hope. How pathetic is that?"

"I thought it was funny," I said.

"But you have a soft spot for Prescott," Demetria countered. "I can take care of myself." She opened the cabin door. "Holy shit…"

I collided with her on the threshold. "What the…?"

I've seen many a trashed room in my day. There was the time Lydia planted fake secret society initiation paraphernalia in our suite. There was the time Gehry's henchmen decided to rearrange Jenny's base of operation this fall. There was the Great Cricket Invasion in January. All paled by comparison to the disaster that lay before me.

All of our clothes were tossed about the room, and most had been covered in splashes of paint. The mattresses had been ripped off the beds and thrown up against the wall. All of Jenny's electronics had been smashed. Most noticeable of all were the words sprayed on the walls and mattresses in neon orange.

Slut
Bitch
Dyke

You know, the usual. At first, I wasn't even sure that all of the curlicues of paint covering the walls were even words. Half of it looked like plain damage, but if you squinted, or turned your head just so, you could make out a variety of threats. *Death to the Diggers. You people make me sick.*

Try wearing that skirt now was scrawled across the remains of Clarissa's designer duds. *Hacker whore* now decorated the cover of Jenny's laptop.

But the one that caught my eye was on the mattress that used to grace my bed.

Keep up your BREAST stroke, or next time you WILL drown.

I hereby confess:
All I could think was,
"Not again."

13.
Meetings

Nothing in this world, not even the depths of the Pacific Trench, is as scary as Demetria Robinson on the warpath. Or at least that's what I figured until Jenny Santos got a good look at the ruins of her laptop. And Clarissa noticed that her Louis Vuitton shoulder bag had been spray-painted orange. I'm sure the conspiracy theorists camped out on the other island thought we were murdering a passel of virgins or something, the screams were so loud.

Salt, who until recently had been little more than a crotchety nuisance in the eyes of my fellow knights, suddenly became a hero. His precautions and policies weren't old-fashioned, unnecessary, and paranoid, but well reasoned, highly advisable, and deeply worthwhile. He was very much in his element.

The males in the club did their best to calm down our half, cracking jokes about the perpetrator's penmanship (or spray-canmanship), and, in George's case, admiring his skilled application of that lowest form of humor, the dirty pun. When Jenny threatened them with her mangled keyboard, they backed off. Harun offered us—or at least one of us—his bed. Jenny responded with the hairy eyeball. Clarissa and I exchanged knowing looks. Something strange was going on there.

Malcolm and Poe arrived, and the latter took one look around the room and marched back out. Fine. Who wanted him here? Who wanted him to even *act* like he cared what happened to her? Not me.

Malcolm stayed to help us with cleanup, and Salt departed to look for clues. Our activities were punctuated with the following exclamations (each on repeat):

1) "Who could have done this?"
2) "When did they get in here? We were here all afternoon!"
3) "Oh my God, my bag/dress/new Gucci!" (Clarissa.)

Eventually, everything got back in (spray-painted) order, and the boys left us alone after an offer to stick around, "just in case," was roundly trounced by Demetria for being some patriarchal, women-are-weaklings, anti-feminist bullshit. She was in rare form.

"I can't put up with this anymore," she said, pacing across the painted floors. "I've had it up to here with Rose & Grave crap."

"This isn't Rose & Grave," Jenny said quietly.

"Oh, no?" Demetria said, swooping down and grabbing Jenny's twisted screen out of the wastebasket. "So you're saying you haven't seen any suspicious e-mails this time around? Aren't keeping any secrets from the rest of us? Where's your poem?"

"That's not fair," Jenny said, then hesitated. "Actually,

it's fair. But no, no I haven't, since you mention it. Give me back my screen."

"The Diggirls being targeted again?" Demetria went on. "Come on, people, open your eyes!"

"There's an easier explanation," Clarissa said.

"Lay it on me."

"It's the people from the other island."

I ducked my head, but Demetria was on a roll. "Bullshit. It's obviously little Mrs. Myers. It's the same old bullshit it's always been since we've been tapped. The patriarchs of this organization are a bunch of racist, misogynist, homophobic assholes."

"But Kadie's not a patriarch," I said. "She's not even a Digger."

"That doesn't mean she doesn't know what's going on around here. You should have heard her talking about Gehry on the boat this morning. Like he was some kind of maligned saint. I wouldn't be surprised if he put her up to it."

"Gehry?" I said. "I hate the guy as much as the next person, but this so isn't his style."

"Yes it is," Jenny said. "Remember what he had his goons do to my room last year?" True. He'd had a guy break into my room as well.

"But he's *hiding out* here," Clarissa said. "Hiding out and praying that he and his wife aren't brought up on charges and that their kids don't find out that their darling nanny's been shipped back to Bolivia. He's not here to start a war with us."

"But he is here, and we're here…" Demetria argued.

"The others are trespassing here…" Clarissa pointed out.

Demetria groaned. "What the hell, Clarissa? You've

been watching too much *Lost*. 'It's the others, it's the others.' It's *not* the others. Occam's Razor."

"Fine," I said. "But Occam's Razor does not explain why a bitch in a snit fit would be the accomplice of a patriarch who thinks as much of women as he does of barbarians. I think it's Kadie, too—and her husband, if you want to go there. She was the one who called us dykes right before she ran off." I pointed at the wall, where the word was still visible despite Kevin's careful scrubbing. "And here it is again. Coincidence? I think not."

"And you're all just going to ignore the possibility that Gehry, who not once, but *twice* has tried to destroy us, who has been known to send his lackeys to break into our quarters and destroy our property, is involved in this little escapade?"

"I'm going to say it's unlikely," Clarissa said. "He's pretty much been a shut-in, hasn't he?"

"The perfect cover!" Demetria paused. "Or maybe he sent his son . . ."

I rolled my eyes. "Yeah, that guy would win Father of the Year. 'Here, son, now I'm going to teach you the fine art of vandalism.' Besides, I hung out with Darren this morning. He's a nice guy." He would not be wrecking my stuff after our dart game.

"You just want to see Gehry, Demetria!" Clarissa exclaimed. "It all makes sense now. You'll blame him if it means you can drag him into the daylight and grill him about everything they haven't covered on CNN."

"What, are you sympathizing with that asshole now?" Demetria asked, turning on her.

"No, but I'm beginning to wonder if you're happy this happened. You've perked right up with all this drama."

Demetria gave her a look that said, *Bitch, please.* "And you don't want to think that your future Junior League co-president is capable of destroying your stuff. Would blaming this on Kadie wreck your debutante sponsorship?"

Clarissa huffed. "That's so unfair!"

"I'm with Amy," Jenny said, straining to steer us back on topic. "Kadie was clearly angry at us back there on the lawn. Let's go get her. I'm thinking full-scale interrogation. Bright lights, Scotch tape on the eyelids . . . She'll cave like an undercooked soufflé."

"Kadie wouldn't have had time to pull this off," Clarissa pointed out. "This kind of damage took more than a few minutes." And more than a few paint cans.

"Well, if she didn't act alone . . ." Demetria was persistent, but we all ignored her.

"And again," Clarissa said happily, "we return to the others."

"No," Jenny said. "Whoever did this *knows* who we are. I say it's Kadie. I say we go all Micah Price on her ass."

"You would," Clarissa said. "You seem to have gotten over him just fine."

"Yeah. He was a jerk. Your point?"

"Nothing," Clarissa said, with an expression that indicated butter would have no business melting in her mouth, as she returned to scrubbing paint off her purse. It was very clearly *not* nothing. And Jenny knew it.

"If you have something to say, Angel, say it."

"Two dollars," said Demetria and I in unison.

Clarissa looked up from her work. "It's nothing, really. I'm just wondering if it's the best idea in the world to rebound with a fellow knight."

"I have no idea what you're talking about."

"Sure you don't," Clarissa said. "But Amy's got a broken heart, too. You don't see her hooking up with another Digger."

I blushed furiously at this, but no one guessed the true reason.

"Amy's already had her taste of society incest!" Jenny cried.

"What, so we each get one? Is that how it works?" Clarissa said. "By my count, I'm the only person here who hasn't tried out the merchandise. Maybe my dad and Kurt Gehry were right. Rose & Grave *is* turning into a dating club!"

"Whose business is it who I fuck?" Demetria asked from her corner. "And, by the way, it wasn't even sex. It was just a couple of kisses—but that's not the point."

"Yeah? Tell us why Odile's not here, then," Clarissa said. "Maybe because it would be too awkward to stay here with you."

"I don't know. I'm hardly her keeper." Demetria seemed to reflect upon how this might sound. "And you aren't Jenny's, Clarissa. She could do a lot worse than Harun. And has," she added under her breath.

Jenny looked appalled. "I really don't know why you keep saying that. I'm not dating Harun."

Clarissa threw her hands up. "Amy, you tell them. Tell them what a mess it becomes."

Oh, it was a mess all right, but not the way Clarissa thought.

"Or doing anything else with him, for that matter," Jenny went on, though no one seemed to be listening.

Clarissa kept pressuring me. "Tell them how you're always fighting with George."

"Oh, yes, do tell us everything about George," Demetria said sarcastically. "Tell us what you did to keep your sordid little affair out of his C.B."

"I figured he just ran out of time and Amy ended up on the cutting-room floor," Jenny offered.

Hey, how did it get to be Bag on Amy Hour? "Guys, please," I began.

"Yeah, guys, please," said a voice at the door. We all looked up to see the object of our conversation standing there. "It takes two to tango. And if you wanted to know something, all you had to do was ask me."

"George—" I started.

But he wasn't going to listen. He crossed the threshold and walked right by me. "I was never one for secrets. It's Amy that likes to keep them, isn't that right?"

I didn't respond.

"But let me tell you, Jenny, since I *also* have firsthand knowledge." George crouched beside her. "Society incest is a really, really bad idea. Just keep that in mind." And then he straightened. "They've called an emergency meeting to deal with the raid. All knights to the tomb. That's what I'm really here to tell you. But if you'd prefer to discuss my sex life, God knows I don't need to go to another one of these stupid meetings."

And, as I stood there, basking in a supernova of mortification, the others gathered up their things and departed. It was obvious that George and I needed a moment alone.

He turned to me as soon as they were gone. "You want to tell me what I just walked in on?"

"We're just stressed because of what happened."

"If you ask me, this is entirely too much stress for Spring Break."

"Well, no one asked you."

"Why don't you just tell them it was you and Jamie on the beach today?"

For a second, I choked. There it was, right out loud. No more innuendo from Mr. George Harrison Prescott. He'd recognized us, and he'd probably recognized what we were doing as well.

"Why don't you tell them?" I chose the offensive. "For someone who hates keeping secrets, you've sure got a lot of them."

"You still don't get it, do you? I like you, Amy. We're supposed to be friends. I don't want to fight with you. I don't want to cause you any pain. And *you* don't want anyone to know how you spent the day, clearly. Understandably! So I'm not saying a word." He shook his head. "It's like you *want* me to be mean. You want that, go talk to your new boyfriend."

Understandably? "He's not my boyfriend, and he's not mean."

"He's a jerk," George said, incredulous. "Have you forgotten? Jeez, you do know how to pick 'em. You'd have been better off with me." George took off down the stairs and broke into a jog to catch up to the others.

I dropped to my bunk, breathing as if George had punched me in the stomach. Everything was moving too fast. George was right. This was supposed to be my vacation, and here I was, fighting with my friends, fending off yet more attacks, and getting involved with a guy I'd made a point of avoiding for months. I should have just stayed at Eli and let Dragon's Head finish me off.

The only time I'd felt remotely relaxed this whole trip had been in Poe's arms this afternoon, and even George, who never had any compunction about hooking up, knew that was a mistake. Not that it mattered; it was over now. The whole thing had been ill-advised, on both of our parts. Whatever there was between Poe and myself, it was built on antagonism, not affection. Not even lust.

Well, okay, a little bit of lust.

But that was the point Clarissa had been trying to make. Like it or not, I was on the rebound. The last thing I should be doing is jumping into a relationship with a guy

I'd never even *liked*. Was I trying to prove something? To Brandon? To myself?

I gathered what was left of my self-possession and walked back to the compound. The light had changed during the time I'd spent in the cabin, and the sun lay low in the sky. Twilight was coming soon. One full day down, five more to go. What a trip this was turning out to be.

———

Because of the heat in the tomb, all the members eschewed robes in favor of street clothes. Between the Hawaiian shirts, folding chairs, and sound of crickets beyond the flimsy doors, it was tough to approach the proceedings with the same air of sobriety and importance we maintained in New Haven.

And yet, we called the meeting to order. There weren't enough chairs for all of us, so the seats mostly went to the more senior patriarchs. Beyond that, it was first come, first served.

Poe stood by the far wall, right next to the china hutch. I stood where it was least likely for my eyes to fall on him. I had no interest in spending the next half hour constantly checking to see if he was glancing in my direction and getting depressed if he wasn't.

No more boys. What a waste of my time. I kept deciding that, and then kept falling back into the trap. But this time, it would stick.

"Didn't you take pictures of the destruction?" one of the patriarchs asked. (For the record, Gehry was not present, despite the summons for all society members to come to the tomb.)

"Why?" Clarissa was asking. "Do you plan to call the cops and file an incident report? I thought we kept barbarian police out of society matters."

"As proof that what you say happened was what happened."

A good eight jaws dropped.

"Half a dozen people here can tell you exactly what it looked like," Clarissa scoffed.

"If you'd gotten your butts over there, you could have seen for yourself," Kevin added.

"Your club seems to get into an awful lot of trouble," said Frank Myer, husband of the much-maligned Kadie. "How convenient is it that intruders broke onto the island and only mangled *your* stuff?"

"That would be awfully convenient, wouldn't it?" Jenny asked. "Because if it wasn't them, I can think of one barbarian on this island who owes me a new laptop." She dumped the remains of hers onto the table, letting mangled bits of plastic, wires, and screws clatter around and roll off the edges.

"Are you accusing my wife of something?" Frank replied. "Because to be perfectly honest, she would have some choice things to say about your behavior to her this afternoon, after we were so good as to let you use our boat."

"Settle down," said another patriarch. "Nobody is accusing anyone of anything."

"Speak for yourself, old man," Demetria said.

"He said, *settle down*," Poe said in a voice that commanded the room's attention. "This is not the way that knights of Persephone address one another, on Cavador Key or off it. Now, it's clear that someone vandalized the women's cabin this afternoon, sometime after the knights returned from their snorkeling trip. I surveyed the damage right after we discovered it and it's extensive, not only to the island's property, but also to the knights' personal effects. We need to find out who's responsible."

"Easier said than done," George said.

"Furthermore, our position on barbarian visitors is very clear. They are here by invitation of the society only. If they are at any time making a knight feel uncomfortable, they will not be allowed to remain, no matter what another knight or patriarch might say about it. That's what our oaths demand."

"Fine," said Frank. "We'll leave tomorrow. With our boat." A few of the other patriarchs looked stricken by the prospect of losing access to the yacht. (Didn't bother me.)

"You'll do what you need to do," Poe said. "Whether that's leaving or making it clear to your barbarian wife that she needs to show more respect to her hosts. *All* of them."

This was being said in front of patriarchs twice his age. Who were *listening to him*. I stared in shock at Poe, but Malcolm hardly looked fazed. Was this how it was back when Poe was secretary of D176? Had people just shut up and obeyed him when he spoke? No wonder he couldn't stand me when we met. I'd never treated him with anything approaching this level of respect.

Poe was still talking. "I spent the last two hours going over every inch of this island, looking for any evidence that we had visitors. I didn't find anything new from the earlier sweep that D177 did. But there are signs. It makes sense that only the women's cabin would have been affected by a raid. It's isolated from the others, and it was empty this afternoon, while the central compound was filled with people. The only other vulnerable area would be the guesthouse, and I spoke to the inhabitants there."

"You can say his name, you know," Demetria grumbled.

Poe ignored her. "They saw nothing unusual. But at least one knight saw strangers on the island early this afternoon." He nodded to Clarissa, who looked vindicated. "I also spoke at length to Saltzman, who is prepared now to give a report of the recent barbarian activity on the island, as well as lay out what he feels are necessary precautions until we get to the bottom of this." He motioned to Malcolm, who tapped thrice, once, and twice on the door to the tomb. Salt entered.

Now I *was* trying to catch Poe's eye. Intruders on the island? What was he playing at? He knew as well as I did that Clarissa hadn't seen anyone but us on the crescent beach. And yet, he was going to indulge in this whole fantasy of visitors?

Was he trying to placate Frank? That didn't make any sense, given what Poe had just said to him about keeping his wife in line. And yet, Poe had no reason to lie. Deny, maybe, but to promote the "intruders" idea? It was Kadie, naturally. We all knew it.

Salt's report was the size of *War and Peace*. Great. Folks started settling in for the long haul, and I was impressed by everyone's patience. I honestly think it's the most fun the caretaker ever had, explaining to a roomful of trapped, if not rapt, society members about how he'd been roused twice on the night of January 27th by a series of strange green lights in the sky.

In the middle of his report on the first week in February, I lifted my head to see Poe looking at me. When he was sure he had my attention, he mimed taking a plate down off the shelf and breaking it over his knee. I stifled a surprised laugh. Where had that come from?

He held my gaze for one moment more, then morphed back into Secretary Poe, serious as a study hall proctor, paying attention to Salt's report as if the dead bird the caretaker had found on his front stoop the morning of February 24th was indeed the portent of doom he claimed it to be.

At long last, the old man wrapped it up and we spilled out of the stuffy stucco box and headed to dinner, as famished as death row inmates with a last minute reprieve.

"Well, that was long and pointless," Demetria said.

"Yeah. At this point, our cabin could have been trashed by Kadie Myer, Kurt Gehry, conspiracy theorist nuts, aliens, marauding pirates, or just really bitter squirrels." Jenny sighed. "Who decided this trip was a good idea?"

Clarissa shrugged. "But I do think Salt had a point. We need to be on our guard. Obviously, people have trespassed here, and I doubt they're afraid to do damage. I think the patrols are a good idea."

"They're a good way to keep us from getting sleep," Harun said.

"I second that. If I wanted to march around in the dark, I'd have signed up for ROTC," said Ben. "I came here to relax."

"How much relaxing are you going to do once they trash *your* stuff?" Jenny asked.

"Touché."

"He was right about not wandering around alone, too," Kevin said. "If I had anyplace else to go, I'd leave Cavador Key tomorrow. I didn't expect us to be under attack here." So much for this being a group bonding experience.

"Well, you can thank Gehry," Demetria said. "That's why there's so much focus on the island right now."

"Then why isn't it Gehry getting attacked?" George asked. "Since when do I have to be that bastard's scapegoat?"

"You, George?" Clarissa said. "Care to show me *your* new bright orange purse?"

Malcolm and Poe sat on the other side of the room during this dinner, and I made sure to sit with my back to them so I wouldn't stare. But I swear, throughout the meal, it was as if I had an internal radar beeping out Poe's position. Now he was at the salad bar, now getting a refill on his coffee, now visiting the table of another patriarch. *Beep beep beep*.

This called for chocolate. I was pouring hot fudge over my ice cream when the beeps started up again. Proximity alert.

"You're drowning your scoop," came his voice from behind me.

"Well, you know me and drowning," I replied without looking back, and put down the bottle of sauce.

His next words were almost too soft to catch. "I'm sick over what that spray paint said about you."

That was unexpected. No, that was . . . mind-blowing. I was glad I was looking away, since it took me a second to recover. At last, I turned toward him. "There was stuff all over, about all of us."

"They knew about yesterday."

"Yeah, imagine that. It's all anyone could talk about."

"So someone sneaking around could have overheard it."

"Why do you think it was an intruder? You know very well—"

"The campfire. The tape recorder. Amy, someone *is* infiltrating this island."

I rolled my eyes. "But they're harmless, like you said. The person who trashed the room is sitting right over there. You know it."

"I've spoken to both of the Myers. They aren't my favorite people, but they aren't violent, either. This was violent."

"You take an awful lot upon yourself, you know."

"Yeah. I do."

"What was up with the meeting today? Why were you acting like you were in charge?"

"Because I am."

"What does that mean?"

He blinked. "I'm in charge. I called the meeting, I ran it. I'm in charge."

"You've barely graduated."

"So? I'm on the board of the Trust."

"You never told me that."

"Every Secretary is the year after he graduates. But I was in the doghouse all last semester, remember? I couldn't even go to TTA meetings. Now, ever since Gehry's been out, I've finally been able to do my job properly. And," he added, "I don't exactly tell you everything about my life."

Or anything at all. I returned to my seat and wolfed down my ice cream so fast, I almost choked.

I'm sick over what that spray paint said about you.

Poe had called the meeting. He'd talked to everyone on the island. Even Kurt Gehry, whom he had more reason to hate than the rest of us combined, considering how Gehry had canceled his White House internship and shoved him off the TTA board. While we were busy scrubbing paint off the mattresses, he'd conducted a full investigation. For me.

George was wrong. Poe wasn't a jerk. But he wasn't like anyone I knew, either.

My internal radar indicated that Poe had left the dining room, and soon after, the girls followed suit, heading back to our semi-clean cabin to finish surveying the damage and make plans for tomorrow, since a yacht trip was clearly off the table. (The regular meeting had been usurped by the emergency summit, and no one had any interest in returning to the stuffy tomb that night.) I found I was too antsy to sit, though, so I grabbed my towel. "I'm going to take a shower." My allotted daily ten-minute shower.

Clarissa looked up from the remains of her purse, which, if not ruined by the paint, had definitely been destroyed by a thorough if unproductive scrubbing. "Wait for one of us. You shouldn't be going anywhere alone at night."

"I'm fine. I'm just going to the compound."

"But you have to walk through the woods."

"Jesus, Clarissa. Let the poor girl take a shower alone." Demetria rolled over and glared at the ceiling.

And with that, I stepped out into the night. Though as soon as I passed beyond the circle of light cast by the cabin windows, I shivered. Maybe Clarissa was right.

No. That was silly. There were no intruders. I didn't care what Poe said about someone targeting me. Those slurs had been written about all four of the Diggirls. And I'd seen Kadie playing Monopoly in the dining hall when we'd left, so I was safe. Yet the deeper I walked into the woods, the more my ears strained for every bit of sound. Every rustle of leaves or snap of twigs. Even the sound of the shells crunching beneath my feet gave me the creeps. There had, after all, been that campfire, though Ben insisted it was more than a week old.

Nevertheless, I was practically running by the time I reached the compound yard. Yellow lights shone from all the windows of the main house, from the boys' cabin, and even from a tiny porch light over the entrance to the tomb. Salt hadn't turned off the generators yet, but the shower house was dark. Natch.

Inside, it was cool and shadowy, and the fluorescent bulb I flipped on was of the variety that gave out only a dim, flickering, violet-tinted swath of illumination. Horror movie lighting. Perfect.

A quick wash later, I was wrapping up in the towel when I *did* hear something outside the window. A definite footstep, then a few more. The door opened.

"Hello?" I called. It was just someone else looking for a late-night shower. Surely. I pushed the curtain aside and tiptoed into the changing area. Maybe they were scared, too.

I tried again. "Hello? It's Amy here."

A figure stepped from the shadows. "I know."

I hereby confess:
Still waters run deep.

14.

Sea Change

I didn't have time to draw breath before hands clamped down on either side of my face and I was pushed roughly against the wall. Fingers tangled in my hair, protecting my skull from the tile behind my head.

"Jamie..." I cried out, as he pressed his mouth to mine.

Poe lifted his head. "Aww, you called me Jamie."

"I don't have that much money left," I said, and pulled him close.

The wall was cold against my wet back, and the knobby weave of the towel cut into my breasts and rubbed hard against my belly and thighs. The fact that, except for said towel, I was completely naked didn't bother me at all. Poe was dressed in slacks and a tee, and I twisted my hands in the fabric of the shirt, balling my fingers into fists as if I could tear it from his shoulders. His kisses were fast and frenetic, moving from my lips to my throat and back again, and he supported all of my weight between his body and the wall. I hooked my ankle behind his knee and arched my back.

He moaned a bit into my mouth and I almost lost it, then and there. This was beyond ridiculous.

1) We were in the shower house. The very open, very public shower house.
2) We were *not* at the point where he should be kissing me in a towel.
3) We shouldn't be getting to that point, ever, what with all the bickering and general not-getting-along.
4) Being stalked is not generally one of my turn-ons.

But my body responded to none of that as much as it responded to the way Poe was sucking stray droplets of water off my collarbone. I sank a bit on the wall, which put the rest of my body into a very interesting position in relation to his thigh.

Okay, this was swiftly getting out of hand. How recently had I promised to instill a moratorium on the Y chromosome? "Wait, wait," I gasped.

He pulled away, doing a bit of gasping of his own.

I tightened the knot on my towel, since I wasn't sure what else to do with my hands. "What the hell? What was that?"

He smiled, a smirk so wolfish that I thought for a second he'd been taking lessons from George Harrison Prescott. "I wanted to make sure. That this afternoon wasn't a dream."

"It wasn't."

"I know that now."

"But this is—what are we doing?"

"I have *no* idea," he admitted.

"All we did today was fight. Fight and make out."

"One more thing than we usually do."

"That doesn't work for me," I said. "I've spent the whole afternoon so confused."

"Yeah. I know the feeling."

"Well, you're not helping. What was that thing in the tomb?"

"What thing?"

I rubbed my head. My hair was in mats. "You know. The *plate* thing."

Recognition dawned on his shadowed face. "It was a joke."

"You don't make jokes."

"You laughed. I wanted to make you laugh." He gave a little self-mocking sigh, as if the very idea of going out of his way to amuse me baffled him as well. "I wanted to make you *look* at me. You'd been ignoring me all day."

Ha! I almost shouted it. "That couldn't be further from the truth."

Up against the wall, once again. And oh my Persephone, it was marvelous. But once again I pushed him away. You know, after a bit.

"We need to talk," I insisted, one hand holding up my towel, the other warding him off.

"I object to that plan on several levels."

"No. We need to talk about this." I hesitated, took a deep breath. "Before it can continue."

Now he looked interested. "What shall I tell you? That I spent the entire day thinking about the many ways I messed up out there on the beach? I mean, you threw yourself at me and I *still* fucked it up."

"I did not throw myself at you," I exclaimed, appalled. "Take that back."

"Done." He smiled down at me, pushed some hair out of my face, and then shocked me anew. "And then, this evening . . . it's been one too many things happening to you recently."

"This happened to all of the Diggirls."

"Being called a slut or having your computer trashed is not the same as a death threat. And that's what you got. A death threat. You, Amy. Not the rest of them. On top of yesterday, on top of this whole semester . . ."

"That was Dragon's Head."

"What if *this* is Dragon's Head?"

"It's not."

"And you know that how?"

Because I trusted that Felicity would keep her word. She'd promised Brandon she'd stop. If he chose her. And he did, but it had nothing to do with me. He chose her because he loved her. He loved her, and he did not love me anymore. I blinked away the tears forming in my eyes before Poe could see them. He'd already seen me cry too much over another boy. "Do you really think they'd devote their last Spring Break to tormenting me?"

"Sounds like a pretty decent time to me. Isn't that what I've been doing?"

I pursed my lips. "Define 'torment.' "

He looked almost ready to grin at that one, but clearly wasn't finished with the lecture. "Someone's on this island, Amy, and you're way too visible. To the patriarchs, to the conspiracy theorists, to Dragon's Head. And yeah, you're the one I worry about. I'm sure the others are lovely girls—except Jenny, who needs to be taken down a peg or two—but you're the one . . ."

He didn't finish that thought. Thank God.

"I can't believe you're taking this so lightly!" he said, changing tactics. "Are you that accustomed to prompting death threats that you take them all in stride?"

"I didn't think of it as a death threat!" I cried. Until

now, of course. "They just trashed our cabin. Nothing violent. You're the one who keeps talking about violence. You're the only person who is taking that spray paint seriously."

"Yeah, and that's *also* unlike you. Aren't you the girl who came to me last year because of a trashed room?"

"No, I went to you because of a missing girl!"

"Well, I'm not going to wait for you to go missing." Said with the utmost finality.

That made me pause for just a moment, but I regrouped. "There is no reason to think this was anything more than standard, senseless vandalism, no matter who's responsible."

Poe just stood there for a second, as if weighing his words. "There's more. Stuff I didn't say at the meeting." He grabbed my hand. "I have to show you something."

I pulled back. "Let me get dressed first."

"Fine." But he just stood there, arms crossed, dark hair falling into his eyes.

"Um, could you please turn around or something?"

A ghost of a smile. "Make me."

I yanked the shower curtain shut between us.

Combed and dressed, but still damp, I let Poe lead me across the compound and down the path to the docks. Our journey was silent, but with none of the awkwardness that had marked our last walk together. Perhaps we stood more closely than usual, but otherwise, there was no sign of the heat that had so recently consumed us both.

When we reached the boats, I drew back. "This is as far as I go."

"The boat won't leave the dock. I wouldn't even know how to do that. Get on."

I groaned and followed him aboard the smaller boat. Poe picked up a flashlight from a box in the cabin and walked over to the railing. "Look at this." He knelt and shined the flashlight at the railing. I saw a series of scratches in the paint around the hole that, until recently, had held the chain in place. The chain I'd broken through as soon as I fell against it.

"What am I looking at?"

"Someone stripped the joint."

"It just wore thin."

"No. You can tell by the markings. It was a screwdriver or something. I've built enough porches and trellises in my time to tell the difference. This thing was going to blow the second someone put weight on it."

I made a face. "There's no way that anyone could have known it was going to be me. It was just a coincidence that I was standing by this rail."

"But you're the only one who could have been really hurt if you did fall."

"Anyone can get hurt falling off a boat."

"You're the only one who can't swim."

I stared at him and everything clicked into place. "Jamie—"

"And there's more," he said.

I crouched beside him and cupped my hand around his chin.

"I have to show you the life jacket. I—"

I shook my head and kissed him. "Stop."

When I opened my eyes, his expression was confused.

"No one is after me. I promise. I know you feel guilty about scaring me at the initiation last spring. But stop beating yourself up about it. I'm fine. I'm not angry at you anymore."

"This isn't about last spring."

"Yes it is. You're the only person who spends any time at all thinking about my phobia. And it's making you read into things." I stood and brushed off my knees. "And that's *me* telling you this. The Diggers' resident conspiracy theorist . . . and pain in the ass. So you know it's the truth."

He swept to his feet and walked across the deck. I stood there, waiting, letting the night breeze blow around my face and cool my skin. Poe leaned against the far rail, staring out to sea and watching the play of starlight on the water. After a while, I walked across the deck and joined him. Minutes passed.

"I just kept thinking that if I hadn't . . . done that to you . . ." he said at last. "That maybe you wouldn't hate me."

"That's silly," I said. "I hated you for much better reasons than that."

"But not anymore?"

I looked down at our hands, beside one another on the rail, and twined mine in his. "Nope. Not anymore."

"Because of yesterday?"

"Stop asking me that." I squeezed his hand once, then let it go. "Ask the real question."

He was silent for a long time. "Fine. *What is this?*"

I shut my eyes tight against the sight of the water and the night, but I could hear the sea slapping against the side of the boat. I could hear Poe breathing, and over it all, I could hear the blood rushing in my ears.

It's Spring Break.

CONCLUSIONS I REACHED LAST NIGHT

1) The view from a boat railing is a lot more enjoyable when the boat is only three inches from land.
2) As with the SATs, if you don't know the answer to a question, you're better off skipping it.
3) I'm not giving up on boys. Not yet anyway.
4) Kisses = Nice.

CONCLUSIONS POE AND I REACHED TOGETHER LAST NIGHT

1) It's very unlikely that anyone is after me, in
   particular. For nefarious purposes anyway.
2) For the time being, we will not mention our private
   time to anyone else.
3) See #4 above.

I know nothing about conclusions Poe may have reached
on his own. Like I said, the boy is very hard to read.

When I finally returned to the cabin, the girls were all
sharing guilty expressions, and for a second I thought they
suspected everything.

"We were just talking," Clarissa said, "and we think we
owe you an apology."

"For what?" I was truly mystified.

"For putting you on the spot about George," Demetria
said. "Glass houses and all."

I looked at the three of them. "It's fine."

"You don't need to avoid us, is all we're saying. We
won't talk about it anymore," Jenny said. She was on the
floor with a screwdriver and computer innards.

"I'm not avoiding you."

Clarissa shook her head. "Come on, Amy, you weren't
in the shower all this time."

I decided to pretend that their apology was acceptable
to me, and that I wouldn't avoid them anymore. Except I
was hoping to get in another swimming lesson with Poe
tomorrow morning. Or "swimming lesson," as it were. I
feared feigning interest in an isolated jog would prompt a
request from Demetria to join me, so I decided to just let
the whole situation work itself out tomorrow, and spent

the rest of the evening learning how to construct a working computer from slightly battered scraps.

Jenny really is a genius.

And as I settled into bed that night, it occurred to me that knowledge of that sort of thing was bothering me less and less as time went on. I hadn't gone to Andover, or Horace Mann or Eton. My high school had been the average kind, and I'd been the best student there. Such was not the case at Eli. Here, I was surrounded by geniuses. I'd figured out early in my college career that there were people like Jenny and Brandon and Lydia and Josh—truly brilliant, truly luminous, whose names would appear in history books that my children and grandchildren would read, and there were people like George and Odile—who through beauty and charm and personality would make the cult of celebrity their own. And then there were people like me. People who, through the arbitrary wisdom of the admissions office, might share space with the big shots for four years, might be their friends, their confidantes, their associates, their lovers—but would live a life well below the global radar. I knew it, and over the years, I'd come to accept it.

And I understood that it didn't make them any better than me. Jenny was a computer genius, but she had enough issues to overcome that I didn't want to trade places with her. Odile might get her name on the Hollywood Walk of Fame, but she also had to deal with every bad hair day being splashed on the cover of a magazine.

But to say that it didn't bother me from time to time? That would be a lie. The biggest problem with being a relatively small fish in the best pond ever is that you start to lower your own expectations. Maybe if I'd gone to a smaller school, or a less prestigious school, I'd have convinced myself that I was still the hotshot I'd thought I was as a high school valedictorian headed to an Ivy League college. Instead, I'd spent three years recalibrating my dreams to fit into the caste that the resident geniuses at Eli had shown me to be a part of. Above-average, to be sure, but not *summa*. Every high school student-council leader gets voted "most likely to be President." Only two or three per decade actually get to be so. When you're at Eli, and you're surrounded by future presidents or children of current presidents, you see what it really takes, and then you get real. Maybe you even overcompensate in the other direction.

And no one had stopped me. Brandon may have loved me, but he'd never once suspected that I'd been looking for advice every bit as much as confirmation when I started talking about my modest ambitions. He was so sure of what he wanted in his life, why would he suspect I was wondering about my own? Why would he suspect that I'd aspire to anything else unless I said I did?

Or maybe . . . the mere thought burned inside my chest, but it must be completed . . . maybe he didn't think I was really capable of anything else. After all, he'd edited the Lit Mag on a lark, while it had been the biggest gold star on my résumé. And all those hours last month ostensibly spent "working" on fellowship applications when really we were just talking or napping? He hadn't actually helped me at all. Maybe he didn't want to encourage me in that direction. Maybe he didn't want to push me toward something where he thought I'd fail.

Perhaps he'd been every bit as shocked as I was when I'd been tapped by Rose & Grave.

What if that was why the society had become so significant in my life, the way Quill & Ink never would have been? It was the one thing about my college career that was really extraordinary. I was a Digger, a member of the most illustrious society on campus, filled with all of the brightest and most promising students at Eli. Proof positive that there was something of that teenaged hotshot inside me still. The knowledge that I'd been a substitute tap had bothered me for quite a while, but perhaps it was time to get over it. The events of the previous year showed that I did have what it took to wield significant influence in Rose & Grave, and—I suspected—beyond. Wasn't that exactly what Poe had said last semester? Long before he had any warm feelings toward me, he'd respected what I could do.

I was never going to be famous. Didn't want to be. But I would be important.

Once I figured out how.

———

With such ruminations lulling me to sleep, is it any wonder I spent the night with shadow governments and secret plans? In my dreams, there was a vast conspiracy afoot, and I was the only person who could bring it to light. I had all the connections to do so, but was afraid of how the consequences would affect the leaders I had come to love. What did I value more: my friends within the conspiracy or the world at large? My unconscious state had a hard time coming to a conclusion about it*, but it was undisputed that my brain had whipped up some really great costumes for us all to wear whilst I fretted.

Costumes are of the utmost importance, as any good society member knows.

I was no closer to a scheme for sneaking off with Poe

* The confessor would like to note that she has studied more than enough literary criticism to pick up on that subtext, thank you very much.

the following morning, and as the clock ticked on inexorably to breakfast time, I began to fret about my options.

1) Spend time with Poe
2) Spend time with my friends
3) ...

I desperately needed a number three. Why was this always the choice when it came to guys? You could either avoid them and spend quality time with your girlfriends (who, let's face it, have all had a longer shelf life than any of your romantic relationships), or you could ditch your friends and do the romance thing, thereby providing you with fodder for the very thing you and your friends spent the most time talking about: boys.

Look at the situation with Lydia. I had a hard enough time tolerating her joined-at-the-hipness with Josh, and I considered him a close personal friend. It was a lot harder to accept a friend's ditching if you actively disapproved of the guy she was ditching you for.

And they would if they knew. I was glad we'd decided not to tell anyone. It was too new, for starters, and too amorphous. He wasn't my boyfriend, wasn't even my friend-with-benefits. How could I explain this whole development to them when I couldn't even figure it out for myself? Plus, they'd all pretty much made their positions clear regarding society incest.

I watched the other girls as they got ready. Jennifer, clearly struck with a bit of hair envy since hers had yet to grow out of its pixie cut (which, if you ask me, suited her just fine, in a sort of Angelina Jolie-in-*Hackers* kind of way), was tying Clarissa's blond tresses into something called a "Dutch braid." Demetria was moaning about starvation and cursing the island policy of keeping food out of the cabins (and thus away from invading hordes of bugs).

None of them knew it, but I was once again living up to my society name: Bugaboo. Clarissa had been wrong. The Diggers weren't devolving into a dating club. Just me. Demetria and Odile may have had a moment or two, but from what she said yesterday, it sounded a heck of a lot more chaste than my little shower encounter. And I had no idea what was going on with Jenny (not a new circumstance, to be sure), but whatever her feelings were for Harun (and vice versa), I doubted she'd acted upon them. No, it was just me who had dipped my toes into Rose & Grave waters, and was now blithely double-dipping. Not only was I the club conspiracy theorist, I was fast becoming the club slut as well.

"I can't take it anymore! When's breakfast?" Demetria said. "This is why I don't live on campus. I like to eat when I want to eat, not sit around like a calf in a feedlot and wait for the dining halls to open."

"Was that your first attempt at a barnyard metaphor?" Clarissa asked. "Because it wasn't half bad."

I doubted any of the three of them had actually seen a barnyard in their lives.

Jenny tied off the end of Clarissa's hair. "This is why we have Starbucks."

"We don't have Starbucks on Cavador." Demetria rolled off the bed and crossed to the dresser. "Whose mints are these? Can I have one?"

I looked up too late and saw that she was ripping open my Life Savers. Poe's Life Savers.

"No!" I shouted. Demetria froze.

It was too late. They were open. Fourteen tiny little white rings exposed.

"I'm sorry," Demetria said, her tone one of pure confusion. "Were you . . . saving these for something?"

"No," I said quickly. "It's fine, go ahead." They were just mints. He hadn't even bought them with me in mind. They weren't a love token, weren't something special. They were a joke. He'd been making fun of me. But they were also the first thing Poe had ever given me.

I didn't watch as Demetria popped one in her mouth, but I heard, or thought I heard, a decided crunch as she crushed the ring between her teeth. She wasn't even going to savor them.

Oh, for Pete's sake. This was ridiculous. They were mints. I hopped to my feet and joined her by the dresser. I pulled another Life Saver out of the package and put it in my mouth, letting the menthol burn against my tongue. Just mints.

Demetria narrowed her eyes. "You okay?"

I ran my finger over the package, trying in vain to pat down the ragged ends of wax paper and foil. "Yeah, why?"

" 'Cause you're freaking me out."

And a moment later, we both almost choked as a voice broke through the morning stillness. "All knights, to the tomb. All knights, to the tomb."

Demetria laughed. "Okay, that's gotta be the weirdest announcement anyone's ever made over a P.A."

And when we finished dressing and arrived at the tomb, it was to greet the solemn face of Salt, who frowned at us all. "It is my great regret to inform you," he said, with vast solemnity, "that I have received a very disturbing report from my counterpart in New Haven."

"What?" George said. "Has something happened to Hale?"

"No." Man, could Salt draw it out or what? "According

to my counterpart, alarm bells went off in the Inner Temple of the tomb yesterday evening at 7:45 P.M. Apparently, the Inner Temple was breached by an outsider."

"Did they steal anything?" Ben asked. Somehow, he'd already snagged himself a cup of coffee and several of the other Diggers were giving it longing glances.

"No," the caretaker announced. "The assailants, however, left a message."

We all waited, breathless, until we became aware that Salt was not about to volunteer the particulars without sufficient setup.

"Let's just call Hale and get the scoop," Jenny whispered to me.

I clenched my jaw. This guy was unbelievable. "What did it say, Salt?" I prompted, and he practically giggled as he read:

" 'It's not over. Dragon's Head.' "

———

Well, Felicity had warned me that the feud hadn't ended as a result of her bargain with "her boyfriend." Just the campaign against me. And that note was a fair warning that though one battle had ended, the war was still raging. Now they'd breached the Inner Temple.

"How convenient for them that we're not on campus," Jenny said.

"Yeah," Demetria replied. "Just like it was convenient for us in January."

"But why didn't they just steal something of ours?" I asked. "Then we'd be even!" Then we'd be forced to tell them about their stupid dragon.

"Maybe they're planning something worse," said Harun.

DIANA PETERFREUND

Ben shook his head. "So we're getting it from two fronts now? A bunch of conspiracy theorists on our neighboring island, and another society back home?"

Harun looked at him with interest. "Actually, do any of us know they are conspiracy theorists on the other island? Maybe that's Dragon's Head, too. Maybe..."

And thus passed another day on Cavador Key. Breakfast in the morning, followed by me resisting a boat trip while the others commandeered the island's craft to check out the neighboring island. (Report from George: "I don't think Dragon's Head members tend to be quite so counterculture as the guys we saw through the binoculars." Retort from Demetria: "So counterculture to you is dreadlocks and facial piercings?") A leisurely lunch, then an afternoon of intermittent siestas and sunbathing, during which time Poe spirited me away for another trip to the crescent beach to practice dog-paddling, floating on my back, and French kissing. (I'm much better at the latter, still suck at the first two.) A long dinner with lots of wine, and a late night campfire complete with marshmallows, hot rum drinks, hot dogs, and ghost stories. (Poe is an excellent storyteller, by the way. Even Jenny and Clarissa admitted to being impressed, and I was glad I had the heat from the fire to explain away my blush.) Still later, the four of us girls tripped back through the woods to our cabin, a little drunk on rum and feeling as relaxed as I could recall being since New Year's Eve.

Way too early the following morning, we heard a distant, rhythmic thwapping, getting steadily louder and louder.

"What now?" Demetria groaned, pulling a pillow over her braids. "God, people, you win, okay! We're trying to take over the world. Now let us get some fucking sleep!"

Jenny threw her pillow at her. "You're making more noise than they are."

Clarissa was sitting up in bed, cocking her head and listening. "Guys," she said.

"Go back to bed, Clary."

"No, guys, I think—" The noise got louder and louder until there was no doubt in our minds what it was. A flyby.

Instantly, all four of us were on our feet and out the door, though Clarissa found time to roll up the bottoms of her silk pajama pants against the morning dew. We looked to the skies, where indeed there was a large white helicopter circling low over the island.

"Salt's gonna freak," Jenny observed. We grabbed our flip-flops from the porch, rushed through the woods to the main compound, and found everyone else hurrying out of the cabins and buildings as well, eyes turned up. Was it a news helicopter? An emissary from the White House, come to exonerate Gehry and invite him back into the fold? Or had the conspiracy theorists finally scraped up enough dough to do an aerial pictorial?

Salt came running out of his cottage, walkie-talkie pressed to his mouth.

"Out of the way!" he yelled over the sound of the rotors, waving his free arm at the assembled crowd. "Move out, move out! You're standing on the landing pad!"

The what? We all looked at our feet, where the path widened into a rough circle. This was a helicopter landing pad? We had landing pads on Cavador Key? And Salt wanted the copter to *land* here?

"Move!" the caretaker bellowed over the deafening roar. The helicopter dipped lower and hovered above us, stirring up massive clouds of dust and sand and whipping hair into everyone's faces.

We moved, and as I scooted back to the fringe of the forest, I couldn't help but glance over to the boys' cabin. Malcolm and Poe stood side by side on the porch, watching the proceedings and leaning on the rail. Poe was dressed in a pair of sweatpants and nothing else. As the helicopter descended into the compound, I saw Malcolm lean toward Poe and cup his hand around his friend's ear to speak into it, and I stiffened.

Hands off, big sib.

Where the hell did that come from! Not that I suspected Malcolm had anything other than friendly feelings toward Poe—and there was definitely no chance of the reverse. That had been made breathtakingly obvious in the last two days. And yet I was as taken aback by the very fact that I had a reaction as I was by the reaction itself. Jealousy? Over *Poe*? This was all moving way too fast.

The helicopter's runners finally set down on the soil of Cavador Key, and the rotors slowed. Every inhabitant on the key waited in awe, their focus turned toward the machine.

And I do mean *every* inhabitant. While they all watched, I couldn't help but notice four figures coming up the path from the house near the docks, forming a small nuclear family knot a safe distance from the group. Even our resident shut-in wanted to see what all the fuss was about.

But before I could nudge Demetria and point to the object of her political obsession, the door to the helicopter slid open, and Kurt Gehry dropped off my curiosity meter.

Out popped a figure in a tight, corset-style top and the biggest sunglasses I've ever seen. Her dark red hair fell past her waist, her smile looked like it was made for billboards.

"Hi, guys!" said Odile Dumas. "Miss me?"

I hereby confess:
Sometimes I think
the whole thing is silly.

15.
Pageantry

Kevin let out a whoop of joy and rushed Odile, and several other members of my club followed. Enveloped in hugs, she laughed. "So I guess the answer is yes?"

"The question is," Demetria said, slapping her a high five, "did you show up because you missed *us*?" We retreated from the helicopter as the pilot set down Odile's bags, waved farewell, and prepared to take off again.

"Yes," Kevin said. "We missed you. What are you doing here?"

Odile shrugged. "Production shut down for a few days and I wanted to see what all the fuss was about this place." She looked at her surroundings and wrinkled her pert little nose. "Bit rustic, huh?"

At least someone agreed with me! I glanced at the other people in the clearing. The younger patriarchs, used to seeing Odile around campus, had lost interest, but their families were still staring and pointing. Any second now they'd start asking for autographs. Poe and Malcolm had disappeared back inside their cabin, but the Gehrys remained on the lawn, watching silently from a distance. Kurt had his hands on his wife's shoulders; she was in turn holding the hand of her little daughter. Darren stood beside them, hand raised to his brow to shield his eyes from the morning sun.

"Hey, Demetria," I said, and nodded in the direction of the family.

"Oh, so he is here!" Odile said. "I'd been wondering, as has the *New York Times*."

"He's here, but it's the first time anyone's seen him!" Demetria exclaimed. "Let's go say hi." She started across the lawn, followed by the other Diggirls, and as soon as he noticed, Kurt nudged his wife as if to encourage retreat toward the house. Mrs. Gehry shook him off and kept staring at our group, and I saw her husband lean over and bark an order at his son before grabbing his daughter by the hand and marching away posthaste.

"Odile Dumas," Mrs. Gehry said when we arrived before her. "My daughter is a huge fan of your work." She looked around, but saw that the little girl was no longer standing by her side, no longer holding her hand. "Where? Where did she go?"

I saw that Darren's arms were outstretched toward his mother, as if ready to catch her.

"Oh, she'll be so disappointed!" Mrs. Gehry said, wavering slightly. Darren's hand came closer. "Darren, darling, go fetch her. Tell her the girl from the dancing movie is here."

"Mom, why don't you come with me?" he asked pointedly, though he couldn't take his eyes off Odile.

Odile caught on. "Ma'am, I'm going to be around for a while, so you can just have—"

"Darren!" Mrs. Gehry shouted, though I now noticed that her eyes were unfocused. "Go get Isabelle. What would your father say if he knew how rude you were be-ing?"

"Tell you what," Odile said quickly, as Darren fought back his blush. "I'll come with you both to meet Isabelle, how about that?"

"No," Darren said quickly. "We can't. Mom, come on, let's go back inside now. I'll bring Belle by later." And with that, he pasted on an expression not unlike his father's at his most inflexible, grabbed his mother by the hand, and started leading her down the path.

"Curiouser and curiouser," Demetria said.

"My goodness," Jenny added. "What's wrong with the wife?"

"Heavy-dose pharms," Odile said with surety. "It's really obvious."

Clarissa nodded. "Antidepressants, maybe?"

"Yeah, but those are like candy." Odile shrugged. "There's a lot more going on there. She was stoned."

"Maybe she's *stoned* stoned," Demetria said. "Prescrip-tion marijuana?"

Jenny shook her head. "I couldn't smell it."

"Ganja cakes," Demetria suggested.

"Or roofies," said Clarissa. "See how she could barely stand?"

"Rohypnol is illegal," said Jenny.

"So is marijuana," I said.

"And so is employing illegal aliens," Demetria finished. "Which, if I recall, was one of Gehry's biggest hot-button issues. So apparently, the law just applies to everyone else. Not him."

And yet, seeing his wife and children in that sad state . . . "I don't know if I can blame her, whatever she might be on. Their whole world has fallen apart."

Demetria toed the ground. "I have less sympathy for her, but I really feel for those kids. Darren must be mortified."

I stared at the retreating pair. Neither of the adult Gehrys seemed in much of a position to provide good parenting, leaving Darren to his own educational devices, and sequestering Isabelle inside. Bet the kids were really starting to miss their usual caretakers. You know, the ones not taking roofies. Or lithium, or whatever it was Mrs. Gehry was on.

Cook emerged from the kitchen and rung the bell on the porch of the main house. Breakfast.

"A bell? This is like a ranch!" Odile exclaimed. "So, fill me in, what's been going on here?"

"All kinds of scandal," Clarissa said. "Amy almost drowned, Demetria is going to beat up a patriarch's wife, our room was trashed by conspiracy theorists, Dragon's Head broke into the tomb in Connecticut, and Jenny has a crush on Harun."

"Do not!" Jenny said.

"In other words," said Demetria. "The usual."

Odile laughed. "Man, I love this society."

———

Darren did not reappear for breakfast, which meant more French toast for the rest of us (except for Odile, who flatly refused to eat carbs). I kept an eye out for him throughout the meal, as the others filled Odile in on the events she'd missed, but the kid never appeared. And as for the other boy of interest on the island, he'd taken a seat with Malcolm and the Myers, and I actually heard him laughing a good half a dozen times during the meal, a sound so unusual that I was surprised everyone in the room wasn't commenting on it.

Another major topic of conversation was the Gehrys, and what could be wrong with the matriarch of the family. All sorts of theories floated around the breakfast table, but our combined lack of medical knowledge kept us from coming to any firm conclusions.*

"She's definitely self-medicating, though," Clarissa said. "Maybe she just can't deal with the loss of status."

"Being stuck on the island all the time with two kids?" Kevin said. "I'd want to get blitzed every once in a while as well."

"I doubt she's just upped the martini intake," Demetria said. "She didn't even realize her husband had taken her daughter." Demetria had grown entirely more subdued since meeting Mrs. Gehry face-to-face. As her work at the Eli Women's Center gave her a vast store of knowledge about various illegal, mood-altering substances, she had spent the meal telling us horror stories about date-rape drugs. "I just hope that whatever it is she's using, she's got a doctor's note."

In addition, Odile was fascinated by my little accident on the way over to the island, and quizzed me far more than I liked about what it "felt like" to almost drown.

"But I'm an actress! A student of human nature!" she protested when Jenny told her to cut it out.

"You're a macabre son of a bitch," Demetria said with a smile.

Odile's lips scrunched into a pout. "Fine. If Amy won't tell me, I'll have to get someone to hold me under so I can feel it for myself."

"Since when are you even remotely Method?" Kevin asked, but Odile changed the subject.

---

* The confessor was relieved that no one used this opportunity to point out that the prior club had tapped a future doctor, but he'd declined joining Rose & Grave once he'd gotten a good look at his ersatz fellow knights.

"And what about these nutballs on the other island?" she asked. "Did they really trash our cabin?"

"Oh, yeah," Clarissa grumbled. "Wait until you see it. I hope you haven't brought anything valuable."

Odile shook her head. "That's awful. We can't let them get away with it."

"That's what I've been saying," said Jenny.

"And what I've been saying is that it's not *them*," Demetria cut in. "But try convincing Clarissa of that."

"Either way," Clarissa said quickly, "they did trespass on our island, and they are camped out over there, spying on us. We shouldn't put up with it."

"Why not?" Demetria said. "We're putting up with a lot of shit around here." She cast an evil glance in the direction of Kadie Myer, who was carrying her plate to the kitchen. Breakfast was ending and the tables had started to clear. I was torn between arranging another rendezvous with Poe and continuing the conversation with the rest of my club. But when I checked the table where he'd been sitting, he had also disappeared.

"So, Jennifer," said George, "on that most charitable topic of revenge . . . what would you suggest?"

Jenny considered it for a moment. "I'm not sure. I don't think we have the resources for our usual pranks."

"I think you'd be surprised what Diggers have managed to pull off on this island in the past."

"Oh?" said Kevin. "Any stories to share?"

George shrugged and swept his last bite of French toast through the puddle of syrup on his plate. "I might have done a bit of sneaking around as a kid, watched a couple ceremonies I shouldn't have."

Poe's words from before came back to me. "I think it's pretty common for the members to put on a little skit for the benefit of whoever might be watching from the other island," I said.

They all turned to me, surprise etched across their features.

"Since when do you know so much about what Diggers usually do on this island?" Clarissa asked.

"I did some poking around in the rec room the day you all went out on the boat with the Myers," I lied smoothly. "There's photo albums and everything." At least, Darren had told us as much. He said he'd been looking through our old records.

"Amy's right." George to the rescue. "I saw the skits in real life. They were awesome. I bet Salt has the costumes hidden somewhere."

"A skit?" Ben asked, his tone skeptical. "A skit is how we're going to pay those dudes back for trashing the cabin?"

"I agree," said Clarissa. "Won't it just rile them up even more? Make them more eager to get over here and see what we're up to?"

"And then we can really rumble!" said Odile. "I love it."

Demetria rested her face in her hands and sighed in frustration, but everyone else seemed to warm to the idea. They were in the midst of discussing plotlines when Poe and Malcolm came back, dressed in beachwear and holding towels.

"Jamie!" Odile called, hopping up and rushing over to my new favorite patriarch. "I'm glad you're here." She was? Since when were they such good friends? "We're going to put on a skit for the PCTs* on the other island. Want to play?"

---

* Paranoid Conspiracy Theorists. Those Hollywood types and their jargon.

Poe smiled. "Depends what you're planning. I was always partial to the story of Perseus and Andromeda myself."

"You would be," Demetria grumbled, beside me.

True. It was a tad on the damsel-in-distress side. And all the good parts belonged to men.

Odile's eyes lit up. "Are you saying we have a sea monster costume?"

"A little raggedy by now, but yes."

Odile squealed and threw her arms around him. "Awesome! You have to help."

I bit my lip, and looked away, so I didn't see when the embrace ended.

"Come on," Odile wheedled. "We had so much fun with the straggler initiation. Remember?"

Oh, right. Well, at least there was one Diggirl who wasn't completely disgusted by Poe. (I mean two. *Two.*)

"Sorry. I'm going on the yacht with the Myers today," he said. "We're leaving right now, as a matter of fact."

My head shot up. Right now? What about our swimming lesson? I watched, stricken, as Poe directed Odile and the other drama enthusiasts to Cavador Key's store of costumes and props, and tried to catch his eye, to no avail. He and Malcolm finished their instructions and waved good-bye to the group, and I followed them out onto the porch.

"Hey," I called as the boys took the stairs to the lawn. Poe turned and squinted up at me through the sunlight.

"Yes?"

"What are you doing?" Poe waved Malcolm on and returned to me. I leaned over the railing and lowered my voice. "You're leaving?"

Recognition dawned. "You have a better offer?"

Than hanging out on a boat with people like the

Myers? I damn well hope so. "I thought we could..." Oh, dear, did I sound clingy, or what? "Go swimming. Again."

"Tempting," he said. "But, uh...I really think I need to do some damage control today. We can't burn every bridge around here, Amy, much as you'd like to."

"Only the ones that lead to bad places," I replied. "Don't try to sell me the 'for the good of Rose & Grave' party line if your sacrifice involves spending the day on a yacht."

"Apparently, that's not the only sacrifice I'm making." He smiled at me, but I wasn't in the mood.

"And what about Malcolm? How can he bring himself to—"

"Unlike some of us, he doesn't believe in throwing the baby out with the bathwater," Poe said. "Besides, he's old hat at dealing with people like that, remember? No one is perfectly good or perfectly evil."

"That's a concept with which I'm becoming increasingly familiar." I rocked back on my heels in dismay. Great, I played my hand and Poe trumped it with *society duty*.

He glanced over his shoulder at Malcolm's retreating form. "Tell you what, come with us."

I blinked at him. Had he lost IQ points during the night?

Reasons That's A Definitive "No."

1) Go with him. *On a boat*. Yeah, right.
2) Go with him on a boat that happened to belong to Kadie Myer, for whom I had no warm feelings whatsoever, and toward whom several of my closest friends held nothing but contempt.
3) Kadie Myer, whose fingernails were probably still a tad orange from her last painting project.

4) Ditch my club and go off very publicly with Poe?
  Was I asking for it?

Poe must have at least guessed the gist of number four, because he added, "Think of it this way: Malcolm's coming. You've hardly spent any time with him."

"Does Malcolm—"

"No." Poe hesitated. "Do any of yours?"

"No." Except for George, but I hadn't been the one to tell him.

"Good." Poe checked over his shoulder again. "So, want to come?"

I shook my head. "On a boat? No way."

"You were on a boat the other night."

"Yeah, docked and not moving. Besides," I added, "three's a crowd. You never get to spend time with Malcolm, either."

"True. But I want…" He trailed off. "Fine. Go make costumes with the kids, Amy. You'll have more fun."

"'With the kids'? Don't be mean."

"I was aiming for cute."

"It doesn't become you."

"Not half so much as mean," he agreed, and when I didn't deny it, he added, "So it's either I leave Malcolm alone in the company of a bigot and her husband, or I stand you up. Neither choice sounds palatable."

"At least you admit she's a bigot."

"Frank's a nice guy. Pity about the wife. I didn't like her at Eli, and I don't like her now. My only hope is that they'll be divorced before they hit that fifty-year mark, when we have to make her an associate patriarch."

"A what?" I cried.

"You didn't know? When they hit their golden anniversary, we give the spouse a guest pass. We even have a little ceremony." He grinned. "There's one argument for keeping it in Rose & Grave, huh?"

I wasn't rising to his bait. "Or killing her off before she's seventy-five."

"Amy!" Odile called from inside the building. "Will you be the back end of the sea monster? It's not a speaking part."

"Obviously," Poe said with a smirk.

"Sea monster seems to denote *sea*, doesn't it?" I whispered to him. "Over my dead body," I replied loud enough for Odile to hear. Turning back to Poe, I said, "Go ahead. I've got an activity director to deal with now."

"Slave driver, more like." Poe's smile didn't dim, and I felt another pang of jealousy. "By the time I get back she'll probably have Industrial Light & Magic on its way."

"Salt would never allow such a thing," I argued.

"True." He stood there for a second or so longer—not moving toward me, not touching me, and certainly not *kissing* me, but possibly thinking about all three—then took off.

I headed back into the library, where I was promptly conscripted into a debate about whether or not Clarissa should play Andromeda. Odile's argument was that, in a white dress, her blond hair and pale skin would sell "virgin sacrifice" across the channel like nothing else. Demetria's stance was that the whole idea of femininity being tied to "whiteness" was a racist position, and that Jenny was not only the most virginal member of the group, but also had the most authentic coloring when it came to portraying a Greek princess. Clarissa said whatever the club decided was okay with her, and Jenny said like hell were they chaining her to a rock, even if it was a fake chain on a fake rock.

"At the risk of having my balls torn off by Demetria," George said, "I vote for Clarissa, white chick or no."

"Yeah," Harun said. "Just because she will be easier to see across the water. Her hair practically glows."

Clarissa glared. Jenny beamed.

"I actually vote for *Demetria*," said Ben. "Sorry, Clarissa. But I see her point, and I think it would be awesome to have a black Andromeda. Very in-your-face, pre-Raphaelites."

Demetria shook her head. "Hell no. I'm playing the sea monster. I don't do damsels."

"Yeah, you do," said George.

Around this time, Kevin suggested he play Andromeda, because he was the smallest member of the club, except for Odile, who had already claimed the part of Queen Cassiopeia, and I decided that, lest I found my ass chained to a rock, I'd volunteer to play the back end of the sea monster after all.

The rest of the morning was spent in scripting and rehearsals. Under protest, Clarissa took the part of the princess, with Ben (the tallest) as Poseidon, Kevin as Perseus, George as the king, and Harun and Jenny as courtiers. Demetria deigned to point out that, with the exception of Kevin, all knights of color were given non-speaking parts, and wasn't that interesting. Odile deigned to respond that the lack of speaking made Demetria's part no smaller in scope, and besides, the intended audience would never be able to hear them from across the water anyway.*

By noon, I'd found myself employed with basting

---

* At this point, the confessor feels obliged to point out that though Miss Dumas might be passing as white bread in the realm of Hollywood, it should not be assumed that her own heritage was purely European. The confessor almost said as much at the time, but wondered if, perhaps, this was the undercurrent to Demetria and Odile's entire argument. Slow on the uptake, that's our girl.

together a scaly tail from the box of vaguely mildewed costumes we'd found in the attic of the main house. The entire sea monster looked, at first glance, like a miniature
version of the kind of dragons they have in Chinese New
Year parades. Pretty cool, actually. Why don't we have one
of these in the tomb at Eli?

A shadow fell over my work. "What are you doing?"

I glanced up. Darren Gehry, holding a box of Popsicles,
was staring down at us.

"Begone, barbarian," Demetria muttered into her
headdress.

"Are those Popsicles?" George asked, jumping up and
taking the box from Darren's hands. "C'mere, man, and
help me with this Gorgon head."

"What is all this stuff?" Darren asked.

"Afraid we can't tell you that," George said, pulling out
an orange pop and handing the box to Ben. "But if you're
really good, I'll let you in on where the best place to watch
from secret is."

"George!" Clarissa exclaimed.

"Oh, come on," George said. "Like you wouldn't have
done the same thing as me when you were his age."

"I guess this answers the question of which of you are
really Diggers," Darren said, as the ice pops made the
rounds.

"Ooh, he's a quick one," said Odile, examining the box
for nutritional info. "Where's your sister?"

"My dad wanted her to stay inside this afternoon,"
Darren said. It was the first time I'd ever heard him mention his father.

"Probably because we're a bad influence," Demetria
said. "Wouldn't want her to get any new ideas about a
woman's place."

"What are you talking about?" I said. "We're sitting here *sewing*."

"Yeah, on a secret project," said Kevin, waving his purple pop in the air like a scepter. "Hate to do this, kid . . ."

George made a face. "It's ridiculous. Darren's a legacy at Eli, and a legacy . . . elsewhere. Is there a word for the opposite of a patriarch?"

"Pretriarch?" I suggested.

"Plus, we're playing a game. Let him join."

"No, thanks," Darren said. "I'm not into dress-up."

"Well then," Ben said. "I recommend you remember this word come Tap Night: 'reject.' "

I laughed. Rose & Grave did require a flair for the dramatic.

"It's okay," Darren went on. "I have an appointment with my father soon anyway."

Appointment? What an odd way to put it. I had appointments with my dentist, or my thesis advisor, not my parents. Then again, Darren was being homeschooled, so maybe he was meeting his dad for half an hour of Socratic dialogue. I could totally see old Kurt going for that.

"Did you get a chance to start on *Monte Cristo*?" I asked him.

"A little," he admitted, ducking his head in guilt. "But I left it in the rec room yesterday. I should probably go grab it."

I stood. "I'll come with you. It's time to stretch my legs anyway."

We walked up to the house and I noticed that Darren was playing with the hem of his grubby T-shirt as he walked. I couldn't imagine the guts it must have taken him to visit the college kids after the scene we'd witnessed that morning, but I wasn't sure whether or not I could even begin to broach the subject. Poe's approach to Darren seemed to be very hands-off, as if the last thing Darren wanted was to talk to anyone else about what was going on in his life, but then again, I had to consider the source. Poe didn't like to talk to anyone about anything. And if Darren really wanted nothing more than to avoid us all, then why did he keep showing up? He'd come to talk to us on the boat, and before breakfast, and again just now.

I figured he was desperate for company in his own age bracket, and the Eli students were the closest he could get. And though I agreed with my fellow knights about keeping Digger activities restricted to Diggers only, I also under-stood George's point. There was a pretty fair chance that Darren would eventually join our ranks, and plus, was our little skit really all that important to the makeup of the or-ganization that we needed to keep it a secret? How juvenile was that?

A lot of times, it seemed like the secrecy of our society just served to hide how boring and pedestrian most of our activities really were.

"You know," he confided in me, "I've seen these things so many times I could probably do it better than any of you."

Well, that answered my question! "I bet," I said with a chuckle. "You want my part? I'm the back end of the sea monster."

"Really?" he asked, surprised. "But you don't swim, and that's the part that goes on the rowboat."

I stared at him. "Rowboat?"

"Yeah," he said. "Aren't you guys using the rowboat?"

Um, not that anyone had told me. Darren's expression had *Amateurs* written all over it, and I began to think that maybe this particular pretriarch had more experience with dress-up than he wanted to let on.

Time to change the subject. "Maybe, if your dad will let

her, Odile can drop by your house this afternoon and meet your sister."

"She'd like that," Darren said. "I think she misses Bettina."

"Who?"

He shrugged. "Our housekeeper. She lives with us and they're really close. We don't even get cell reception on the island, so Isabelle hasn't been able to talk to her since we've been here."

That wasn't the only reason. I opened my mouth and shut it again, unable to formulate any type of response. So there it was. Darren didn't know.

"Got it," Darren said, picking up *The Count of Monte Cristo* off an end table. I noticed a bookmark a good third of the way into the novel. Ah, a fellow speed-reader.

"You must be liking it so far," I said, pointing at the bookmark. There. Books were a safe topic. Weren't they?

He flipped through the pages. "It's okay." He looked out the window at the rest of my club, then returned his attention to the book. "Hey, I heard something happened at your cabin the other day."

I nodded, eager to steer the conversation far, far away from Bettina. "It was outrageous! Someone broke in, trashed the place, and wrote all kinds of nasty stuff on all the walls and mattresses with paint."

"Wow," he said, though his face was still buried in the pages. "Anything of yours get ruined?"

"Not mine, luckily. They totally destroyed Clarissa's new purse, though."

"Designer?"

"Louis Vuitton." Not that he knew what that meant.

"That's my mom's favorite," he said. Once again, Darren surprised me. Was there anything this kid didn't know?

"You know," he said. "I don't think George is right."

"About?"

"Me joining Rose & Grave. Wouldn't it be cooler to, like, join Dragon's Head or something? I bet they'd love it, all the secrets I could tell them. Aren't they the big Digger rivals?"

"I may have heard something like that once," I said. I was *so* the wrong girl to ask about Dragon's Head, the bastards. And to bring them up now, after yesterday's news . . . I wondered how much this pretriarch actually knew about society happenings. "But still, that's uncool—to join another society just because you have the goods to betray this one." Not that I was biased or anything.

"What else am I going to use this info for?" Darren asked. "It's not worth anything if I just become another Digger."

"You've been reading too much Nietzsche," I replied. And here my inner Digger was rising up in defense. We were giving this guy room and board on the island, and this was his idea of gratitude? Maybe we should rethink the whole barbarian invite policy.

"Whatever. I probably won't even end up at Eli anyway."

"Really? I think you're pretty much a shoo-in."

He shrugged. "I might go to Oxford or something instead."

"That would be cool," I agreed, glad to get back onto topics that wouldn't raise my ire at the teen. Who knew what I might let slip if that happened? "I've never been to England." But one of my fellowship applications would take me there. If I got accepted. (Cross fingers!)

"I have. And Oxford's a better school than Eli, even."

I bit my lip to hold back a smile and nodded. Okay, now he was just trying to piss me off. Join Dragon's Head to screw with the Diggers. Go to Oxford because Eli wasn't good enough. Maybe he was more like his dad than I'd thought. Or maybe he was just a teenager bored out of his skull and trapped on Cavador Key. Either way, I think he'd cashed in his last sympathy point with me, and I was relieved when Odile appeared a few moments later in search of a spare broadsword.

"Greeks didn't use broadswords," Darren volunteered. "Their swords looked very different. Besides, they used spears mostly, and I'd definitely have some with me to kill a sea monster." He pretended to catch himself. "Oops, did I reveal too much?"

I rolled my eyes. The little snot.

Odile, however, was much taken with the young know-it-all, and took him on board as a "story consultant." He looked very much in his element instructing George on the proper way to tie a toga, which apparently was something the latter had never learned in all his youthful spying on Cavador Key.

"Of course," the teenager was saying, "a toga's pretty anachronistic as well. Perseus would have been wearing a chiton."

"Oh, really?" Odile said, practically batting her eyelashes at him. "Do you know how to make one of those?"

Beside me, Jenny snickered. "You're so *knowledgeable*," she mocked. "So big and strong and masculine, with your ancient costuming know-how."

Demetria smothered her laugh in a pile of scales. "Aww, have pity on the poor guy. He's starstruck. It's a story he can tell his friends at school."

"He doesn't have a school," I said.

"Or access to the Internet," Jenny added. "Or he'd be the most popular kid on MySpace."

"Screw MySpace," Clarissa said. "He'd have some mighty fine pictures to sell to the tabloids if he wanted."

And I believed Darren would do just that, given our conversation in the rec room earlier.

Done convincing Darren of his profound desire to finish all the hems, Odile sauntered over to the Diggirls and plopped herself down. "So, Amy," she said, "what do you think of this whole break-in situation? You were so quiet during breakfast. It's not like you to keep mum on the subject of a conspiracy."

I shrugged. "I haven't a clue. It's either the guys on the other island, or Kadie. Honestly, I'm starting to lean toward the other island."

"Not you, too," Demetria groaned.

"Why?" Odile asked me.

Because Poe had promised me that Kadie wasn't involved. Then again, Poe had told me last fall that Kurt Gehry had nothing to do with Jenny's disappearance, though it turned out that the older man knew exactly where she'd gone and even a good chunk of the reason why. And Poe had been protecting him, as well as the secret of Elysion. Poe, who even now was enjoying an afternoon on Kadie Myer's boat.

Remind me why I was kissing this guy?

"I don't know. It just seems a bit sophomoric for her."

Odile blew a strand of hair out of her eyes. "I don't know her that well, but I'm inclined to agree. I remember she had quite the ice queen rep on campus when we were freshmen."

I hadn't run in Kadie's circles at all, and she'd passed the torch to a new generation of well-bred queen bees (like Clarissa) by the time I understood the social strata of Eli enough to figure out who she was or what she was like. I'd have to take Odile's word on that one.

"The temper tantrum bitch-fit wouldn't appeal to her," she went on. "She's more likely to slip poison in your afternoon tea than get her hands dirty with a paint can."

"How . . . vivid of you."

Odile laughed. "Well, someone's got to pick up the slack if you aren't going to provide the theories, *chica*." She cast me a concerned look. "Still hung up on Brandon?"

"Still?" I echoed. "How quickly do you want me to get over it?"

"Quick. I half expected you to be in the middle of a rebound right about now."

I swallowed. "With whom? There's no one here but us Diggers."

"Never stopped you before," Jenny snapped.

"I thought we'd tabled this conversation," Demetria said.

"Huh?" Odile looked at Demetria, confused.

"Society incest is a bad idea," I said. "In summation." She didn't need to know that a rebound was a pretty darn good description for my latest trip to the shower house. "You missed the Diggirls' last debate on the subject."

Odile let out a delicate snort. "*Society incest* might be the most ridiculous term I've ever heard," she said. "Fuck who you want to. It's not illegal. If you worried about 'incest' in L.A., no one would ever get laid."

"So clearly," Demetria said, "it's not something you've ever worried about."

"Can we please change the subject?" Clarissa asked. "I never thought I'd say this, but I really wish Mara were here to encourage us to talk about something other than our sex lives."

"Or lack thereof," Jenny corrected. "Please."

Demetria groaned. "Am I getting that bad? Really? Clearly, I'm the one who needs to get laid."

Odile shrugged and rose to her feet, brandishing the anachronistic broadsword a bit more skillfully than one would expect for an actress who'd never appeared in a period piece. "Isn't that what 'social networking' is really code for? Besides, we don't *just* hook up with one another and talk about sex. We also play dress-up and commit capers. And then sometimes we have those boring political debates." She sheathed the sword in a leather scabbard. "I prefer the sexy stuff."

Clarissa dropped her face into her hands and sighed. "Where's a gang of conspiracy theorists when you really need them?"

I hereby confess:
I wanted to believe
it could be that easy.

16.
Sunstroke

Midafternoon, our club was engrossed in rehearsals for the evening's skit, Darren had returned to the Gehrys' house, Salt had reported back from his patrol that there was no sign of any trespassers having infiltrated Cavador Key that morning, and the Myers' boat pulled into the slip with a rather impressive catch of shellfish. We were all surprised when Kadie approached us on the lawn. She walked right up to Demetria.

"Hi," she said with perky purpose. "I wanted to apologize for my behavior yesterday. It was pretty inexcusable. Also, we caught a couple of snappers and as many lobsters as our license will allow, and we thought maybe we could all have them for dinner?"

Demetria looked incredibly amused, but before she had gathered her wits enough to cop an attitude, Clarissa accepted on the club's behalf. After all: lobster.

"Look at it this way," George said when Demetria protested later. "She's apologizing. Extending the olive branch. Isn't that a step forward?" He turned to Jenny. "Explain the whole forgiveness thing to her, will you?"

"To forgive is divine," Jenny said. "Especially when it involves drawn butter."

"Yeah," Harun agreed. "Not that I eat shellfish. But it's true. She's not saying, 'Accept my bigoted principles and join me at the table.' She's saying, 'I was a homophobic bitch and I'm sorry. Lobster anyone?' There's a big difference."

"And now that we've endured this very special episode of *On Cavador Key*," Odile said, "can we get back to rehearsals?"

Sighing, I climbed back under the rank tail end of the sea monster, inwardly grumbling about being hidden from sight when Poe and Malcolm came by. Soon after, George staged a mutiny, and the whole party adjourned to the beach to relax for the rest of the afternoon. I gave in and joined them (with the stipulation that I'd stay way back on land). Ben and Harun went to coax a cooler full of drinks out of Cook, and we all took off for the nearest stretch of sand, toting reading material, sunscreen, board games, beach blankets, and a few weathered boogie boards.

I donned sunglasses and lay on my blanket, flipping idly through a back issue of *The New Yorker* and watching my fellow knights play in the surf. From this distance, it even looked like fun, all that splashing and awkward balancing on the board. The water was almost turquoise in the sunlight, like the inside of a swimming pool, and looked just cool and inviting enough to counteract the afternoon heat. Maybe if I just dipped my feet in . . .

"Yo." Malcolm plopped down beside me. "You keeping dry, Amy?"

"You know it," I said. "How was the boat?"

"Awesome." He stretched out beside me, and from behind the safety of my sunglasses, I saw Poe standing above us, shaking out another beach blanket to my left. "Frank taught me how to use a speargun."

Poe chuckled. "*Tried* to teach you, you mean." He opened a book onto his lap, but I wasn't quick enough to catch the title. It might have been in French. "We very narrowly missed making a slight detour to the local hospital, the way Mal here shoots."

"Hey," Malcolm said, sitting up. "I figured it out. Eventually." He looked at my back, bare except for the strings of my bikini top, and pressed his thumb against my skin. "Amy, are you wearing sunscreen? You're going to burn."

I glanced over my shoulder at the mark Malcolm's fingertip had left. "Oh, I forgot."

"I have some," Poe said quietly.

I looked at him over the rim of my glasses. "Do you want to get my back?"

He never got a chance to answer, as Clarissa returned, dripping wet and on a mission. "Did you see where Jenny went?"

We all looked up at her. "No," I said. "She's not down at the water with the rest of you all?"

"No," Clarissa said. "She's gone."

Oh my God. Undertow. I shot into a kneeling position and scanned the shore for signs of her dark head. "Oh, no! Is she a decent swimmer?"

Clarissa rolled her eyes. "I don't think she drowned, loser. Harun's disappeared, too."

Oh. How foolish of me.

"I mean, who does she think she's kidding?"

I sighed. "Clarissa, why is this such a big deal for you? Let them have their fun."

"Yeah," Malcolm agreed. "Are you jealous of them or something?"

Clarissa huffed.

"I think you are," Malcolm went on, a smile tugging at his lips. "If you had a little Spring Break luvah of your own, you wouldn't be half so uptight right now."

"I care about the reputation of this club, is all," Clarissa said. "Jenny already threatened it once last semester. I don't want her risking things again."

Malcolm stood and swung his arm around Clarissa's shoulders. "You know what we're going to do right now?" He started leading her up the path to the house. "We're going to break into the kitchen and I'm going to show you how to make a patented Cabot Cuba Libre using a recipe that, I kid you not, my grandfather got from Fidel Castro himself."

"Wouldn't that make it a patented Castro Cuba Libre?" Poe asked. Malcolm shot him a look and led Clarissa away.

"So what do you think is really her problem?" Poe asked me when they were out of earshot and we were, once again, alone.

I shook my head. "No idea." But she'd always been a tad on the pissy side. Maybe she was just angry that we were harping so hard on Kadie Myer. After all, they had been friends since Kadie was a senior.*

"Do you still want me to get your back?"

I glanced up at him. "What do you think?" I sat up, slid back until I was facing away from him, and pulled my ponytail out of the way. Seconds later, his hands were on my shoulder blades, spreading the cool lotion over my sand-flecked skin. I scooped up some sand and let it fall between my fingers. "So, I was thinking," I began. "I don't really know much about you."

---

*The confessor is pretty underwhelmed by her fellow knight's choice of companions. Felicity and Kadie don't rank high on her list of potential friends. But then again, Clarissa's not the one making out with Poe.

"Yeah you do."

"I mean, I know about your parents and stuff...but you have that whole file on me. It's hardly fair."

"And it should be fair?" He slipped his fingers under the tie at my back, spread a thin film of lotion there, then moved on.

"Fairer than that," I said.

"What do you want to know?" His hands were now tracing circles on my lower back, and I was pretty sure that this was the most thorough suntan lotion application ever. "This tattoo of yours..."

"I know, I know...*discretion*." I circled my fingers in the sand to mirror Poe's hands on my skin. I sneaked a peek at him over my shoulder and found his eyes glued to the ink. "Don't tell me, that kind of devotion to the society gets you all hot and bothered."

He lifted his gaze to mine and smiled in affirmation. The moment had *kiss* written all over it. But the rest of the club was only a few yards away.

"Let's go have that lesson now," he whispered, and I shivered, despite the warm Florida sun.

"And put up with the same grief as Jenny and Harun?" I asked.

"I'll go one way, you go another, and we'll meet up," Poe said.

I ratified the plan and watched as he packed up and headed back to the compound. For appearances' sake, I took the slightly longer route past the girls' cabin. As long as I was planning a rendezvous, I might as well pause for a quick application of lip gloss. But when I reached the cabin, I found Darren Gehry standing at the door.

"What are you doing?" I asked.

He ducked his head, ashamed to have been caught. "I just wanted to—"

"What?" I strode up to him. "You wanted to what? Break in?" Hadn't we had enough of that already?

"No!" he said, looking hurt. "God, no. I just wanted to see what had happened. Everyone's been talking about the damage. I just wanted to see it. Jesus." He stuck his hands in his pockets and looked past me.

"Oh, well." I frowned. "Come on, let me show you." I leaned past him and undid the brand-new combination lock Salt had installed on our door. Thankfully, the code was something other than 312. Salt's devotion to all things Rose & Grave clearly couldn't overcome the fact that Master Locks come pre-programmed.

Darren followed me inside and took in the dingy surroundings. "Wow, you guys must have cleaned a lot of this up."

"Why do you say that?"

"Well, don't kill me for saying so, but it's not nearly as bad as what I'd been hearing." He traced a line of paint on the wall. "You washed off the swear words, at least."

Swear words. How cute.

"Which one is Odile's?" he asked.

I smiled. Someone here had a cru-ush. "The one where the blankets aren't covered in paint," I said, gesturing to the freshly made-up bunk.

He looked at her luggage, her pillow (I resisted pointing out that she'd never actually slept on it) and the traveling clothes she'd tossed on the bed.

"Were you expecting something special?" I couldn't help but ask. "Something other than a Samsonite roll-aboard?"

He shrugged. "Am I being a big dork?"

"No," I said. "Just normal. I bet I'd be a mess if I met some of the politicians who come to your family's Christmas parties."

"That's different."

Yeah. Condoleezza Rice hadn't yet appeared in lingerie in *Maxim*.

Clarissa materialized at the door, and clutched a hand to her chest. "Oh, Amy! It's you. You surprised me." She glanced over at Darren. "Hi."

He waved back. "Thanks for showing me around," he said to me, and brushed past her and out into the sunlight.

Clarissa came inside. "That poor kid," she said. "I mean, I'll never forgive him for ruining my top, but I suppose in the scheme of things..." she waved halfheartedly at her destroyed bag, "it could have been worse." She took in the sight of me applying lip gloss and still scented heavily with lotion. "Are you done with the beach?"

"I was thinking of—"

"Can I talk to you?"

I looked at her. For the first time in I don't know how long, I really examined Clarissa. Her hair had split ends. Her manicure was chipped. She'd actually put on a couple of pounds (though I thought it looked fabulous on her). Clearly, Clarissa's Spring Break had been no more relaxing than mine, and she seemed to need a vacation even more than I did. I recalled her short temper since we'd arrived. "Sure," I said. I'd deal with Poe when he showed up.

We sat on the porch and Clarissa clasped her hands in her lap. "I haven't told anyone," she said. "Felicity...I couldn't. I mean, we're friends and all, but it's like we're rivals, too. Always trying to one-up each other. With grades, with toys, with men..." She glanced at me. "Until Brandon of course. I think she really does love him."

"I know she does," I said flatly. *Ixnay on the Andonbray, huh?*

"I'm sorry."

I waved her off. "It's fine. I don't want to talk about it. What's going on with *you*?"

She was silent for several long moments. "I don't know what I'm going to do next year."

My brow furrowed. "I thought you were going to work for McKinsey?"

"I lied." She buried her face in her hands. "I couldn't really tell anyone. But I didn't get offers from any of the places I applied."

"Oh, honey," I said, and threw an arm around her. "It's only March." And heck, I didn't know what I was doing, either. Who was I to comfort her?

"No," she said. "I'm not going to get a job. It's like college applications all over again." I felt her shake underneath my arm. "Except this time, I don't have my *daddy* to bail me out." She expelled a pent-up breath. "God, I'm such a spoiled brat. I've been sailing by all these years, convinced that I'd proven myself. But it's starting all over again. And I don't even know if I *want* to be a consultant. But that's what you *do*, you know?"

No, I didn't know. "I'm not going to—"

"Amy, what am I going to do? I need to find a job." She looked up, her eyes red. "I can't spend the rest of my life living off my family. Just looking at Malcolm earlier—I envy him so much. He gave his family the finger, went off, did his own thing. And he made it work."

"He's working on a fishing boat," I pointed out. I could hardly envision Clarissa with a chum bucket.

"He's going to grad school!" she cried.

"You could go to grad school," I said.

"And do what?" she said. "I can't let it be an excuse, like everyone else does. A reason to put off the future for a few more years."

I dropped my hand to my side. Was that what my

applications were all about? Putting off the future? After all, it wasn't like I saw myself in academia on a permanent basis. I wasn't interested in becoming a professor.

"I'm sorry," she said. "I shouldn't have said that." She swallowed. "I shouldn't have said a lot of the things I've been going on about. It's just—you were right. I'm jealous. Jenny was such a mess last semester, and now she's got it all together. Happy, and starting her little company, and in love—no, I don't care what anyone else says, there is something going on with them. And you know what? I don't really care. It's just that I think about the things my dad said about us, about how we'd turn into a singles club or a soap opera, and I wonder . . . maybe he was right? And if he was right, then why did we bother fighting the patriarchs? If we hadn't fought, maybe I wouldn't be . . ." She trailed off, looked out into the woods.

I followed her gaze and saw Poe standing there, watching us. I waved at him and he waved back, then melted into the trees.

"And everyone keeps slamming Kadie," she went on. "Like she's this total worthless witch, and Demetria keeps acting like I'm just like her—"

"That's not true!" I said. "You're not like Kadie in any of the bad ways. Demetria's just a little brash when she gets upset."

"And I think, is that all I'm cut out for? Like Kadie? Just be a vicious, backstabbing, little society wife, and forget that I've got an Eli diploma in my closet? Like maybe that's my unavoidable fate? Or just easy enough that there's no point fighting it?"

And much as I hated to admit it, some of that rang true. This is the problem with being both really smart and a little screwed up. You're able to concoct the most believable self-defeating positions.

"No," Clarissa said, as if coming to a decision. "I don't mean that. I just can't help it—my dad's voice echoing in my head all the time. I don't want to be that person. But I'm not sure I've figured out an alternative. And I hate all you people who have."

I sighed. Well, *I* hadn't. "We're not what your dad predicted we'd be, Clarissa."

"No?" she said. "I am. I'm treating the girls here like I do my friends everywhere else. I'm jealous and competitive and awful."

"You're not awful," I said, recalling how, even a year ago, I thought the exact opposite. "You're ambitious—even if you don't know what for—and that comes with a strong sense of competition. It doesn't make you evil to think bad things about your friends from time to time." At least, I hoped it didn't, or someone should fit me for a black hat and a twirly mustache. I was regularly jealous of Lydia, and vice versa. But we loved each other, and we stood by each other when it counted.

"My dad didn't do that. Not with the Diggers."

"That's crap," I said. "Diggers are the same as everyone else. You don't think they stab one another in the back? You don't think they choose other concerns over this society? Kurt Gehry screwed P—Jamie over when he didn't agree with him. The President tossed Gehry to the wolves last month. No matter what our oaths are, we're not always going to be friends with someone just because they're Diggers. And it's not just this year, not just the addition of women. It's all of us. Look at your dad and what he did to us."

"Dad didn't think we *were* Diggers."

"He was wrong. He's wrong now, too. We haven't devolved into a dating club just because some of us have hooked up." I put my hands on her shoulders and faced her. "You are going to figure out what you want to do. And when you do, I pity the people who get in your way."

She smiled then, weakly, but still with a hint of the Cuthbert spark. "I'd better," she said. "Because I don't have any more Monets to give away."

I chuckled at that, but was still worried. In this atmosphere of sharing, should I reveal my own secret?

"I wonder what Jamie was doing lurking around here," she said. "You notice he's always hanging around? I kind of got the idea on the beach earlier that Malcolm was trying to get away from him. Guess he finally wised up about that weirdo."

Maybe not.

And I wondered if Clarissa was right in one respect—if Malcolm was trying to leave us alone with each other. Poe said he hadn't told his friend about us, but that didn't mean Malcolm couldn't figure it out for himself. George had.

"Actually," I said, and took a deep breath. "I'm supposed to meet with Jamie right about now. He's helping me with swimming." Okay, so not the whole truth.

Clarissa's expression flashed from confused to polished almost instantaneously. "Really? That's . . . nice. I didn't know."

"Yeah." *And we've been making out. Quite a lot, to be honest. And he's a pretty good kisser. And funny, which you don't realize at first, but yeah. Really funny. I think I'm starting to like him, Clarissa. Also a lot. So stop calling him a weirdo.*

And yet, none of those things made it into verbalizations. I slipped my feet in and out of my borrowed flip-flops.

"Shouldn't you go catch him?"

"Are we done talking?"

Clarissa tossed her hair back. "I'd say so. I've never been one for endless therapy sessions." She squeezed my hand as I stood. "But thanks, Amy. It felt really good to get that off my chest."

"I know the feeling," I said. But the truth was, I only wanted to.

———

The afternoon passed quietly. Poe actually did take me for a swimming lesson—a real one, and for the most part, we kept our hands off each other. He taught me to blow bubbles, to float on my back, to tread water, and, finally, to do something incredibly scary called the dead man's float.

"Breathe, Amy. When you breathe, you're lighter than water," he said as I spluttered to the surface again, saved from hysteria as much by Poe's sure hands at my waist as by the fact that we were only chest-deep. "The reason this is good to learn is that it doesn't take much energy to just float, unlike treading water. So if you ever fall off a boat again, you can do this for a lot longer."

"Yeah, but I can't hold my breath!" I said. "Just thinking about it freaks me out. Why can't I float on my back instead?"

"Go ahead," he said. I did, and promptly got a face full of water. "Oops, guess there was a wave."

I coughed, scrambled to my feet, and splashed him back. "I call foul!"

He splashed me again, angling his palm against the water to produce maximum effect.

"Not fair!" I cried, pushing water back at him. "You've had a lot more practice than me."

"You can say that again." He placed his fist on the surface and squeezed, sending a cunning little stream right at me. I hopped, and splashed back, but my own waves fell short.

Poe kept advancing, both fists now squirting jets of water in tandem.

"Stop!" I cried, laughing and wading away as fast as my feet would take me. But Poe was quicker, and then he leapt for me and we both went under.

I held my breath this time, and when he pulled me to the surface moments later, I wasn't coughing at all.

"There," he said, wrapping his arms around my waist as we bobbed. "You can do it."

I pulled him close. Amazing how much less afraid of water I was when it became my preferred make-out spot.

———

Since we planned to put on the pageant before sunset ("The better to let them see us with, my dears," as Odile said), the club of D177 congregated in the main house for an early dinner. The Myers were there, of course, presiding over their seafood feast, and some of the other patriarchs showed up to enjoy the atmosphere as well as the drawn butter. Salt was in a great mood, and Malcolm and Poe convinced him to whip up a batch of his apparently infamous Bahama rum punch, which tasted strongly of Campari and dyed red the lips and tongue of anyone who tasted it.

"Watch out for these," Poe whispered to me on the sly, as I finished my first serving. "They're sweet and you can drink them like water, but there's a reason they call it 'punch.' "

"Party pooper," I said, reaching for the almost empty pitcher. I refilled my glass with the dregs.

"I'll get more!" Darren volunteered, laying down his fork and grabbing the pitcher out of my hands.

"Good pretriarch," George said, and ripped into another tail. We'd invited Darren to join our table for dinner, since he'd given us so much help with the preparations for the skit.

A few minutes later he returned and grabbed his own glass first.

"Uh, uh, uh," Jenny said, lifting the filled-to-the-brim pitcher out of his hands. "The last thing we need is to get in trouble with your folks."

"Any more than we already are?" Clarissa said. "Let the poor kid have a drink."

"Yeah," said Odile. "Drinking ages are for wussies. It's not like he's about to get in a car or anything. There's no safer place to experiment."

But Jenny handed the pitcher off to Ben, on her other side, and Darren watched it make the rounds without him getting so much as a taste.

I just rolled my eyes and sipped (carefully!) at my drink. Interesting flavor, but I think I preferred the tang of our official drink, the 312, to the bitter/sweet taste of the punch. Darren pouted for a few moments, then brightened when George sneaked him a flask and a can of Coke.

Thus fulfilling our quota of illegal activities for the evening, we settled down to dinner. I dug into my blackened snapper and watched Ben and Clarissa have a lobstercleaning contest (Ben won, but admitted he was still ashamed at the trouncing he'd received from Demetria on the tennis court that afternoon).

As the mountain of seafood dwindled and the bottle of Campari started running low, we all drank a toast to our providers, Malcolm, Poe, and the Myers, and packed up for the hike out to the crescent beach. It was decided that Ben and Demetria would take the skiff out around the island, since I wasn't yet comfortable enough around water to play navigator. I'd only get in the rowboat once they'd pulled it into the relatively shallow zone of the lagoon.

So off we went, into the gathering Florida dusk. The roar of crickets and other insects in the woods drowned out the sound of the waves from the nearby shoreline. I kept my eyes turned toward the treetops, hoping for another glimpse of the ospreys, but we were all making too much noise for them to show themselves.

Odile had a steady lecture going as we walked. "And then, Kevin, you have to make sure to angle the sword so it gets the light of the sun, or they won't be able to see it. You don't need to move fast—it's more for looks than any—" She froze, covered her mouth with her hand, and gagged, shoulders convulsing so hard that she lost her balance and fell to her knees on the path, gasping as she began to vomit into the bushes.

Moments later, everyone else joined her.

I hereby confess:
Everyone, that is,
except me.

17.
Suspicions

There were several occasions, during the horrible quarter of an hour that followed, that I thought I, too, was going to be sick to my stomach. Projectile vomiting is not something anyone can watch with impunity. I almost lost my cookies just from listening to them.

Eventually, they recovered enough to stagger back to the main house. The skit was clearly off, even if half of our costumes hadn't been ruined in the deluge.

Oh. Ick. Amy... Would it be okay if I just skipped the details? Suffice to say I can go a long, long time without seeing anything like that again. Or hearing it. Or... smelling it.

"Food poisoning," I gasped out to Salt as I deposited my last semiconscious fellow knight on the porch. "I think they all need water. Or Gatorade. Or something."

Actually, I thought they all needed to be airlifted back to the mainland to have what was left inside their stomachs pumped.

Why hadn't I gotten sick? True, I'd stuck to the snapper rather than the spiny lobster, my Midwestern roots expressing horror at the idea of eating things with obvious eyes.* But still, every single lobster would have had to have been contaminated.

Harun was standing there, shaking his head at the carnage before him. He looked ill, to be sure, but then again, I bet I hardly looked the picture of health myself at that moment. Had he gotten sick?

"How do you feel?" I asked him.

He shook his head. "Sympathetic dry heaves. I can't stand watching people throw up. Otherwise…fine." He met my gaze and we spoke in unison. "What did you eat?"

Frank and Kadie Myer appeared on the porch, aghast at the sight before them. "What happened?" the patriarch asked in dismay.

"Your seafood, that's what," George replied, rolling onto his side. "Christ, what did you do? Ferment that shit in a shed?"

"How dare you!" Kadie cried, stepping forward (but not, I noted, near enough to be in smelling distance). "We had those fish in ice the moment we caught them! Why do you blame everything that happens to you on someone else?"

"Specifically, on us," Frank said. "I'm getting sick and tired of the prejudice this club harbors against its patriarchs."

Clarissa moaned. In the distance, I saw two more figures emerging out of the dark. Demetria and Ben, arms wrapped around each other for support, heaving their way up the path.†

---

* The confessor can do tails alone, but add the entire body, complete with green tomalley, and the deal is off.
† The confessor is not above the occasional pun.

Poe and Malcolm arrived on the scene soon after, looking none the worse for wear. "What happened?" my big sib asked, while Poe pulled the seething Myers aside and began talking to them in low voices.

"You don't want to know," I said, almost gagging at the thought. "Disgustingly vicious food poisoning."

Salt arrived with a giant pitcher of water and a stack of paper cups and we set upon rehydrating the troops. Luckily, the worst seemed to have passed. No one was looking green anymore, and there were no more relapses into uncontrolled... well, you know.

"Did anyone else eat the shellfish?" I asked. "Have you spoken to the other patriarchs?"

"Darren," Odile rasped. "Someone check on Darren."

"I'll go," Kadie said with a dismissive sniff. "You people smell like trash anyway."

"Don't be long, honey," Frank called after her. "We're leaving first thing tomorrow morning." Poe looked as if he was about to say something, but Frank stopped him. "No," he said. "I mean it. I'm sick of this. We have done everything we could for these bitches, bent over backward, humbled ourselves like you wouldn't believe, and they still treat us like we're somehow the enemy. I'm not going to stand here and be accused of things again and I'm certainly not going to let you keep insulting my wife like this. It's disgusting. You should all be ashamed of yourselves. And that goes for you, too, James. Where's your pride? You should be ashamed of tapping a club of Diggers such as these." And then he stormed off.

Salt poured another cup of water for our invalids, who were lolling about on the porch steps, clutching their stomachs. Harun returned from the kitchen with a packet of crackers and started doling them out (Jenny first). Poe clomped down the porch steps to where I knelt patting George comfortingly (yet gingerly) on the shoulder.

"Hey," I said softly as he passed. "Don't listen to him."

"Why not?" he snapped, loud enough for everyone to hear. "He's right. You guys are pathetic, ungrateful brats. Those two were trying to be nice to you and you spat all over them."

"To be fair," Demetria said, "we vomited. There was very little spitting."

"We were somehow supposed to help ourselves?" Ben said. "We got food poisoning. It wasn't their fault, but it happened."

"I suppose you expect us to swallow it, lest we appear ungrateful?" George said.

"Food poisoning, my ass," Poe said. "You're all just drunk."

"Leave them alone!" I said, standing and facing Poe. "Haven't they been through enough?"

Poe shook his head. "I ate as much lobster as the next person and I'm fine. Malcolm's fine. The Myers are fine."

"Lucky you," Jenny said.

"So what are you saying, that *we* did this to you?" Poe said in a low, dangerous tone.

"No!" I said quickly. Dude, what was with the misplaced guilt? "It was an accident. It was just a really, really sucky accident. Everyone thinks so—right, guys?" I nudged Demetria with my toe and she nodded, weakly.

"So why did you jump down their throats?" Poe asked.

"Because it was their seafood, man," Ben said. "Your seafood. You caught it."

"But we didn't do anything to it!" Malcolm said.

"No one is saying you did!" I tossed up my hands. "That's the definition of 'accident.'"

"It wasn't the food," Poe insisted.

"Well, it wasn't the alcohol," I said. "We were all drinking."

"Not all of us quite as much, though," Poe said. "It's not possible that you all just *happened* to get bad lobster and no one else did."

"Dude," Demetria croaked, "I don't feel drunk."

"What you did manage to accomplish, however," said Poe, in vintage frost, "was to alienate yet another of the patriarchs with your groundless accusations."

"That's uncalled for," I said. "No one is accusing anyone of anything here. And when we did, we had plenty of grounds."

"You just told the Myers they tried to poison you."

"No, we informed them that we *were* poisoned. Agency unknown."

"By *their* olive branch."

"If the shoe fits..." I said.

"Jesus, you two," George groaned from the porch steps. "Get a room already."

Poe stiffened and addressed the assemblage (while I did a quick check to see if anyone else had noted George's comment). "I'm getting a little sick of cleaning up your messes."

"Don't go into the woods, then," Jenny said.

"It's not our fault that they took it too personally," I cried. "Don't you think it's the people rolling around on the ground here who are the real injured party?"

Poe looked away, and I reached for his arm.

"Look, I know you spent time mending fences today, and it's appreciated. But this? This is all a misunderstanding—I'll go explain it to Frank if you want."

He shook me off. "Go tend to your wounded, Amy."

I bit my lip, torn between snapping back at him and just letting it go. It was clear where Poe's loyalty lay. He'd protect any slight against the society, even a perceived one. The shaky truce he'd engineered between the Myers and D177 had backfired, big-time, and he'd decided it was somehow our fault. Poe brushed past me and he and Malcolm retreated to the boys' cabin.

Kadie appeared at the base of the path. "Darren isn't feeling well, either," she reported. "He apparently went to bed early."

George dropped his head into his hands, no doubt remembering the flask he'd handed over. Alcohol certainly couldn't have helped matters if Darren, too, had been victim to the food poisoning. Demetria staggered to her feet and approached Kadie.

"Hey," she said, her voice strangely subdued. "Thanks for checking on him for us. I'm sorry if anything we said came across as confrontational. We know you only meant well when you offered us dinner."

Kadie narrowed her eyes. "Whatever," she said, lifting her chin in the air. But as she brushed past Demetria, she paused. "You know, Frank lives in this dream world that no one in his life knows what's going on. But I know everything. The very idea that he and the rest of you all can bring barbarians to this island belies that. Your secrets aren't really what make you interesting. It's your dedication to this organization—the one you make for life. The one you make for the good of everyone that came before you. But that's not something I see in your class."

"No," Clarissa said. "When we stand, it's with one another. And you would, too, if you'd been through what we have."

"Oh, boo hoo," Kadie said. "The rebel Diggers. Disavowing patriarchs right and left for every slight—whether real or imagined. You don't even know what you've done, do you? At first, you had every patriarch in the country terrified that you'd repeat the process on them, but now they just don't give a shit. You people don't matter. You're not playing the game, you're not part of the team, and you're missing out on the whole point of joining a society. Aren't you supposed to be networking for the future? All you're doing is burning bridges. In another month or so, you'll have tapped a new class and then it will be *you* who are disavowed, from everyone." She shook her head and looked us over. "Just a little friendly advice." And then she was gone.

Afterward, we all sat there in silence for several long moments, and then George said, "Way to kick us when we're down, bitch."

Demetria snorted. "Can I go beat her up *now*?"

A few chuckled, but Clarissa still looked worried. "Do you think what she's saying is true? Maybe that's why no one seemed to be particularly concerned when our cabin was broken into. Because they all hate us and don't take us seriously."

At least one patriarch took it seriously, though. Poe.

"I don't care," George said.

"Easy for you to say," Kevin said. "Your dad is always going to be on your side."

"And I'm always going to be on yours," George said. "If getting patriarch support means kissing the asses of Frank Myer or Kurt Gehry, then I don't need it. I never needed this society, and I can't think of another person here who does, either. We've all got our jobs, we've all got our graduate schools. Fuck them."

Clarissa looked down and let her long hair fall around her face.

"You're right," said Odile. "We don't need it—not now anyway."

"Not *you* anyway," Clarissa muttered.

"But we've apparently gotten a reputation—and I don't think it's just among people like Gehry and Myer," Odile went on.

I thought back. When was the last time I'd spoken to Gus, who'd given me my internship last summer? Had we really been neglecting patriarch relations—even the friendly ones? If only Josh weren't in Spain. He'd have a much clearer picture of how things were actually going.

"Any way you cut it, though," Harun said, "no one is to blame for what happened tonight. We weren't being rude, and the Myers weren't working against us."

"Yeah," Jenny said. "If you ask me, they were just looking for an excuse to leave. Maybe we made it easy on them, but it didn't take much for them to blow up in our faces."

"I think we're all agreed on that much," Clarissa said. And she didn't add (though she didn't have to) that it didn't make Kadie's accusations any less of a fact.

So what was Poe's excuse? Yeah, he'd stuck his neck out and it hadn't worked, but he wasn't stupid enough to believe it was our fault. So why had we been on the receiving end of his attack? Why had *I* been on the receiving end?

"Let's get out of here," Odile said. "I totally need a shower after all that."

"The sick or the lecture?" Clarissa asked.

"Both!"

"How are you all feeling?" I asked.

Ben shrugged. "Fine. I guess I got it out of my system."

"I know the righteous anger burned all my nausea away," Demetria said. "And, I reiterate, can I go kick her ass now?"

"I have no problem with that." George pushed to his feet. "And I second the shower idea."

Clarissa laughed. "Not together, bonehead."

Though I didn't exactly feel my freshest, I'd already

used up my shower points for the day, and certainly didn't need them as much as my fellow knights, so I let them commandeer the island's meager water supply and walked with them back to the cabin, where they left me behind (after thorough toothbrushing all around) and I contemplated the logistics of a cold sponge bath.

I was just stripping down when there was a knock at the screen frame. I tossed on a fresh shirt and went to the door.

"Amy," Poe said.

I crossed my arms and glared at him. "What do you want?"

"To talk. Let me in."

I shook my head. "Don't think so."

"Okay." He took a deep breath. "Are you all right? I can't believe I didn't ask you that before."

"You're not the only one." I chewed on the inside of my cheek.

"I'm sorry. I shouldn't have yelled at you."

"You shouldn't have doubted us," I prompted.

"I—" He sighed. "No, you're right. I shouldn't have. It was just . . . reflex."

"Reflex!" I said, incredulous. "Reflex to attack my club?"

"Reflex to get screwed over by people I'd been trying to help." He narrowed his eyes. "Remember last fall, when you topped off my horrible year by kicking me out of the tomb?"

I blinked, but my eyes started to burn. "Yes," I said softly. "I do. And you repaid me by casting your lot with Elysion."

"I wasn't the only one." But he'd been instrumental in getting that group founded. He'd been the one to tell them about the secret meeting spot inside the tomb. He'd been the one to lie to my face about it when I'd gone to him for help. And yet, I'd forgiven him. I'd forgiven all of them. The club was reunited.

Of course, Poe wasn't in our club.

"Jamie, that's water under the bridge by now." Wasn't it? He had to believe that.

He looked away. "All I know is that this isn't the first time you've told patriarchs to go fuck themselves when they're not convenient to you. So I'm sorry for jumping to that conclusion, but you should at least recognize why I did."

I put my hand against the screen. "You're not *convenient* to me, you know."

He laughed, mirthlessly. "I know that. Believe me, Amy. It's painfully evident how difficult it is to work me into your schedule."

"That's not what I meant."

He turned his gaze to mine. "That's what I mean, though. Your friends can't stand me. And you'd pick them in an instant."

"I'm not picking anyone!" I said, though at that moment, all I could think of was Clarissa telling Kadie that our club stood on our own. "Or rather, I'm picking everyone."

He looked at my hand on the screen, then back at me. "Yeah, right."

The Diggirls would be back soon. I opened the screen door and stepped out onto the dark porch. "Let's take a walk."

Poe didn't miss a beat. "Fine," he said, in a voice that meant *See?* but still he followed me out into the darkness. We went to the edge of the forest behind the cabin and stood there, alone except for the sound of night insects and the scent of ocean breezes. "I told Malcolm," he said abruptly.

My heart raced. I was tempted to ask Poe why he'd spilled the beans, but I knew the reason. Society oaths trumped all. And if he was confused, who better to go to than his favorite brother? "Oh?" was all I could trust myself to say.

"He says he never thought I'd be this stupid."

The words were like a slap in the face. Why would my big sib say something like that about me? It was as bad as Lydia and Josh. "That's not—"

"I think he's wrong, for the record."

"Oh?" I repeated, eloquent as a rock.

"I can definitely be this stupid."

I looked at him, heart breaking. Malcolm was right. I never should have dragged Poe into this. Not if he liked me the way Malcolm believed he did. And from the past few days, I was starting to believe it, too. "This was supposed to be easy," I whispered. "Like back on the beach that day."

"When I said I'd smash the Nazi plates in the tomb for you?"

"A lover's token?" I said with a little laugh.

"Yeah, but for that kind of vandalism, I'd expect a lover's reward." Now he laughed, too, right before he got serious again. "I wish it could be easy, Amy. I do."

I nodded, slowly.

"Sorry."

Not as sorry as I was.

———

The rest of the evening passed with relatively little drama. Whatever affliction my fellow knights had suffered, it was entirely gone by the time they were back from their showers, and everyone was in high spirits again. There was even talk of returning to the crescent beach and actually doing the stunt, but as soon as we surveyed the damage to the costumes, we nixed that idea flat.

Good thing, too, because apparently Ben and Demetria hadn't turned their faces over the side of the boat when they got sick. They said the sea monster was a real mess.

Instead, we settled into the couches of the rec room and sampled the meager offerings of Cavador Key's video library. And I do mean video, as in VHS. Let's put it this way: I had no idea that Steven Seagal made as many movies as he did.

"Are you kidding?" Demetria exclaimed, pushing the first into the ancient VCR. "He's a legend! He's an eco-warrior!"

"And a vegetarian Buddhist," Kevin added.

"And so not as hot in real life," Odile said.

Everyone stared at her.

"Well, he's like sixty now," she said in her own defense.

"And not hot . . . like ever!" Clarissa pointed out.

Jenny looked at the screen, tilted her head to the side, and made a noncommittal grunt. I noticed she was sitting next to Harun, their shoulders all but touching, and began to feel some of that jealousy Clarissa had mentioned.

Wait a second . . . vegetarian? Wasn't Poe one as well? I'd certainly seen vegetarian cookbooks in his apartment last fall, and I'd never actually seen him eat a piece of meat. When we'd gone out for pizza that time, I'd been the one to try the white clam, while he'd stuck with tomato, basil, and mozzarella on his slices. Furthermore, for all Malcolm's talk of spearguns, I never got the impression that Poe had taken part in bringing in the catch.

And yet, he said he'd eaten "just as much lobster as the next person." Either he ate seafood after all or . . . he was lying.

The only question was, why?

I hereby confess:
I never saw it coming.

18.
Sweetness and Light

I didn't sleep well that night. Every time a twig snapped in the woods, I was sure it was the vandals, back to finish the job on our cabin. Anytime one of my cabinmates rustled on her bunk, I was positive I was in for another round of bearing witness to their retching. And every time I started to drift back into unconsciousness, a single thought nagged at me: Poe had lied.

He'd fed me this big lecture about how I wasn't being fair to him, and all along, he'd been handing out bullshit of his own. He'd lied before, too, whenever it worked in his favor. Keeping secret his pact with Gehry, going all over town to help me find Jenny, without ever once admitting that he wanted to find her to see what she knew about Elysion. He did it so smoothly that I hadn't caught him in the act until it was way too late.

But what would he gain by lying about eating lobster? What was the point? It made no sense. If he wanted to prove that all the lobster wasn't contaminated, he could have pointed out that Malcolm and Myer had eaten it, too, not to mention several other patriarchs.

There was another rustle from the vicinity of the bushes outside, and I rolled over and pulled my pillow on top of my head. That sounded way too big to be a night bird or a reptile. Were there raccoons on this island, or had Salt taken that "night patrol" suggestion to heart? Maybe it was the people from the other island. If so, I wished they would keep it down. Vandalism was one thing, but the least the intruders could do was let me get a good night's sleep.

———

At breakfast the next morning, I watched carefully to see if Poe added any bacon to his plate (he didn't). There was, however, milk in his coffee and he seemed to have no problem downing a pile of scrambled eggs. But all that meant was that he wasn't a vegan.

And perhaps that I watched him a tad too much.

The members of my club were famished, seeing as how they'd all emptied their stomachs the previous evening. The Myers were back at their table, pointedly ignoring the students. They'd even placed their luggage between their table and our own, like a monument to their affronted attitude. Demetria merely rolled her eyes when she saw it. In her opinion, she had informed us that morning, folks get one chance to apologize. Kadie's had been when she offered us lobster. Demetria's had been last night, when she tried to explain that they hadn't thrown it all up on purpose. When Kadie didn't accept, the gauntlet had been tossed.

"What did you do," Jenny asked. "Drill holes in their hull?"

But Demetria wouldn't tell us. "Don't want you implicated in my crimes, *chicas*," she said with a wink.

"Ten bucks, she slipped a snake in Kadie's toiletry bag," Clarissa said.

But if Demetria had left the cabin this morning, I hadn't seen it. As I said, I was up almost all night.

All during breakfast, Kadie Myer spoke in whispers to another patriarch's wife.

"Talking about us, I assume?" Clarissa muttered into my ear.

"No," Jenny said, in a voice almost too low to hear. "Shhh..." She pulled out her Sidekick and started typing away. It took the rest of us a moment to understand she was transcribing:

K: Thy ddnt evn no whr ther son ws. F he ws evn in house.

O: No!

K: Gry ws thr, lukin v ragged + strnge. Lk he ws on drugs.

O: Lk wife?

K: Xact. + I sed thr ws prob w/ food, ws D OK? Wife ddnt luk 4 hm. Sed = daren? = lk she ddnt no who he ws.

O: Thrs sumfin rely f* up w/ thm.

K: U sed it! + Thn ltl grl went upsters 2 chk, cme bk + sed he ws n bed + sic.

O: Wht parnts do?

K: Lukd releevd.

"How can you understand them?" Clarissa whispered. "How can you even hear them?"

Jenny just rolled her eyes and kept typing. They looked relieved that their son was ill? What kind of parents were the Gehrys? Or were they merely relieved that he was in his bed, since apparently, prior to that, they hadn't the slightest clue. Poor kid. No wonder he'd been vying for attention all week. He certainly wasn't getting enough at home. "Appointments" with his father, indeed!

Jenny's uncanny sense of hearing further revealed that the inside of the cottage was relatively neat, with a few exceptions. The couch in the living room was a mass of bedclothes. "Someone's not sleeping in their bed," Kadie mocked, in a voice loud enough for all of us to hear.

Around this time, I excused myself from the table to get another grapefruit half off the sideboard. I think I'd miss the citrus when I left Florida. My timing sucked, however, and I found myself reaching for the sugar canister at the same time as Poe, who'd come for a coffee refill. His fingers closed around the glass a split second before mine. Our thumbs almost brushed.

"Good morning," he said.

I kept my eyes glued to the sweetener packets. Maybe I should just grab a few Splenda and call it even.

He held the sugar out to me. "Ladies first."

I grabbed blindly at the canister and dumped some on my grapefruit. "Thanks." I shoved it back at him.

"You look tired."

And now I did turn my face to his, eyes blazing. "That's a hell of a compliment to give a *lady*."

His brow furrowed. "What's wrong?"

But I just clucked my tongue and turned away. Were all men as daft as that?

I felt his gaze on me all the way back to my seat.

After yesterday's debacle, everyone in the club decided to keep it low-key that morning. We packed a cooler of food and drinks and headed out to the closest beach. I floated the idea of returning to the crescent beach because the lagoon was shallow enough for me to splash around in, but since it meant going back on the path, no one wanted to take the chance of seeing (or smelling) the mess they'd made. Nevertheless, I gathered every scrap of courage in my system, and played, knee-deep, in the surf for a full ten minutes.

One SoBe, two issues of *U.S. News & World Report* (the most recent grad school guides), and a bag of pretzels later, it was time for lunch. Maybe this was what Spring Break was supposed to be. Forget romantic dramas or society intrigue. All you needed was a beach blanket and some junk food.

"Wow, you got some sun!" Malcolm said as I passed him on the path back to the main house.

"Did I?" Someone should hire Malcolm for some sort of skin cancer prevention squad. Dude was obsessed. I examined my arms. Crap. Sunscreen. I pressed my fingers against my skin and lifted them away, watching as the oblong white marks darkened to a decidedly pink tone. Not so bad. It would fade, but not peel. I hadn't quite hit lobster territory yet.

Lobster. That reminded me. "Can I talk to you for a minute?" I said to Malcolm as the rest of my club passed me and headed up the steps to the rec room. I waved them away.

His face fell. "If it's about what I think it's about, then no."

I grabbed his arm and steered him away from the others. "It's not, but if it were, I'd have every right to be pissed with you."

"And I wouldn't have the right to be pissed at you?" Malcolm replied in a low voice. "I told you all that stuff in confidence."

"And I kept your secret!" I said. Like always. "Tell me how I broke my promise."

He ran his hands through his blond hair and looked at me incredulously. "Are you kidding me? You . . . *acted* on it.

You made your choices based on the private information I gave you."

"So?"

"So, you promised me you wouldn't do anything."

"No," I corrected. "I promised I wouldn't humiliate him."

He snorted. "Well, you haven't done that, have you?" He patted his shirt and shorts. "Where in the world did I put that gold star?"

"What is your problem?" I asked. "Aren't you the one always encouraging me to hang out with him?"

"A mistake I won't be making again, I assure you. I don't offer my friends up as sacrificial lambs."

"Oh, no?" I said. "Isn't that exactly what you're *known* for doing, you and your string of fake girlfriends? You even wanted me to join their ranks."

"That was different."

"You bet it was!" I crossed my arms. "You used people terribly. I never lied to anyone, and what's more, I was having fun, too." Which was more than I could say for Malcolm and his beards.

"Oh, so because you lay down all your parameters in advance, that makes it okay? Guess George Prescott taught you a lot after all."

My mouth dropped open. "How dare you try to take the moral high ground with me? You broke Genevieve's heart. Willingly. Cavalierly." I shook my head. "Are you saying the difference is that she wasn't a Digger, and so wasn't supposed to have the same courtesy? Is that why you didn't tap her?" Is that why I was standing here right now?

Malcolm was silent for a moment, and when he spoke, all the anger was gone from his voice. "I regret so much what I did to Genevieve. I cared about her a lot, and you're absolutely right. I hurt her, and I shouldn't have. It was a cruel thing to do and I will never do something like that again." He scrutinized me. "So you see now—"

"No," I said. "It's not the same." And it didn't matter anyway. Poe and I were through.

He sighed. "Fine. Screw it. You don't listen to me, he doesn't listen to me. I'm not a fucking babysitter. What was it you wanted to ask me?"

"If Jamie's a vegetarian."

He stood there for a second, blinking at me. "Yeah, you clearly care for him *so* much. You don't even know something like that?"

"I thought I did." And in my defense, he wasn't exactly the most forthcoming individual on the planet.

"He is. Why?"

"Did he eat the lobster last night?"

Now Malcolm stepped back, eyes wide, face a mask of disbelief. "What the hell is your problem? Let it go already! So you all got food poisoning. What's the big deal?"

"Did he?" I pressed.

"I have no idea! I don't calorie count other people's plates."

"Try to remember," I said, urging.

Malcolm threw his hands in the air. "Probably not. Vegetarians don't tend to go for things with faces, remember?" At least that was something we had in common. "Why do you ask?"

I shrugged. "Because he told us all that he had been eating it. Last night when he was busy insisting we were a bunch of paranoid freaks. Curious, don't you think?"

And I walked away.

————

I don't know if Malcolm talked to Poe before lunch, or if the seed I planted had any effect at all on my big sib. But, as

I lingered over my grilled-cheese-with-tomato and chocolate milk, I noted the following:

1) Malcolm and Poe were sitting on opposite sides of the room.
2) Jenny and Harun were the only knights of D177 who hadn't made it in for lunch.
3) Frank and Kadie Myer had not yet left.

The dining room was packed to the brim, as if no one wanted to miss out on a hot lunch and be relegated to fending for themselves with questionable deli meat for the rest of the afternoon. They'd planned an island-wide barbecue for dinner, and Salt had only recently returned from the mainland, the small boat packed full of ribs, steaks, burgers, and fixings. Even Darren Gehry was present again, having apparently recovered from his bout with food poisoning as well. I watched him finish his third cupcake—iced in Eli blue frosting—and proceed to sweet talk Cook into letting him into the kitchen to lick the bowl. I chuckled when she capitulated. Apparently, she had a soft spot for boys with attitude problems.

"Change your mind?" I overheard another patriarch ask Frank toward the end of the meal. "I'm so glad to see it!"

"Nah," Frank said. "We're just having a little bit of engine trouble and I want to take a look at it before we sail out. Just in case."

Engine trouble? Why in the world would Demetria do something to the Myers that caused them to remain on the island? And even if she had a good reason, it seemed a bit beyond her to dismantle a ship's engine. When I looked back at Demetria, her grin had vanished, and as I watched, she excused herself from the table. I pursed my lips. Could no one in this organization be trusted anymore?

(Yes, okay, fine, it's not like I haven't kept my own secrets.)

"Dee, wait up," I said to her on the porch. "What's going on?"

"Nothing," she said without looking at me.

I took the steps down to the path. "This is going to sound crazy but…you didn't sabotage the Myers' boat, did you?"

She stopped and looked at me. "Amy, please, like I'd want them here any longer?"

"That's what I thought but…we all know you did something."

She bit her lip, then leaned her head in close. "Yeah, I did, but you can't tell anyone."

"That's what my oaths are for," I said, putting my hand over my heart.

"Okay, so the idiot left her shampoo in the shower house last night. Her name was right on it in black marker. Some designer product, sixty bucks an ounce. I just refilled the bottle with Nair."

I clapped my hand over my mouth to stifle a giggle. "You didn't!" Maybe I was growing paranoid after all. Why in the world would I suspect my fellow Diggirl of doing something so hard-core as destroying a yacht?

"Who knows if it will work, but I couldn't resist getting back at her." She glanced over her shoulder at the shower house. "But now I'm worried that she forgot to pack it."

"Let's double check!" We took off for the shower house, laughing all the way. This was what a society prank was really like. No nonsense about sabotaging gazillion-dollar boat engines. Just some hair remover in the beauty products. No vast, month-long conspiracies against the girl trying to steal your boyfriend. Simply break into her society's tomb and wreak havoc.

We'd just reached the door to the showers when a shout rent the air.

"Nooooooooo!" We froze, looked around. Where was that coming from?

"Oh, no! Help! Help! This is a travesty! This is the last straw!" On our left, the door to the tomb burst open and Salt came running out, his face a mask of hysteria, his shouts so loud they were almost hurting my eardrums.

At the main house, people had moved to the windows or spilled out onto the porch to see what all the fuss was about. Demetria and I trailed Salt up the path, where he'd ground to a halt at the base of the steps, still shouting at the top of his lungs, but so incoherently I couldn't follow a word he was saying. He held something white in his hands, but was waving it around so fast I couldn't get a good look.

"Total destruction...last straw...how could they... abominable...really have to call the police this time..."

"Salt, Salt," Malcolm said, hands extended, palms down. "What are you talking about? Did someone break into the tomb?"

"Yes!" And now he threw whatever he was holding onto the steps, where it struck with a loud *crack* and shattered. And I saw what they were. Broken bits of china. With little tiny swastikas on them.

"The whole set is smashed. Destroyed."

Oh my God. I looked up at Poe, and he was staring at me, too, his expression utterly unreadable.

"Eww, what is this, Nazi memorabilia?" Demetria said. "Good riddance, I say!" Guess she hadn't seen them on the tour after all.

"Miss!" Salt said, turning on her. "This is the island's

property. It's a monument to the hard work and sacrifice of one of our own in service to our country."

Jenny looked confused. "Hitler?"

Harun patted her on the shoulder. "I think he means a Digger in the army during World War II."

"That's not the point!" Malcolm said. "Someone broke into the tomb. That's the point."

Poe nodded, but he hadn't taken his eyes off me. "Was anything else destroyed, Salt? The cabinet? The furniture? The paintings?"

"No," the caretaker reported. "Just the china."

Poe's lips compressed to a thin line. "Call a meeting. I want every member of the Trust in the tomb in ten minutes."

"Of the Trust?" Demetria said. "What about the rest of us? Don't we all have a right to know who is on the island and why?"

Poe dragged his gaze away from me. "I think we've put on enough of a spectacle for the barbarians in the group. Everyone, go back to lunch. I'll take care of this."

Okay, what were the chances? Poe and I had been joking about smashing that china all week. He hadn't done it, had he? In some bizarre attempt to get my attention?

"Take care of what?" George scoffed. "Nothing was stolen, nothing was ruined that shouldn't have been, if you ask me. Change the locks and call it a day. Why does everything have to be such a big deal?"

Poe whirled on him. "Because someone has been systematically infiltrating both this island and the tomb back home. I want to know who it is, I want to know why, and I want it stopped, now."

"Why do you think it's the same people?" I asked, baffled. Clearly, Dragon's Head was responsible for the break-in at Eli, whereas the likely culprits here were the conspiracy theorists on the other island. I mean, if it hadn't been Poe himself.

And now he looked back at me. "I don't," he said simply, then announced at large, "Ten minutes," and walked past us all to the tomb, belying all of my suspicions. If he'd smashed the china, why would he need to see it for himself? Unless he was trying to cover those tracks and pretending to be more upset than he was. Salt hurried behind him, along with some other Diggers and patriarchs, all eager to see the extent of the damage. The barbarians and the rest of the knights clustered, whispering furiously to one another. George rolled his eyes and sat down on one of the rocking chairs, which seemed to me to be the most sensible reaction I'd seen so far. Like he'd said, what was the big deal? So a couple of really macabre bits of Digger booty got wrecked. So what?

Still, I stood there, in the middle of the path, completely unmoored. My mind spun with possibilities, lies, suspicions. *Was* Poe responsible for breaking the china? And if so, then why was he launching some big meeting to deal with the situation? Why would he lie like that? Why would he lie about eating that damn lobster?

And then I remembered our conversation on the moored boat that night, when he was so determined to make me believe that someone was after me and he was the only one who recognized it. It wasn't possible that this was for me, was it? That if I saw him taking charge of the situation, directing people, acting the part of avenging angel, that I'd somehow be impressed?

No. That was way too manipulative, even for someone who'd bought in to the Digger party line.

So why couldn't I shake my suspicions?

For that kind of vandalism, I'd expect a lover's reward.

Had he done it hoping I'd . . . reward him?

A hand clamped down on my wrist. "I need to talk to you," Poe hissed, and tugged me off the path. I had to almost run to keep up with him, and he pulled me around the back of the main house, away from any open windows, and into the shadow of its walls.

I whipped my arm back and crossed both over my chest. He stood across from me, eyes wide and disbelieving.

"What the *hell* were you thinking?" he asked.

"What the *hell* are you talking about?" I snapped back.

"Why did you do it? It's not like I care. I'm glad to see that shit gone. But how am I supposed to defend you to the Trust?"

I let out a bark of laughter. "Me? You're kidding, right?"

"Amy," he said, "this is no coincidence. Not after our conversations."

"Oh, I agree," I said, my tone dripping with sarcasm. "You practically promised me you would. For a *reward*."

He did a double take. "You think *I* did it? That's ridiculous. I was joking. I have a lot more respect for society property than that."

"Oh, and I'm just the one who tosses all our traditions to the wind? That's what you think of me, isn't it?"

"You hardly even *looked* at the plate pieces Salt had. You had no interest in checking out the damage. That reeks of guilt to me."

"George wasn't interested, either!" I said in my defense. "Because you know what? *It's not a big deal.*"

Poe clenched his jaw so tight, his cheekbones stood out like knife blades. "George," he said, and almost smiled, though it was the scariest smirk I'd ever seen. "Of course. How stupid of me. Especially given the nature of your 'reward.' Tell me, was the big plate smash part of the foreplay or just something to pass the time between bouts of mind-blowing in-tomb sex?"

I gasped. Actually gasped. And from the expression that flashed across Poe's features, he didn't believe he'd said that, either. But almost before I had a chance to register the look, it was gone, replaced again by the cold, calculating mask.

Every inch of my face burned, but whether with anger, shame, or sadness, I couldn't tell. I could hardly breathe, could speak not at all.

"What, no denial?" he said in a mocking voice.

"I wouldn't dignify it with one," I whispered, since that was the most I could manage. George was right about Poe. He was a jerk. I swallowed, and for a moment I thought I'd never done so before, it was so hard. "But because you're about to go into that meeting with who knows *what* kind of theories, let me at least put your mind to rest about one thing: I never touched those goddamn plates in my life."

And then I was back in the sunlight, back in the compound, surrounded by friends and fellow knights, but a red haze had settled over my vision. I stumbled blindly past them, shook off their hands and Amy-what's-wrongs? and Are-you-okays? Through the compound, down the path to the beach, where the afternoon sun was already glinting on the water. But I felt cold. My shoes flopped hard against my soles and eventually filled with sand, but I kept running. Through the trees, where pine needles and bits of bark scraped at my ankles, through a grove of mangroves, where I crushed roots in my rush, sloshing through muck and onto another beach. The one where Poe had given me those swimming lessons. I must not be far from the lagoon. At the edge of the water was a large, bulky shape caught upside down between sand and shore. The skiff.

Eyes still stinging with unshed tears, I waded into the water, fully clothed, up to my thighs and yanked at the boat, tugging until I pulled it all the way back onto the shore. I found one oar stuck in the sand nearby, another flung beyond the tidemark close to the path that led back to camp. So this is where Ben and Demetria had come in the previous night. Not far from the second oar was a pile of material. The ruined sea monster costume, currently festooned with buzzing flies. I kept my distance, picturing last night's scene in the woods.

I piled the oars inside the boat and stood, breathing hard and unsure of what else I could do. Part of me wished I could cry, just get it out, but tears didn't come. The burning coal inside my chest refused to erupt into outright sobs.

Why? Why can he hurt me so much? Why do I care?

I wandered back up the beach and dropped onto the sand, leaning back against the roots of a tree that skirted the edge of the woods. I pressed the heels of my hands against my eyes, but still, no tears.

I'd been the one saying over and over that I couldn't take any of this seriously. It shouldn't bother me in the slightest that he thought I was sleeping with George. It should even work to my benefit—proof indeed that this was nothing more than a Spring Break fling.

And yet, Jesus Christ, it hurt. Not that he figured I'd broken the plates—that would be kind of cool, actually— but that I'd do it behind his back, with another man. After we'd joked about it repeatedly. It was *our* thing. Like Life Savers.

Our thing! Damn, Amy, get a grip. Jamie Orcutt was a liar, a manipulator, and a jerk. And I didn't really know anything about him. I didn't trust him; he didn't trust me. Malcolm had been right. It was stupid for us to think of getting involved, given our long-standing mutual dislike. At least with George, we'd always been friendly. Now there was a guy you could have a casual affair with.

Poe wasn't fling material.

I leaned my head against the wood and took several long, deep breaths, but the pain in my chest didn't diminish one iota.

Crap. At this rate, I was going to need another entire Spring Break to get over the heartbreak of this one.

After a while I saw a figure making his way up the beach, but due to the angle of the sun, I couldn't see him until he'd gotten close enough to speak.

"Hey," Darren said. "What are you doing out here all alone?"

"Just thinking," I said, hoping my eyes didn't look too puffy.

He nodded. "Mind if I join you?"

Yes, I thought, but then I remembered the time I'd ditched him to go off hiking with Poe. Remembered what he was dealing with at home. Thought that maybe his little sister wasn't the only one missing their housekeeper.

"Sure," I said, and scooted over to give him room to sit between the roots.

He sat and pulled off his backpack. "Bit of drama back at the camp, huh?" He yanked out a Tupperware container filled with a few more of those cupcakes from lunch and a bottle of electric blue sports drink.

"You know I can't talk about that," I said with a rueful smile.

He rolled his eyes. "Please. No one was being really quiet about it."

"True," I said. I pointed at the sweets. "Gonna share those?" He held the container out to me and I took one.

"Thanks. I didn't get a chance to have dessert at lunch." I took a big bite. Wow, it was sweet. He uncapped his drink bottle. "Are you going for a blue theme today?" I asked him, pointing at the energy drink.

He shrugged. "Something like that. Maybe I'll go to Eli after all."

I laughed and kept munching the cupcake. It really was too sugary and rich for my taste, but I couldn't very well not finish it after he'd shared with me. "So, how have you been liking *The Count of Monte Cristo*?"

"Pretty good. Drink?" I nodded and took the bottle. The cloying taste had made me thirsty. "Makes me want to find a buried treasure, that's for sure."

"I know, can you imagine?" I took a huge swig.

"What would you do with a treasure like that?"

"Just what the count did," I said. "Take revenge on anyone who ever wronged me." Maybe I'd start with Poe. Or Felicity.

"Oh, you don't need a treasure to do that," Darren said.

I giggled. "Experienced in the ways of revenge, are you?"

He smiled. "I try." We talked about the book for a few minutes more. Darren was a smart cookie. His grasp of literature was pretty well developed for a kid in the early years of high school.

Even the energy drink was too sweet. What I wouldn't give for some regular water. It was like the more I drank, the thirstier I got. "You know," I said, "if you're going to be trapped somewhere, there are worse places than an island in Florida." Oh, wow. Had I said that out loud?

"Oh, yeah?" Darren said. "Name one."

"Connecticut in February's pretty sucky."

"Anyplace is pretty sucky when you live with two parents who don't speak to you about what's going on."

I stared at him. It was, quite possibly, the most vulnerable statement he'd ever made to me. "Darren, I'm so sorry. I know I shouldn't be getting involved, but if you need to—"

He looked away. "Forget it," he said. "Is that the boat from the skit?"

"Yeah, it must be where Ben and Demetria pulled it up last night."

"You didn't get sick, though," Darren said, abruptly.

I shook my head. "How do you know that?"

He smiled again. "I know all kinds of secrets."

"Like what?" I laughed again. This kid could actually be kind of charming if he tried.

"Like what they were saying about you in the tomb just now."

The words took a few seconds to sink into my brain. "How do you know . . . that?" I repeated, dumbly.

"There are ways into the tomb other than the front door," was all he said. "I told you, I've been here for a while. I've seen it all."

"And you were . . ." I blinked. The light was starting to hurt my eyes. "Listening?"

"Yep. I listen to a lot of things."

"What did they say?" I asked, but at that moment, I wasn't sure I cared. The sun had become too warm, the sand too bright. Where were my sunglasses? Why didn't I care more?

"That you were the one to break the plates." He dropped his voice. "But I know that's not true."

And for the third time, I pushed the words out, and this time each syllable was a struggle. "How do you know that?"

"Because I did it."

I hereby confess:
I can't remember
anything after that.

19.
The Other Island

When I opened my eyes, it was dark out. I was lying on my side in the sand, back to a log, mouth filled with cotton balls.

Okay, not that last part, but man, it felt that way. My mind screamed for water. I tried to put a hand to my head, and discovered the following:

1) My hands were bound behind my back.
2) My feet were tied together with thick rope.
3) Every muscle in my body ached.

I shoved myself into a sitting position and my head began pounding so hard I almost lost my cookies into my own lap.

"You're awake," said a voice on my left. "Thank God. I was really worried."

Very gingerly, I turned my head toward the voice, but I saw little more than shapes in the dark. "Darren?"

"Yeah," he said. "How do you feel? You've been out for hours."

"What happened to us? Where are we?"

"The other island," he said. The direction of his voice changed, as if he was looking out at our surroundings. "This is where those people have been camping."

"Are they here? What...happened? I can't..." Oh God, what had happened to me? I felt like I was covered in bruises. I wanted to throw up. I'd never been so thirsty in my life.

"Shhh," he whispered, his voice closer now. "Stop talking."

Okay, think. Forget the pounding in your head. We'd been kidnapped. We'd been kidnapped by insane, violent, paranoid conspiracy theorists who thought that we were responsible for all the evils of the world. And Darren was just a kid, pretriarch or not.

"How did we get here?" I whispered back.

"The boat. You don't remember?"

I shook my head, and was rewarded with even more acute pain. It felt like my skull was being crushed between two sharp stones. Had they come up behind us on the beach and hit me over the head? I wished I could feel around for bumps or cuts. I slowly tilted my head toward my shoulder, and felt like the contents were sloshing out of my temple. My hair, crusted with something chunky and smelly, pressed against my cheek. Oh, no. Vomit.

"I can't remember anything. How many of them were there?" All of a sudden, even worse fears clawed their way into my muddled mind. Darren said I'd been out for hours. Plenty enough time for them to—bile rose in my throat, and I remembered Brandon's words from long ago.

Stop overthinking.

There was no time to be afraid, or freak out about what

had already happened. We needed to get out of here. I needed to keep Darren and me as safe as possible until we were rescued. Surely the Diggers would have noticed by now that I was gone. Even if Darren's own parents didn't much worry about his whereabouts, my friends would expect me to be back by evening. It wasn't that big of an island, and I'd never been one for wandering around after dark. Except, that's exactly what I'd been doing the past few days, wasn't it? At least, that was the story I'd let the Diggirls believe while I made out with Poe.

Or maybe they all believed Poe's theory about me breaking the plates and thought I'd taken off. Of course, how could I take off? Where would I go in a place surrounded by water?

"Amy?" Darren's voice came out of the darkness. "Have you fallen asleep again?"

He'd never answered my question about the number of our attackers. And... yeah, now I could remember. He said *he'd* been the one who'd broken the plates.

"This would be the third time, you know," he continued. "Which is pretty tiresome."

I remained silent. He'd never *said* we'd been kidnapped.

"This isn't at all like I thought it would be."

I swallowed, tried to work up some saliva in my mouth. I tested the strength of my bonds. There wasn't any give at all.

"It's just so... fucking... frustrating," he said. "Nothing's gone right."

After that, he was silent for so long I thought maybe he'd given up on talking to me. Finally, I decided to speak up. "Darren..." I rasped.

"Yeah?"

And once I started, I couldn't stop. *"What did you do?"*

"They were supposed to still be here. But the fuckers up and left. The Diggers were supposed to find you here and blame the guys on the island."

"Find me?" I said, a sob rising in my throat. "Like... my body?"

"Jeez, no!" His tone was offended. "But it took forever to row out here. And then you wouldn't wake up. You were so heavy, I couldn't even get us to the camp. And now it turns out they aren't even here. Cowards."

"What did you do... to me?" I was too groggy. There was no filter between my mouth and my brain. "I was nice to you."

He didn't respond. I wanted to scream, but I didn't have the energy. And it would have split my skull in two.

"So now I have no idea what the fuck I'm supposed to do."

"How about untie me?" I said, hating the pleading note in my voice. I'd been drugged. I could hardly move; it was the only explanation. I'd been drugged. Four years of watching my drinks at every frat party I'd ever attended, and I'd wound up roofied by a fourteen-year-old with Gatorade and access to his mother's medicine cabinet. If this kid had so much as laid a finger where it didn't belong I'd tear him limb from limb.

As soon as I sobered up. For now, though, I rasped my wrists against each other, trying to work the knots loose, to no avail. My skin screamed as the rope tugged against sensitive nerve endings. Oh God. Oh God oh God oh God oh God... I pushed back against the waves of panic in my battered brain.

"You've done the whole initiation thing," he said suddenly. "What am I doing wrong?"

"*What?*" I whispered. "This isn't anything like initiation." That had been all fun and games. Yeah, there had been a few moments here and there that scared the heck out of me, but now, now that I knew what *true* terror was, Poe and his shenanigans with water guns and coffins seemed like child's play. "Please untie me." Please please please please please. I rubbed my feet past each other, and the skin on my calves must be tougher or something, since it didn't hurt quite as much. Was I creating any give at all?

I wondered if the others were looking for me. How well did sound carry across the water? Would they hear me if I screamed?

I tried it. "HELP!"

Within moments, Darren had me pinned against the sand, my shoulder blades twisting in agony under the pressure of my bound position.

"Ow!" I sobbed. "Please, please, get off me, you're going to break my arms, get off me! Please!"

"Shut up," he said, but he let me go.

"Darren, this isn't a joke," I said, my face still in the sand. "Untie me. Let's go back."

"My dad said they used to play games like this all the time," he said, as if in argument. "Kidnapping, hostage situations..."

"Games?" I croaked. Okay, clearly Rose & Grave was a little different in the olden days. But I didn't think Darren had any idea what he was talking about. For all I knew, his dad had just puffed up tales about a few rousing rounds of Capture the Flag. "No, not like this." *Nothing like this, I swear.* "Please untie me."

"And then what?" he asked.

"And then we go back," I said. I kept working my arms and legs against each other, ignoring the pain in my flesh, in my head. *Don't think about it. Just go. Just go.*

"And *then* what?"

And then someone locks you up and throws away the key, you devil spawn. "I don't know," I lied. "Just untie me, okay, and we'll figure it out."

No, wrong. Too much. Darren had to be the one to figure it out. He had to be better. I could almost feel his distrust.

I mean, "What do you want? Whatever you want."

He snorted. "I got what I wanted. Revenge."

Like *The Count of Monte Cristo*. That's the last time I recommended that book to anyone. "Against who?"

"D177, of course," he said. "What are you, retarded?"

I swallowed. My head felt worse. I was so dizzy. And the knots around my limbs weren't budging. "Why did you want... revenge against us?"

"I thought you guys would fight back more. I heard about what you did to that kid last semester."

Micah? "Fight back?"

"But you're all such pussies. I can see why Dragon's Head takes advantage of you."

I fought to wrap my head around what he was saying. "I can't fight... unconscious." And tied up. Okay, my feet were definitely looser now.

"Against the pranks I pulled."

I blinked, slowly. My head felt so heavy, so fragile. "You did the cabin."

"And the drinks last night." He sounded proud. "No one even guessed! That's the part I'm no good at. Half the time, people don't even notice. Like last night, when I short-sheeted all of the boys' beds. No one even mentioned it at breakfast. Do you think they slept on top of their sheets?"

Likely. But I was still a step behind him. "The drinks?"

"It wasn't food poisoning," Darren said. "It was ipecac syrup. I read about it once on the Internet, but I never saw it before until we got here."

Ipecac? Did people even make that anymore? Gross. Only on some backward, out of the way island like Cavador.

"That's how I knew you didn't get sick. You didn't have any of the pitcher I made."

And neither had he. So he'd been faking in his bed last night. And he'd already drugged the Diggers once, and gotten away with it.

"This is why I would join a society like Dragon's Head instead. From what I hear, their pranks are so much better."

Their pranks were *pranks*. Crickets and sodas and library fines. Darren could have really hurt us. Maybe he already had. But the more he talked, the more I doubted he'd done anything untoward to me while I'd been unconscious. He really thought this was equal to Dragon's Head's attacks. He sincerely believed that drugging and kidnapping a woman was no different than short-sheeting a couple of bunk beds. "Maybe that's what's going on now," I said, weighing my words carefully. "Maybe the Diggers just don't know that this is a ... prank."

"I'm thinking that, too," Darren said, his voice as casual as if he were remarking on climate change.

"Darren," I said. "Let's go back. I think I'm really sick. Please? Just untie me and I'll help you row back to Cavador. It will go much more quickly if we each take an oar."

"I can't do that," he said. "You'll have too much of an advantage."

What? I could barely stand. I probably wouldn't be able to row, even if he did give me a heavy, blunt object to wave around at will. Oh, God, please let me have an oar.

"How much longer are you willing to wait around here, though?" I asked. "I mean, what if they think I just ran off? Because of the plates?"

"Oh, they'd never think that," Darren said. "You're too afraid of the water."

The words broke through the fog of my mind like a spotlight. "What?"

He sighed and spoke again, as if annoyed. "They wouldn't think you'd leave of your own accord, because you're too afraid of the water."

"How did you know..."

"See what I mean?" he said, his voice filled with frustration. "No one even noticed I'd rigged your life jacket! You guys are such losers."

I almost fell over. He had tried to kill me. He'd been trying since before I arrived on the island. And he was wrong—one person had noticed. Poe. And to think I'd called him paranoid.

Now I really was losing it. My hands and feet hurt from lack of circulation, my head felt ready to explode, and I was alternately fighting to stay conscious and to keep from throwing up. "Darren, do you think I could have some water, at least?"

"Sorry," he said. "I didn't think ahead. I'm thirsty, too."

"Then let's go back," I said, fighting desperately to keep the sob out of my voice. "Please, please, please!" Dammit. There it was. And once I started, I couldn't stop. My mouth turned sour, and the tears started pouring from my eyes. "Please," I cried. "Let's just go back to Cavador. We could go back to the crescent beach. It's really close, and I'll stay out there if you want. You can still...play hostage. Just, back on our island. Maybe you can write a ransom note or something..." Anything. Anything, just get me within screaming distance. No one would ever find me out here. And once we were back on Cavador Key, the chance that he'd get tired of the game and go home rose considerably.

"Yeah," he said. "But there's no cover on the crescent beach."

"There is!" I said, hope blooming in my chest to replace the panic. "There's that grove of pine trees. You know, where the ospreys are nesting. We could go there. It's nice and thick. No one would ever see us."

Either my eyes were starting to adjust, the moon had come out, or I was hallucinating, because I thought I could make out Darren's skeptical expression. "I don't know..."

"It's a great idea," I said. "It's like what we've done in the past. In the tomb." Crap, was that too far? Should I have said it's like what Dragon's Head would do? I couldn't concentrate.

Darren seemed to weigh this idea in his mind. "Fine," he said at last. "But you're getting off easy, I think."

If I weren't so scared, I would have laughed.

"But you are going to have to row," he went on. "I'm too tired."

He was too tired? Rich. Still...I held out my legs "Are you going to untie me?"

More hesitation. "No, not until we get in the boat. And then just your arms."

I didn't know I could be more terrified. He was going to put me in a boat, tied up?

But first, he made me hop down the beach. *Hop.* My head felt as if it were going to implode with every leap. I practically bit through my lip trying not to scream. How in the world was I going to row back to Cavador Key if I could hardly move?

When we got to the boat, I fell into it sideways, banging my hip and knees hard against the bench. "Owww," I moaned.

"Move," he grunted, trying to push the boat into the water. "I'm sick of dragging you around."

Then don't drug me next time! Don't render young women unconscious! Don't—I felt blood in my mouth from biting my lip. *Just get through this.*

The boat tipped and rocked hard as it hit the water, and I held my breath. Thank God I was unconscious for the trip over. How could I stand this? How could I do it? Water sloshed against the side of the boat and over the rim as Darren pulled himself inside. I was going to die. I was going to die. I was sitting inside a thimble, bound from head to foot.

"Untie me, please!" I cried, no longer able to keep the hysteria from my voice.

"Hold on," he said, annoyed, then leaned across me to undo the bonds on my hands. I felt the boat tilt as the weight inside shifted, and he fell against me. I froze, so terrified that I barely noticed the sick sensation of his body on mine. *Don't tip, don't tip* ... And then, sweet relief as the pressure on my wrists eased.

If I were James Bond or Jason Bourne or Sydney Bristow, I would have punched him while he was still off balance, then hit him upside the head with an oar. But I could barely feel my fingertips. I shook my hands as he sat down, trying to get sensation back into my limbs. And as he settled himself on the far bench, expression wary and watchful, I made a few grabs for the oars. A quick glance behind me showed the sandbar of the crescent beach, several hundred yards away, nothing more than a lighter gray stretch against black water that might as well be an endless chasm.

The first stroke was torture. Every muscle in my arms ached. When one of the oars hit the sandy seafloor, the resulting jolt almost knocked me to my knees.

"I can't," I cried, letting my hands drop.

Darren snorted. "You're such a whiner. I don't think the boys would be breaking this easily."

Is that what these hypothetical hostage games of the Gehrys were supposed to do? Teach the hostages not to break? What was this, a way to prepare young Diggers for the rigors of war? Make them into little spies? I clenched my jaw and picked up the oars again. Fine. I was in Rose & Grave. I could do this.

Don't think about the water. Pretend it's knee-deep the whole way across. I started again. *Pull. Pull. Don't look. Pretend every stroke sends you sailing.*

Still, it was endless. "You'll tell me if I'm off course, right?"

Darren said nothing. He was staring out over the water, eyes narrowed.

I looked over my shoulder to see what it was that had caught his attention.

A light! A boat. And there it was, the sound of an engine in the water. Still so distant, but if I was correct, it was coming from the dock at Cavador Key.

"Here!" I shouted, dropping the oar to wave. "Over here! Help!"

Darren smacked me in the dark. "Shut up!"

"Game over," I mumbled, and leaned down to undo my feet. The knots weren't budging. "Help!" I shouted with all the strength left in my voice. "It's Amy! Help, I'm hurt! Please! Darren—"

And then he landed a real blow and I fell over, my head pounding. The boat tipped wildly, and a small wave crested the side and splashed over my face, stinging the raw skin there.

Darren shoved me out of the way and tried to grab the oars.

"Darren, just stop," I begged him, even while I fumbled for the rope around my feet again. "You can't outrow a motorized boat. Come on."

"Shit!" he exclaimed. Now I could hear voices, along with the motor and the light.

"Help, please! Please help me!" I kept screaming it over, and over, screamed it until my voice gave out. The light kept getting bigger, the voices louder. They were yelling, yelling my name.

"Shit!" Darren said again, and then he was standing.

"No!" I said, and grabbed his arm, just as he dove over the side. The pressure of my hand on his threw him off, and he hit the edge of the boat with a loud, metallic thud.

The boat tilted far to the left, and then to the right.

And then, once more, the world turned upside down.

I hereby confess:
I no longer care
what anyone thinks.

20.

Seaworthy

In the night, underwater might as well be deep space. Just as cold, just as black. I heard nothing, saw nothing. I kicked my legs, but the knots remained. I could move my feet within the bonds, but not enough to pull them apart. The skin around my ankles burned, the only warmth in all that freezing water.

And then I broke the surface, not coughing, and sucked in air. The cold had shocked me awake.

Why was it so quiet? Where was the other boat, where were my rescuers? Where was Darren? I heard no splashing but my own, and the soft susurrus of waves against the side of the boat. I grabbed for it, but my fingers slid off the smooth underside of the hull, and then it slipped away. So cold. So cold.

No! I was turned around, or something. I couldn't see. I couldn't see anything, could barely tell where the water met the air. And my arms. My God, my arms. They hurt so much. I couldn't do it.

"Help!" I screamed, and promptly went under.

Breathe, Amy. When you breathe, you're lighter than water. Who had said that? Poe? In his silly little swimming lessons? Dead man's float. What an awful name. I clawed my way to the surface once more, took another deep breath, and let my face sink into the water. And amazingly, miraculously, it worked. The blood rushed from my ears and I could hear again. The motor was close now, people were shouting. I could see the light playing on the water from behind my eyelids. I lifted my face and breathed again. "Over here!" I shouted, and breathed again, quick. My arms, my arms...

There was a huge splash next to me and then an arm around my waist. Someone shoved something under my armpits, something that lifted me up out of the water.

"Amy, are you all right?" George's voice. There was a light in my face.

I opened my eyes. "My feet..." I said, "...tied."

I could see George's expression flash to horrified. "Oh my God."

And then I was being dragged against the side of the boat, hands on my wrists, scraping against the skin there, and I remember saying the word "Darren," and then there was more splashing. I heard them say they'd found him, and then they covered me with blankets and I remember Jenny and Demetria holding me in their laps and crying, and crying, and crying...

"Her face..."

"...hypothermia sets in."

"Keep her awake, keep her awake..."

George's voice, in the midst of some unthinkable rage. "Tied her up. *Tied her up!*"

"Drink this." I think it was Jenny, holding a mug to my mouth. I batted it away. No more drugs.

"Amy, please, it will warm you up." I breathed in some

sickly sweet smell and it was too much. I rolled onto my side, retching, coughing.

And then, I felt hands on my face, pulling my hair back against my neck, caressing my forehead and my cheeks. Demetria's voice was very soft, and very firm. "She's been drugged. Look at her eyes. This is what it looks like. The motherfucker..."

And then there was more screaming that broke through the fog of my brain. I blinked my eyes open. I was lying on the deck of the boat, and two people were holding Demetria back from attacking a bundle on the other side of the deck. Darren. He was wrapped in a blanket as well, holding a dark red towel to his head. No, it wasn't dark red. It was just turning...

"He's bleeding," I said to Jenny, but she didn't respond.

And now Demetria was screaming at the man driving the boat. "Take us right to the mainland," she shouted. "Right to the police."

"Too late," Salt said, and steered us into the dock of Cavador Key. "We're going to work this out right here."

"Over my dead body," Demetria said. "I bet he already got through to the coastal unit or whatever they're called."

"We'll see, miss." He turned off the engine.

Ben was crouched by Darren's head. "The bleeding is worse than the cut," he said. "Head wounds. But he'll probably need stitches."

Darren said nothing. He was looking at the dock in fear.

Every light was on, and a crowd had gathered. I saw the remainder of my club. I saw Malcolm and a host of other patriarchs. I saw the Gehrys standing there, waiting to climb aboard the boat the second Salt threw over a rope.

Or maybe not even that long. Because here was Mr. Gehry, right on deck.

"Darren!" he bellowed. "Son, are you okay?"

"Yeah, Dad," he said.

"What the hell were you thinking? What were you do-ing? You could have killed this girl! Have you gone mad?"

Everyone was silent. Darren looked at the assembled crowd, and then at me, and then, at long last, at his father.

And burst into tears.

"Dad..."

"How could you?" Kurt shrieked. "Considering what we're dealing with?"

"Dad..."

"Knowing everything we've been through?"

"Dad..."

"Is this how we raised you?"

"But I don't know!" Darren snapped. His father stepped back. "You won't tell me anything. No one will! You leave your job, you send me and Mom and Belle here, and you don't let us watch TV, and you don't let us make phone calls, and you don't let us have our computers..."

"It was for your own good, son. You're too young to understand..."

"I understand everything!" Darren shouted. "Do you think I'm stupid? I read it all on the Internet before you made us come here. It was D177's fault. They ruined it all for you. He asked you to resign...he asked you to resign, and it's all their fault. It's because they don't have any re-spect for you. These stupid college students dismissed you, and you lost your job because of it! How could I let that stand? They need to recognize what we can do! That's what you always told me. That you need to show them how dangerous you can be."

Kurt Gehry stood there for several moments, then he dropped to his knees in front of his son and pulled him close. "No. No, Darren." He sighed. "No. That's not why

I resigned. I'm so sorry if I let you believe that. I'm appalled that I let you listen to those rumors and didn't tell you the truth. It's my fault."

"Then why is Mom like that?" Darren sobbed. "Why is she always—"

"Darren?" Mrs. Gehry's face appeared over the side of the boat, and she, too, scrambled aboard. "Oh, God, Darren, what did you do? You stole my medicine, you ran away, you've been hurting people!"

"Hush, Gail," Kurt said, leaning back. "He made some pretty serious mistakes, but he thought he was doing it for us." He looked back at Darren. "Son, we love you. We'd do anything for you, anything to protect you. I don't know what you were thinking, but I promise, you don't need to do anything to prove yourself to me. You don't need to protect me. I can protect myself."

"Tell me the truth!" Darren cried. "Tell me why we're really here! Hiding . . . Why did Isabelle and I have to leave school? Why are we stuck here? Why are you ignoring us?"

"Not here, son. We'll talk about it, I promise, but not in front of these strangers."

"Bullshit!" Demetria yelled crossing the deck from my side to the family's. "We all know anyway. And your stupid secrets almost got Amy murdered tonight. She was certainly assaulted. And certainly kidnapped. Don't you think you'd better explain it to Darren before he has to face the police?"

"No!" Kurt Gehry said, and rose. "I will not have you using your hatred of me to destroy my son."

"How about my hatred of your son?" Demetria said. "There is no way I'm letting this get swept under the rug. He did who knows what to Amy, and I think he did it with the help of drugs that you or your wife obtained illegally. I don't need a doctor to tell me what she was on tonight. We've seen your wife on the same shit. Rohypnol, huh, Darren?" she hissed at the boy, and his mother held him closer. "Pretty smart of you, with the blue Gatorade. Quite the date rapist in training. Now you're in real trouble, and there is no way I'm letting any of you get away with it."

"Demetria," Clarissa said.

"You will do nothing of the sort," Gehry insisted.

"How you gonna stop us?" Demetria said. "You can't do anything. You can't keep us here."

"Listen, you bitch..." Gehry said.

"You have no idea what a bitch I'm going to be," she replied.

"Stop." I pushed to my feet, wavering, and they did stop. I looked at Darren, tearful and bloody, on the other side of the deck. I looked at his mother, cradling him in her arms, the blood from his head soaking into her sweater. She looked all too sober right now. I looked at his father, broken, battered, and crazy with concern over his child.

That was a first. Clarissa's dad would humiliate her in front of all his Digger friends. Malcolm's father had dropped him the second his son had declared anything that jarred with his own worldview. But Kurt Gehry, evil patriarch, hypocritical lawmaker, all-around jerk—everything he'd done had been to protect his children, however misguided, however damaging it had ended up being. And nothing had changed. Even after seeing what Darren had done, he was still fighting for him. He'd been a real dad.

No wonder Darren loved him so much. No wonder Darren had gone to such insane lengths to protect his father, in turn. The teen looked so tiny, so lost in the shadows on the deck. I remembered playing darts with him, making costumes. He'd been trying so hard to impress us all. Too hard.

"I'm not pressing charges," I said.

"What!" shouted voices all around me. I put a hand to my head.

"I'm not," I said.

"Amy, you aren't thinking clearly," Demetria said. "You've been drugged—"

"Nothing happened," I said. "It could have. I'm not going to lie about that. But . . ." I tried to shake my head and failed. "This was a really bad mistake."

"It was a crime!" Demetria insisted.

"There are a lot of those going around."

A couple of months ago, I was terrified that Dragon's Head was going to call the police because I'd broken into their tomb. And yet, I'd never once considered pressing charges against the society members for ruining my textbooks or pouring drinks all over me. It was all fun and games. Part of the package for society members. Last semester, we'd broken into Micah Price's apartment and filled it with rats, and none of us was facing jail time. This was society culture. This was what Darren had been taught to idolize. He was just too young to see the distinction between mischievous and truly dangerous.

And maybe there was no distinction. Poe had ended up in the hospital after we'd broken into Dragon's Head. What if his wounds had been worse? What if Micah'd had his finger bitten off by one of those rats? What if I'd slipped on the icy sidewalk Dragon's Head had left for me and broken my neck? What if any of our supposedly innocent society pranks had gone horribly wrong? Would it be one of us trying to figure out if we could plead down from felony to misdemeanor and wishing we still had the parachute of under-eighteen to keep us from ruining our lives? Except Darren wouldn't have that parachute, either. He was too famous. The son of Kurt Gehry was media fodder, and if he

DIANA PETERFREUND

got arrested after his father's fall from grace, given his father's notoriety, well, he would be destroyed, plain and simple.

Don't get me wrong, I was angry at him. Furious! And every time I thought about those terrified moments on the other island, every time I remembered the feeling of tipping over the side of the boat, every time I recalled the very large suspicion I'd had that I would not be surviving the night, I wanted nothing more than to see him eviscerated. By the press, by large, mangy dogs—whatever.

But looking at him lying there on the other side of the boat, broken, frustrated, desperate...looking at the whole family...He'd already been eviscerated. What more could a juvenile court probation accomplish? I thought about how he was fourteen, and he thought he knew everything. And how I was eight years older than that and I couldn't even imagine how much I didn't know.

Darren had been so wrong, but what he'd showed me was that a lot of what we did in Rose & Grave without even thinking about it was every bit as wrong.

"Amy, please. I'm begging you. Reconsider this," Demetria said.

She could. She could reconsider it, once I told her that Darren had poisoned them as well. I took a few shaky steps past her, to Kurt Gehry, and spoke in low tones. "You're going to fix this. Whatever it takes."

"Yes."

"For real. If you decide to ignore it, forget it...well, I won't."

"I understand." He grabbed my hand as if to seal the bond. "Thank you." I winced when his fingers closed around raw skin, and he dropped my hand in horror.

"I want to leave."

Demetria was shaking her head. "Amy, please, please..."

"I want to leave." I wavered on my feet. "Please." I looked around the boat at my friends, but their expressions were unsure. Where was Poe? Jamie would help me. Wouldn't he?

Except, where was he now?

Demetria sighed. "Fine." She turned to Kadie Myer, still on the dock. "Have you used your shampoo?"

"What?" The older girl's eyes narrowed. "No. Why?"

"Don't. I'm buying you a new bottle. Will you take us off this island? Tonight?"

Kadie looked at her husband, who spoke up. "As soon as we can get the boat. Yes. Anyone who wants to go."

Demetria turned to Jenny. "Can you pack up?"

Jenny nodded. "Absolutely." She and Odile took off.

I sat down on the deck again and leaned my head back. Good. We were leaving.

"As soon as we get the boat back..." Frank was saying to Clarissa, and in the distance, I heard sirens.

It was over.

———

But of course, it wasn't over. I slept through the police boat's arrival and subsequent dismissal, but from the story that Kevin told me later, they were all too happy to get off Cavador Key as soon as they were told the police call was a misunderstanding, a "boating accident." "Salt and Gehry put on an Academy Award level performance," he said. "Quite astounding, really."

"And the rest of them?"

"Stayed out of it!"

I remember getting on the Myers' yacht, but not why it took so long, and blessedly, I don't remember a single moment of the trip back to the mainland.

Somehow, I wound up in a fine hotel suite in town (possibly on Jenny's dime and Odile's reputation), cocooned inside a massive white comforter, while my fellow knights debated about whether or not to send me home to Ohio. I remember that conversation for sure. Because I remember sitting up and telling them no.

"I don't agree with a lot of your judgment calls lately, Amy," Demetria said.

"I don't care," I replied. If I went home now, I didn't know if I'd ever come back again.

"But, Amy," Clarissa said, "you have to tell your parents."

I compromised and told my folks I'd been in that alleged boating accident (true) and got tangled up in some ropes (also true), and was banged up a bit, but was okay now (remained to be seen). My mother started crying, and my father begged me to spend the rest of Spring Break at home, where they could keep an eye on me. I basked in their parental love and concern, but I told them I'd rather go build houses in Louisiana with my friends, as planned.

Within a day—thanks to Odile's no-fail detox diet—I felt back to normal, with nothing more than the scabs on my wrists and ankles to show what had happened to me. From what I was conscious for, there had been a lot of debate among the other members of the club about whether or not they could pursue a case against Darren Gehry without my consent, or barring that, if they could just leak it to the media.

The oath of fidelity was invoked quite a lot. It was my secret, and they were sworn to keep it. As soon as I felt up to the argument, I told them all about Darren's confession to me on the island, and explained his strange conviction that everything he was doing was par for the course in society pranks.

"But how could he possibly conflate kidnapping and what we do?" Clarissa asked, baffled.

"What we do?" Demetria said, and I practically saw the bulb light itself over her head. "Like breaking and entering? And robbery?"

"And vandalism," said Ben.

"And hacking and stalking, and...assault." Jenny bit her lip, and I could see the figure of Micah Price looming large before all of us. "We're pretty bad."

No one wants to be shown just how low their moral high ground really is. After that, most of the others came around to my way of thinking, and those who didn't at least respected my decision.

It bothered me a lot that Poe never called. I don't remember seeing him on the dock that night, but then again, I couldn't remember much beyond the stricken faces of the Gehrys.

I stopped Clarissa the following afternoon. I was sitting on the couch of the suite, pretending to watch videos and veg out while I fretted over the situation. "Do people... know where we are?" I asked.

"Malcolm called yesterday," she said. "I thought you wouldn't want visitors yet. He's going back to Alaska, but I'm sure..."

"No, that's fine," I said. Malcolm had called. But what about Poe?

That evening, while we were repacking to leave for Louisiana, Josh and Lydia phoned from Spain. The knights had left him a message earlier, asking about the legal ramifications, and Lydia was frantic to know that I was okay. I allayed their fears and reiterated to Josh that there was no way I was pursuing charges against Darren, but all the while I wondered what our patriarch who was *actually* in law school thought about the matter.

During the long drive up the Gulf Coast with the other Diggers, I finally got to hear bits and pieces of the story from the others' point of view.

WHAT I KNOW FOR SURE

1) They *hadn't* decided that I'd broken the plates in the tomb that day. In fact, Poe had never even brought it up. They were still blaming the campers on the other island by the time Clarissa and Odile reported that I was missing late that afternoon.

2) In his rush, Darren had left his backpack (name conveniently sewed inside) behind on the beach, along with the bottle of bright blue Gatorade and my flip-flops, which must have fallen off when he dragged me to the boat. Inside the backpack was the empty bottle of ipecac syrup and some broken pieces of china. "Trophies," Demetria had said with a shudder.*

3) They'd gone to the Gehrys to see if Darren knew where I was, but found the Gehrys had little clue as to their son's whereabouts, which is when Demetria and Ben put two and two together about the location of the backpack and the missing rowboat.

"But how did you know that he'd taken me against my will?" I asked Demetria.

"Well, Amy, it's not exactly a secret that you don't like the water," Jenny said.

Odile looked up. "It was Jamie. Jamie knew you weren't about to get into a boat."

---

* The confessor suspects Darren was desperate for recognition of his pranks by the time he resorted to kidnapping.

"Where's Jamie now?" I asked.

But no one knew the answer to that question. And I wasn't sure if I wanted to ask them where he'd been while I was being rescued that night. Would they find it odd that I cared? And, more important, would I hate the answer?

———

Two days later, I was enjoying the catharsis one derives from a well-stocked nail gun in a small bayou town in Louisiana. The days were long and no one in the Diggers' crew (who, for the purposes of the trip, were undercover as nothing more than a group of friends) was going to win any cuisine awards at the end of the week. Still, the work and lifestyle kept my mind off all the things I wanted to obsess about: the future, Darren, and Poe. I'll tell you this: I hadn't had one nightmare about drowning since I'd started sleeping on a church floor with fifteen other ersatz construction workers. (And only once had the memory of Poe and me in the shower house made me flush red from something other than the southern sun.)

I was stacking roofing tiles when George approached, hands in pockets. "Your tattoo is showing," he said.

I yanked my tank top down in back, but then wondered why I'd bothered. Clarissa had been sailing around all week with her shoulder-blade symbol flying free. Demetria's tattoo was almost always on display, but you barely recognized it in the midst of all her other ink. And still, no one had seen Jenny's. I was starting to suspect she didn't have one.

George looked at the ground for a second. "Have you spoken to Jamie recently?"

"No."

He nodded, slowly. "I was just wondering what he thought about the no-pressing-charges thing."

"Yeah, I was wondering myself," I said, then laughed. "He's probably fine with it, though. He's so gung ho about our status above the law. Wouldn't want me to do anything to hurt the society."

George's expression turned confused. "What do you mean, Amy? He's the one who called the police."

"What?"

George shook his head. "Didn't you know? Jenny couldn't get any reception with her battered cell phone, and Salt wouldn't let anyone use the radio on the island's boat. He insisted he be the one behind the wheel if we went out to the other island to look for you guys. Such a bastard. I can't wait until we're on the Trust board and can fire his ass."

"But...Jamie?" I asked. *Stay on subject, George.*

"Yeah, so we figured Salt was trying to protect the Gehrys at that point, and we were all pretty angry, but when Salt wouldn't budge, Jamie jumped on the Myers' yacht and released the rope so Kurt Gehry and Salt couldn't follow him aboard. It drifted out and he radioed the police. That's when we left to get you."

"And he couldn't get back?"

"Well, docking's pretty hard," George explained. "Even for people who have driven boats before." And Poe hadn't. "Malcolm had to actually swim out to get him, I heard. By the time they came back to the slip, you were asleep, I guess. Didn't you talk to them when we got on the boat to leave?"

I shook my head. I didn't even remember getting on the boat. Had I brushed past Poe without even acknowledging him, without even thanking him for trying to help?

No wonder he hadn't called me! After he went out of his way to get to the police, endangering himself and a significantly pricey piece of the Myers' property, I'd refused to press charges.

"I'm surprised you haven't talked to him," George said. "Considering."

I bit my lip. "That's over." More like a nonstarter.

"Oh."

"What, does that surprise you?" I said, getting annoyed now. "You're the one who told me he was a jerk."

George looked at me in surprise. "Do you really care what I think?"

No. No, but... "I don't want to talk about it," I said at last. "Not with you."

"Fine," he said, and picked up a box of nails. "But you should know that I don't think he's a jerk anymore."

"Thank you," I said. As he turned to go, I touched his shoulder. "And thank you, also, for saving my life."

George smiled his gorgeous smile. "That was cool, huh? I've never done anything like that before."

"It was very, very cool."

He walked away and I stared after him, watching various women on the crew drifting in his direction. I smiled. They absolutely couldn't help it. Gorgeous, funny, charming, and in his spare time, he saved the lives of innocent coeds. And yes, I was completely grateful for that. But I didn't feel the slightest compulsion to sleep with him again.

I put down the nail gun and grabbed my cell phone, dialing the number from memory. It rang and rang, and when at last the answering machine played Poe's voice, I hung up. What I had to say didn't belong on a machine.

———

"I'm never going to get the feel of powdered drywall out of my hair," Clarissa whined. "And my manicurist is going to shoot me for what I've done to my nails."

"Do you regret it?" Demetria asked, pulling off I-91 and onto the quiet streets of New Haven.

Clarissa grinned. "Not a minute."

"You'd better get it together," Jenny said in mock warning. "I don't want a CFO who isn't presentable."

I smiled out the window. While others had used the road trip to get their futures in order, the drive up to Connecticut had given me too much spare time to ruminate on all the questions that remained unanswered. How long had Darren been spying on Poe and me to overhear our hypothetical plate-smashing plot? Would Gehry keep his promise to punish, rehabilitate, and, moreover, help his son? And what in the world would I say when I saw Poe?

As the van rolled down Danbury Road, I came to a decision. "Hey, Demetria, can you pull over?"

Demetria checked me out in the rearview mirror. "What? Why?"

"There's something I have to do." I saw Poe's block on the left. "Right here."

Odile checked out the neighborhood. "What do you have to do here? Buy crack?"

"Isn't this graduate student housing?" Jenny frowned and Harun covered her hand with his. "Oh."

George looked at the house. "Amy, do you think he's even home?"

"Who?" Clarissa asked.

"Jamie Orcutt," George said softly. He looked at me. "I'll get your bags back to your room."

"Thanks," I said, sliding open the door and slipping out. My sneakers sank into the last of the March slush. I felt through the fabric of my purse for the remainder of the cylinder inside. Life Savers.

"I'm not leaving her down here alone," Demetria said. "We can wait to see if he's there."

But we didn't have to. The door opened, and there was Poe, framed in the screen. He was wearing khakis and a dark blue Eli hoodie, and his arms were folded across his chest. I waved back at my friends and headed up the path to the porch. I didn't even see them take off.

"Hi," I said. "Can I come in?"

He stepped aside and I entered the apartment. It was much as I remembered it from last semester. The same worn furniture, the same bookshelves and red-bound law texts, the same giant aquarium with the giant snake. Lord Voldemort, if I recalled correctly. And next to it, the smaller cage for the little white mice Poe fed the snake. Except now, when I looked, I saw only one mouse in the cage, and a hamster wheel, and a little colorful ball. I leaned in closer.

"I named her Reepicheep," he said abruptly.

"What?"

"The mouse. I named her Reepicheep."

"Reepicheep was a boy mouse."

He shrugged. "Details." He joined me in front of the cage. "He was a really brave mouse. Brave and noble and dutiful, and a little bit too much into self-sacrifice."

I swallowed. Well, there was answer number one.

"And anyway," he went on quickly, "I couldn't very well feed her to anyone after that lecture you gave me in November."

I nodded. "And after naming her."

"Right." He looked at me. "What do you want?"

"To see you."

He turned away from the cages and sat down on the sofa. "Okay."

"And talk to you." I turned around, too, but there didn't seem to be anyplace to sit where I wouldn't touch him. There didn't seem to be anyplace to put my hands, anywhere to look that wasn't at his face. I focused my eyes on the bookshelves, on the vegetarian cookbooks there, and I remembered why we'd fought that day. I felt so stupid now. He had eaten the lobster that night. He'd eaten it as a peace offering to the Myers. Poe was also a little too much into self-sacrifice.

"I'm sorry," I said.

Jamie's eyes went wide. "*You're* sorry? Christ, Amy, what for?" He shook his head in disbelief. "I can't even look at you right now. I've been dreading seeing you again, after what I said to you. After what happened."

"Why?" I asked. This was like in January, when he'd avoided us all after he cracked his head open during the Dragon's Head raid. "I heard about what you did, stealing the boat to call the police. I'm sorry I wasn't able to thank you then and there."

"But that's not what you wanted." He wasn't looking at me, and I think I might be getting a bit better at reading his expressions. Disapproval, resignation, carefully reined frustration. I remembered what he'd done to Micah Price, and that poor boy had only spit at me. Gehry would do well to keep his son away from Poe.

I came closer. "You didn't know that when you did it. Hell, *I* didn't know it. You didn't know anything but that I was in danger. And you chose me over the society."

"No."

"Yes." I sat down next to him. "Like it or not, Mr. Patriarch, you broke the third oath."

He looked down at his hands and shrugged. "Details."

Exactly. Amazing how silly they seemed in context. Present a good enough reason, and you realize that the things you thought were important go right out the window. The society was just the symbol. It was the people inside who really mattered. Put me in a room with a man like Jamie, and my well-reasoned case against dating seemed ridiculous. And all the specific arguments against dating him evaporated like frost in the sun.

We sat in silence for a few minutes, and then he spoke again. "Still, it was a pretty stupid move. It took me right out of the game. I wasn't able to rescue you. I heard it was ... George."

And how that must have grated on him! "You know George is long over, right?"

He nodded. "Yes. I knew it at the time. I don't know why I said that stupid—"

"I don't care." I did then, but it all seemed so petty now. "You were angry. We all say stupid shit."

"That's not even it," he admitted. "It killed me that *I* wasn't there to save you. Like I didn't have the right to be."

"Actually," I said, smiling, "I kind of saved myself. A week earlier, I would have drowned long before the boat got to me."

And now he did look at me.

"I think I must be a pretty good swimmer now, if I can do it tied up and drugged."

"Amy ..." All incredulous.

"Here's the thing," I said, quickly, before I lost my nerve. "I've made a lot of mistakes. About the society, and about my relationships—everything." He was still staring at me, and the words came out in a rush. "And come on. We've had so many battles, and you're just so damn prickly all the time. And my friends would think I'm nuts for ..."

"For what?" he cut in. "Making another mistake?"

"No," I said, and took his hand in mine. "Doing something that might make up for all of them."

Jamie stared at our hands for a moment, then pulled away. "No. I tried, on Cavador Key, but I hated it." He caught my stricken expression and amended his words. "I couldn't—I can't pretend this isn't important. I can't act like it doesn't exist. It's ironic, but true. There are a lot of things I'm really good at keeping secret. But I've learned I'm not too good at that with you. I can't pull it off. I don't want to just hook up. I don't want a secret relationship."

"Well, that's a relief," I said, grabbing for both of his hands and holding on for dear life.

Doubt started giving way to recognition, but he needed to hear it. "Why's that?"

"Because I'm really sick of secrets."

Acknowledgments

FOLKS I'D LIKE TO THANK

1) The readers of *Secret Society Girl* and *Under the Rose*

2) The Venerable M.A.E., footnoter extraordinaire

3) Tracy Devine, master titler

4) Pam Feinstein, Lynn Andreozzi, Carol Russo, and all the others on the Bantam Dell Team

5) Deidre Knight (and the gang at TKA), who always rooted for Poe

6) The Sistahs, TARA, WRW, CLWOW, and the Non-Bombs, for being the only societies I need

7) Holly Black, Libba Bray, Cecil Castellucci, Margaret Crocker, Cassandra Clare, Maureen Johnson, Jaida Jones, and Justine Larbalestier, for the (in)sanity

8) Marley Gibson and Cheryl Wilson, who always have my back

9) Erica Ridley and Carrie Ryan, for screaming in text and in person at the shower scene

10) Julie Leto, who saved my storyline

11) The bloggers, blog readers, and lurkers galore

12) My family, family-in-law, and friends

13) Fellow sons and daughters of Eli

14) Those fabulous secret sources

15) My husband (!!!)

About the Author

DIANA PETERFREUND graduated from Yale University in 2001 with degrees in geology and literature. A former food critic, she now resides in Washington, D.C. Her previous two novels, *Secret Society Girl* and *Under the Rose*, are available now from Delta. Visit the author's website at:
http://www.dianapeterfreund.com.

AND WATCH FOR

The Conclusion of Diana Peterfreund's *Secret Society Girl* Series

On Sale Summer 2009

Please turn the page for a special advance preview.

I hereby confess:
Everyone wants
to be one of us.

You arrived in a state of awe, of wonderment. Maybe you're the latest in a long line of your family members to matriculate to our fine university. Maybe you're a celebrity, or foreign royalty, or a sports star, or a genius at the near-lost art of lute playing. Maybe you're a Westinghouse scholar; a national debate champion; or the valedictorian of your elite, East Coast boarding school where your name was on the register from the moment you were born. Or maybe you're none of the above. Perhaps you're just handy with the SATs, rocked grades nine to twelve, and charmed the heck out of the middle-aged lawyer who interviewed you one evening in his satellite office on behalf of his alma mater. Whatever way it happened, you ended up at Eli.

And from the moment you stepped on campus, you heard about us.

For all that we were secret, we remained one of the constants of your college career. You could hardly get to your dorm freshman year without passing our tomb. And you wondered, even if you wouldn't admit it to your roommates or your singing group friends or your lab partner, what it would be like to be one of us. What we did at our weekly meetings—sequestered, sacrosanct, silent except for the occasional scream.

You hoped that someday you'd find out.

The season is upon us. We, the members of Rose & Grave D177, are graduating and are thusly charged with the tapping of new souls to fill our robes, take up the torch of our traditions, and stand beside us as members of this illustrious, rarefied order. It is a lofty invitation and one that no man (or woman) should accept lightly. We are the standard bearers of a New World Order. We are the key that will unlock the life you've only imagined.

You will be judged. Will you be found worthy?

For this *is* what you've always wanted.
Isn't it?

I hereby confess:
I like being his.

1
Pledges

As many of my friends (and a few of my enemies) will tell you, I have a tendency to overanalyze. I'm aware of this characteristic within myself, and I do my level best to overcome it. As a result, I have occasionally been known to make snap decisions that, in retrospect, were probably mistakes.

But here's what I think now. Life is a bit like a standardized test. Not putting down an answer because you fear it could be wrong *will* lower your overall score. So remember what those nice folks at the Princeton Review told you: Make an educated guess. But be careful. You never know where that decision is going to take you.

Almost a year ago, I accepted the tap from Rose & Grave, Eli University's most powerful, exclusive, and notorious secret society. I knew my life would change. What I didn't realize was how. I figured my induction into their order would net me some contacts in my preferred field of business, add an extra *oomph* to my résumé, and provide an insurance plan for the future that loomed just beyond the next set of final exams.

What I didn't expect was that it would open my eyes to a whole world of my own potential. I no longer even wanted the job I'd once hoped Rose & Grave would help me get. I also didn't know that I'd have a host of new friends, some of whom I'd never dreamed of associating with before—a few of whom I'd actively disliked. But now I'd move mountains for any of them. I certainly never knew how much danger one little club membership could net me, though I'd spent the last year being threatened, thwarted, chased, conspired against, and even once—bizarrely—kidnapped.

But most of all, I didn't realize that the following March, I'd be sitting on a couch that looked like it had been fished out of the trash, staring at a guy I'd never even have looked twice at, and wondering if I dared take a risk answering the following:

AMY HASKEL, ARE YOU IN LOVE?

a) Yes
b) No
c) Insufficient data to answer this question

Oh, hell, it's c, which is why there was no way I was going to let our Spring Break fling end. He couldn't do the secret hooking-up thing anymore? Fine. Let's try something new.

"I'm really sick of secrets," I said, and kissed him.

Brilliant as Jamie Orcutt is, it took him several seconds to parse the meaning of my statement. And when he did, the kiss turned from hesitant to heated in no time at all.

Somehow, we shifted on the couch, from a relatively decent and G-rated side-to-side to something that rated the sort of parental supervision we had zero interest in at the moment. And, say what you will about how the couch looked, it certainly felt comfortable once I was sandwiched deeply between the cushions and Jamie. I clung to his shoulders as if I were drowning and he knotted his fists into my shirt, sliding the material away from my skin as his mouth moved south over my throat.

"Ja..." I said on a sigh, and then, as his tongue flicked over my collarbone, "Puh..."

He lifted his head. "You are never going to get it straight, are you?"

"Unlikely." I slid my hands down his back, to where his sweatshirt ended and his skin was bare. "It's already a tough enough effort to think of you as Jamie and not as—" *Poe.* I stopped myself in time to avoid a fine.

"This is troublesome," he said. "But then again, that's your society name." He tapped my nose.

Bugaboo. Yes, and he'd probably chosen it, too, now that I thought about it. "You want to know what's even more troublesome?" I scooted up. "Our real names rhyme."

He chuckled. "Yeah, they do. I never thought of that."

"People are going to laugh whenever they say things like, 'We should invite Amy and Jamie to the party next weekend' or 'Let's go on a double date with Amy and Jamie.'"

He frowned. "I'm now required to go on double dates with your friends? Maybe this isn't such a good idea."

Neither was bringing up my friends, the majority of whom had no particular love for him. "I'm just saying, 'Amy and Jamie' sounds a bit lame."

But he was smiling. "I was just thinking how nice it sounds."

I blushed, and just as quickly, the concerns started crowding into my head. What kind of person gets into a relationship less than two months before graduating from college? Was I mad? Jamie was in law school, here, at Eli, for the next two years. I had no idea where I'd be. When I left town at the end of May, there's no way our relationship would be ready for the long-distance thing (if it even lasted until then), and I had no intentions of sticking around New Haven for a boyfriend I'd just started dating. This was silly. I was setting myself up for an even worse heartbreak come commencement.

"I should go," I said.

"What?" he shook his head in disbelief. "I don't think so. You can't just show up on my doorstep, drop this bombshell on me, then disappear."

"I have work to do...." I began vaguely.

"You just got off a twenty-hour car trip." He caught my hands in his. "You have relaxing to do." His thumbs slid over the scabs on my wrists and we both winced. He looked down. "I'm glad I wasn't there that night," he said softly. "I don't think I would have trusted myself."

"You? Mr. In-Control Poe?" Crap.

He wagged his finger at me. "See? And yeah. I might have killed that kid."

"You wouldn't have been alone." Half my club had wanted to kill Darren Gehry for drugging me and dragging me off in a twisted, dangerous version of what the teenager had convinced himself was a society prank. I was the only person who understood that we might have been to blame for giving him that impression.*

My hands had somehow escaped Jamie's and become balled in my lap. He noticed, in that way he had of noticing everything.

"Stay here for a while," he said. "I'll cook something for you, and we can talk. You can ask me all those personal

* And some of my friends were still muttering the word "Stockholm" in my vicinity.

questions you've been so relentlessly curious about, and I can…" He trailed off.

He could what? Give me a foot massage? Seduce me? Lecture me about the importance of tofu in cuisine? He knew everything about me already. He had researched my past exhaustively when they'd tapped me into Rose & Grave. Scary thought. I'd never before dated a guy who could name all my elementary school teachers, who knew every one of my worst fears and how best to exploit them.

It's kind of like dating your stalker.

"We're a little past first-date conversation where I'm concerned," I said. And then it occurred to me. Back when he'd done all that research, he'd felt nothing for me but contempt. In Jamie's opinion, I hadn't been good enough for Rose & Grave. He'd changed his mind now, though. Right?

He cupped my face in my hands and kissed me, and all my fears dissolved. "We're a little past first dates, too."

———

After dinner, Jamie walked me back to the gates of Prescott College. I swiped my proximity card at the sensor and pulled open the door. "Well," I said.

He rested his hand on the bars. "Well." A flash of memory: Jamie's hand gripping these bars as we shouted at each other. I wouldn't let him in, and I'd left that evening with George.

"Come up for a minute," I went on. "You've never seen my suite."

Here's something new: When Jamie looks at me now, his eyes, those cold gray eyes of his, almost smile. I didn't know eyes could do that.

We wandered through the courtyard, which remained

mostly devoid of students. Spring break came to a shuddering stop, as folks drifted back to campus on their own schedule. Some of the lights were on in suites, but the room I shared with Lydia remained dark.

Jamie caught my hand as I crested the steps to my entryway, and he tugged me back into his arms.

I laughed inside the kiss. "If this is supposed to demonstrate our new ability to kiss in public, you picked a pretty pathetic venue. No one's here."

"Baby steps," he said, as I unlocked the door and pulled him inside. As I wrestled with the doorknob to our suite, he nibbled along the neckline of my shirt. I flicked on the lights to the common room, but Jamie showed no interest in our décor, he just pulled me onto his lap on the couch and started kissing me for real.

A moment later, someone cleared a throat.

I looked up to see Lydia and Josh standing in the doorway to her bedroom. The former looked amused, the latter, gobsmacked.

"Amy," Lydia said. "You're home!" She looked at Jamie. "And you have a guest."

I slid off Jamie's lap and we stood, knees knocking against the coffee table. "Just got home," I said. "I didn't realize you were here."

"Clearly," my best friend replied, not even trying to hide her glee. She shoved her hand at Jamie. "I'm Lydia, Amy's roommate."

"I've heard about you," he said. "Jamie Orcutt."

"Nice to meet you."

He then turned to Josh. "Jamie," he said, and stuck his hand out.

Josh shook himself free from shock. "Um, Josh," he said, a moment too late, and with a complete lack of believability.

Lydia rolled her eyes at the boys. "Give it a rest, you

two. I know where Amy spent her Spring Break. Where else could she have met him?"

Jamie looked at me, eyebrows raised in disapproval. But Lydia wasn't about to let an opportunity like this pass her up. "So, what college are you in, Jamie?"

"I'm at Eli Law, actually," he said.

"Oh." Lydia frowned. "I thought you were a...*senior*." Meaningfully.

And now Jamie did smile. "I was a...*senior*. I graduated." He looked at me. "Your definition of *secret* differs from most people's."

I shrugged. "Some things are impossible to hide."

"Apparently!" Josh blurted. Everyone stared at him.

"I guess you want to catch up with your friends," Jamie said. "I have some reading to do, anyway."

I thought of him walking all the way back to his apartment, alone, in the dark. But what could I do? There was no way I was about to invite him to spend the night. He gave me a quick kiss. "I'll call you."

As soon as the door closed, Lydia let out a strangled squeal. "Oh my God, Amy!" she grabbed my hands and led me over to the couch. "That was a boyfriend 'I'll call you.' You have a *boyfriend*. I leave you alone for two weeks and you have a boyfriend. And he's cute! And he's tall! And he's at Eli Law, which means he's brilliant, to boot! Tell me all about it."

"Lydia," Josh said. "Leave her alone. She's had a traumatic week. She's not—"

"Thinking clearly?" I finished for him. "Is that your theory?"

Lydia waved her hand at him dismissively. "Shoo. We're having mushy-wushy girl talk now."

But Josh was not the type who could be shooed. "Who else knows?"

I lifted my chin. "Whoever wants to." George, to start with, and probably anyone else who'd ridden back to Eli with me in the van. "It's no secret." What, did he want me to make a formal announcement?

"I want to hear everything!" Lydia pressed. "Did all this happen before or after . . . you know."

Before or after I was kidnapped, she meant. I wonder what else in my life is going to fall under that before or after. I don't want it to be like that.

"We've known each other for a while," I said. "And our feelings just . . . grew."

"They didn't have far to fall," Josh said with a sniff.

Lydia whirled on him. "Would you get out of here? You're ruining her story."

"It's okay, Lyds," I said. Josh's reaction was the one I expected. "We can talk about it later. Tell me all about Spain."

"Spain was great," Lydia said. "But I need to hear about your adventures."

"Specifically, the one where you were almost killed," Josh added.

Ugh. Maybe I should have stayed with Jamie.